## IN THE DIM LIGHT, HIS HAIR SHONE WITH LIVING FIRE. HIS EYES WERE LIT BY GOLDEN SPARKS OF DESIRE. . . .

Sweeping her up, he carried Hetta to her room while she struggled to banish thoughts of a pale creature with silver-blond hair—a beautiful remote Englishwoman— by pulling open the buttons of his jacket one by one until her own dark hair stranded across Alex's chest.

"You have never been so with her?" she demanded fiercely.

"No," he protested.

"Swear it."

"I swear it. *I swear it!*" She read in his eyes the denial of the whole world in defense of that moment. The fire raged in them both, and when the leaping flames dwindled, she lay against him with tear-dampened cheeks while he told her of the precious gift she had given him. . . .

# THE
# BURNING
# LAND

by
**EMMA DRUMMOND**

A DELL BOOK

Published by
Dell Publishing Co., Inc.
1 Dag Hammarskjold Plaza
New York, New York 10017

This work was first published in Great Britain
by MacDonald Raven Books.

Dell ® TM 681510, Dell Publishing Co., Inc.

ISBN: 0-440-10274-X

Printed in the United States of America

First U.S. printing—October 1979

## Author's Note

The hamlet of Landerdorp has never existed, but the
events that occur there might have happened in that place
and that time. . . .

All characters apart from historical figures are purely fictional.

# PROLOGUE

That summer of 1882 was a succession of long hot days of adventure, and nights that sped past in loglike sleep untroubled by the cares of adulthood; in fact, it followed the usual pattern of summers enjoyed by young boys. Until one day in the middle of July.

To Alex, the lake—mysterious, enigmatic, forbidden, and shimmering like a silver circle fringed by dark firs—seemed irresistible on an afternoon of beating sun that had turned his skin browner than ever and parched his throat. Pulling on the reins of his small pony he looked across at Miles, expecting him to do the same, but his brother seemed lost in thought.

Alex was irritated by this mental absence which separated them so often lately. Miles was at public school; he was quite remarkably clever and had a brilliant future ahead. Everyone said so, especially Father. Alex knew it was right, for Miles had been given the brown gelding he now rode as a reward for an excellent school report. And Miles always *knew* about things, no matter what one asked him. He was hopeless at cricket and jumping, which was some consolation to an athletic younger brother. Even so, he wished all those brains did not make Miles so dreamy when they were out on an adventure. It was uncomfortable to ride beside someone who had forgotten you were there.

"Let's go down to the lake," he said in a loud voice.

Miles came out of his reverie. "Eh?" He shook his head. "Much better not. The Guv'nor wouldn't like it."

That was another thing. Miles had taken to calling their father "the Guv'nor," something Alex dared not do to his face. Somehow the expression sounded wrong on the lips of an eight year old who was tutored at home. Miles, four years older and already a handsome young man in his Eton jacket, said it with assurance and approbation. The young boy felt a sudden need to assert himself.

"*I'm* going down there. I'm hot and tired, but if you prefer to continue on your own, that's up to you."

Miles laughed good-naturedly. "All right, go and dangle your feet in the water, if you must."

"Good," cried Alex and urged his pony into an unwilling canter to the edge of the lake, whooping at the top of his voice for having gotten his own way.

"You know, you're getting frightfully grown-up, Miles," he commented as he slithered from the saddle. "If you get any worse, I shall find you unbearable."

With that, he was seized by the collar and marched forcibly down to the water's edge where his brother threatened to toss him in and push his face in the mud. There followed one of those tussles beloved by boys, which showed their affection for each other by the fierceness of blows. Alex had deliberately promoted it without really knowing why, but was delighted when his suspicions proved correct. It would not be long before he would out-wrestle his slender brother.

The fight ended when Alex spotted the punt and proposed a voyage in it. "It will be the most tremendous fun," he added. "You *can't* think of an objection."

"Yes, I can," Miles told him, dusting himself off as he looked at the boat tied up a few yards away. "The lake is out of bounds; you know that quite well."

Alex made a disgusted face at his brother. "Has that school turned you into a girl!"

Miles retaliated quickly. "It has nothing to do with school, you toad. The Guv'nor says the lake is dangerous."

Alex looked at the smooth enticing expanse of water. "But it's so calm. There's not even a ripple on it, so how can it be dangerous?" He wanted to sail out onto the sun-struck water and trail his fingers through the silver-and-black shaded patches. After riding his pony across the estate the thought of a cool glide across the forbidden surface urged him to plead with Miles.

"It can't be dangerous on a day like this. Just a *short* voyage." He added an extra inducement. "You can be captain and I'll be crew, I promise."

Miles hesitated. "I don't know. We've been told to keep away."

"That was when we were small," said the eight year old. "Father doesn't expect us to keep to those rules now. Of course, if you're too *scared* . . ." he whispered tauntingly.

"Come on, then," Miles decided swiftly. "But you'll jolly well have to do as I say."

Too excited to disagree, Alex scrambled into the long flat-bottomed boat and immediately hung over the edge to put his fingers in the water. The movement broke a mirror reflection of his face so that it broadened and quivered into distorted expressions on the green-black ripples beside the bank. He grinned into the water, and the reflection was even funnier.

"Why does it do that, Miles?" he asked without looking up, and received a patient and informed reply. "Water is funny, really," he went on idly, as the punt broke into the sunshine beyond the overhanging trees. "It isn't any color, and yet it can be anyone of them. If it's poured onto the ground it soaks away, so how does a lake ever grow? And why can a boat float on it and not a person?" He squinted up at his brother as he wielded the punt pole. "Don't you think it's funny?"

"Not really—not when you know the science of it."

Alex wished his own voice would change into that deep scratchy tone his brother had acquired last term. It would be easier to call Father "the Guv'nor" then. He rolled over to hang across the other side of the punt and stared into the transparent water, that showed floating greenery below.

"It isn't in the least dangerous, is it?"

"If you keep squirming about like that, it will be, you idiot. Boats can overturn, you know."

Alex lay on his back and stared at the sun to see if he could beat his record at looking at the blinding light.

"Not this boat."

"This very boat," said Miles in a significant tone. "It was from where you were sitting that a housemaid fell into the lake and drowned a hundred years ago."

Alex tried to keep his gaze on the sun, but his eyes were watering and he had to wipe them. After that the brilliance seemed to be exploding in ever-widening circles. "This boat wasn't made a hundred years ago. Only castles last as long as that. Besides, that girl jumped in on purpose." A thought so strong occurred to him it seemed more important than breaking his sun-staring record. Miles was only a long dark streak against his dazzled eyes, but he asked, "Is it frightful to be *wronged* by someone—frightful enough to want to jump into a lake and die?" Miles took so long in answering, he went on, "What do they mean by wronged, Miles? I mean, he was one of us, wasn't he?"

"Our great-great uncle, to be exact," said the envied deep voice. "But she was only a servant, you know, and it was quite usual for . . . oh, you'll find out later on. Actually, I think she was frightfully stupid to drown herself. It probably wasn't Sir Gavin at all. More likely some village rip."

"*What* was some village rip?"

"The one who wronged her," said Miles with a touch of drama. "Her ghost walks in the village, so it stands to reason . . ."

"*Ghost?*" Alex sat up straighter. Miles was getting clearer now; he could make out the features on his white face.

"They never found the body. It was too far out in the lake and tangled in the reeds below the surface."

Alex took his fingertips from the water as if it scorched him. "Why does the ghost appear in the village if the body is still in this lake?"

Miles narrowed his eyes cunningly and plunged the punt pole into the water. "The ghost appears here, too. In fact, on a still day like this, it's sometimes possible to see her hand come up through the water, trying to hold onto something. They say if anyone is near, she'll clutch him and pull him under."

Alex swallowed. There was a piece of wood sticking up a few yards away that looked remarkably like a hand, gnarled and beckoning. The bank seemed a long way off. Suddenly, he had had enough of this voyage.

"I suppose we should be going back," he said as casually as he could. "The ponies will be cooling off too quickly, and Roberts always makes a frightful fuss over things like that."

Miles dug the pole in again and had a job to bring it up. "You're the crew, remember? I think we should investigate the spot where the body is supposed to lie, all tangled up in the reeds. We might even see the hand come out of the water. That really would be an adventure."

The young boy began to feel slightly sick. The sun had been very hot that afternoon, and he had thrown off the white linen hat he had been told to wear when they'd been only a hundred yards from the stables. All at once the lake seemed immense; its glassy expanse sinister in its stillness.

"Miles, we seem to be a long way from the bank. Perhaps Father meant it was dangerous to go too far."

The older boy feigned surprise. "You said just now that those rules no longer applied now that we're older."

"Yes, but . . ." He got no further. Miles had drawn up the punt pole with difficulty and plunged it back into the water just ahead of his standing figure, but there was no anchorage for it and his momentum sent him headlong after the pole. The punt glided slowly onward leaving a thrashing figure in the water.

It was a moment before Alex could believe what he saw, then he shouted his brother's name in a high scared voice.

"Miles. *Miles!* I can't stop the boat. Swim over here."

The boy in the water was splashing furiously and getting nowhere. "Alex," he gasped. "Help me."

The gap between them was widening. Alex jumped into the water, knowing only that he needed the comfort of his brother's company. It was icy cold, as if the friendly sun had no power against the frozen colorless lake that hid so many secrets.

Completely possessed by fright, he struck out with flailing arms. But the sailor shirt he wore had ballooned out, hampering his inexpert swimming strokes. With fear as his propellant, he reached his brother in a state of breathless relief.

The relief was short-lived. Miles was white-faced with fright, and clutched Alex with desperate hands.

"I can't move. There's something around my legs," he gasped. "Get me out, Alex."

The young boy had not realized how strong Miles was. When they had wrestled earlier that afternoon it had seemed almost an even match, but now those gripping hands locked onto his shoulders, dragging him down until the water rose above his nose. The next minute he was beneath the surface and it was black everywhere. He could not breathe. Things touched his bare legs with slimy insidious strokes, and he thought of the housemaid lying lifeless here for a hundred years.

Breaking the surface, he gasped in air and swallowed the water churned up by their struggling bodies. Miles still held him in a vicelike grip, and he knew he would go under again any minute. It was worse the second time. Blood pounded in his ears and put a red mist over his eyes. The slimy fingers began to wrap themselves around his legs. He kicked out in terror and felt his brother's body against his feet. Miles was holding him under. He must break free.

Using all his strength he pounded with his fists and feet until the hands that held him down let go, and he bobbed up to daylight. Miles was looking terrible—pale and large-eyed with fear.

"Pull me out," he shrieked. "Get me out of here!"

Crazy with terror and knowing it would be fatal to go within reach of his brother's grasp, Alex flailed and splashed his way toward the punt with the idea of pushing it over to Miles. The despairing cries kept him going even when he began to retch and sob with effort.

The boat had drifted away. He thought he would never reach it and sobbed all the more. "God, please help me," he cried.

By the time he reached the punt, nearly all his strength had left him. He tried to push it in the other direction, back toward the place where Miles still struggled, but could not make it move. Sobbing, gasping, praying, he struggled helplessly to climb aboard, and would have failed if his leg had not touched a submerged branch. It felt like the bony fingers of a hand. Giving a shuddering cry, he fell over the shallow side onto the bottom and lay there fighting all kinds of demons until the painful wrack of his breathing had eased a little.

Then he remembered Miles and struggled to his knees to lean over the side and paddle with his hands. The boat merely swung idly round to the left as a result of his furious effort. He was too small to reach both sides at once, and the circling continued until he realized it had grown very quiet. Full of fear, he stopped cupping his hands against the water and turned his head. Miles had vanished.

Shaking from head to toe he stared at the calm empty surface and knew he must be having one of his periodic nightmares. At any moment he would awaken to feel the reassuring warmth of his bedclothes and see the familiar bedroom furniture glowing with a mellow sheen from the low light in the lamp always left with him.

He sat huddled in his wet clothes, saying every prayer he knew, and any words he could remember from the rector's sermons that always set him fidgeting. *Dear God, let me wake up soon.* The ponies on the bank whinnied—a sound of reality that had somehow found its way into his horror dream.

As evening shadows lengthened, the lake seemed to grow in size until it was a sea that had swallowed up the world. Everywhere he looked there were hideous things protruding from below, and he dared not peer over the side of the punt into the blackness surrounding his floating island for fear of what he might see there. A breeze sprang up to put goose pimples on his body, and the light began to fade. Tears ran unheeded down his face. He missed Miles with a pain he could hardly bear. When it was completely dark he knew he was not going to wake up this time . . . ever!

Shouts and bobbing lanterns entered his black purgatory. Although he heard his own name and his brother's, his throat would not allow him to make a sound. They came in a boat with a sweeping lamp that showed the mist swirling above the black water. Carter, the handyman, reached out for him, then he knew nothing more until a figure standing ten feet tall in a dark swirling cloak, his face yellow and strange in the lantern light, took his shoulders and shook him until his head wobbled.

"Where is Miles? Answer me boy! Where is your brother?"

The tongue that usually prattled on happily was stilled; the lips frozen. Father had suddenly become a menacing figure, like the devil, looming high above him in the night beside a huge black horse. Petrified, Alex buried his face in Carter's coattails, and the man said, "He's sufferin' from shock, Sir Chatsworth. You won't get no sense from the little lad yet."

But he was wrenched away and held in hands that reminded him of someone else gripping him around the neck. He began to shake again until his teeth chattered. He wanted Nanny; someone soft and kind who smelled of flowers—someone who made everything come right.

"Stop crying, boy, and tell me what happened to your brother. *Where is he?*"

Alex could not stop crying; he tried, but the tears kept flowing. His father was all part of the nightmare, for he had become a demon with a cruel yellow face and a voice that did not seem to belong to him.

"Sir Chatsworth, your son's hat is in the punt," said a quiet voice. "I think we must assume he was with the boy on the lake."

Alex was dropped immediately, and his father gave a cry that was hardly human. "Dear God, my son. *My son!*"

"We'll get all the boats out as soon as possible, sir," said another voice. "I've sent to the house for more lanterns. If he's out there, we'll find him."

The group moved off in a circle of yellow light leaving the boy alone. All alone—the sudden realization broke him finally, and he leaned against the warm hide of the horse, the only comfort available. He remained there, gripping the girth with hands that had to be pried open, when someone eventually came for him with a blanket and kindly words.

"There now, Master Alexander, you come up the house with old Samson. You don't want to stop here no longer now, do you?"

The heavens opened on the day of the funeral. It was as if the summer had ended with Miles Russell's departure from the world. Alex stood in a black suit that clung wetly to him and watched through the stream that ran down his face. The ceremony meant nothing to him; it was just a polished box being lowered into a hole; the whole ritual, dark and incomprehensible, frightened him.

But the nightmare had not ended. People looked at him oddly, and he had never felt more alone in his life. Even Nanny spoke in whispers and kept crying. She was normally so jolly and comfortable to be with. Every time he closed his eyes he saw a hand coming up through black water . . . the same ghastly apparition that kept him awake each night, staring at the lamp. He wished Miles would come back. Surely term must be over by now.

The next day was heavy with unshed rain, but Sir Chatsworth was determined that his order be carried out. The man selected for the duty reported failure. Before he had reached the lake Alex had shown such terror, he had turned back.

"By George, did no one tell you it is fatal to give in to weakness?" thundered Sir Chatsworth. "When a child has been tossed from a pony he must be put back in the saddle immediately, or he will never ride again. The boy must be *made* to go into the water, d'ye hear? His brother drowned after saving his life; he must never be the cause of such a tragedy again."

So Alex was carried kicking and screaming into the lake

and held in the water by force, although it broke the servant's heart to do it. After a few minutes he could stand no more and brought the terror-stricken child out. Later that day, another man was sent with the boy, though more hardhearted than the first, he nevertheless returned within a quarter of an hour to report that Master Alexander seemed to be ill.

That night Alex developed a fever and lay seriously ill for several weeks. When he was back on his feet again, they told him arrangements had been made to send him away to school. His father had gone back to London, so the estate manager saw him onto the train and wished him success with his studies.

Alex was home for the Christmas holidays when his twelfth birthday came around. Staying with him was a school friend whose parents had gone abroad. Sir Chatsworth rarely came to Hallworth Manor during his son's school holidays and, when he did, had no contact with him except during dinner when each sat at the long table in comparative silence.

Surprisingly there was to be a tea party to celebrate the occasion. Alex suspected it was the instigation of his two aunts who were bringing Cousin Judith and her school friend.

"Rather jolly to have two girls, Russell," said Percy Calthorpe when he heard. "Are they pretty or are they fun? I have always found that girls are one or the other—never both."

"I don't know, Calthorpe. I haven't seen my cousin for absolute years, and her friend could be ugly and disapproving, for all I know."

The girls were pretty and flatteringly overawed by two boys who already showed signs of being strapping sixfooters. But what promised to be an entertaining afternoon fizzled out into a dull and embarrassing visit. They had arrived and duly divested themselves of fur-trimmed cloaks before handing Alex a splendid telescope as a birthday gift.

"I say, thanks most awfully," he said with enthusiasm. "It's jolly unusual for girls to think of something like this. They more often give boring things like soap."

They all laughed and promised never to give him soap. The four young people were having a fine time spotting landmarks from the French windows when Sir Chatsworth walked in. Alex, who had been busily organizing the rota with the telescope, fell silent and his change of mood affected the others. The laughter went and was replaced by polite conventional behavior.

The tea was splendid and revived the youngsters a little until Alex was obliged to blow out his candles, and Sir Chatsworth said, "I recall your brother's last birthday—it was his twelfth, also. I remember it as if it were yesterday instead of four years ago. Miles extinguished the candles in one breath. See how well you do, Alexander."

One candle remained obstinately alight, and it suddenly seemed significant beyond all proportion to everyone in the room as the boy looked at it in despair before pinching it out with his fingers.

Into the silence came a clapping as Judith applauded. "Shouldn't we give a birthday cheer?" she asked, but her mother commented rather hastily on the tasteful decoration on the cake, and the general awkwardness increased.

"He would have been sixteen now, and thinking about his approaching entry into university," Sir Chatsworth reflected. "He had a brilliant mind, that boy."

"Chatsworth," said one of the aunts softly, "it's Alexander's birthday—a *happy* occasion."

But the laughter was forced from then on, and Alex had grown very quiet. Judith commented on it as the four young people walked through to the library where they proposed playing spillikins.

"Aren't you enjoying your birthday, Alex?"

He looked at her quickly. "Of course. That was a first-class present you gave me."

"It was my idea," she said shyly. "You don't seem very happy, though." It was said with the frankness of a ten year old.

"I'm sorry. Have I been rude?"

She smiled. "No, silly . . . it's just that you were laughing until it was time to blow out your candles. Did you mind doing it? I mean, is it something boys find rather . . . well . . . childish?"

He nodded. "Yes, that's it, I expect."

Behind them Percy Calthorpe was telling Judith's friend in an audible whisper, "It's all rather grisly, actually. He drowned in the lake saving Russell's life. Bit of a touchy subject, of course."

"Ooh!" said the friend with an awesome giggle.

"There was also a housemaid drowned there. One of Russell's ancestors had wronged her, you know. Her ghost walks this corridor quite frequently, as it happens."

"Ooh!" gurgled the friend in fright.

Judith said quickly, "What did your papa give you for your birthday?"

"A rather grand set of encyclopedias."

"That doesn't sound very exciting."

"It's a splendid edition." It was said defensively.

"Oh, I see."

"Very useful, too. My examination results were not too good this year, so the Guv'nor thought . . . I mean, it will save going down to the school library every time I want to look something up, won't it?"

"Do you like school?"

He seemed startled at the question. "I have never thought about it. It's something we have to do, isn't it? The school is a frightfully good one. My brother went there. His name is on the roll of honor, you know."

"Perhaps yours will be there one day."

He shook his head. "Oh, no. I shouldn't think so." He opened the library door and stood aside for her to pass through—a gesture she liked—and indicated the spillikins box. "It's a bit childish, but I daresay we can make something of it. There's nothing much else to do, I'm afraid."

Percy Calthorpe came up then. "If it were freezing we could skate on the lake. That's great fun."

The spillikins fell from the box, and they all had to gather them up from the floor. Judith noticed Alex's fingers were shaking and felt an inexplicable urge to slap Percy Calthorpe. But he was too busy trying to hold her friend's hand to notice the furious look she gave him.

"But, sir, I might never get the chance again," Alex protested.

"Do not treat me to wild dramatics, if you please. Germany is not at the far end of the world, and no doubt the Black Forest will still be standing when you have finished your studies."

Son stood facing father almost eye to eye. At seventeen Alex was nearly six feet tall and built in proportion. His voice was deep and confident, his nature good-humored but determined. Yet, the minute he stood before Sir Chatsworth his assurance evaporated, and he was a small boy again—a boy who should have died instead of his brother.

"It seemed such a good idea to join Chalmers on this walking trip as I shall be in Germany for the foils championship." It was a last stand, and he knew it.

"I beg to differ. You will not be in Germany for a . . . *foils* championship. A lot of fancy nonsense with outmoded weapons. I will not finance you for such an effeminate pastime."

Alex reddened. "A great deal of skill and strength is needed, sir. If you would only attend a contest . . . believe me, the Germans are excellent, but we believe we have their match this year. It's a matter of prestige, sir. I thought you would . . . well, I thought you would be pleased by my inclusion in the team. Seventeen is young for . . ."

"Seventeen is an age when a young man should be devoting himself to his future, not wasting his time with namby-pamby pursuits more suited to Frenchmen. Alexander, do you give no thought to your duty? Tragically your brother has not lived to inherit what should be his, by right of birth. The least you can do in honor of his memory is try to emulate him—however unsuccessfully."

The young man looked desperate. "Sir, I can never replace Miles."

The old hawk-face hardened. "I have been aware of that since the day your brother was lost. He was brilliant and also supremely aware of what was expected of him. It would never have entered his head to follow selfish desires at the expense of his duty. If this *championship*," he said the word bitingly, "is the best you can do by way of distinguishing yourself, I suggest you devote the vacation to your books. The coming year is a vital one, and if you are to enter university you plainly need to improve your present deplorable standard."

"I have already indicated that I shall be able to form one of the British team," said Alex miserably.

"Then you must indicate that you misinformed them," was the cold reply. "It's a great pity that your present passion for athletic pursuits was not in evidence nine years ago. Your brother might still be alive."

He left the room, and his son moved across to the window overlooking the estate that would be his someday. God knew he would give anything to be worthy of Miles's sacrifice, but whatever he did seemed to fall short of expectations. He was too old to cry, of course, but he pressed his forehead against the cool glass and closed his eyes. He had set his heart on going to Germany.

"Alex, I can't. My courage has evaporated."

He looked into the blue eyes that always gave away her secrets, and felt his heart melt. He loved her to the exclusion of all else. The past term had found him unable to concentrate at lectures, skipping study periods, and trying to write a thesis in the early hours with her perfume still in his nostrils, and her soft dark hair against his throat a vivid memory.

To his intense joy she loved him the same way, and he could go on no longer. She was an assistant in a Cambridge confectionery shop—a high-class one—and had respectable and strict parents. Taking a room in a quiet hotel for a weekend was out of the question. Besides, he wanted more than that where she was concerned. Last week, over muffins eaten before a roaring fire, he had asked her to marry him, and they had planned their future. He would leave university and start a career with the railways—something in which he had a great interest. One of his fellow undergraduates had an uncle who would surely give him a start in that line, so it only needed an advance from Sir Chatsworth to buy a little house, and they could be blissfully happy.

She had been dubious of such an easy path to paradise, but Alex had ardently assured her his father would only have to set eyes on her to be as captivated as he was. Even so, the thought of meeting a "sir," as she put it, and taking tea with him at the Houses of Parliament was an ordeal that filled her with dread.

Alex had laughed and kissed her hard. "He's only a mortal man, darling, not an ogre."

He laughed again now as they crossed Westminster Bridge, but felt his own heart thudding with apprehension. Knowing it would not be the easiest of tasks to get his father's approval on the railways idea, he had written asking if he might bring Miss Aspel, a very special friend, to meet him. The invitation to take tea with Sir Chatsworth at the House had been sent by his secretary—a rather discouraging response—but Alex still felt confident Alison would charm even his stern father, who was never at ease in the company of ladies. However, his confidence was now be-

ginning to evaporate, as it always did when he was trying
to explain himself to his father.

The tearoom was dark and hushed, with only a few
members eating cress sandwiches, or toast and Gentlemen's
Relish. The two were shown to a table in the corner where
they sat for three-quarters of an hour. Twice a steward
asked if they would care to order, but Alex assured him
they were waiting for Sir Chatsworth Russell. They ran out
of conversation. Alison looked pale; Alex felt awkward and
angry. He cleared his throat and said he expected the debate had gone on longer than usual. Trying to appear calm,
he got up and walked across to ask for a message to be
conveyed to his father's secretary.

Twenty minutes later Sir Chatsworth walked in and
looked around him before going to the only table left occupied. "Alexander, what's so urgent that it brings you here?"
He ignored the girl.

The unexpected approach caught Alex on the wrong
foot. "Sir, I wrote . . . I understood you had invited us . . ."
He broke off to turn to the girl. "I particularly wanted
you to meet Miss Aspel. I explained the reason in my letter."

"I never read letters unless Frederick hands them to me.
He deals with all routine ones. Must have been a mistake
somewhere." There was no apology, no regret, and no pleasure on seeing his remaining son.

The introductions were made, and Alison could not have
been more gauche and nervous. In a flash she had turned
into a mumbling, awkward shop girl, flaunting her inferiority with every word. He ached inside when she said, "How
do you do, Sir Russell"—he had told her countless times
she should say *Sir Chatsworth*. Even her voice sounded
wrong now that his father was there with them, and he
could see how she must appear to the older man. Because
of it his own nervousness increased. It was all going so
badly.

They were all standing, since Sir Chatsworth had made
no attempt to join them at the table. Now, he looked at
Alex. "I assume Miss . . . ?"

"Aspel," Alex supplied woodenly.

". . . Miss Aspel has a problem. Is she from my constit-
uency?"

The room seemed to be closing in on him. Why did the
girl he loved so desperately suddenly look like one of his

father's constituents? She stood with humble awe written all over her. Where had the warmth and loveliness gone? He struggled to retain his command over the situation.

"Miss Aspel is a special friend of mine, sir." There was silence so he plunged on. "We love each other."

Sir Chatsworth subjected Alison to the barest flicker of a glance before raising his eyebrows. "Dear me!"

"Could we all sit down?" Alex asked through tight lips. "I'd like to talk to you, sir."

Sir Chatsworth took out his pocket watch with great deliberation and stared at it. "You have caught me at a most inconvenient time, I fear. Your message brought me away from a vital debate on the Transvaal gold question, and as a man with investments there I am expected to speak with first-hand knowledge. Is it really important, Alexander?"

In that moment Alex knew with absolute certainty that Frederick Stacey, his father's zealously efficient secretary, would have shown his employer a letter from his son, would have arranged the tea invitation with Sir Chatsworth's consent; the engagement would have been entered in the diary and mentioned on his arrival in Westminster that morning. He grew desperately angry.

"Yes, it is important. It concerns my future." He took Alison's hand. "*Our* future."

The older man frowned. "Your future has already been decided. You will finish your studies at Cambridge, then take a post in the city that will attempt to fit you for the responsibility of running the estate and its accompanying wealth when the time comes." He looked at Alex beneath low brows. "Since you survived and Miles did not, it is incumbent on you to ensure his sacrifice was not in vain. Have you really not yet grasped that fact?"

Alex was sinking fast, and there was nothing to support him. The girl beside him was picking up her gloves from the table with hands that were trembling, yet all he saw was the neatly darned patch at the end of one of the navy blue fingers.

Sir Chatsworth took his attention again. "Perhaps I was not as harsh as some people thought when I decided on twenty-five as the age at which you will take control of your own finances. It is my hope you will have passed the age of indiscretion by then." He looked at his watch again. "You really will have to excuse me. This trouble in South Africa over the Boer franchise is quite vital to the country

. . . and to the family." He began moving away. "I shall see you at Hallworth for Christmas, no doubt. Good afternoon, Miss." With a hint of a bow he left them standing in the far corner of an empty room.

They left the parliament buildings in silence. Outside on the pavement Alison told him she would prefer to return to Cambridge alone, and he thought she had never looked lovelier than with tears on her lashes.

"I love you," he told her raggedly.

She nodded, not looking at him. "I know. Good-bye, Alex."

He wished her distant figure would vanish but he could still see her cherry-colored coat five minutes later. The bustle of traffic was all around him—the clopping hooves and shouts of drivers, the clatter of trams and bells—but he heard none of it. He was on the bridge looking down at the Thames, filled with a strange kind of desperate pain. The water was brown, swirling along in greasy eddies, cold and sinister. As he watched, it seemed to rise and engulf him as it had once before. After thirteen years his brother had put up a bony hand and dragged him under.

# PART ONE

# CHAPTER ONE

London's West End was seething with merrymakers. The theaters were packed with lower-floor toffs in diamonds, furs, and silk opera hats, satins, velvets, and starched shirts; while the upper-floor crowds sported Sunday best, and the new ties and gloves received at Christmas.

In the elegant houses of Belgravia and Park Lane champagne was flowing and young ladies were growing indiscreet. In Stepney and Clerkenwell effects of too much ale were much in evidence, and girls were accepting a kiss and a cuddle from any man in sight. In the Old Kent Road they were blissfully dancing in the street, while in Trafalgar Square, tail-coated men-about-town were whooping it up with bottles of bubbly.

The new year was 1898 and it was trembling on the brink of birth with all of London celebrating England's greatness and prosperity. Under Queen Victoria the Empire had grown and developed; men had dared and achieved as never before. Trade was booming, and Britannia ruled the waves. Railways, the cloth industry, and steel were pounding the once-quiet island with the roar of pistons, wheels, and flying shuttles. Smoke poured from tall chimneys in the North, and horses plodded ceaselessly between furrows of rich soil only a few miles from the clatter of factory clogs on wet cobblestones.

For the rich it was splendid; the poor went on as before. But for Britons of every class and station there was a sense of being on the crest of a wave that would never break—the only small hazard was the jagged rock of the Transvaal, where talk of war was growing. However, South Africa was a long way from England, and British troops were garrisoned there for such alarms. Majuba had not been forgotten, and the British public would welcome an opportunity to avenge their dead by giving the Boers a thrashing next time.

But New Year's Eve was not a time for heavy thoughts. Instead, it was time to eat, drink, and be merry—for to-morrow we shall do it all over again. Alex was having a night to remember. Tom Standish had led them all up a staircase of a house to join a party that had reached the carefree stage, and then discovered that he did not know the host, after all. They had already given their cloaks to the man and it seemed rather foolish to leave again; no one objected to a few more in what was an overcrowded room.

Alex took a glass of champagne and tossed half of it back immediately as his eyes studied the female guests inti-mately. He and three friends had been to the theater after a snappy dinner in someone's rooms, and paid homage to Lottie Lavenham. The little minx had refused their com-pany to attend a party with Archie Molyneux, even though they had all given her a jolly decent present. Alex could not remember exactly what his present had been—probably a jeweled garter—but they had all felt very cut up about her treatment of them. It was then that Tom had remembered that a friend of his was throwing a party. Pity he had forgotten exactly where, but one was as good as another . . . and the girls just as beautiful!

After ten minutes he had discovered that the host was called Freddie and approached a girl who reminded him painfully of Alison. She had the same kind of soft dark hair and big eyes, and knew he was headed in her direction even though she pretended not to be looking.

"Hallo, old fellow," he greeted the strange man with her. "Freddie told me I should find you over here. It's dashed good to see you after all this time."

"Nice of you to come over, old chap," replied the stranger. "Life treating you well, is it?"

"Can't complain." He smiled at the girl. "Won't you pre-sent me?"

"But my dear old friend, you must already know . . ."

"Marion," supplied the girl, giving Alex a wide-eyed invitation to know her better.

"Must already know Marion," said the other man heart-ily, having no idea who she was.

Alex took her gloved hand to his lips in a drunkenly exaggerated gesture. "Any friend of Freddie's cannot help knowing Marion. You look more beautiufl every time I see you."

After a while the stranger moved off, and it was not long

before Alex skillfully maneuvered Marion toward the terrace where it was more secluded. When he kissed her she did not object, so he kissed her again.

"Are you sure your name is Marion?" he asked thickly.

"Are you sure you are Sir Chatsworth Russell's son?" she countered softly.

He nodded. "Oh yes, there's only one of us. My brother is dead, so I can't be him. He drowned saving my life."

"Brave man!" Her eyes glowed for a moment. "So the family name and fortune rests on your shoulders alone, does it?"

He did not like the way the conversation was going. It was a night for whooping it up, not for maudlin introspection. He kissed her again. "You do look frightfully like Alison, you know."

Her eyes glowed even more. "Are you fond of her?"

*"Was,"* he said with alcoholic drama, ". . . three years ago."

"What happened?"

"The Guv'nor didn't approve." He nibbled her ear. "He'd like you."

She held him off in a tantalizing fashion with soft hands against his chest. "Jealous of the family name, is he?"

"Who?" he asked, trying to kiss her neck.

"Sir Chatsworth . . . your father."

"Oh yes. Family honor . . . carrying on the old traditions . . . all that kind of thing," was the expansive reply designed to impress her. "It all rests on me now. When I am twenty-five I take on all that Miles should have inherited." He gave a wicked grin. "But until then I am going to have a damned good time."

She let him draw her closer then, and he felt his words must have done the trick for she was much warmer than before. They drank a lot of champagne, and if she kept filling his glass from her own it did not seem to matter as long as she remained by his side. Her face grew more and more like Alison's as time passed and he began calling her by that name, believing in his fuddled brain that she had come back to him.

He grew more amorous. "I can't believe my luck in meeting you again, Alison," he whispered against her shoulder. "Isn't it wonderful?"

"Wonderful," she agreed. "Who would have thought such a ripe plum would have fallen into my lap tonight."

Her words went over his head. He was too busy following with his mouth the line of her dress where it crossed
her smooth white shoulders. She resisted him with a low
teasing laugh. "Not here, my sweet. There are too many
people about."

"Let's go somewhere else, then," he suggested ardently,
but it had reached midnight and all the guests burst onto
the terrace to sing Auld Lang Syne. After that, Tom Standish suggested they should repair to Trafalgar Square to
drink Nelson's health.

About a dozen of them crammed into a carriage armed
with bottles and glasses. Alex had the girl on his lap. He
could not remember when he had had such a grand evening—in fact, he could not remember much at all. The
square was alive with revelers who were past caring what
they did and whom they were with. Each one was filled
with goodwill and brotherhood; he loved his neighbor with
all the extravagance a bottle could produce. People surged
around the fountains singing songs ranging from the pa-
triotic to the latest naughty music-hall ditty—each ren-
dered with equal fervor—arms linked in comradeship.

Alex and his friends spilled from the carriage to join the
throng, and he was soon urged to open a bottle of champagne. With his silk hat on the back of his head and his
opera cloak askew he complied amidst laughter and encouragement. When the cork flew off they all cheered, and
Alex's sleeves were covered in foaming liquid before he had
a chance to pour any in the waiting glasses.

"Whoops!" he cried drunkenly. "Keep those glashes
shtill!"

Most of it went on the pavement and was immediately
lapped up by several scavenging mongrels.

"A toasht!" proclaimed one of the young men in the
group. "A toasht to Alex who has managed to get himshelf
shent down from Came . . . Cambridge five months before taking hish degree. He hash joined our ranks at last.
We thought he would never do it in time but . . . but he
did." It was said with great deliberation. "He dashed well
did!"

"To Alex," cried the group, plus anyone else who felt
inclined to join in.

"Have you really been sent down?" the girl beside him
asked.

"Yes," he said with a fatuous grin, and cuddled her to

him. "Too many girls, the dean said. Good thing he didn't see you, Ali . . . Alishon."

The girl seemed to be swaying, so he held her tighter, but there were hands seizing him from behind, and she faded away. With the whole of Trafalgar Square spinning around in a flash of colored lights and discordant voices his boisterous companions lifted him shoulder high as they marched around in procession.

Highly pleased with such distinction Alex waved his arms wildly and drank from the champagne bottle to celebrate his success at being dismissed from Cambridge to join a long list of distinguished miscreants. The world was a wonderful place up there on his friends' shoulders. Lights, people's faces, the sparkling fountains, and tall colonnaded buildings spun 'round and 'round until they merged into a dizzying blur of color that accompanied a growing sense of well-being and self-assurance. He was a fine fellow, everyone was his friend, and his achievement would go down in history. Alexander Russell had been worth saving from a watery grave all those years ago!

The fleeting thought of that summer afternoon cleared his vision for a short moment to show him, in smooth, menacing, light-reflected blackness, the stretch of water around Nelson's Column. In that moment he knew what his friends were about to do. His senses were almost dulled to a stupor and his reactions at their slowest, before he realized they were at the edge of the ornamental lake. He began to struggle like a man possessed. Ghosts and horrors rose out of the water with skeletal beckoning fingers; trailing slimy fronds lurked beneath the surface to wrap around his legs and drag him down. In that water were unspeakable things he could not face—had been unable to face for sixteen years.

He was fighting madly against the hands that clutched him, but those bearing him aloft laughed all the louder as they began swinging him back and forth in preparation for the ducking. Seized with debilitating terror he tried to tell them, but the crowds were cheering and singing, corks were popping, and the muscles of his jaw were locked rigidly to prevent any sensible words from forming.

The next minute, he was flying through the air to hit the water with a smack. The cheers of onlookers increased a hundredfold into a great deafening roar as his head became submerged and everything turned black. He could not breathe, the dread water pressed him down, further down until his ears rang and his heart thumped throughout his whole body. When cold air filled his nostrils once more he fought to get upright. Fear triumphed over Bacchus, enabling him to stumble with water-sogged haste toward the stone wall encircling the lake, pushing off the reaching hands of the others who had decided to join him and were reluctant to see one of their number go.

Shaking from head to toe he fell over the low wall, gripping it with iron fingers to prevent himself being dragged back by a hand reaching out from the past. Vague pictures of a boat and himself beating the water with his hands mingled with the tantalizing nearness of recollection of something a small boy of eight had banished from his mind by shock. The brink of a traumatic memory was strong enough to set him scrambling over the wall to the solid pavement, and he pushed through the crowds to get as far as possible.

His panic grew. All those revelers who had been his friends in inebriation now appeared menacing; the slap on the back, the comradely arm about his shoulders were now gestures of threat. If he did not get away they would put him back there. As he was a big man no one tried to argue with him in his new fighting mood, and he charged through the crowd with sick desperation until he found himself up against a gray stone wall. He leaned against it with outspread hands, feeling the safety of its ancient solidness. Slowly, he conquered the sensation of having stared at death in the face. When a hand touched his arm he spun round aggressively.

"Easy, darling. Are you all right?"

She looked beautiful in the half-light, just as Alison had when she said good-bye to him. Splashes of water had put drops of silver on the girl's eyelashes so that it looked as if she were crying, too. He could only stare speechlessly at her.

"I think you had better come with me," she said softly. "It's not far, and you look dreadfully ill."

She led him to a carriage and gave the driver an address. Alex was exhausted beyond measure and lay back against the cushions with his eyes closed. He hardly noticed the outside of the house; he merely handed the driver a fistful of silver and followed the girl who was Alison and yet was not.

The first-floor room was warm and softly lit. He swayed and had to steady himself on a chair. The girl had vanished to return with a large brandy balloon.

"Drink this. You have had a shock."

He took the glass, but just looked at it reflectively.

"Was it the water?" she asked softly.

His eyes focused on her again, and he felt the pain of that parting beside Westminster Bridge. "Yes. Do you find that fainthearted?"

She moved closer. "Not in the least. Drink your brandy."

He downed it in one gulp and felt the warmth reaching his frozen limbs. She refilled the glass and handed it to him. He made a wry face. "I'm making your carpet exceedingly damp."

She walked to a door and opened it. "Go in and take off your wet things. I'll arrange for them to be dried. You'll find plenty of towels and blankets."

It was difficult to navigate the doorway without hitting the sides. When he did, he found himself in a large bedroom that surprised him with its good taste. He had not expected that kind of girl to live in such a house . . . but such thoughts were only fleeting as he downed the second brandy before stripping off his wet clothes.

As he was toweling himself, he found the room suddenly spinning, and had a distinctly dizzy feeling similar to what he had experienced prior to going into the water.

"Damned fool!" he muttered to himself, losing his grip on the towel and reaching for one of the blankets on the bed. "Brandy after champagne is . . . is . . ." His brain could stretch no further, and he sat on the edge of the bed in the hopes of steadying himself. It was worse. The bed rose up to meet him, and the blessing of oblivion enveloped him.

Much, much later—or so it seemed—Alex was brought to a half-aware state by hands moving over his body in a tantalizing fashion, so that he struggled to lose the alcoholic lethargy weighing him down. All he could manage was a heavy arm across a waist clad in silk.

"Alex," whispered a voice in his ear. "Are you awake?"

"Mmm," he managed after an effort. His head was a stone, but he turned his face into her soft hair with a contented grunt.

"That's quite enough, darling," the voice said with amused firmness. "You won't forget Marion, will you?"

"Mar . . . ion." The name fell like a word spoken by someone in a trance, then her lips were on his softly and fleetingly.

"Thank you, Alexander Russell, for everything . . . especially your terror of water. You have been the answer to a prayer, my sweet."

Her warm nearness was suddenly withdrawn, but his brief visit to reality had ended and only his inner spirit called for her return. He half heard her words, but saw nothing of the girl in a silk evening gown who took her fur wrap and left the house with a smile of delighted satisfaction on her beautiful face.

In the morning, a manservant brought Alex tea and his evening clothes cleaned and pressed. He seemed completely unsurprised at the guest and spoke as if his master—a Mr. Jermyn—habitually played absent host to friends who needed lodgings for the night. Of the girl Marion there was no sign, and the man made no mention of her. Alex played along with the expected role and left as soon as possible, feeling Mr. Jermyn might not intend his hospitality to extend to his mistress.

To salve his conscience he sent an anonymous case of whiskey to his unknown host, which took a chunk from January's allowance. He was delighted, therefore, when Tom Standish invited him to his uncle's place in Italy where the gambling tables of the wealthy would give him the opportunity to restore his bank balance. He would also have a breathing space in which to think over his future. The railways still appealed to him very strongly.

They still appealed to him very strongly when he arrived back in England, but regrettably, his bank balance only enriched by a pile of notes of hand. Luck had run against him. So it was with a sinking heart that he found a letter from his bank awaiting him.

It contained far worse than he imagined, for he was not only quite heavily in debt but the manager regretted to inform him that as of January Sir Chatsworth had discontinued his son's allowance. It was a blow that brought a premonition of trouble far exceeding what he knew was inevitable when his father discovered he had been kicked out of Cambridge.

All his confidence vanished and was replaced by the old feeling of guilt and worthlessness. It stayed until a summons arrived in reply to the message he had sent by hand to his father's town house. Then, the imperative tone of the summons forced a determined bravado to firm his steps as he approached the front door.

The old house was too full of the past. Trent greeted him as Master Alexander, which turned him into a boy immediately. The familiar dark-paneled hall and heavy somber staircase echoed with childhood memories. Timidity sat upon him once more, as it had so many times during his life when he had trod the thick carpet leading to his father's first-floor study. With a sense of disgust with himself he halted outside the door and remembered he was a man of twenty-four who could shape his own life.

One look at his father's stern face, carved in lines of long-standing loss and sadness—all caused by himself, he knew—was enough to fill Alex with the usual need to offer himself up as a sacrifice to atone for his sins. The thud of his heartbeat increased as he drew nearer the old man and saw in his expression a contempt that exceeded any ever written before on those gaunt features. Although now an inch taller than Sir Chatsworth, Alex felt at that moment that the old man was looming over him in the same sinister manner that he had that black night beside the lake. The half-memory made him shiver, as if cold had just invaded him. It hung over him like a specter passing above his head—a memory of huge black horses and lights bobbing about in a mist of terror—then it faded leaving him still chilled. It was a fancy, a dream he must once have had that returned to him quite often in moments of stress, yet never lasted long enough to take a definite shape.

"Even you should have had the sense and courtesy to leave a forwarding address at the bank," Sir Chatsworth began. "Or was it excessive cowardice that sent you running instead of facing the consequences of your actions like a gentleman?"

The savageness of the attack knocked him off-balance. His father's anger had always taken the form of controlled contempt. Now he was using words that were unthinkable between mere aquaintances—to his son they were unforgivable. Shocked into silence Alex could only stand in the oak-lined room lit by the harsh March daylight while Sir Chatsworth's anger flayed him.

"From that terrible day I have sought to understand the will of the Lord, that he should take Miles so tragically. Right from the start you made it clear there was no sense of gratitude, no moral obligation, none of the pride *he* felt so strongly. God knows, I have worked unceasingly to make something of you, even when I knew in my heart I was building on quicksand, but even in my darkest moments I did not dream it would ever come to this! Does the name of Russell mean nothing to you? Has your family's distinguished past never raised a shred of pride in you? Is it possible you could contemplate dragging us all through the mud without a qualm? By God, sir, have you not done your family enough harm without *this*?"

Staggered by the manner in which his father was taking the news, Alex found himself offering a hot defense. "Sir, my great-uncle was expelled from Eton. He never even went to Cambridge."

"Damn, you, I am not speaking of Cambridge, but Lady Lorimer."

"Lady . . . Lorimer?" He was completely confused.

"Lady Marion Lorimer. Were you too inebriated even to . . . ?" Words failed the elderly man.

Alex could see his father's hands shaking and doubted he would ever see him in a greater state of rage than he was at present. With foreboding he remembered New Year's Eve when he had been extremely drunk, and had met a girl called Marion . . . but she was a . . . surely his father would not know someone of that nature?

"I'm sorry, sir, but you must have made some mistake . . . be under a misapprehension . . ."

"I wish to God I were, but your record over the past three years leaves me with little hope—undesirable company, deplorable drinking habits, and young women by the score. I was prepared to allow that immaturity and long-standing weakness of character accounted for this . . . this degeneracy," he said, "that it would pass when it had run its course. I believed you were responsible enough to get your degree at least. With only five months to go you throw away years of study for the sake of an immoral liaison—several, in fact—which could have been conducted in a discreet hotel. You knew the college rules; one would think you deliberately flouted them."

There was no point in interrupting. It was basically true. Something told him a storm was about to break. All this wrath over his dismissal from Cambridge was only preliminary thunder.

"I see you have nothing to say for yourself." The mouth that formed a bitter slash across a face that was handsome, despite harshness of line, grew tighter. "Then I will have an answer from you on *this*. Did you, on New Year's Eve, accept help from Lady Lorimer who took you to the nearby house of a friend, and there assault her while intoxicated and force your will upon her?"

Alex remembered that water, and a woman who gave him brandy in a warm room. He had been seized with a terrifying fear of that water, the strength of which had consumed his every thought until her hands on his body returned him to humanity. They had been in bed together— she in something soft to the touch and he naked—that was all he remembered. His quick impulse was to deny taking her by force. He had never done that to any woman. He opened his mouth to speak, then closed it again. Surely that girl Marion had been of easy virtue. She had played up to him all along the way. How did his father know of the incident, and why should he call a woman of that nature Lady Lorimer?

"I am waiting, Alexander . . . or am I to take your silence as an affirmative?"

"No, sir."

"You deny the incident?"

He hesitated. "I deny doing anything in which the . . . lady . . . was not a willing participant." He tried a faint smile. "She made it quite plain that her mode of life included . . . er . . . immoral liaisons, I believe you called them, sir."

Sir Chatsworth grew cardiac red. "You damned fool! Her mode of life includes entertaining at the highest level, acting on many committees—one of which is for fallen women—and assisting her husband in his public life. She is the wife of Sir Giles Lorimer, a man of infinite talent and a fellow member of parliament."

The information hit Alex like a blow in the stomach. If Sir Giles was charging him with violating his wife all hell would break loose in the courts, and society in general. How could he possibly defend such a charge?

"Why didn't he come to me?" he asked harshly. "If I am man enough to commit what he suggests, I am man enough to handle his charges."

"Sir Giles is in South America—has been for six months. It was Lady Lorimer who paid me a visit."

Thinking of that sweet face with the innocence of Alison, but the lure of Delilah, Alex found it difficult to imagine how his father had handled such a woman.

"She claims you as the father of the child she now carries," continued the voice that was famed for its oration in the House. "With understandable reluctance to bring such a sordid affair to public notice, she asked only for a suitable sum to enable her to retire to the country until after the birth of the child, and to arrange for suitable foster-parents." His glassy eyes flashed with the anger of a clever man who knows he has been forced into a corner. "You may thank your stars she applied to me and not to you. I already have a list of your debts."

Alex was roused to anger at that. "She would have received nothing from me, in any case. Surely you can see it is blackmail. She might be Sir Giles's wife, but I told you all along she was no better than a . . ."

"Do you take me for a fool?" Sir Chatsworth roared. "Of course it is blackmail. She has undoubtedly been indiscreet while her husband is away and is looking for a way out. Were you intimate with her at anytime?"

"I . . . it is possible."

"*Possible!* Damn you, what kind of answer is that!" He strode across the room slapping a hand against his leg. "This is as much as I am prepared to suffer—as much as any reasonable man might be expected to tolerate from his son. You will not commit any further outrages, I swear."

"There is no way of proving I am the father of her child," Alex said tautly.

His father swung around and thumped the desk with his fist. "That, sir, is not the point. It is that you allow yourself to become involved in tawdry affairs that lay you, and everyone connected with you, open to scandal. If you must satisfy your masculine appetites you should have the sense and decency to do so discreetly and with sober knowledge of whom you are with." He approached to within two feet of his son and looked him over with withering disparagement. "Never in my life have I been subjected to such distaste as my interview with Lady Lorimer. I never would have believed a son of mine could vanish after failing so miserably at university and leave no trace of where he might be found. I might eventually find it possible to overlook weakness of the flesh, but lack of courage to face the consequences of such weakness I will not tolerate from someone who has to substitute for my rightful heir. You are a disgrace to his memory."

With whatever anger, whatever defense Alex might have countered his father, that last left him standing before a yawning chasm of honor, duty, and guilt. The truth was slammed against him. By saving his life his brother had placed on his shoulders an inescapable obligation. His short revolt against the legacy Miles had left him had been futile and disastrous. He was not his own man and never could be.

With his jaw working he forced himself to say, "I am sorry, sir."

"Sorry!" Sir Chatsworth exploded. "By throwing away the career in politics you should have pursued after coming down from Cambridge, you leave me no alternative but to arrange the only other course open—one you are damned fortunate to find. I have spoken to your tutors, and to my old friend Colonel Rawlings–Turner, who has agreed to accept you as a subaltern in his regiment on the showing of what work you *did* do at Cambridge. It is not one of those elite regiments whose officers are pampered nobles whiling away the time because they have nothing better to do. It has a reputation for discipline and loyalty, and its officers are jealous of the colors they serve. You will find yourself up against tradition, endeavor, and integrity—things for which you appear to have no appreciation." He coughed lengthily, showing how the cold winter had stricken him. "As far as I can see," he resumed a little thickly, "the only thing in your favor is that you shoot extremely well. In a rifle regiment it will be a great advantage. The rest you will have to learn the hard way." He coughed again and went to poke the fire before standing with his back to it. "The army will make a man of you, and marriage will steady you down."

"*Marriage!*" The word burst from Alex in the midst of his frozen state.

"Your present way of life will cease on entering the Downshire Rifles. An officer and gentleman is not expected to amass debts, disobey rules, or smuggle young women into his quarters. I can control the first, the regiment will control the second, and a wife will control the third." He rocked back and forth on the balls of his feet. "You will report to the Colonel at the end of this month."

Rallying the impulse to fight for survival Alex heard himself say, "And if I say I do not care to?"

Sir Chatsworth took his time in answering. "I shall renounce all ties with you. They will declare you bankrupt, and you will run the risk of facing Lorimer's charge, with a possible prison sentence." He sank down in his chair by the desk like a man bowed by age and despair. "Alexander, your mother died to give you life; Miles surrendered his for the same reason. Do you not owe them something for their sacrifices?"

What could any man answer? He knew it was over. His question was born of his despair, "I suppose you have someone in mind for my bride?"

"Of course. I have only to settle the details before the engagement can be announced."

Judith Burley was writing letters at her escritoire. She had just refused three invitations, thought better of it, and accepted each one—all for the same evening. The action was born of cynicism. If her company was so much in demand, she could afford to be precocious. Think how disappointed two hostesses would be when she did not arrive—and how jealous of the third!

She sighed. The thought no longer appeared amusing, and she really did not wish to go to any of the functions. Her letters went into the wastepaper basket to join several others. For a while she sat staring from her windows at the passing couples—pretty girls and attentive young men enjoying a stroll in the late April sunshine. They looked happy to be together; they reveled in the coming summer days. There would be boating on the Thames, canters in the park, picnics, and flirtations that blossomed during long balmy evenings. Girls found pleasure in donning pastel muslins and lace, with tiny waists and full flowing skirts, frills beneath the chin, and cartwheel hats in romantic style that put a tracery of light and shade upon faces that teased and tantalized ardent companions.

Summer brought a rash of engagements and marriages, as young men yielded to spring fever. Bells pealed from church towers; paper petals showered dewy-eyed guests; veils and blushes covered the brides; pride and pink-tipped ears distinguished the bridegrooms.

At twenty-two Judith was still unattached—still untouched by the emotion that seemed to conquer others so easily. Where some girls were showered with proposals of marriage in theater-boxes, drifting punts, blossom-filled conservatories, and secluded arbors—even by post—Judith had not been called upon to fight off ardent embraces, nor exercise tact and understanding in refusing an infatuated young suitor.

Watching the flirtatious procession in the street below as lovers headed for the park, she sighed again. The escritoire was covered with invitations she did not want, to the sort of affairs that always ended the same way. She was heartily sick of being paraded before eligible young men by hostesses who only emphasized what their designs were by their elaborate attempts to hide them. Young men, Judith found, fell into two groups—those foolish enough to throw themselves at her feet, and those foolish enough to allow her to stop them from doing so. Charming, handsome, wealthy—even amusing, sometimes—they might be, but all had that same fatal weakness. She did not want a man at her feet; being a tall girl her preference was to have a partner to whom she could look up to—in every sense.

For three seasons she had borne the ritual of foolish, pleasure-ridden boring events where dalliance was the main attraction. Most young people played the game with mutual pleasure; Judith found it vastly disappointing. Was there no more to life than the frothy pleasures of her set? Would she finally marry one of the mild young men and continue the social round with hair that turned grayer and grayer?

It was thoughts such as these that Mrs. Burley interrupted by her entry, and Judith's restlessness increased. Her mother was wearing an unmistakably flustered expression, which was usually the result of an upset with her sister Pansy, and the young girl was not in the mood to hear the usual long tirade of grievances.

Judith had passed the stage of feeling guilty over wishing she had been her aunt's daughter. Aunt Pan had wit, common sense, and courage; her mama was rather self-centered—an indecisive feminine creature who should never have remained a widow for so long. Living in an all-female household was a strain, at the best of times; when two widows crossed swords—more frequently than not over Judith herself—it became intolerable. Alicia Bur-

ley and Pansy Davenport were complete opposites, yet
both made the same mistake of not quite understanding the
young girl in their charge. Mrs. Burley imagined her
daughter to be a copy of herself; Mrs. Davenport tended to
guide and advise her niece with affectionate wisdom but a
touch of mastery. Judith had a mind of her own that was
pulled apart by the difficulty of dutifully trying to please
both matrons. To her mother, she tried to show compassion for her many invented ailments and struggled against
the clinging possessiveness that demanded a compensatory
devotion to a selfish woman deprived of a husband's attentions. Judith should have been a joy, not a whipping boy
for a cruel fate that had taken away the widow's pillar of
strength.

With Aunt Pan it was more difficult to put a finger on
the problems. Apart from feeling a duty to defend her
mother against Aunt Pan's scathing, but mostly accurate
disparagement, Judith felt extremely close to her aunt, and
in sympathy . . . yet she sometimes had a vague sense of
being manipulated by the strong-minded woman. Aunt Pan
was a remarkable woman. Judith was not certain she also
wished to be remarkable—just independent, perhaps.

Mrs. Burley often bewailed the absence of a man in the
household, but none of the three women in that imposing
house at Richmond regretted it more than Judith. Her own
life would have been so very different and far less sheltered
with a father or uncle to bring a little humor and common
sense to tense situations, and to act as escort for those functions for which a male chaperon was essential. The presence of a father or uncle might also have produced the
acquaintance of more interesting young men than the season's crop of "eligibles."

Now knowing it would be useless to confess her own
restlessness Judith steeled herself to answer her mother's
greeting with pleasant composure. Mrs. Burley was not in
the least composed, however.

"Judith, something quite extraordinary has happened. I
really cannot imagine how to tell you. Pansy is extremely
calm and vigorous, as usual, and I fancy Chatsworth is
finding her quite impossible." She fluttered her hands. "Of
all the times I have wished your father were here to support me . . ." the sentence tailed off on a note of pathos.
"I miss his excellent advice, you know."

"Mama, you have been a widow for fifteen years," said

Judith. "You should be used to making your own decisions."

"But in this case . . . oh, my dear, I do not know what to do for the best. One cannot help being flattered, and yet it seems a little unusual these days. I know it was quite the thing when Chatsworth was a young man . . . and I am never certain how you feel about . . . I mean, there is the de Marny boy and that handsome Clive Raglan." She paused for breath and put a fragile smile on her face. "You have never confided in me, even though I have been your only parent for so long. Is it any wonder I sometimes feel you are a stranger?"

Judith went across to her soft, sweet-smelling, pink-and-white mother and embraced her. "That is complete nonsense." she said. "If it seems that I do not discuss everything I do and feel it is because I know you have quite enough to worry you. See how upset you are now."

"Not upset, dear, simply uncertain what will be the best for you. I do not deny the future prospects are quite dazzling, but if you take one of your strong aversions to the scheme I can see naught but disaster coming of it."

From long experience Judith knew her mother was liable to run on and on without making any sense, so she put her arm behind the corseted back and urged her toward the door. Since the cause of her agitation appeared to be something concerning herself—and in some obscure way, Duncan de Marny and Clive Raglan—Judith felt it would be best to descend to the sitting room where Aunt Pan was apparently being impossible to her cousin Sir Chatsworth Russell, and try to clarify the situation.

When they entered, Mrs. Davenport was heavily engaged in a conversation concerning the money she had invested in South African gold shares at her cousin's suggestion.

"It seems the height of foolishness to allow Englishmen in to dig the gold and settle in their new country, then refuse to treat them as citizens, Chatsworth. The Boers are of farming stock without education. Now, I'll allow that they probably know best how to run a farming community, but no one with any sense could say they are fitted to govern an entire province that has . . ." she broke off at their entry and said, "So, you have taken my advice, Alicia, and decided to let the girl speak for herself. Judith, before Sir Chatsworth puts his extraordinary proposal to you, I wish to make it clear that if you were my daughter he would have been sent on his way long ago. I think the whole notion is impudent, extremely unflattering, and quite outdated. Since I am no more than your aunt, all I could do on your behalf was to prevent two ridiculous people from arranging your future without any reference to your wishes. Let me impress upon you, my dear, that you have only to refuse and the matter will be very speedily dropped. I will see to that," she concluded firmly.

If Judith was curious before, she was speechless now. She shifted her gaze from the bristling lady in dark green to the tall autocratic man she saw only at intervals, and whom she had always rather feared for his satanic appearance.

He was extremely courteous, as usual, but, taken aback by Mrs. Davenport's declaration, greeted her with a certain amount of awkwardness. Judith was too anxious to hear what he had to say to bother much about his discomfort.

"Good afternoon, Sir Chatsworth," she began. "It is quite some time since we met, and I cannot imagine how your visit can have caused such a stir and concern me so strongly. I hope I have not offended you in anyway."

"Quite the reverse, my dear young lady. I have always felt you possessed admirable qualities."

Judith was surprised. He had not seen her often enough to form such an opinion, unless it was based on hearsay from her mother and aunt.

"That is very kind of you," she said politely. "In what way can I help you?"

To say she was astonished would be too mild, for he was not the kind of man she would connect with matchmaking. As he gravely put forward all the reasons why he thought she would make an excellent wife for his son, how Alexander had recently taken a commission in a rifle regiment, and laid out for her the advantages of becoming Mrs. Russell, she felt the afternoon had taken on an even stranger quality than before.

No one attempted to interrupt Sir Chatsworth, but the minute he finished speaking Mrs. Burley said, "He is so eligible . . . *such* a good match! If only your father were here to handle this."

"Nonsense," said Mrs. Davenport. "There is only one person who can handle this, and I know Judith well enough to be confident she will give the sensible answer."

"Quite right, Aunt Pan," said Judith. "The answer is Yes, Sir Chatsworth."

The two widows sat open-mouthed, but Sir Chatsworth merely gave a small bow.

"I am greatly relieved, Judith. I shall tell Alexander, and he will make the formal proposal as soon as it can be arranged."

"I shall look forward to it," she replied. It was as if she were speaking of a social engagement.

## CHAPTER TWO

After their guest departed Mrs. Burley burst into joyful tears, thrilling herself with rambling vocal visions of bridal veils, an archway of swords, handsome uniforms clothing even handsomer men, and herself as the fragile, widowed mother-of-the-bride. That thought produced another bout of weeping for memories of her own wedding day and the long-lost husband who would have been so proud today. Mrs. Davenport, sorely tried by her romantic and completely impractical sister, put in her own more down-to-earth comments.

Judith sat gazing from the window in something of a daze. In a matter of minutes she had sealed her future. If she had felt the need for action earlier this afternoon, no one could say she had not responded to that need. On an impulse, the direction of her present life had been violently altered—in a way that had not even remotely occurred to her even in daydreams.

The decision had not been made by her; the word "yes" had come of its own accord, surprising her as much as the two ladies. It was as if there had been no choice in the matter. The notion of predestiny appealed to her; the suggestion of being mastered by the inevitable brought an almost erotic pleasure.

*Mrs. Alexander Russell.* Marriage would give her release from this house of women with its tense atmosphere, its emotional outbursts, irrational reactions to normal events, and the exhausting demands the three, so unlike women made on each other.

*Mrs. Alexander Russell.* The wife of an army officer could expect a life full of color and incident. She would almost certainly travel—perhaps even to India—and lead a sophisticated life her stay-at-home sisters would never know. The military set were usually breezy, outspoken, with conventions peculiarly their own. The social round was always more lively when uniforms graced ballrooms and salons, and nothing was gayer than a military review with brass bands and pageantry.

*Mrs. Alexander Russell.* She would be a married woman—someone with status. Her house would be filled with clever, charming, and influential people. It would be an elegant place in the best part of town, furnished in style, and she would be its sole mistress. She would also have Hallworth as the country seat. The old mansion was a trifle somber, she remembered, but her own touch would transform it into a mellow rambling home whose rooms glowed with color and traditional comfort.

It was only at this point that she gave any thought to the person who was to give her all this. She had not seen her distant second cousin for four or five years because he had been at university, but she knew him as a quiet, well-mannered person with a hint of sadness about him. Someone with breeding and intelligence. She recalled a birthday party when he had had an obnoxious friend staying with him. She had been in love with Alex for a whole term after that—encouraged by the envy of her friends who thought the tragic incident concerning his brother and him most beautifully romantic—and envisaged Alex as the prisoner of fate.

He had been replaced in her affections by the new music master, and the next time she had been in his company his companion had taken all her attention, whisking her away to a secluded bower and quickening her heartbeat with the first words of love she had received from a man. At the age of seventeen, she found a practiced flirt very exciting, and all she could remember of Alex was a very tall and broad stranger who said polite things in a deep voice.

He would be twenty-four now. In her mind there rose a picture of her future husband. Tall, deferential, a young man of intelligent and quiet nature who would be an easy companion and provide her with stimulating conversation. His friends would be bound to follow suit, and their evenings would be enlivened by culture and interest. His duties might require him to be absent from her side a great deal but, as a married woman, she would have freedom, a great deal of wealth—and no further need to be paraded before eligible young men.

*Mrs. Alexander Russell.* Her pale pink mouth curved into a dreamy smile. How could she have known this day would bring such unbelievable good fortune?

The room settled into silence, bringing her from her reverie, and she turned to find her mother gone and Mrs. Davenport looking at her very penetratingly.

"Your mama has found it all too much," said that lady with her usual crispness.

"Poor Mama." Judith had almost forgotten mother's outburst; she was far too busy enjoying the sensation of having been granted three wishes.

"Have you had a brainstorm, child?"

The question startled Judith into studying her aunt's expression for the first time. It was very serious. "Why do you disapprove so much?" she asked in puzzlement. "It is a very advantageous marriage."

Mrs. Davenport rose to her feet in a surprising show of agitation. "If one is talking of material wealth, I suppose you are right, but my dear, dear girl, I never dreamed you would be so foolish." Pacing back and forth, her green silk dress rustling with every step and the sun lighting the fading golden hair as she passed the window, she presented a picture of concern Judith would not have associated with her. "Your haste to accept is beyond my comprehension. It was almost shameful."

Judith felt herself growing pink. "Aunt Pan, I am twenty-two—past the age of coquettishness. You have always taught me to be direct."

The older woman put her hands to her temples. "Direct, yes . . . but not foolhardy! If you were a girl impossibly in love there might be some excuse, and I cannot think it is merely for wealth and position. You must have had a dozen opportunities for both during the past two years."

Judith absorbed her aunt's words. Why had she not jumped at the chance to marry other young men of wealth and position? The answer did not materialize.

"Chatsworth appears at our door after an absence of

many months with a preposterous expectation that you will immediately do what he wishes, and you do!" she cried in exasperation. "Without a moment's hesitation or thought, you do!"

"Aunt Pan, are you angry because I agreed, or because Sir Chatsworth got his own way?"

Mrs. Davenport gave her niece a strange look, and sat down again. "Can you give me your reasons for accepting the offer?"

Judith thought for a moment, then sighed. "It came at a time when the future seemed dull. It spelled excitement . . . I don't know . . . I can't really say why I accepted. Can you give me your reasons for believing I should have refused?"

"You will be marrying a man, Judith, not an abstract name. Alexander Russell is a human being, with vices and virtues, likes and dislikes, and a will of his own. What do you know of him?"

Judith smiled. "He is about twenty-four, very polite and serious, his manners are quite delightful . . . and I should imagine he has not lost that slight air of reticence, since his father had to stand proxy for him today. I suspect he will make a painful job of the actual proposal."

"I see," was the reply. "You gave your assent to this marriage because of the young man you describe? How many times have I heard you deplore men who cannot speak for themselves?"

Judith sighed again. "I said Yes because it seemed absolutely right to do so. It still does."

"When did you last meet Alexander?"

"At a garden party. I was seventeen and terribly taken with one of Alex's friends who was dark and dramatic." She laughed. "Poor Alex was left standing when we slipped away to an arbor of roses."

"Really?" Mrs. Davenport commented dryly. "He has changed a lot since he was nineteen. At the end of last year he was sent down from Cambridge after two earlier warnings for nonattendance at lectures, drunkenness, and misbehavior with young women. He is almost habitually in debt, and his father has just paid a considerable amount of money to avoid a terrible scandal involving Alexander and a married woman." She raised her eyebrows in an inimitable gesture. "I doubt 'Poor Alex' would be left standing now!"

"It can't be true! How do you know this?" Judith cried in alarm.

"I visit Chatsworth frequently to discuss our investments. The maid is a particularly confiding old soul who does not need much prompting."

Knowing her aunt well enough to believe she was telling the truth Judith stammered, "But if he is really that type of man why is he allowing Sir Chatsworth to arrange his life for him? Why would be agree to a marriage like this?"

"Because he has no choice. I imagine Chatsworth has given him an ultimatum. He still controls the Russell money until Alexander is twenty-five. That is a very strong hold to have over a young man." She paused to let the information sink in then said, "Judith, my dear, this marriage is being forced upon an unwilling and resentful man. That fact alone, apart from his mode of life, points to a desperately unhappy time for the bride, don't you think?"

The spring sunshine made Judith shiver. What had happened to the quiet boy she remembered? "What am I going to do?" she asked numbly.

Mrs. Davenport smiled gently. "Learn by this lesson to be a little more cautious, I hope."

She blinked at her aunt, unable to believe she was now taking the situation so lightly, but the older woman rose and came across to take her hands.

"The answer is absurdly simple, dear girl. When Alexander makes his formal proposal, you charmingly and regretfully turn him down."

It was mid-June before Alex was given leave, and Sir Chatsworth invited the three ladies to Hallworth for the weekend. For Judith, the intervening weeks had been like riding on a seesaw. One day she was apprehensive that it might not be so simple to go back on her word to Sir Chatsworth, the next, she was burningly angry that he should have expected her to marry his degenerate son. First, she was full of disparagement for Alex who would allow himself to be bullied by his parent, then sighing with disappointment over the Alex of the past. One week she filled her hours with a hectic round of social engagements, the next week she was mooning about the house filled with regret for the dreams she had had of life as an army officer's wife.

Unable to bring herself to tell her mother it was all a

mistake, Judith found Mrs. Burley's constant talk of weddings almost more than she could stand. It was difficult enough to persuade her no public mention of it could yet be made, and it was not until Mrs. Davenport was quite severe with her that she admitted the need for secrecy.

As the weekend drew near Judith found herself growing nervous and wished she could write a note instead. She suggested this course to her aunt who told her very sternly that she had precipitated the situation and must have the courage to remedy it.

"It is impossible to go through life without making bad errors of judgment, and if one is to have any character at all one must face the consequences. I made the tragic mistake of urging your uncle to endeavors he was unable to withstand. When he collapsed so suddenly I was determined to see his death was not in vain. James is following in his father's footsteps in excellent manner and making the American company one of the best. I have doubled your uncle's fortune and enabled young men of talent to pursue their goals by backing them with his money." For a moment the tranquil face saddened. "I hope I have atoned, Judith. I hope I have."

The girl smiled fondly. "What would I do without you, Aunt Pan?"

"Very well, I daresay . . . but I like to think you have learned some common sense from me, even if you have inherited your mother's romanticism."

Perhaps that was the trouble, Judith reflected on the way to Hallworth. Sir Chatsworth's out-of-the-blue proposal had been romance in its most colorful guise—not the valentine and forget-me-not variety, but the kind that hints of excitement and unknown adventure. An unwilling, resentful bridegroom who would pursue a rakish path did not fall into either category, and it would take a hard, ruthless girl to survive such a marriage, let alone win him to her side. Who, in her right mind, would accept such a challenge?

Sir Chatsworth greeted her warmly, making a guilty reticence govern her during afternoon tea. Alex was not expected until the early evening train, for which Judith was very thankful. As it was, her hands had begun to tremble while she was dressing for dinner. If only it were over and she was on her way back to London!

The three dresses she had brought were spread upon the bed for her final choice, and it seemed the most important decision of her life, for some silly reason. The blue satin flattered and deepened her eyes, but it was rather décolleté. She did not wish to spend the evening feeling his lecherous glance lingering on her shoulders. The caramel taffeta was beautifully embroidered with gold thread, and the sleeves puffed so wide they emphasized her tiny waist. It was a dreamy romantic dress to enhance her fair coloring, but she did not wish to present a picture of fragile submissiveness to a man who exploited such qualities.

When the two widows arrived at her door it was to compliment her on how regal she looked. With her ash-blonde hair dressed in a superb Scandinavian style, and the white stiff-silk dress scattered with rhinestones Judith could have been a legendary Swedish princess. She was tall, and it was easier to be elegant than fetching. The classic lines of the virginal dress could not have suited her better. That she was paler than usual only served to add to her cool attraction, and Mrs. Davenport said softly, "Just the right touch, my dear. A little saintliness will add to your cause."

Judith smiled and relaxed a little. Her aunt always put things in their right perspective. Alexander Russell was just a man, after all, and she had dealt with quite a few without difficulty.

Father and son were standing by the tall windows that overlooked the rose garden, each with a glass in his hand, yet it was quite apparent that their close proximity meant nothing. There was a heavy silence hanging in the room—a silence that had probably only been broken by the chink of a decanter on glass. At first glance Judith had an impression of two tall men with rigid shoulders, staring across the summer lawns, right hands holding glasses, left hands clenched behind their backs, feet planted aggressively apart. Then they turned and came forward to greet the ladies.

Sir Chatsworth could be charming when he chose. Now, he complimented his guests and found them seats. Alex did no more than dutifully kiss the hands of his second cousins, whom he always addressed as aunts, before turning to Judith, who automatically offered her gloved fingers for his salute.

He held her hand near his mouth and paused, casting a glance at her from beneath thick dark lashes. "Judith, I would not have known you as the girl I last saw five years ago. I regret having kept you waiting so long for this, but my life is ordered by the regiment these days . . . you probably know that already."

The room spun. The romantic dreams of freedom, wealth and travel, social position and personal independence all dimmed. His libertine habits, his failures and intrigues, the pain in store for the bride of this marriage were all swept aside by triumphant, unashamed glorious desire that had her sighing for the décolleté gown in her room and wide sleeves that suggested fragile submissiveness. Unbidden, came a great tidal wave that set her body tingling and vitally aware of itself. A feeling she had never known before. Alexander Russell had captured her with just one glance!

The stunning truth kept her silent as she sat in her chair sipping sherry. Out of the blue had come that emotion she had thought so elusive, the recognition was painful. Was this how they felt, those happy laughing girls who flirted along the towpaths all summer long? They appeared enlivened and joyous; she was breathless and melting with weakness. Here was the man who had no intention of throwing himself at her feet, who would stand tall before her and apologize for nothing.

Burning like a person with fever, she studied the man. His uniform of rifle-green laced with silver gave him an air of knight errantry to her inflamed senses. Dark auburn hair lay in waves across his brow and put irregular tongues against his neck above the stiff hooked collar of the jacket. His face was lean and secretive, a fascinating look to the girl who knew so little of him. Shadowed anger in his eyes gave the green a darkness that formed amber flecks, and the long auburn lashes framing them emphasized their intensity of expression. Judith found herself catching her breath every time he looked her way.

She watched his fingers as they curled loosely around the glass he supported on the arm of his chair and imagined them curling around her own fingers, protectively. He arched his neck in unconscious gesture against the restriction of his tight collar, a movement that set her wayward thoughts on a breathless path. There had been men who amused her, some who aroused sympathy inside her sensitive heart, others who commanded her respect . . . but no man had ever filled her with such longing for physical contact with him.

When dinner was announced and he took her elbow to

assist her, she trembled beneath his touch. He raised his eyebrows sardonically. "Cold . . . on a mid-June evening?"

Any answer was shocked from her mind by the certainty that he could hurt her beyond words if he once guessed the power he held over her. When she accepted his proposal it must be with calmness and in the same manner with which he made it . . . or she would be lost!

The conversation over dinner was mostly of Ascot or Henley; Lord's and Goodwood; Windsor and Carlton Terrace. But Sir Chatsworth only attended social functions as an obligation to his profession. The two widows found his participation rather half-hearted and turned to Alex. His response was just as disappointing.

"For the past three months I have been engaged in learning how to form a body of men into a column, then into lines; how to ride a horse in military fashion; how to outflank an enemy—and what to do if I don't succeed. My evenings have been spent in studying manuals and diagrams—when I have not been enduring long boring dinners sitting beside elderly boring colonels." He took up his glass. "Army life leaves me with no time for social frivolity, Aunt Pan . . . but I daresay my father has already explained all that to you." The rest of the wine was drunk quickly, and he nodded to the servant to refill his glass. "I hear we are to have a ball for midsummer. If I can struggle through the welter of books of instruction in my quarters I should be pleased for you all to attend. I am sure you would find an evening with officers and gentlemen an uplifting experience."

Mrs. Davenport treated him to one of her calm stares. "My dear Alexander, at my age I have no desire to be uplifted . . . and if they are all elderly boring colonels or impudent young men like you, your officers and gentlemen are quite liable to be forced to partner each other at your midsummer ball."

Alex drew in his breath, then smiled, delighted. "I was ungracious . . . as you pointed out. Please forgive me. I promise the colonels will be neither elderly nor boring when they set eyes on you, Aunt Pan . . . but the young men will certainly be impudent."

To Judith's astonishment her aunt chuckled. "Then we must certainly accept your invitation."

"Of course we shall accept," gushed Mrs. Burley. "*Your*

invitations would naturally cancel out any others we might previously have accepted . . . am I not right, Judith?"

"I really cannot remember what social engagements we have for next week," she said as coolly as she could, and Alex flicked her with his eyes.

"We'll try again next year, if necessary," he said with disinterest. "It is not as if I shall be leaving the regiment."

The dishes were cleared then, and they rose to go to the drawing room for coffee. As there was no hostess, the gentlemen could not linger for port and cigars, although Judith was hard put to imagine these two sharing the after-dinner custom with any enthusiasm. They had not been long with their coffee cups when Mrs. Davenport broached the subject that was worrying her considerably.

"Chatsworth, what is going to happen in the Transvaal? There was that terrible affair at Christmas when an Englishman was shot by those police maintained by the Boers —an affair that filled the newspapers for a week and set everyone talking about justice—and yet the situation seems to have reverted to what it was before. Can we not get rid of that terrible man, Kruger?"

"Short of assassinating him, no!" said Sir Chatsworth.

"Will he never see that all citizens are entitled to vote and govern the state they helped to make prosperous? Without their gold they were a mere poverty-ridden farming community."

Alex leaned forward intently. "That is all they wish to remain, Aunt Pan. It is the basis of everything they do. The Dutch trekked north to get away from the English as much as a century ago. They are simple people who farm as a way of life. They found the Transvaal perfect for their kind of community. Each man can have a farm large enough to avoid meeting his neighbors more than he needs; there is abundant wildlife to provide the food for his family; he can till his land, raise his children, and observe the good book in a healthy clime. No sooner did they find this than the very people they suffered so much to flee from, came flocking into their paradise."

"But the English gold diggers do not want to farm," Mrs. Davenport pointed out. "It is not as if they are depriving the Boers of their living."

"It is not their living but their way of life which they feel is threatened, I think," said Sir Chatsworth. "The Dutch

are religious fanatics. They live by the word of the Old
Testament in its strictest sense."

"Hm," clucked Mrs. Davenport. "Then why do they
treat the poor natives so badly? Is that a Christian attitude?
A religious man sees everyone as his brother, surely."

"That is an idealistic viewpoint, Aunt Pan," said Judith
without thinking. "It is easy for us to believe such a thing,
but poor people are selfish. It comes from a need to survive."

"I would say it was the other way about," Alex put in
dryly. "A man with nothing should find it easier to share
with his neighbor than people like us. A rich man holds on
to his acres and wealth jealously for fear of losing status
with his fellow. Those at the bottom can relax with their
brethren. A happy state, indeed."

"Then it is as well *some* of us are prepared for endeavor
through life, or we should all be wallowing in self-
indulgence," snapped Sir Chatsworth. "It is time you recognized that fact."

There was a short embarrassing silence which Alex filled
by studying a Gainsborough as intently as if he had never
seen it before.

"If this silly attitude provokes the war that is constantly
being predicted, it will be men like Alexander who will
have to risk their lives," remarked Mrs. Davenport, breaking the silence. "Can a person make greater endeavor than
that, I wonder?"

Judith sat trembling, wishing she had her aunt's audac-
ity, her uncanny instinct for saying all the right things
where Alex was concerned. He seemed so aloof, so out-of-
reach sitting three feet away from her. How could she begin to learn how to touch a man like him?

"All this talk of war," cried Mrs. Burley. "I sometimes
wonder if people create them simply for the sake of attract-
ing attention to themselves."

Her sister gave her a withering glance. "My dear Alicia,
that is a singularly naive observation. One could hardly
have a war in secret!"

Sir Chatsworth stirred restlessly and looked at his son
with a stern eye. Then he cleared his throat pointedly.

"I am sure Judith does not wish to sit here all the evening, Alexander. Were you not intending to show her the
rose garden?"

An electric silence charged the room until Mrs. Burley

laughed nervously. "How nice of you, Alexander. Judith is
very fond of roses . . . aren't you, dear?"

She swallowed, remembering her aunt's words: *This
marriage is being forced on an unwilling and resentful man.*
The moment had come. Sir Chatsworth had made it plain
to his son—and to everyone in that room—that the formal-
ities must be observed so that the engagement could be offi-
cially announced.

Alex was standing dutifully before her. "Do you need a
wrap?" he asked. His eyes, all green and amber fire,
mocked her.

"On a mid-June evening?" she countered coolly. "Why
ever should I?"

They left the drawing room, and its expectant silence,
through French windows. The sun was throwing gilt edges
around fingers of pink cloud in a sky that promised another
day of drenching heat. This was England at its glorious
best. The evening air was unbearably full of suggestions
and fancies: the smell of sun-warm honeysuckle; echoes of
lovers' laughter, crisp bread straight from the oven eaten in
the open beneath the shade of trees; strong white teeth biting into rosy apples; dogs chasing their tails from sheer
exuberance; sleek feline tabbies treading delicately through
waving grasses, intent on a field mouse garnering for his
family; men and women working in the fields; and spotted
handkerchiefs for carrying bread and cheese or for tying
beneath the chin of a sweetheart. Summer!

All this hung in the air of that June evening as Judith
and Alex strolled across warm terrace flagstones, down the
old stone steps and across velvet lawns soon to drink the
blessed dew. Hallworth sprawled behind them in distinguished splendor, and the stables to their right were tinted
with scarlet highlights as the dipping sun bade the walls
farewell. From their direction came the steadying voice of a
groom as he led a horse along the ringing cobbles, then the
clatter of a pail being set down.

For some unaccountable reason Judith was moved to
tears by it all. Something inside her was bursting for recognition. Her eyes followed the flight of a vee of homing birds
and loved everyone of them. The oaks bordering the far
paddock stood as they had for a century or more, noisy
now with starlings. A colored ball rolled across the gravel
at the east end of the house, and a small boy ran out to
retrieve it before returning to the kitchens. He was so

young; the oaks so old, yet they would still be there when the child became dust beneath the earth of England . . . or in some foreign land, if he became a soldier.

The idyll vanished abruptly, and she looked at the man beside her in quick anxiety. He came to a halt and turned to her.

"I think this is a suitable place for the ritual, don't you?"

Taken unawares, Judith realized they had reached the rose garden without having exchanged a word, and he was indicating a rustic seat in an alcove. An unwilling and resentful man? Yes, he was all that at this moment—determined to do his duty to Sir Chatsworth but fighting every step of the way. He was waiting for her to sit. She remained standing and her thumping heart told her he must not guess he had only to snap his fingers and she would come running. That must remain her secret until . . .

"If you decline to sit it will make the whole thing even more ridiculous when I sink onto one knee," he said cuttingly. "Which knee is correct, by the way? There must be a convention governing the choice."

It hurt already—more than she imagined. With him as master of the situation there seemed no way of answering.

"Perhaps you would prefer to do the asking," he was saying, "since there are no palpitating hearts to take into consideration, I suppose it doesn't matter who actually pops the question."

Judith flinched. The expert with a foil knew how to pierce his adversary in the most vulnerable place, but, she knew, the wounded adversary always reciprocated. Now Judith began her long duel with the man who had tonight claimed the woman she was underneath. Looking steadily into his militant eyes, she said clearly, "Will you allow me to do you the honor of becoming your wife?"

His mouth twisted. "Touché, Miss Burley. Unfortunately, I am unable to give you the opportunity to tell me when I must prepare myself for the honor, for that has been dictated by my father and the regiment. Father and Colonel Rawlings-Turner have decided it shall be next March when my training is completed, and I am able to apply for permission to marry." He put up a hand. "Have no fear. Permission will definitely be granted."

"I never doubted it," she replied. "Sir Chatsworth would not have slipped up on a detail like that."

A gleam of some emotion appeared in his eyes. "Bravo!

You have it all worked out, I see." Before she was aware of his intention his arm slid around her waist, pulling her against him with a confidence that did not expect opposition. "However, just because it is to be a marriage to order, there is no need to dispense with the trimmings."

His other arm enclosed her shoulders as he bent his head. It was not a savage kiss, but a firm salute of possession that went on and on until voices within her told her to give him more, much more. On the brink of surrender, she came to her senses and grew angry. What a fool she was! One kiss and she had forgotten what kind of man she was taking on. A flight to the stars in his arms was, to him, merely one more conquered female to add to the list.

Pulling away she said, "No, Alex. You cannot have it all ways. As you said, there are no palpitating hearts in this contract. Sir Chatsworth has arranged a marriage of convenience. Let's keep that in mind all the time."

His mouth tightened and the anger that had been subdued all evening flared. "How wise of you to make your position quite clear at the beginning, Judith. Let's hurry back with the glad tidings so that they can get to work on the financial details. It is those in which you are mainly interested, I take it."

That was the worst thrust so far, and pain made her snap back, "That was not only very ill-mannered, it was quite unnecessary. You, of all people, have no grounds for graceless behavior. Keep it for your dissolute friends."

His whole body stiffened. "By God, a pillar of piety into the bargain. Let me make *my* position quite clear, also. I am prepared to give you money, position, and the honorable name of Russell that rests now on my shoulders alone, but I will tolerate no self-righteous directives. You are embarking on a marriage, not taking up good works."

She began to tremble. "Your views on this marriage are somewhat one-sided. Is it not a case of the pot calling the kettle black?"

"With one difference. I have no choice; you are selling yourself of your own free will."

"How dare you say that!" she gasped, out of her depth completely. All her experience with young men had been with reliable and affable beaux. Not one had spoken to her in such a manner. Never had she witnessed a flare of temper like this or known a man at war with himself. Women's tears and tantrums she understood only too well, but this man before her was dealing blow after blow and she was unprepared for it.

"Why else would you have accepted my father's very insulting proposal?" Alex said. He leaned back against a low stone wall and studied every inch of her statuesque beauty. "He assured me you leaped at the offer."

Standing there in the growing dusk beneath the scrutiny of a man struggling against a yoke he had no wish to wear, Judith realized he was right. She *had* only thought initially of the material things this marriage would bring her. Now, she could not tell him she had intended turning him down until a glance from beneath his thick lashes took her breath away and all her resolution with it.

With her eyes on the glow of his burnished hair as the last sun rays caught it, she said tonelessly, "Sir Chatsworth called at a time when I was particularly restless. Living with two aging widows is very restrictive. His offer spelled freedom."

He did not move, or change his expression. "Really? You are quite remarkably beautiful, I have to acknowledge. I cannot believe you could not have escaped to freedom with any of a dozen others well before this."

Trapped completely, she spoke in haste. "Any other man might have demanded more than a business arrangement."

For a moment he took in the severe hairstyle, the chaste cut of the white dress, and her slender elegant figure. "I see. That explains why you agreed to the liaison even though we had not met for five years." That twist was there on his lips once more. "If those are your terms you must allow me mine. My *dissolute friends* will provide what you are unwilling to give."

She felt color steal into her cheeks. How wrong, how very wrong he was! But she had no intention of ranking with all the others. Before she gave him any sign of the sudden and unexpected emotion he aroused in her—the ultimate emotion between man and woman—he must see her as a woman apart from any other—the only woman in his life.

"I should like to go back to the house now," she told him coldly. "I think we have said all that is necessary."

He straightened and threw out a hand. "Certainly. This way will be quickest."

They walked side by side, not touching, as he said, "I shall contact Garrods to tell them you will be calling to select an engagement ring. I daresay my father will be pleased to accompany you."

She looked at him quickly. "And you?"

"Alas, duty calls," he said with smooth alacrity. "I am sure you can manage without me. Father is an excellent organizer, and you seem to be supremely certain of what you want."

With the color high in her cheeks she allowed him to put a hand beneath her elbow as they mounted the steps and entered the drawing room. They found the older people playing cards. The game ceased at their entry and three expectant faces looked up.

"I hope you have the champagne on ice, sir," said Alex woodenly. "It can now be safely opened."

Sir Chatsworth's severe look eased and he actually smiled as he went to take Judith's hand. "Thank you, my dear. I shall ensure that you are happy."

"It is for Alexander to see to that, surely," giggled Mrs. Burley. "My dear girl . . . such a proud mother . . . if only your dear father were here to see it!" Tears replaced the giggles. "A spring wedding, I hear. How romantic!" She folded Judith to her bosom with a long sigh, then moved on to Alex. "I had not realized until tonight how very handsome you had grown, Alexander. A gallant soldier serving Queen and country . . ." She sniffed and brought out a handkerchief to wipe delicately at her eyelids. "There, I am quite choked." Her bosom heaved. "You have never known a mother, dear boy, nor I a son. Let us hope that we can be that to each other from now on." In a burst of emotion she stood on tiptoe and enfolded him in an embrace.

Alex looked startled, but manfully endured it. He kissed Mrs. Davenport soundly on the cheek without asking permission and slyly asked, "Are you going to be a second mother to me?"

"Certainly not, young man," she replied crisply. "I doubt any woman could mother you." Her glance went to Judith. "I trust you realize how fortunate you are. My niece is a girl of very unusual qualities."

"So I have discovered," was the reply, and only Judith knew what he really meant.

The champagne was brought in and, under cover of popping corks and bright conversation, Mrs. Davenport spoke in an undertone to Judith. "Have you taken leave of your senses? I tried to catch your eye as you left, but your gaze never left his face for a moment. Oh, don't worry, child, he is too busy being truculent to notice what I saw quite plainly."

Judith stared at her. "You knew I was going to accept?"

"Of course, I knew. My dear, he is quite irresistible—I had not realized, for I have not seen him for some years—and there is not a woman alive who does not adore a black sheep, but it does not alter the facts one jot. I warned you what you would be taking on."

"But you have just admitted he is irresistible," Judith protested, still stunned by the events of the evening.

"So he is . . . and a challenge to any woman with courage and determination. If I were thirty years younger . . ." She sighed. "You have determination, Judith, and courage, when you choose to show it . . . but unfortunately your mother has endowed you with a strong dash of her own romantic sensitivity. Whereas I might enjoy a confrontation of this nature, I am very afraid you will be hurt in the process."

Judith looked across the room to where her future bridegroom was drinking a toast to the marriage—a marriage that was being forced upon him, and that he would fight all the way.

"Perhaps I shall, Aunt Pan," she said softly, "but I have no choice."

## CHAPTER THREE

Alex returned to barracks deeply unhappy. The weekend had been worse than expected and had eaten into his dwindling pride with greedy teeth. Letting himself into his quarters he barked at his servant who was carrying his bag in.

"Good weekend, was it, sir?" was the harmless question that drew Alex's wrath.

"I pay you to clean my gear and see that I am comfortable, not to pry into my private life," he snapped.

"Yes, Mr. Russell, I'll remember that," he replied, stiffly. "I'll be along later for your uniform and shoes."

Alex opened the cupboard where he kept a bottle for this sort of occasion. "I'll leave them outside the door," he said. "I don't wish to be disturbed again tonight."

"Right, sir." The soldier dumped the bag as hard as he dared on the case rack and left without another word.

He hates me, Alex thought dispassionately, as he poured a drink. No doubt he will apply for a transfer before long. The brandy warmed his frozen stomach and he let out a long breath before slumping into a chair and putting his head back to stare at the ceiling.

He could still see them all standing around the prize exhibit with glasses of champagne—his father proud of his achievement, Aunt Alicia coating the whole thing with pink icing, Judith cold and virginal in the sparkling ice dress. Only Aunt Pan had been different. There had been a warmth about her that had saved the weekend and he had homed to it like a stray cat seeking the hearth.

He drained the glass and poured another draught. What a pity Judith had not inherited her aunt's personality. Even a copy of her mother's silliness would have been better than that haughty holier-than-thou disapproval she had displayed. Reproof on his bad manners, accusations of gracelessness, disparagement of his friends, and sharp-tongued retorts to his testing questions. He frowned. No man would deny she was very beautiful, and he was still uncertain why she was doing what his father wanted. If it was freedom and wealth she desired, why not marry an old man who would conveniently die soon after the wedding leaving everything to her in his will?

Brooding on what had passed between them in the rose garden he downed another brandy and sat with the glass swinging between thumb and forefinger. To hell with her! If she wanted a passionless marriage she could have it. He preferred dark girls with laughing eyes and a heart he could reach. Pale remote creatures left him as cold as themselves . . . although he almost believed she had trembled with surrender in his arms. There were not many girls who did not!

Misery washed over him. How he hated this place. The rules and regulations were worse than university, and the punishments for breaking them designed to browbeat the offender into submission. Every time he walked into the officers' mess or turned out on parade, he was conscious of the Colonel's eyes on his friend's recalcitrant son. Every move he made was strictly controlled. He was being disciplined—made into a man, his father had said—and taught to do exactly as he was told.

With his allowance cut to a minimum by his father, and the Colonel ready to pounce if he incurred a debt, he was obliged to lead a monastic life—so much so that he was taunted by the other subalterns. He was an outsider. That did not worry him. He had no wish to join a set of fools who prattled on about the honor of the regiment, an Enlishman's duty, and military tradition until he could stand it no longer.

His unpopularity pleased rather than upset him. The army was a ridiculous institution, as far as he was concerned. Most of the officers were the sons of former officers, who bored on about battles and heroism until he put a stop to their stories with a few well-chosen but unacceptable words.

He tipped up the bottle again and reflected grimly on the growing war between himself and a fellow subaltern called Forrester. That it would come to a head soon was inevitable. The fellow was the son of a general and as steeped in regimental tradition as it was possible to be. He was the blue-eyed boy of the mess—of the whole bloody regiment, possibly—and took pompous and active objection to the disrespect he felt Alex showed to long-standing traditions.

The room was bleak and chilly. He had not attempted to improve it with his personal things. Gazing around his uncomfortable quarters, Alex wondered how much more he could stand. Full of self-disgust he lurched to his feet and went to run a bath. He had allowed himself to be thrust into a profession he kicked against for its suggestion of teaching naughty boys how to behave, and spent every day in the knowledge that the Colonel and probably most of the senior officers disciplined him even as they despised the weakness that let a man of twenty-four be ruled by his father.

He had felt the same thing this weekend. *The pot calling the kettle black* she had said. He deserved a wife like Judith when he bowed to his father's commands so meekly. How could the army make a man of him when he was no man at all but a weakling who had survived while his mother and brother died? Pouring another drink he gripped the glass until his knuckles tightened. *I wish to God you had let me drown, Miles.*

A knock fell on his door and he walked to open it with the glass in his hand. Neil Forrester stood outside.

"Yes?" said Alex.

The dark-haired young officer made a point of looking at the brandy before asking, "Might I have a word with you?"

"Go ahead."

"Inside . . . if it is not too much trouble."

Alex stood aside so that his unwelcome guest could enter, but deliberately left the door open to suggest that he did not want the visit to be a prolonged one. Neil came to the point immediately; he had no intention of staying longer than he had to.

"Your horse is in my stable. I should be glad if you'd move it."

Alex leaned against the door jamb, smiling faintly. "If my horse is in it, it must be my stable."

The young man in impeccable dinner jacket raised his eyebrows. "That is a common mistake made by the bourgeoisie—possession being nine points of the law."

Alex's eyes hardened. "Have you purchased that particular stable?"

"I have no need. It is mine by tradition."

"By God, not another of your endless traditions! What is it this time—your uncle's second cousin's grandfather once took a pot shot at Napoleon while hidden in that stable? Pity he missed. We might have been spared several hundred other such reminiscences by later generations."

Neil Forrester reacted by flushing and taking a step nearer. "I am getting a little sick of your constant sneers, Russell. I happen to be very proud of my ancestry and its connection with the regiment."

"So I gather. I have heard you say so with such boring regularity."

The other man controlled himself with difficulty. "What are you doing in this regiment if you have so little respect for it?"

"I have every respect for the regiment. It is the members of it I find so ridiculous."

"I don't mean to waste any further time with you. You're drunk, Russell. The Colonel doesn't allow subalterns to keep spirits in their quarters. You know that, don't you?"

"Oh yes," said Alex. "It's the same at Eton, but nobody pays any heed."

The suggestion that he was behaving like a junior school-boy finished Second Lieutenant Forrester. He walked back to stand beside Alex in the open doorway.

"That stable must be vacated. It always houses the horse that wins the regimental steeplechase cup, and I intend putting Rapscallion in it tomorrow. It is a tradition that has lasted over a hundred years."

"Time it was changed, in that case."

His visitor pushed past him in anger. "See that your horse is moved, or else."

Alex laughed. "Threats, Forrester? Awfully bad form to threaten a junior officer—even one who is only three months behind you. It might incite a retaliatory action leading to a court-martial. *That* is a tradition older than the hills, old chap."

Neil fired a last shot. "You'll never last in this regiment, Russell. Sooner or later you'll go too far."

Alex closed the door behind him and leaned against it to down the last of his brandy. If he had lived his brother would have been like Neil Forrester. Heavy with maudlin self-pity he walked into the bathroom to find several inches of water on the floor. The bath had run over, while he had been having that immature confrontation with an upright and reliable young scion.

Turning off the tap with a vicious twist, he returned to the bed and stretched out on it fully clothed. He would have to move his horse. However much he might loathe this life he must stick to it somehow. Next spring he would have a wife to support—to help steady him down. Next spring he would be bound hand and foot, and his father would finally feel compensated for his losses. He closed his eyes in despair. Next spring he would be only twenty-five. And what would he do with the next fifty years of his life?

The officers of the regiment were disappointed if they hoped to meet Second Lieutenant Russell's fiancée at the Midsummer Ball, for a summer cold kept her away, and the newly entered subalterns departed soon after for specialist training at the School of Musketry in Kent.

For the first time, Alex found a degree of pleasure in his

new profession. He was an excellent marksman with a keen eye and very steady hand. Yet, inexplicably, his outstanding prowess, a talent that would have been loudly and generously acclaimed in someone like Neil Forrester, was only greeted with disapproval by his fellow trainees. Hitting the bull's-eyes time after time was regarded as immoderate showing-off which, of course, was extremely bad form.

Alex accepted it philosophically. For years he had been put in his place; showing-off had been stamped out very early in his life, and he was amazed that they should regard his success in that light. However, he got tremendous pleasure from handling the military rifles as if he had been born to it, and was gleefully amused to notice that Forrester, his long-standing adversary, could not hit the target even when it was stationary.

It was this that led to the head-on collision that had been foreseen by them both for a long time. For over a week they had all been lying on their stomachs for two hours every morning and afternoon firing at regular circular targets, cut-out figures, and moving shapes, and still young Forrester was failing to hit the target more than once or twice. In consequence, he had grown tense and nervous and took an inordinate time to fire his required rounds.

On Friday afternoon they were all looking forward to a free weekend and hoping to get away early, in time to make the six o'clock train. As they could not leave the firing range until all shooting was over, Neil was showered with requests to speed up his performance. More tense than ever, and knowing he must get a minimum number of hits on each target before it would be lowered, he took even longer trying to line up his sights.

To his astonishment, and that of everyone but Alex, his target went down very speedily. The success continued throughout the afternoon until a flag was suddenly waved to halt the firing. The sergeant told his pupils to stop shooting and went to speak on the field telephone connecting the target pits with the firing line. He came back looking smug and bristling with importance.

"Mr. Russell and Mr. Forrester, I'd like a private word with you, if you please."

The two officers rose from their prone positions, one smiling, the other puzzled. The sergeant looked at Alex boldly.

"You don't seem to be at your best today, sir. Only half your shots are hitting the targets."

"I had a late night," Alex said easily.

The sergeant scowled before he turned to Neil. "You, sir, have made outstanding progress. Could it be because you had an *early* night?"

He smiled faintly. "I was bound to improve, wasn't I?"

"Yes, Mr. Forrester. You could hardly have got worse," he answered caustically. "However, there is something very strange going on, it seems. Although you have been hitting the targets quite well, your usual number of shots are still going wide." He paused for dramatic effect and rolled back on his heels as he looked at the dark-haired subaltern. "Now, sir, either you have been firing more than your quota of rounds, or someone else has been firing at your target as well as his own." His eyes swung to Alex. "Well, Mr. Russell?"

He stared back calmly. "I understood everyone wanted to get away early."

No one got away that day at all. Alex was taken from the firing line and set to cleaning guns. Neil Forrester was obliged to start from the beginning with fresh targets, and was so angry that he was still trying to get the required number of hits when the six o'clock train left the station.

Dinner was a quiet meal with the majority of diners seething for revenge. Alex soon sensed that something was afoot and was not really surprised when he was approached by the senior subaltern at the conclusion of the meal with a request to accompany him to his room. However, he was surprised to find the rest of the subalterns there, perched on the bed, table, and chest of drawers, and all looking at him with great animosity.

He had not gone through public school and university without suffering indignities of varying kinds, so it was not hard to guess this was some kind of punishment committee. His mouth curled. How typical! Another of their juvenile traditions they should have outgrown by now.

It followed the usual pattern. He was accused of unsporting behavior of the worst degree, of humiliating a fellow subaltern, of flaunting his prowess as a marksman in a manner no gentleman could tolerate, and, inevitably, letting down the regiment. There was a lot more besides; the many witnesses who came forward lost no opportunity to

air the marked dislike they all felt toward him, a man they
regarded as an outsider.

He stood in the center of the room like the accused at a
trial. When asked for his defense he offered none. Experience of such occasions had taught him the victim would
suffer whatever defense he offered. Instead, he pointed out
in a calm voice that they would benefit far more if they
stopped this nonsense and asked him to give Forrester a
few lessons on how to shoot. They shouted him down and
called for a verdict.

The senior subaltern then spoke. "You have been found
guilty on all counts, Russell, and I shall pronounce judgment."

Alex thought he would probably be deprived of his trou-
sers and dumped head first in the pig swill, or lathered all
over with shaving soap and locked in a broom cupboard all
night—two popular ways of dealing with offenders. He was
wrong.

"You will be taken out to the lake on the east boundary
and thrown into the center thereof."

The room tilted. The sea of faces blurred into a pale
zigzag; the green uniforms seemed to close in on him. Fear
both terrible and overmastering blotted all else from his
mind and he made a desperate dash for the door in his
panic.

"Look out, he's bolting!" came the cry. He was brought
down by a rugby tackle.

"My God, what a coward!" exclaimed an indignant
voice. "He was running away."

From that moment, Alex stood no chance whatever.
Cowardice! It was the most damning accusation anyone
could make. Alex was outnumbered eleven to one and they
were determined to have their revenge. The fear of water
pushed the blood through his arteries with such speed Alex
felt sick and giddy. His heart pounded, his body broke out
in a sweat. Kicking and lashing out with his fists at those
who held him, the desperate need to get away making him
stronger and more vicious as he fought to break from the
restraining hands.

In the midst of a struggling mass he was dragged along
the corridor, down some steps, and across a courtyard.

"For God's sake, no," he rasped. Hands were pulling at
his jacket and his tight collar threatened to strangle him.

The next minute, he was pushed face downward onto a

hay trolley used for transporting fodder, and half a dozen men promptly sat on him. He could not move any part of his body. His arms and legs were pinned down, and his face pressed into warm scratchy hay that threatened to suffocate him. Painfully, he managed to twist his head to one side, enough to breathe freely, but it was pure instinct.

His mind was full of horrors—slimy things against his legs; hands pulling him down into black oblivion; gnarled branches like skeletal arms reaching up for him; and mist hiding the world from sight. He was drenched with sweat and all his strength had suddenly gone. The shouts of those around him as they dragged the hay trolley reminded him of the clamor he had heard on New Year's Eve. His captors were pounding his body unmercifully into certain submission, and his stomach clenched with pain. It seemed as if his entire body was twitching with his heartbeat, and his head was bursting open.

The trolley halted; the weight left his back. With a speed created by the subconscious he rolled off the hay and tried to run, but hit a wall of rifle green that closed around him. Highly excited voices shouted conflicting orders, hands pushed him in opposite directions, and he lost his balance and was hauled up by his collar. The water lay black and gleaming before him for a few nightmare seconds before it was around his ankles and lapping further up his legs. Pinioned and helpless, the night became a whirl of black starstudded sky and shimmering water as they forced him down and under.

He was choking, struggling, gasping. The body of the wronged housemaid floated toward him with open gaping mouth and staring eyes. Then it seemed to be a man he knew with gleeful gleaming eyes and a mouth that was shouting with excitement, against a background of cedars and night sky.

"Again, again . . . give it to him . . . duck the coward again!"

The sky faded and the roaring fearsome noise was in his ears once more. Something was holding him below the surface. The punt was drifting away. *Miles! Miles!* A high childish voice echoed in his brain, but then he was breathing again and the elusive phantoms faded.

"Once more?" asked a hoarse sadistic voice.

"YES!" came the roar.

It was worse this time. He was being strangled by something tight around his neck and the world was receding. Voices rang in his ears. *She was wronged, you know. Miles, is it frightful to be wronged—frightful enough to want to jump in a lake? Her hand comes up out of the water sometimes.* He thought it should be sunny, but it was as black as the grave with only a hand sticking out of the water. It was an empty box they were putting in the earth; Miles was in the lake with the housemaid.

Now, he was alone in that land that hung between life and death. There were lights bobbing and voices calling his name and his brother's. A giant figure in a swirling black cloak rose up before him. The devil? No, it was his father standing beside huge black horses. *If the Lord had to take one of my sons why did it have to be Miles?*

Alex knew he was drowning and, this time, Miles would not save his life. They had hold of him now, those whose spirits moaned and wandered beneath the inviting surface. Something told him Miles was there; he would soon see him. He *could* see him. There, on the edge of truth hung the echo of a fantasy that drifted fitfully through his head without substance, never staying long enough to reveal itself. Now, he was to see the revelation of that phantom.

At that moment the calling voices grew louder, the bobbing lights exploded into a shower of stars and the night hung above him again. The hovering past faded away, leaving him abandoned and bereft; all alone on this vast earth. Dark figures were drifting away, and there was only himself and the gruesome menacing pull of those who floated in the lake.

Shaking uncontrollably he clawed and scrambled on his hands and knees up the bank, retching as he went. He had never felt so ill. The world did not seem to be the prize he had always imagined it to be; gladly would he abandon it forever at that moment. Already he was in the dark underworld that led to eternal oblivion, and the small spark of desire to return to life was flickering dangerously.

The water was behind him and there was something in his path that was solid and warm—something that would anchor him against the lapping greedy ripples. Falling upon the sweet-smelling substance his quaking hands gripped a round solid bar with a hold guaranteed never to break, and he lay with his face in the sharp comfort of something he knew, riding out the deep-seated terror to which water always subjected him.

The hands gripping the bar were ice cold like the whole of his body. The tight-fitting mess uniform he wore had stiffened with saturation and clung to him like embalming bandages. Water ran from the hair plastered to his head and sent runnels against his face that set his stomach crawling afresh. His grip tightened in a superhuman effort to hold on. His whole body was growing rigid with the strain. He had the nightmare feeling that he was screaming aloud but finding no sound coming from his throat.

Then, a voice from far above him said, "All right, take it steady, old chap. It's over now."

A hand fell on his shoulder in comfort instead of aggression, but Alex was still a long way from life. Speaking gently and with confidence the voice urged him to take deep breaths and let himself go limp. What an impossible request!

"Come on, old fellow, ease off. Relax those fingers and let the trolley take your full weight."

Gradually, painfully Alex began to return to sanity with the help of his companion. Turning his face sideways made breathing easier and, once that happened, his muscles automatically relaxed. There seemed no further need to hold the bar, but the effort required to bring both arms down from above his head was too great. He lay limply, face down and longed to go to sleep.

"For God's sake give me some help, somebody," the voice called in anger, and soon there were hands taking hold of him again. "Steady . . . *steady*," soothed the voice. "We are simply going to get you into a sitting position."

Leaden-headed and past caring what they did to him, he let them lift him up until he could sit leaning against the barred end of the trolley. He stared at the pale face in the night and thought he might have seen it before. It looked as white as death.

"It's over now. Everything is all right," the man repeated. "I wish to God I had been a bit quicker to recognize the symptoms. I'm sorry, Russell. We had no idea."

Alex could not take it all in, so continued to stare in perplexity wondering where he had seen the man before.

"I'm with the medical department, if you remember," said the subaltern whose name, Alex recalled now, was Caxton. "I should have been more observant at the start. I've seen this sort of thing before, but not with water."

Drained, unbearably tired, and aching in every part of his pumeled body, Alex sat silently looking at the medical man. Then he turned to gaze at Neil Forrester who was standing beside him, looking as white as a ghost.

"We . . . we all thought you were trying to funk punishment," he stammered. "If we had known . . . I mean . . . well, we don't like rotters in the regiment, Russell."

Sitting there feeling like a man who has glimpsed the grave, Alex wondered just how much longer this crazy night would last.

It was not until three days later that Neil Forrester knocked on his door and asked if he could have a word with Alex. Since the "subaltern's trial," relations between Alex and the other men had been quiet and guarded, with a general air of dejection hanging over those on the musketry course. The weekend had passed quietly, with most of the officers going to town, and Monday had found all the young men firing very earnestly at their own targets.

The visit from Forrester took Alex aback. Although the man had assisted the medical subaltern in getting him back to his quarters that night, Neil had been in the midst of the mob while they were dragging him to the lake, and Alex was not in the mood for his company. However, he stood back.

"I see you were studying," Forrester said as he entered. "This will only take a minute."

Alex waited in silence.

"Did you mean that about giving me lessons in shooting?"

It was the last thing Alex expected. It took a moment or two before he said cautiously, "If you are serious, yes."

"Thank you." There was an awkward pause, then, "You see, I have three brothers who are excellent shots . . . and I don't make a very good showing against them."

"Three brothers! You must find that rather difficult."

Neil gave a pale smile. "It gets a bit competitive at times."

Alex nodded. "I daresay." He hesitated, then offered, "We could go out tomorrow. There's sure to be somewhere we can do a little target practice."

"Yes." The dark-haired man walked rather self-consciously to the door. "Tomorrow, then."

Alex went back to his studies but saw nothing of the

page at which he stared for so long. He had almost called
that fellow Miles. Since Friday night he had been thinking
of his brother a lot and trying to recall something that
stayed just out of reach of his memory.

The engagement ring had been on Judith's finger for six
months. It did not seem possible, for she had seen her unwilling fiancé on less than a dozen occasions since that evening in the rose garden, and did not feel she had penetrated
the barrier between them at all.

The diamond—pure and chaste as Alex had called it—
had been chosen with Sir Chatsworth, who had allowed his
son to pay for it. There had been a family wedding at
which they had met, two weekends at Hallworth; a review
at the regiment's barracks to commemorate a renowned
battle, after which the guests had taken tea in the officers'
mess and Judith had charmed every subaltern except the
one she was to marry. Twice she had watched Alex play
polo, and both times had left her longing for him in a way
that thrilled yet shocked her. Polo was a physical game and
Alex was a very physical man. No woman could ever be
*half* in love with Alex, she was certain.

On one occasion she had persuaded him to escort her to
a ball—an evening of mixed delight and anguish—and on
another to the ballet, which had been an utter failure. Alex
had found the male dancers hilarious, and she had grown
angry, accusing him of having no soul. He had retaliated
by saying it was better than having no heart, and her fear
of earning even more scorn led her to treat the remark with
hauteur when she really longed to show him how very
wrong he was.

She often sat gazing at the ring for minutes on end. He
had not helped to choose it, neither had he slipped it onto
her finger, but it was the object that tied her to him and
therefore precious. In three months they would be married.
He rarely referred to the fact: She thought of nothing else.

They all spent Christmas at Hallworth and no one could
say it was a wild success. The relationship between Sir
Chatsworth and his son cast its dark shadow over them all.
The older man poured constant criticism on Alex, who
smoldered beneath the surface, and when she attempted to
defend him to his father, smoldered even more.

Longing to reveal her love, yet too afraid of his ridicule
Judith spent the entire three days aching for his touch, taut

at his nearness, and dark-eyed from lack of sleep. She was
jumpy and nervous, her senses drawn like the strings of a
bow. Alex did not appear conscious of her need for him,
but Mrs. Davenport was a woman who had suffered and
recognized the symptoms.

She watched her niece for as long as she could bear, then
sought her out on the afternoon of Boxing Day as she sat
on her window-seat in the bedroom. Judith was pleased to
see her, but only a wan smile betrayed the fact.

"Aunt Pan! How nice. I was hoping for someone to talk
to."

Mrs. Davenport crossed the room to a brocaded chair
and sat arranging the skirt of her bronze silk dress around
her. "What has happened to your fiancé that you are here
all alone on a bright afternoon? It is very wicked of him to
abandon you in this way."

Judith lifted her shoulders. "It is not his fault this time,
as it happens. Sir Chatsworth sent him off to a tenant's
cottage to sort out an argument between the husband and
wife. It seems the husband spent all his wages in the inn
on Christmas Eve, and the wife is unable to pay the
butcher for the goose she ordered. The butcher has a
shrewd suspicion that the money is gone for good and is
holding onto the bird. The wife locked her husband in the
outhouse and will not let him out. The prisoner managed to
get a message to Sir Chatsworth through a passerby."

"Dear me!" smiled Mrs. Davenport. "What a splendid
woman!"

Judith relaxed a little. "There's more. The key to the
outhouse has been hidden by the wife, who refuses to say
where it is."

"And poor Alexander has been presented with the impasse?"

"Sir Chatsworth says he must know how to deal with
such problems. The estate will be his eventually." Judith
shifted her position on the window-seat to glance out over
the snow-covered grounds. "I think Hallworth is quite
beautiful."

Mrs. Davenport nodded. "But you are not marrying
Hallworth, my dear." She paused long enough for her re-
mark to hatch an answer. When none came, she asked,
"How are you handling him? It does not make you happy,
I can see that."

"How can anyone *handle* a person like Alex," Judith

cried. "He sees me only as a girl dedicated to gaining a share of everything he owns. I am never with him long enough to show him he is wrong and, even if I did, would he believe it? He is so very cynical."

Mrs. Davenport raised her eyebrows. "From what I have heard it has not been difficult for a girl to persuade him of her feelings. The last adjective I would use of him is cold."

Judith avoided her aunt's eyes. She was longing to explain, to throw herself into her aunt's arms and beg for her advice. But it was impossible to confide even to the person closest to her what had passed between herself and Alex on that June evening in the rose garden.

"I can only suppose I do not have the skill others have when it comes to affection."

"Nonsense!" Mrs. Davenport's lively face adopted a determination Judith had often seen when her Aunt Pan was dealing with people who had less confidence than herself. "I have seen the extravagant gifts from admirers that arrived for you in the past. Those suitors had no difficulty in reading your feelings."

Judith sighed. "I had no feelings for them to read. This is different. Aunt Pan, I couldn't share him with anyone, and I think I should die if I lost him."

"Then you must fight on, whatever the cost. Some people might think you have just made an extravagant statement; others might think it insincere. Sometimes, it is desperately true and the poor unhappy souls cannot face life alone. Make certain you are not one of those."

Judith left the seat and sank down on the floor beside her aunt's chair. "He uses duty as an excuse to avoid meetings, yet mocks the regiment and all it stands for. He does only what he absolutely must, and no more. Presents arrive on appropriate occasions, but they are items selected by highly trained staff in the best shops. My letters go unanswered unless I have asked specific questions." She spread her hands helplessly. "How can I draw near him?"

Mrs. Davenport rested her head against the cushions in a moment of reminiscence. "Only when he decides to stand still. At present, he is retreating before your advance. Sir Chatsworth has exerted heavy pressures on him. I think he can take no more, for the moment." She smiled gently. "All you can do is wait."

"For how long?" Judith sighed.

"Oh, my dear, my dear," her aunt said, "how well I re-

member the age when a week seemed a lifetime. If you love
him as you say you do, you will wait forever."

With that comfortless thought Judith dragged to her feet
and returned to her scrutiny of the grounds of Hallworth
Manor. After a moment she said, "I feel I could not wait
that long, but the alternative is unthinkable."

The rustle of skirts announced that her aunt had risen.
The next minute, an arm went around her shoulders. "I do
not for one second think you will have to wait that long.
Let him build his defenses, if that is what he wants. In
three months you will be married and have every right to
his company each day . . . and night," she added softly.
"Judith, he is very human, and you are very beautiful. I
think you will find the battle will not last very long."

Judith felt her cheeks flame and was glad her aunt was
standing behind her. Of what use would be the right to
Alex's company at night when she had led him to believe
she wanted no such overtures from him. In his own words
he would take from his dissolute friends what she was unwilling to give. What would she give to have that evening
over again. . . . But would it have made any difference if
she had melted in his arms? She had seen the way he
looked at other women when they were out together. How
much more unhappy she would be now if she had revealed
her true feelings that night! He would despise her even
more.

"What do you say to a short stroll down the drive, my
dear?" asked Mrs. Davenport, bringing Judith back to the
present.

She smiled faintly and agreed it would be nice to get out
for a while. They made their way downstairs, Mrs. Davenport saying, "Who knows, we might meet Alexander returning from the cottage—unless that enterprising woman also
has him under lock and key by now." She laughed gaily.
"What a heaven-sent opportunity *that* would be for you, my
dear."

They walked in the gardens for an hour. Alex did not
appear.

The incident with the tenant's wife was recounted that
evening over dinner. Judith asked Alex how he had dealt
with it.

"Very cautiously, I assure you," he replied. "I knew an
offer to settle the butcher's bill would have insulted her and

put her poor husband in more trouble, so I offered to buy the key to the outhouse."

"The key?" Judith repeated curiously.

"I explained that it would be necessary to call in a locksmith to remove and replace the existing lock if her husband was to be set free and suggested I give her that money for the existing key. It saved her the indignity of unconditional surrender, or the disgrace of a locksmith being called to release her husband. The money was enough to cover the butcher's bill and it went into her hands, safe from the till at the local inn."

"How very clever of you, Alexander," said Mrs. Burley. "I'm sure I should never have thought of such a scheme."

"She agreed?" Judith asked.

He cast her a deliberate look. "She jumped at the offer. For money she was prepared to suffer the company of a husband for whom she has no affection." He continued, "The poor fellow was released, and no doubt, will not be allowed to forget his moment of folly for a very long time."

Mrs. Davenport cut into a slice of melon and said casually, "I notice you have all sympathy with the husband who spent the money on selfish pleasures, and nothing but contempt for the wife who was unable to provide a decent meal on Christmas Day, had to face the wrath of the butcher, and almost certainly would have suffered the effects of the husband's drunkenness on his return from the inn. Do you always adopt so harsh an attitude toward marriage?"

It made him pause, but a smile soon broke through. "No, Aunt Pan, but one can't help feeling that a man who would drink himself insensible on Christmas Eve in the local inn cannot bear the thought of spending it at his own hearth. What man would neglect comfort and a loving wife for the loneliness of the tap room? Besides, you did not see the woman." He laughed. "I am amazed the butcher had the temerity to withold the goose at all."

"Speaking of marriage," Sir Chatsworth put in heavily, "I think we should take this opportunity to discuss the final details of your own. I have directed Frederick to draw up a list of guests. Let me have the names of those fellow officers you wish to be included. I think a dozen would be fair and suitable to the occasion."

Judith saw Alex's face grow still and pale, and wished

she were able to spare him something he would rather discuss in private—or not at all.

"I have been with the regiment too short a time to form any friendships close enough to warrant an invitation, sir."

Sir Chatsworth frowned, his heavy brows almost meeting. "Nonsense! You cannot have lived with other young men for nine months and not . . ." He sighed. "Very well, I will have a word with Colonel Rawlings–Turner on the subject. Of course you must have representatives from your regiment. It is the expected thing."

"An archway of swords," Mrs. Burley pleaded. "You must have an archway of swords, Alexander. It's so romantic, and Judith has set her heart on it, haven't you dear?"

Still looking at her fiancé's stony face Judith wished her mother were not so foolish. "No, Mama. It was simply an idea I had . . . a thought . . ." she trailed off, hearing the ice in her own voice.

"I spoke to Lord Harbinger about his lodge in Scotland," Sir Chatsworth continued. "He is prepared to make it available for three weeks at the start of April. There is plenty of good shooting, riding and hunting there, besides an ideal opportunity for highland walks."

Judith began to burn with anger. Alex was allowing his father to arrange everything without a word of protest or reference to her wishes. She was to be the bride, after all. At the moment, she could imagine nothing worse than three weeks' isolation in the midst of heathery glens with an unwilling groom. She could not believe even the nights would melt a man surrounded by gaunt rocky heights, spartan comfort, and sudden mists. Her only hope was to get him somewhere warm, with beauty and the lure of balmy evenings to relax the defense he mounted whenever they were together.

"I should prefer to go elsewhere, if you do not mind, Sir Chatsworth," she said as calmly as she could. "I do not shoot nor hunt . . . and one cannot walk constantly for three weeks."

Sir Chatsworth looked astonished, as much by what she said as the fact that she had said anything at all. "Where do you suggest as an alternative?"

Caught unawares she blurted, "Italy." Then, emboldened by the stand she was making turned to her fiancé. "Do you agree, Alex?"

He was angry, she could always tell by his eyes. "I think

the destination does not matter. A honeymoon is reputed to be bliss wherever it is spent. However, as Aunt Pan feels my views on marriage are rather harsh, I suggest you state your preferences to my father before he arranges something for which you don't care."

It was another way of saying the marriage was none of his doing, and it hurt her anew. It did not seem likely that a gold band on her finger and the right to be with him would be any help to her. The pain would grow worse if she lay night after night waiting in vain for him to come to her bed.

Later that evening, the three older people tactfully left them alone. Into the icy silence between them, Judith began guardedly chatting about the regiment's New Year's Eve Ball.

"Do you really have no friends in the regiment, Alex?"

"We don't really have a lot in common," was the short reply.

"Do you still hate the life?"

He took his time in answering. "How could I when it is designed to make men of its members."

He was bitter and in his most difficult mood, but she would not give him the satisfaction of leaving so soon.

"Wasn't there a Lieutenant Forrester in the polo team who knows you quite well?"

He smiled grimly. "Oh yes. Neil Forrester is an excellent fellow. His father, a general, was speared by the Zulus. There are three younger brothers, all destined to follow him into the regiment and, no doubt, all as *frightfully* upright and earnest as Forrester Major. I gather the Colonel has already accepted the three brothers, but they don't like rotters in the regiment, you know."

His attitude fanned her anger. "Do you despise everyone and everything?"

He remained unmoved though the question was flung at him with great heat. "On the contrary, I admire the man. He is loyal and proud of his heritage. He is prepared to give his life in the service of his country. Men like him are the backbone of England and the Empire." There was a short pause. "My brother would have been another like him, if he had lived. God only knows why he didn't." He put his hand beneath her elbow and led her toward the stairs in a move to end their tête-à-tête. "Actually, Forrester was quite taken with you. He would make a far better husband than I shall. The Forresters are an old and distinguished family, and wealthy. Of course, it has to be divided among four sons—which would be a disadvantage from your point of view—and Neil is ridiculously old-fashioned over institutions like marriage. He would expect his wife to give him some affection."

Roused to heedless anger she replied, "Then he would not do at all. As you are well aware, all I require from a husband is a vast fortune, a noble name, a position in society . . . and his constant absence from my side. In short, my dear Alex, you fit the description admirably. I cannot wait until March when I shall achieve my ambition so easily. Good night."

She turned and put her foot on the first stair, but that was as far as she got. He was there beside her, his hands clutching the banister on each side, so that she was forced back against it with no escape. There was an explosive tension in his body that alarmed yet elated her, and his eyes glittered darkly.

"No ambition is worthwhile unless achieved against adversity," he said bitingly.

It bore no resemblance to the kiss he had taken in the rose garden. Then, he had been coldly angry. This time, there was a fire within him. With fierce carelessness, he held her pressed against him, with one arm twisted behind her and her head in an aching tilt. It was impossible to twist away from a mouth that was determined on punishment. Judith's own anger flared dangerously.

Struggling free at the first slackening of his hold she cried through her attempts to catch her breath, "I will not be treated like one of your long line of women," and began to run up the stairs away from him.

He caught her two steps later and swung her around against him. This time there was a grim smile on his face. "You might be almost as good with a little more practice."

With provocative and exciting deliberation he brushed her lips roughly several times. Then, the possessive pressure of his mouth turned her anger slowly through all the stages of a woman's battle with herself until her desire was dangerously inflammable. In a moment she became a willing prisoner longing for everlasting captivity, but there was still a small voice that told her surrender at this stage would be fatal.

Desperation to escape before it was too late stiffened the body that was beginning to melt and brought her hands up to push against his chest until he released her. Trembling from the danger she had so narrowly avoided she began backing up the stairs, holding the rail for support as she tried to retain her dignity.

"I see now why your father has taken you in hand—to put a stop to this kind of behavior."

He followed her step for step as she felt her way up the flight, not daring to turn her back on him. Her heart almost whispered its beat, and her legs grew weak as she read the unmistakable expression on his face that silenced the warning voice. His slow steady pursuit had a quality of heady excitement that quickened her breathing and tingled every limb, so that when his hand on her wrist halted her retreat, her whole body was aching for what was to come.

"I have to sacrifice everything in this marriage," he breathed. "I don't see why you should get off scot-free."

It was as if he knew her resistance had gone. He bent over her with almost gentle insistence as she lay back against the banister, and let his gaze wander over her bared shoulders.

"Alex . . . please . . ." she began, but her protest died as he put a hand beneath her head to hold it steady while his other arm drew her up to him. This was what she wanted—had wanted since the evening in the rose garden. There was no further thought of resistance. Everything within her cried surrender. Her mouth grew soft and submissive; her hands moved against the soft cloth of his jacket as she gave herself up to the ecstasy of complete capitulation.

Only when she was melting and limp did he release her and step away down one stair. He gave her a long look that took in the elegant white velvet dress, diamond-drop pendant, and piled ash-blonde hair.

"You might think you call the tune, Judith," he said, "but the piper has to be paid now and then."

He ran down the stairs and strode toward the library, his hair glowing darkly auburn in the gaslight and his back still rigid with anger. Judith was left holding the banister for support, feeling empty and bruised. Slowly she turned and climbed the remaining stairs but, at the top, caught at the huge sturdy pillar with trembling hands as she fought for control of the tears that were already on her cheeks. She would pay the piper—again and again—if he would only call the tune, as he had just done.

On New Year's Eve Judith prepared for the regimental ball in a mood approaching apprehension. They had parted under strained circumstances after Christmas. That night on the stairs had awakened in Judith a throbbing desire to confess her love and risk the outcome, but Alex had been moody and unapproachable the following day. The desire was still there, locked inside her and ready to burst the bars, as she wondered how he would be when he called for her. She and her mother were staying with friends in the garrison town, and Alex was invited to dinner before escorting her to the ball.

The gown she had ordered especially for the occasion was a deep warm apricot instead of the white he seemed to dislike so much, with a half-train trimmed from waist to hem with knots of creamy flowers. It was a romantic dress guaranteed to charm any man, but would it conquer Alex? The death of one year and the birth of another stirred the blood of most with its sad wistfulness and promise of a new beginning. That was what she was determined upon—a new year and a new beginning.

When Alex arrived it seemed as if her wildest hopes might be realized. There was a glow of admiration in his glance as he said, "You look very beautiful tonight. I shall be lucky to have one dance with you."

She drew in a quick breath. "Thank you, Alex. You are very flattering."

His dark lashes drooped over his eyes, tantalizing her. "Not at all. I have never denied that you are extremely lovely."

Desire flowed through her. There was something about him tonight that was superlative. He always looked particularly striking in the green uniform with its elaborate embellishments in silver on collar and front of jacket, but tonight he was vitally alive as she had never seen him before. All through dinner she watched him with bemused eyes. Health almost burst from him; his eyes were vivid with golden lights; he smiled with unrestrained spontaneity that was sweetness to her soul; and he was generous with himself. For the first time she felt he was not holding back from her. She sat watching him, hardly daring to believe time had given him a different view of those kisses on the stairs, that he was now as enslaved as she.

The ball was a grand affair held in the local assembly rooms, and no expense had been spared. The hall had been decorated with hothouse blooms arranged in twelve tableaux depicting the months of the year, and every guest spent some time admiring them. Color was everywhere in the ladies' dresses, and rifle-green uniforms dotted here and there with the scarlet of visitors from other regiments. The regimental orchestra was polished and sparkling, the music festive and gay.

Judith was soon surrounded by would-be partners eager to sign their names in her card, and she was enjoying the admiration in many an eye. Surely the golden glow in Alex's green ones signified the same?

It was only when the music struck up the first waltz and Alex took her in his arms that she realized he had no intention of dancing with her. Once around the floor and he was guiding her through the arched way to a snuggery where a fire blazed, throwing dancing shadows over the velvet-covered settees around it. Her heart leaped. Was he so enchanted tonight he could not wait to be alone with her? She sat prettily, her soft apricot skirts billowed around her and looked up into his lean face as he stood before her in the firelight. *How I love you,* she thought. *Will I ever find the words to tell you?*

"Judith, I can't delay any longer in telling you something I should have said earlier. Your mother's presence with her friends prevented me."

"I'm sorry. Mama sometimes lets her tongue run away with her. I could see you were anxious to get away. I wish you had overruled her earlier," she added softly.

"She was rather determined."

"Yes, she was . . . but we are alone now, and I shall not care if we don't return to the ballroom all evening."

It was heady to be able to say such words at last. He was flushed with flame-glow; young and eager. She yearned to be drawn against him once more, and her mouth felt swollen from the need for his kisses.

"It was essential that I should tell you this at the beginning of the evening," he said. "Before you heard it from someone else."

"Someone else?" Her heartbeat held suspended.

"The regiment is going away."

"Away?" Was that all she could do—repeat his last words in the hope that they would be unsaid?

"Funny, isn't it?" he mused. "My father forced me into the regiment as part of his plan, and that same regiment has given me freedom from it all. We sail for South Africa at the end of the month."

She sat looking at that same eager young man and knew a woman could be no greater deceiver than to herself. He had never been enchanted; he was alight with the thought of freedom from her.

"The wedding will have to be postponed, naturally."

"No!" The cry echoed the pain of waiting and the hope that had just died. "There is time before you leave."

"Hardly. Duty to Queen and country—not forgetting the dear old regiment—must come before all else. Even my father must agree on that!"

His delight was barely disguised and crushed her into the ground. *An unwilling and resentful man.* There had never been a moment when he had reconciled himself to the marriage; she had meant no more to him than a stone around his neck. Fight for him, her aunt had said, but it was not even a battle any longer.

"How long will you be away?" she asked in monotones.

"Two years. That is the usual posting." He paused long enough for it to register fully with her. "If you feel that is too long to wait for the things you wanted from our marriage I am prepared to take back the ring. It will not cause too great a stir. Many a brave soldier has been jilted on the quayside."

His mockery was the last straw. She rose, ignoring the hand outstretched to receive the ring. "Oh no, Alex, you do not wriggle from this engagement so easily," she told him in a voice that shook with emotion. "You allowed your father to force it on you; you will find I am determined to hold you to it. The only way I shall take this ring from my finger is if *you* withdraw from the bargain—and I shall immediately sue for breach of promise. And somehow, Alex," she added, "I cannot see you braving your father's wrath in such an event. Strength of character is hardly one of your virtues."

With the great diamond on her left hand digging into the palm of her right, she swept past him to the ballroom where the strains of the Forget-Me-Not Waltz were heralding in an evening of gaiety. And if the swirling couples grew blurred it did not matter. Alex was behind her and too lost in his own freedom to see the sparkling drops on her lashes.

## CHAPTER FOUR

The departure of a great liner is an event that stirs an emotion peculiarly its own from those who stand and see the gap begin to widen, knowing there is no turning back. For those on board there is a voyage and a new life ahead to compensate for the slow agonized breaking of bonds. A train draws quickly from the station; horses gallop at the flick of the reins. A ship takes its majestic time to tear relations and lovers from their last sight of each other, and it does so with bands playing, streamers linking decks with quayside, sirens hooting, and excited emotional crowds waving until there is only a dark hulk in the distance.

Judith had decided quite definitely that she could not bear to see the departure of the Downshire Rifles for Durban, yet she traveled to Southampton on a bitter gray day at the end of January along with many other women burdened with the same desperate need to have one last glimpse of a beloved face.

Once there, she wished she had not gone, for it made his going away so much more real and desolate. The overtones of duty and glory put a lump in her throat. The sight of columns of marching men weighted down with full kit suggested a serious side of military life she had never seen before. To add to her apprehension boxes of ammunition, guns, equipment, hospital supplies, and several hundred horses were being winched aboard amid a roar of shouted orders, squeaking cogs, protesting beasts, and swearing sailors.

Officers were supervising their personal equipment and the chargers they owned, besides dealing with all the things that inevitably go wrong in what should be a clockwork

operation; N.C.O.'s were barking orders and generally calling on their grandmothers to witness what they had to put
up with. The troops marched hither and thither knowing
they could have embarked with no trouble at all if they had
been left alone to just walk up the gangplank and sort
themselves out.

On the pier, great-coated soldiers were hugging weeping
wives and handling children with alarming ferocity in order
to cover their own need to weep. At times, it was hard to
be a man. Mothers were clinging to the hands of rosy-
cheeked young men, seeing only the small boys they had
raised—the men themselves, looked away, torn between
sentiment and embarrassment.

Sergeants bade their womenfolk farewell with brisk directives to look after themselves and the children, then
walked off tugging their moustaches and blinking rather
obviously. Officers and their ladies stood apart from the
hurly-burly. The men remained stoic as was expected of
them; the ladies smiled to make parting easier but their
eyes said all their upbringing forbade them to put into
words.

Judith stood with a fearsome heart. The mass of uniforms, guns, horses; the tramping boots and roughly barked
orders; the white-faced women and frightened children who
did not understand why papa was acting so strangely—all
suggested something she did not want to face. Surely they
would all come back? These men were not going to war.
There had been talk of such an eventuality for years—since
the conflict of 1880 against the Boers—but there was no
reason to suppose it would ever develop. The Downshire
Rifles were going for a normal two-year tour of foreign
service, that was all . . . and yet there was a note of desperation about the farewells that no one tried to hide.

For a while she made no attempt to seek out her fiancé.
She had seen Alex only once since the ball, at the farewell
dinner party given by Sir Chatsworth in his house in town.
It had been a strained and uncomfortable affair. Alex had
been terse, painfully impersonal. It had been obvious at
once that the very worst thing she could have done was to
apply further pressure to a man already tightly shackled.
She had regretted her outburst at the ball from the moment
it had been made. Alex had begun flirting with his partners
and made the most of the wine that flowed freely all evening. As the new year of 1899 came in, all the men had

kissed their partners, including Alex. She had frozen in his arms and he had taunted her with, "My dear Judith, one more kiss will not commit you to a lifetime of passion."

"I hope that applies to both participants," she had replied coldly.

"You make your rules; allow me to make mine," he had come back quickly, with wine-smooth tongue.

His official good-bye, made in privacy, was short and formal. At one point she had almost feared he was going to shake hands with her, like a male acquaintance. Numbed by his hostility she had been unable to say any of the things she had rehearsed time and again in her room—apologies for what she had said about his strength of character and how much she would miss him. And so she had come to Southampton, unable to resist another chance of putting into words what he could not possibly guess. She had been so near to becoming his wife—even three months had seemed an eternity—and now the thought of two years tore her apart. The diamond on her finger would grow heavier and heavier with the waiting.

Suddenly, she saw him. It was a distant glimpse over the criss-cross of caps and flower-trimmed hats, and she started forward with his name on her lips. It was difficult to find a way through to him with all the confusion on the pier, and when she broke through he had gone.

Urgency filled her as her eyes searched every face beneath a uniform cap. Walking slowly along the pier with the great white side of the ship towering over her, she grew more desperate. She *must* see him. Surely here, with the atmosphere of last confessions, she would find the right words to tell him. All she felt, all she had ever hoped for, all he did not guess was there on her lips to be said. She could follow him and they could be married in Durban. Once he knew the truth he would see he did not have to escape to be free. Once he knew she loved him it would be the foundation on which they could build their happiness. Once he knew the true reason for her holding on to him . . .

The clamor grew as she neared the gangplank. Soldiers were being detailed off to march in single file onto the ship; women and children were weeping noisily. She stopped and knew she could not weep like the women around her, even though Alex was there at the top of the gangplank consulting with a fierce-looking sergeant major.

He had left England already. Way out of reach above her Judith knew she had lost him after all. There was no way she could go aboard, and he would not come back to land again now. If she were a working-class woman, a soldier's sweetheart, she would shout and wave until his attention was drawn to her, but ladies of the upper class did not betray their feelings, except in private—and sometimes not even then. Officers did not have young women running after them, calling their names out loud and creating a scene in public, no matter how desperate they were.

He was so near—so achingly near, yet out of reach. All she could do was pray he would glance her way and have enough generosity to come down to her. Somehow, she knew it would not happen. He was expecting no one to be here, and the business of command was occupying him fully.

For long minutes she stood, a tall girl in dark-blue trimmed with soft gray fur, willing his eyes to leave, just for a moment, the supervision of the stream of green-clad men flowing onto the ship, or the sheaf of papers held by the sergeant major. It did not seem possible that the strength of her will did not reach him, yet she stood on and on without success.

At last, he turned his head casually to look at the scene below. Her heart leaped. His name hung on her breath as his eyes met hers . . . then traveled on through the entire panorama. Satisfied with what he saw, Alex had a short word with the other man before walking along the deck, ducking his head beneath a low bulkhead, and disappearing below.

No, he could not have seen her. Even Alex would not treat her so badly. There was no point in lingering until the ship sailed. Alex had gone; the slow drawing away of the vessel could only hurt her more, if that were possible. Holding back sobs she made her way through clusters of pale drawn women with faces wet with tears. There were others like her, elegant, serene in their fashion-house clothes smothered with fur. They had said good-bye to the confident young men who had filled England's public schools until recently—men who were following in the wake of gallant ancestors with a record of service to their country únequaled anywhere. Judith looked at them and wondered if she had their same calm air . . . but how many had come away having received no comfort, as she had?

The floating reflected images of changing countryside passed outside the carriage window as Judith stared from it. She saw nothing of Hampshire's rolling meadows and tiny farms as they traveled toward London; copse-clad rounded hills and winding white roads leading to quaint medieval market towns. All she saw was her own face, like a misty, accusing ghost trapped in the pane of glass.

The softly-shaped, perfect contour that marked her heritage and stamped her as a classic beauty was what he had seen when he looked at her. Smooth knots of pale hair twisted regally on top of her head to add another inch or two to her height, added to her elegant swaying slenderness, and blue eyes, clear and light with none of the disturbing depths his contained, must have suggested lack of emotion. He thought her cold and uncaring: There was nothing in what he saw to persuade him otherwise.

The moment they had met, she had reversed her intention to decline his proposal. Overwhelming physical attraction swept aside all other considerations with a firm and committing hand, so that she was helplessly governed by desire stronger than she had dreamed possible. Around that she had built instant defenses because she dreaded his scorn of it. His scorn had been for her apparent lack of it, she saw that now.

She had remembered Alex as a quiet polite boy who was eager to please. Suddenly, he had changed dramatically—thrown away his university degree, involved himself in sordid scandal . . . and she had made no effort to discover why. Her aunt had said Sir Chatsworth had given his son an ultimatum—enlisted him in a regiment against his will, and arranged a marriage in his absence. Alex was an aggressive virile man. He fought her; he fought the regiment. In fact, he fought everyone but his father—and she had made no effort to discover why.

Instead of trying to help him she had been too busy protecting herself against the natural instincts that might have led her along that path. She had wanted him physically—had wanted him to miraculously want her—yet had not even tried to understand the man he had become. That was not love. Love was this present inner weeping for an unhappy man who had given all the signs of desperation and found them all unheeded. The rattle of the train pounded in her head, and memories of angry eyes and bitter words emphasized the truth. A man like Alex would not beg for help. He would fight his battles all alone if no one offered to join his cause.

For a week Judith was feverish with activity. To his surprise she called on Sir Chatsworth for no apparent reason other than to chat about his son's youth and activities at university. It was a short visit since Sir Chatsworth was anxious to go to the House. He had very little to say about Alex. On Cambridge he said nothing at all, except how the years had been wasted by irresponsible behavior and the subject was still too painful to discuss. She left with an impression that Sir Chatsworth had spoken of Miles Russell more than Alex—a fact that left her deep in thought if it did not answer any of her obvious questions.

Next, she tackled Mrs. Davenport, who appeared to know *how* Alex had behaved, but not why. All she could offer was that young men who had been reared as strictly as Alex often went off the rails at the first opportunity.

"Fortunately, Chatsworth took care to retain his control over the family wealth and no one, however determined, can be a man-about-town with an empty pocket, Judith." She looked thoughtful. "I have known Chatsworth for some years. He was always a taciturn man, although Cissie softened him for a while. Her death due to complications after Alexander's birth embittered him and made him very strict with his sons. When Miles drowned after saving his brother's life, I suppose it was natural not to want the boy around as a reminder. I should have thought it to Alexander's advantage, since it got him away from the severe atmosphere of Hallworth."

Judith asked about Miles Russell and was told he had been a very handsome boy, favoring his mother, with a brilliance that was already obvious by the time he was ten.

"Such a tragedy as a result of boyish disobedience," she concluded. "For a while after it happened they feared the shock had affected Alexander's brain, but he recovered from it, in time."

"I remember thinking it all very romantic in the way one thrills to tragedy at the age of ten," reflected Judith. "We had been to Hallworth for Alex's birthday, and I had heard the story anew. I think I fancied myself in love with Alex then—or maybe with the courageous Miles. I can't remember which."

"Do you know the answer now?"

Judith looked at her aunt. "Yes, I know the answer now.

Aunt Pan, you once advised me not to become one of those
poor souls who cannot face life without the one they love,
but the thought of two years before I see him again is unbearable. I have to talk to him. Letters will not suffice."
She bit her lip. "I . . . I went into the shipping office
today to inquire about the cost of a passage to Durban." A
faint sad smile touched her lips. "Even that seemed to
bring him nearer for a while."

Restless and unhappy she rose and walked to the window of her aunt's room. Swinging around to face her aunt
she went on, "Would it be so terrible to make a voyage
alone?"

"For a young woman of your circumstances, yes," was
the firm answer. "You, my dear, have been reared under
sheltered circumstances. You have no notion how to cope
on your own. It is abundantly clear you would be besieged
by unscrupulous young men if you traveled unaccom-
panied. Besides, a young woman of your station does not run
half across the world after an errant fiancé."

"Then what does she do?" Judith cried.

Mrs. Davenport gave her a straight look. "I fear she ac-
cepts the situation with dignity and a serene countenance,
letting no one know her true feelings. That is the penalty of
being a lady."

Judith said nothing more. She knew her aunt spoke the
truth. She also knew there was little sympathy to be had
from someone who felt she had mishandled the engagement
right from the start. That Alex had gone off leaving the
wedding up in the air for two years had all been her own
fault and, although Mrs. Davenport had never paid a word
about it, Judith was certain her aunt had lost patience with
her.

But each passing day made Judith more restless and un-
settled. Far from accepting the situation with dignity and a
serene countenance, time only made her desperation to see
Alex harder to bear. Soon, she grew pale and devoid of
energy. At night she lay awake cursing the rules that
obliged women to remain at home while their menfolk
went away. *Two years, two years*, she cried silently, tossing
and turning. She could not wait quietly for his return. By
then she surely would have lost him for good.

A month after Alex sailed Judith was a shadow of her
former self. Mooning around the house, silent and listless,
she longed to do something, *anything* rather than accept

the futility of her situation. Alex would be in South Africa by now, free from obligations to his fiancée, free to entertain other women as much as he wished, while she had his diamond on her finger and was expected to remain true to the promise it signified. Not that she wanted other men—they all appeared less than real in comparison with the one with whom she longed to be.

By the middle of March the situation was even worse. A letter had arrived from a place called Ladysmith where the Downshires were garrisoned, and Alex had managed to convey his delight in the country, the new life he had found, and his pleasure at the prospect of two years in such a place, all in polite sentences spaced well apart in order to fill the page quickly. Judith reached her lowest ebb that evening.

They sat with their coffee in the pretty sitting room she had begun to hate. *Three females with not a man among us*, she thought bitterly. *I think I shall never do more than this all my life unless I shock society . . . or enter a nunnery. Oh, Alex!*

"It really is too bad," Mrs. Davenport said suddenly. "Those dreadful Boers will not see reason at all."

"I beg your pardon, Pansy?" said her sister. "Whatever has led you to utter such a statement on such a quiet evening? You know I do not understand such subjects."

Mrs. Davenport turned her beautifully coiffeured head to study Alicia Burley. "It's time you did, my dear. The world does not consist of this house and Fanny Bartholemew's drawing room, as you seem to think."

Mrs. Burley bridled. "That is most unfair of you. You must know as well as I that some of us are born with heads, and some with hearts. I happen to fall into the latter category. I am soon affected by emotion and suffer for others who are in distress. No one was more upset over Alexander's call to duty that obliged him to postpone the wedding when it was so near. I still have not recovered from the distress of the news. It would not do if we all abandoned our natural role in order to study world affairs."

Mrs. Davenport laughed gaily. "On no account would I expect you to abandon a role you so obviously enjoy, Alicia, but it does not mean you must bury your head in the sand."

"What about the Boers, Aunt Pan," Judith asked quietly.

Mrs. Davenport set her coffee cup upon the table and

made herself comfortable. "They appear to be extremely complex. First, they claim to be God-fearing folk, yet look upon other people with contempt. Far from embracing the world as their brothers, their declared intent is to make the Boers supreme.

"They are poor farmers struggling to make a living in a vast land containing vicious tribes of natives. The women are expected to work as hard as the men, besides producing children at regular intervals. Their food is what they grow and what they can shoot—spartan fare, in the extreme— and they live in roughly built huts, for the most part."

"I really cannot see what concern they are of ours," complained Mrs. Burley. "They cannot be very different from those unpleasant people who gather on the heath each August. I always pass quickly and look the other way. One feels the slightest encouragement would have them asking for money . . . or worse." She shuddered.

"The Boers are not Romany gypsies, Alicia. They are a people desperate to settle—to *stop* moving on all the time. They have chosen an area in South Africa and are determined to make it their own, with no intention of sharing it with anyone."

"That sounds supremely selfish."

Mrs. Davenport tried to keep her patience. Alicia had been foolish all her life and saw no reason to change. "Would you not think most people would welcome the discovery of immense wealth on their land? To poor people it should be a godsend, but these farmers curse the gold that lies beneath the ground of their chosen state and wish it had never been found."

Judith recalled a conversation similar to this one on the night of her engagement. She remembered vividly every word Alex had said.

"Only because it has attracted all kinds of other settlers—mostly English—when the Boers had crossed the whole of southern Africa to get away from them. They wish to be left alone to live their own kind of life . . . at least, that's what Alex said."

"Perhaps Alexander will learn a little more about the situation now he is on the spot," said her aunt with a touch of asperity. "It sounds quite ridiculous to me. Gold will provide growth and industry for the whole of Africa. The Dutch are not the only people in the area."

Alicia Burley rose. "All this is giving me a headache.

You will have to excuse me, Pansy. Regardless of what you say, I fail to see why I should concern myself with some unpleasant farmers on the other side of the world." She crossed the room in a cloud of lavender water, her rose-pink dress sweeping gracefully behind her thickening figure. "I shall be glad if you will come to me in a short while, Judith. If my headache worsens, your soothing fingers will work wonders."

"Yes, Mama," said Judith with an effort, while her inner self screamed a protest. It was unbearable to be here, with her demanding pretty mother when she should be with Alex. Her original wedding day was only a week away, and his absence was all the more marked the nearer it drew.

After her mother left the room Judith felt unable to sit still. She went to the piano with the intention of soothing herself with some music, but got only as far as lifting the lid before she realized it was not what she wanted at all.

"They are happy enough to let the English mine their gold for the benefit of the country, in general, but will not allow them any rights, nor a voice in the government of the state," Mrs. Davenport continued as if the interruption had not taken place. "It does seem completely unreasonable that those who work hard to extract the wealth of a land should be regarded as inferior citizens and treated with humiliating authority, while a parcel of farmers who do nothing except for themselves set themselves up as rulers. I am not at all surprised the English are growing a little tired of such treatment. To be forced to bow to a government that has one rule for the Dutch and another for anyone else is beneath the dignity of any Englishman. After all, somebody has to get the gold up."

Judith had reached the end of her tether. "Why? Is it so important that we have to worry about it here in England?"

Her aunt looked stern. "Of course it is important. I, for one, have invested a great deal of money in it."

"I'm sorry . . . it's just that . . ."

"I have invested a great deal of money," repeated Mrs. Davenport, "and Chatsworth has been making inquiries on the situation in Johannesburg on my behalf . . . and his own. Russell money is backing the mining industry to the hilt, also." She rose and went toward Judith at the piano, her slender figure well molded in red silk. "For all his influence as a member of parliament Chatsworth cannot seem to obtain a firm answer on the success of the venture, nor any information on the whereabouts of the mine manager who was arrested last month for causing a disturbance at a meeting to demand the vote for English settlers." She reached the piano and stroked the glossy black lid with a gentle hand. "Chatsworth is a busy man with affairs in England, but I have time on my hands. It seems to me the most sensible thing would be to go there and see for myself what is being done with our money." Her eyes met Judith's. "I could not possibly travel to South Africa alone, could I? Can you suggest a suitable companion with interests of her own in that country?"

The tears were already wet on Judith's cheeks when she took her aunt's hands. Words were not necessary between them. They never had been.

## CHAPTER FIVE

South Africa was a land of splendor and riches. It lured adventurers, rogues, opportunists, settlers, and escapists. In all these men were the qualities needed to conquer the unknown: in some such qualities were ruthless and self-centered, in others they bred great strength of character.

From across the oceans came white men in search of the things they had never yet found in their own countries. From the sweltering center of Africa came black men seeking fresh pastures for cattle and homelands for their rapidly increasing numbers. The indigenous people of South Africa, the Hottentots, were too thinly scattered to keep their prize to themselves. Month after month, the ships arrived bringing Europeans, while Africans poured down to the more moderate plains.

Down at the Cape the Dutch set up trading posts, and the British soon followed suit. At first, there appeared to be room for everyone, but the two trading nations did not take long in discovering they had irreconcilable differences of opinion. The British thought the Dutch narrow-minded and unfriendly; the Dutch thought the English decadent and far too interested in getting the biggest share of their new country.

Trouble came to a head all too quickly. Englishmen were old hands at colonizing. Their tongues were too smooth for the simple Dutch settlers who found themselves being ruled by the people they hated. For a while they stuck it out, but when their new masters ordered them to free the black slaves they owned, it was too much. Outnumbered by the English they began moving inland to set up their own colonies. Into the unknown they trekked in long columns of wagons, believing the words of their Bible that pointed to them as God's chosen people in a land He intended they should inhabit. But, no sooner had they settled in new pastures than the British followed, and the pattern began again.

During the next hundred years both British and Dutch moved steadily north, unaware that the black tribes were approaching just as steadily south. The inescapable confrontations were bloody, horrific, and bred in the Dutch a lasting hatred; in the English the urge to subdue and rule. For a while the white men were united against the black, the trekkers depending on the vast British army to defeat the savage tribes. The hinterland was opened to all settlers but only after the slaughter of thousands. The Dutch who died did so for the land they wanted so badly. The British soldiers made the final sacrifice merely in response to orders.

An uneasy peace reigned between black and white. It was then that a new element entered the scene. The earth beneath the new settlements revealed its secrets. Gold in quantities seldom before seen, and diamonds of great size and value. Only saints could have remained peaceable. The English and Dutch did not.

For the first time, British and Dutch took up arms against each other, the red-coated soldiers so skilled at putting down native tribes finding themselves out-foxed by the wily trekkers. In a disastrous battle at Majuba Hill the Dutch, now known by their own word for men of the land, massacred the British who grudgingly had to agree to waive their claim to sovereignty over the two states settled by the Boers.

It rankled, and the situation simmered uneasily. The British did not like playing second fiddle, and the Boers made very sure they had to. For the following decade and a half, red-coated troops garrisoned their own two states, not only to emphasize their rule but to temper their farming neighbors who had turned the tables and made it plain they would be happier with the British out of South Africa altogether. It was a vast country to garrison, and men from gray industrial towns of England or those used to the soft green, rain-blurred images of rural landscapes often found themselves isolated in outposts both wild and inhospitable.

The hamlet of Landerdorp in Natal was such a place. A straight dust road ran between scattered tin-roofed shacks, and a tiny church stood at the end of it. A stream provided water, an occasional tree gave shade from the blistering sun. On the outskirts, a native village of thatch-covered huts straggled in unplanned fashion in a hollow, giving an exotic note to the tiny settlement.

All around stretched the veld—the endless yellow-green plain of South Africa. The veld was wild and compelling, luring men to cross it for what might lie beyond. Many never reached their goal. In summer the burning sun shriveled the grass and dried up rivers: Winter brought bitter winds and temperatures that froze everything to iron hardness. Autumn storms trebled the volume of rivers to form unfordable torrents racing through the earth's gashes, yet those same storms in spring brought forth instant carpets of brilliantly colored flowers in an unsuspected profusion of fertility.

It was that same savage terrain that also provided some of the most compelling landscapes the English had ever seen. Used to lush green meadows, scented blossoms, white winding lanes that led through villages, and rounded hills buzzing with bees as they took the pollen from yarrow and buttercup, the grandeur of great flat-topped *kopjes* rearing into a sky bluer than they could credit took their breath away. For miles there was no sign of habitation, only the spread of veld that sometimes sang with the wind, and the heights covered with spiky aloe where creatures they had only seen in zoos roamed free. There were no smells of baking bread from the farmhouse, night-scented stock, milk fresh from the udder, or ale drawn from a barrel in the tap room with its familiar odor of tobacco and hay. This countryside smelled only of fresh, pure air and the good earth. While they dreamed of home and the sounds of hounds baying, children playing by the village pond, cattle pulling

the sweet grass in juicy tearing grunts, and the jangle of the
bell on the door of the thatched shop, the area around Landerdorp rang only with the crack of shots as the officers
hunted the wild beasts. At times, they also heard the desolate cries of the *aasvogels* as they circled high above a distant spot, waiting to descend on whatever lay breathing its
last below them, and at night they tried to shut their ears to
unearthly, animal shrieks and cries from the *kopjes* circling
their tiny garrison. Not one would admit he enjoyed his
situation, yet after he had left for those things familiar and
beloved, the memory of vastness, the colors of nature, and
the untamable beauty of Africa haunted him on nights
when dusk hung too long in the air and conjured up fantasies.

Landerdorp could never be mistaken for anything but a
poor hamlet in a stretch of wild, sparsely populated country, but it boasted an importance beyond its appearance
because it also served as a depot for the railway between
Ladysmith and Johannesburg. Supplies were off-loaded at
the railway station, and farmers from a wide area around
rode there in ox carts to collect their simple provisions.

There were no bolts of expensive silk, for the women
wore homespun clothes suited to their life close to the
earth. Here merchants sold no elegant lamp shades, bird
cages, ornaments, perfumes, and lacy parasols, luxuries the
tillers of Natal's land would not have understood, for they
were people whose world consisted of their own acres and
occasional glimpses of strangers who got off the trains to
stretch their legs for a while.

The farmers were not all of Dutch extraction—there
were occasional English-speaking South Africans who tried
their hands at making a living from the land—and not all
Boers were fanatical adherents to the Boer creed, but the
isolated, harsh existence endured by the hardy folk who
had trekked across the great continent tended to breed a
distrust of strangers and strange ways. In some, however, it
bred curiosity—the desire to learn. But all had one thing in
common—tenacity.

Alex had reason to reflect on that quality as he emerged
from his quarters one afternoon late in March and saw a
girl seated in an ox cart, resisting all overtures made to her
by a young subaltern in the engineers who had reined-in
across her path. He smiled to himself. Cuthbertson would
get nowhere with a Dutch girl. They had courage and de-

termination—and very little time for British soldiers. Their tongues were sharp, even though it was impossible to understand their confounded language, and many a man had felt the thong of a whip on his hand, or the weight of a wheel across his foot as an unwilling girl urged forward her oxen with a Boer word of command.

Alex had to admit they had cause for their attitude. After the garrison town of Ladysmith most Englishmen found outpost duty at Landerdorp very dull and tried to enliven their existence in any way they could. The British soldier had a sense of humor the Boers did not understand and the pranks that were commonplace in the ranks of a British regiment were regarded as decadent by the local populace. The joining together of two ox wagons standing back-to-back did not amuse the farmers who tried to drive them in opposite directions, but the watching soldiers fell about with laughter.

The women visiting the stores were profoundly shocked when a highland corporal strode in to purchase a pair of drawers and tried them on for size over his brawny legs. Tired of suffering from sunburned knees exposed by his kilt he had dreamed up an ingenious remedy. His friends thought it hilarious; the Boer wives thought he was touched by the devil.

The natural friendliness of the British soldiers went too far for the subcontinental farmers—especially when it came to their wives and daughters. Their resentment was not without foundation.

The officers tried to stop it, but were often worse offenders. Their sense of arrogance was excessively greater than the rankers, many of them finding the farming folk less educated and intelligent than their tenants on large estates all over England. With nothing else to do they relied on the bottle to pass the time, the resulting inebriation produced a series of risky and idiotic capers.

A captain was invited to visit a leading burgher of Landerdorp, and rode his horse right up the front steps and along the *stoep* before dismounting at the front door. A lieutenant full of drunken bravado jumped his horse clean through a goods wagon forgetting there was a downward slope on the other side. He broke an arm, but declared it had been "dashed good sport." The "dashed good sport" declined a little after a subaltern was drowned while trying to ride across a *drift* blindfolded. There had been a storm the night before and the river had risen six feet, making the ford impassable.

Alex watched such incidents with cynicism, holding himself aloof from regimental buffoonery. However, he had flirted with young women at Ladysmith and been a companion to Bacchus on many occasions. He still drank heavily at Landerdorp, but left the women alone. They were, English or Dutch, mostly neither young nor attractive. Against his fellows he had one overriding pleasure in his command at the outpost: the railway. Although the Royal Engineers had a small detachment supervising the yards, he was able to spend as much time as he wished with Guy Cuthbertson who was the engineer in charge, and his interest in railways grew. He had even borrowed some manuals on the subject from the subaltern and read them with absorption.

His friendship with Guy did not prevent him from deploring the fellow's morals, however, and he watched the girl in the ox cart being pestered that afternoon with growing irritation with the man. Had he nothing better to do than make himself obnoxious to girls who wished only to be left in peace? Guy was a notorious charmer, of course, with a heart as fickle as a butterfly. For a few minutes he watched through eyes narrowed against the glare of Natal's brilliant autumn sunlight. The girl seemed flustered, unable to handle the situation.

He started to move away; it was none of his affair. The wooden *stoep* outside the two-storied building used as quarters by the officers groaned beneath his boots. He was a big man with a heavy tread that threatened to go through the rotting planks. He must get Guy to arrange for its repair—better employment for him than aggravating relations between the Boers and the English.

Two steps led to the ground and the corner, around which lay the stables. His horse was saddled, as ordered, and he swung onto it with indecision filling him. He was off to check his outlying guard posts, but it was such a perfect afternoon he would much prefer to make a gentle hack over the *kopjes*. In the three weeks he had been at Landerdorp there had been few opportunities for such pleasure, for he had discovered Captain Beamish, who commanded the detachment of the Downshires, was a man who believed in delegating responsibility to his subalterns to the extent of leaving himself none. He was a weak foppish man with little understanding of the present situation, and his two subordinates crossed swords with him perpetually.

Setting his horse at a trot into the street Alex came upon a scene that made him slow down. Guy Cuthbertson had seized the reins of the ox cart and was tormenting the occupant by inviting her to take them, then holding them out of reach. He had dismounted and had one foot on the cart, bringing him near enough to the girl to make her edge nervously away along the seat. She looked about her for help. Alex decided to intervene.

He trotted up. "You appear to have been assisting this young lady for a considerable time, Guy. Is the axle broken . . . or is something else preventing her from leaving?" he asked pointedly.

Then he turned to salute the girl and found the answer. She was not more than eighteen with a bloom on her cheeks that had not yet become toughened by the sun and rain of the veld. Large dark eyes stared at him fearfully, in case his presence would only double her predicament. Dark hair was braided and wound round her head, reminding him of senior girls at boarding school.

"Good afternoon," he said, more warmly than he intended. "Since my colleague appears to have difficulty in assisting you I am very ready to lend my services to his."

She made no reply, staring at him as if shocked by the arrival of yet another tormentor.

"God, I wish I could speak their abominable language," Alex cursed. "It's obvious that you have successfully convinced her your intentions are dishonorable, but there seems no way of putting over that mine are just the opposite." He looked back at the girl and smiled encouragingly before saying to Guy, "I suggest you round up some of your sappers to reinforce the *stoep* outside our quarters before I put my foot through it."

Guy grinned amiably. "I happen to be well-occupied here."

From his advantage on horseback Alex looked down on his handsome colleague. "I am not one to pull rank, old fellow, but I was commissioned three weeks before you. I am taking command of the situation as senior officer."

"Ha!" Guy exploded with amusement. "That's no use. First, I am off-duty. Second, I am out of uniform."

Alex took another look at the wide eyes regarding him.

"Look, clear off, Guy. I don't think she appreciates your attentions."

"As you please," was the genial reply. Taking his foot from the wagon he gave the occupant a mock bow before preparing to lead his horse away. "I think you are in for a bit of a surprise, Alex," he said in parting, "but as senior officer, I daresay you are equipped to handle it."

Alex watched him saunter off, then smiled at the girl, saluted, and prepared to go on his way.

"Thank you," she said in English. "You are very good."

He was nonplussed, trying to recall what he had said in the belief that she could not understand him. Then, the humor of the situation overcame him and he laughed.

"You wouldn't say that if you really knew me. I can be very wicked, at times."

"Oh yes, you are a good man. Of that I am sure," she said with great seriousness.

He studied the smooth face and eyes that were still wide with some kind of shock. "Why did you allow me to speak to my friend in the belief that you understood no English?"

She sat very straight. A small figure on the seat of a heavy ox wagon, yet looking somehow proudly dignified. He was intrigued.

"At first I thought you were like the other. I was frightened. Afterward, I liked hearing you speak."

He grew more intrigued. "What I said was rather forthright, if I remember correctly."

"Are you the Commandant of Landerdorp?"

Tempted to lie, he found himself saying instead, "Regrettably, no. I am merely a humble subaltern."

"Subaltern?" she repeated hesitantly.

He smiled. "A lieutenant."

Her answering smile was a little shy. "You see, I do not know so much English. But I can say 'thank you' . . . and also 'goodbye.' I must now go."

The sight of the young girl handling the cumbersome vehicle mesmerized him for a moment, then some impulse made him turn his horse to move off alongside her. "Must you leave immediately? It seems a pity now we have discovered we can communicate."

Although she did not turn to look at him, nor offer any answer, he felt she did not object to his riding beside the wagon. Until she told him he was unwelcome that was where he intended to stay.

"Where did you learn your English? There are not many Dutch ladies who speak it."

"Oh yes," was the grave reply. "Many know it quite well, but will not use it because their men forbid it . . . or because they . . ." she broke off suddenly.

"Because they hate us?" he asked. "We know they do." He sighed. "Perhaps we often deserve it."

They traveled in silence for a short distance until the shacks were left behind. She was taking the track that led through the *kopjes* out onto the open veld. It was an easy decision to make when choosing between inspecting his outlying guards and continuing beside this girl who looked so charming in a long dark skirt and simple blouse.

"Do you have far to go?" he asked.

"It is a four-hour ride, that is all," she told him with the nonchalance of people who thought nothing of spending all day roaming the wild beautiful countryside of their chosen land.

"But it will be dark before you are half way there! Allow me to escort you."

"No." It was swift and tinged with apprehension. "It would not do . . . and you have your duty."

He decided not to press the point, but asked why she was all alone on such an errand. "I have not seen you in Landerdorp before, of that I am certain."

Unaware of the compliment in his words she replied, "My brother Franz has injured his hand in the machine and cannot drive the team. It is some time since I was in Landerdorp. It has changed."

The sun was beginning to sink, giving the land an evening vividness, and the road ahead lay like a streamer that had floated down to settle on a rich green carpet after the noise and excitement of a party. To Alex it seemed just like that. The noise of the railway yard, and the exchange of voices above the hissing steam; the guttural shouts of Boer farmers and vendors; the laughter and hoofbeats of British soldiery had all been left behind for a quiet bewitching atmosphere he had never before noticed in the surrounding hills. A strange feeling of blessedness washed over him. It was a long time since he had thought of God in a reverent sense, but vague memories of the stained-glass windows in the school chapel came to him suddenly—memories of a small boy wondering if his mother had looked anything like the angels depicted there. Sir Chatsworth always described

her thus, and said she had gone to heaven with his brother.
For a long time he had imagined the Virgin and child to be
the two—saintly and out of reach.

He shook off the disturbing recollection and breathed the
clear sparkling air that put health into a man's lungs. The
very wideness and grandeur of this country brought a man
nearer himself and his Maker, he had noticed. Small wonder the wandering Boers had felt it their perfect destination.

"Do you not have duties, Lieutenant?"

Her sweet husky voice brought his eyes around to her as
if recovering from a dream.

"None that need urgent attention. If you have no objection I will ride a short way with you." He smiled. "It seems
that you don't hate the English as much as your sisters."

"I have no sisters." The serious answer charmed him
with its innocence. "To hate people is bad, I think. It is
better to try to understand them."

"Yes," he said bemused. She drove the creaking ox
wagon with skill, although her hands were small and unsuited to the heavy harness she held. The general stamp of
Boer women was somewhat muted in her, although the
young face had signs of determination in the mouth and
eyes, and had the striking profile common to Dutch
women. But this young girl's face was smooth and clear-
complexioned; her dark hair well-groomed; and her
clothes neatly washed and pressed. Perhaps it was her
youth. Time and age might eventually drag her down into a
careworn, overworked woman who knew nothing but toil
and sacrifice and childbirth. The thought displeased him.
As she was, he found her interesting, enigmatic, a simple girl
with the wisdom of scholars. It would be infinitely sad if
she were to change.

They were approaching a *nek* or pass through the range
of hills encircling Landerdorp in a horseshoe shape, and
Alex could see the sun still shining in the distance where
the veld lay flatter for miles around. Dusk had come to
Landerdorp, but on the other side of the hills it was still
afternoon.

The girl glanced at him and commented on the way
ahead. "You see, it is quite easy for me. Once past Devil's
Leap the road is very good."

"Devil's Leap?" he asked. "Where is that?"

Her laugh was soft and beguiling. "You live in Lander-dorp and do not know Devil's Leap, Lieutenant? They tell me Englishmen look and never see anything."

"Do they, indeed." He felt a warmth creeping right through his bones. "Perhaps we should see a lot more if we had a charming guide to show us her homeland."

She looked a little uncertain what to say next, so he helped her by saying, "Should you mind explaining to me what I should already know? I have been in Landerdorp for only three weeks. Perhaps it will excuse my failure to identify Devil's Leap."

"I should not have said what I did. Why should you know the old legends we are taught? You are not one of us."

"I am sorry for that," he said before he could stop himself.

For a long moment she looked at him with her lovely brown eyes full of new lessons learned that day. The wagon lurched on, the oxen knowing the way by heart, as he rode beside her lost to the sudden dimness thrown by the high walls of the pass that cut off the sun. Alex had forgotten his outlying guards, his fellow soldiers, and his obligation to return. All he could see was a face he should have known long ago.

Neither spoke as they traveled through the pass, but it seemed a natural silence, as if the hills knew their thoughts, and the clopping hooves echoed their heartbeats. At the far end, the girl eased gently on the reins and the beasts stopped.

Alex brought his horse round to face her. "What is wrong?"

"It would be better for you to return now," she told him gravely, then nodded to herself. "Yes, better."

Wanting to extend the moment he said teasingly, "Am I not to be told about Devil's Leap after all?"

"Of course." It was a quick breathless phrase before she turned rather self-consciously to point back along the pass. "There, where the ledge stands out from the *kopje*. That is Devil's Leap. You see how it overhangs the *nek* with nothing beneath?"

Dragging his eyes from a study of her profile, Alex saw a narrow shelf several hundred feet up the steep slope forming the right-hand side of the pass. It overhung a sheer

drop to the stony ground below. Right now, the dying sun
caught the underside of it, putting a glow like fire upon the
rocky surface. It was aptly named.

"The black people believed it was a magic place," she
said in a far-off voice. "When anyone had been accused of
sinfulness, the tribesmen brought him to stand on that
ledge. They waited for the signs of justice. If the man was
possessed by devils, those devils would persuade him to
climb back up and continue his wickedness. Those lying in
wait killed such men with their spears. If he was blameless
the gods would bear him safely down when he leaped into
the *nek* and send him happily on his way."

Alex smiled faintly. "A very neat way of dealing with
offenders. We call it 'between the devil and the deep, blue
sea.' "

She turned back to him with lips that wanted to curve
into a smile but dared not. "Now you must explain to me,
please."

He took a deep breath to steady himself. They were
alone and there was magic in this silent, beautiful place. "It
means there is no choice but disaster. Once a man set foot
on Devil's Leap he was lost, whatever happened."

She took a long time in speaking. "You make it sound
very sad."

"It is."

"I must go." The decision was sudden, and the oxen began to move forward in their lumbering, nod-headed manner.

"Shall you be coming to Landerdorp again?" he asked
quickly—too quickly for her not to notice the note of anxiety behind the question.

"On Thursday I shall come. Good-bye, Lieutenant."

It was a moment before he trotted after her. "May I
know your name?"

She hesitated then said, "Hetta Myburgh."

"Thank you." His horse sidled beside the cart as he began turning. "I will watch on Thursday in case I can be of
service to you, Miss Myburgh."

The wagon rolled on into the setting sun, blinding him to
the sight of its passage across the veld. It seemed deserted
out there. Where was she going? For a long time he leaned
on the pommel watching the distance. The vivid glow of
light from the west put a veneer of unreality upon the great
stretch of grass so that it charmed his senses with luminous

beckoning freedom. Out there the air was clean. It smelled of early dew and sun-soaked nature. When the wind blew the soft pressure on one's face held a hint of distant mists above water, and the scent of mimosas mingled with the pungent warmth given off by animals' pelts. To Alex, it all stirred the captive spirit within.

His eyes, narrowed against the glory of dying day, fastened their gaze at the point where the golden-rose skyline touched the earth. It looked but a few hours' ride away, yet he knew a man might be lured by it for days at a time and never find what he sought. The black people lived out there—their strange beehive huts took one by surprise when traversing lonely areas—and it was possible to see them straggling along the distant horizon with their bony-hipped cattle until they were swallowed up by sheer space. At this hour of super clarity Alex could make out the far-off smoke from dung fires and knew they were there.

Still bemused, he turned in the saddle to study the hills hanging above him, already caught by approaching night. They were not the gentle, green hills of home, but tall eruptions of the land that stood in uncompromising continuation of the veld. They challenged, rather than invited which, to a man like Alex, aroused more response. The gray-green slopes dotted darkly with spiky, aggressive aloes reared away from the spot where he sat his horse, up into the heavens as if some precious prize at the top must be defended from despoilers.

Their sheer might at once overawed him, yet gave birth to a feeling of defiance. To conquer them would make him a man among men, yet the hush and extraordinary isolation now that the ox wagon had gone gave him once more that sensation of nearness to his Maker that brought humility of spirit.

The sun vanished below the earth's rim: the darkening veld had swallowed the girl in her cart completely. Full of disturbing sensations Alex trotted back through the *nek* beneath Devil's Leap feeling he had been enchanted. It had not entered his mind once that this was the day he should have married Judith Burley.

# CHAPTER SIX

Hetta had traveled across the veld all her life. It was part of her heritage; its wildness was in her bones; its freedom burned like a flame within . . . yet an inexplicable loneliness enveloped her as she drove the wagon toward the farm. She could resist the temptation no longer and at last turned to look back. He had gone through the *nek* and was hidden from her view.

If, unlike Alex, she was unable to recognize enchantment when it surrounded her, the memory of the British officer still dominated her long ride home and she made no effort to drive it away. If a small feeling of guilt rose up she ignored it. There was nothing sinful in speaking to an Englishman. This one could hardly be held responsible for the deeds of the past, and she could not have ignored him after he had been so . . . been so . . . The right word escaped her.

The other man with flashing eyes had alarmed and dismayed her with his refusal to let her leave, although he had not meant her any real harm, she was certain. Then, the lieutenant had appeared from nowhere on his beautiful horse, so suddenly that it had taken her by surprise. A little lurch somewhere inside her breast accompanied the memory. Surely she could be forgiven for thinking him to be the commandant, for he spoke with such authority to the one who was beside her wagon and sent him on his way so easily.

A faint smile touched her lips. His voice was beautiful—deep, and with a way of making English words softly gentle on her ear. She had not wanted him to stop speaking. A Boer man would have confronted another in such a situation with aggression and harsh words, and then only if she was his woman. Why had the Englishman put himself out over an unknown Boer girl?

The lieutenant was unlike any man she knew or had ever

encountered. Unbearded, his face had fascinated her with its firm lines that suggested a peaceful and sensitive nature. Most of all she had liked his mouth—clearly defined and infinitely attractive when he smiled. Piet had thick lips that showed moist and red through his luxuriant dark beard.

Veering away from thoughts of Piet Steenkamp Hetta thought again about the man from Landerdorp. What had prompted him to ride beside her when it had been unnecessary? How was it possible for a person to be gentle and commanding at one and the same time? He had done nothing, laid no hand on the first man, yet a few words had freed her—a few words and a steady glance. He had green eyes. She remembered them vividly. Not pale, like Piet's, with the light of crusade in them, but dark green and mottled with golden flecks—sad eyes, she now realized.

Something told her he was a lonely man. Lonely within himself. No doubt he had friends among the others stationed at Landerdorp—soldiers were friendly people, as a rule—but he probably never revealed his true identity to any but those closest to him.

She had seen women like that—women on farms they never left year in, year out; women who lived a frugal relentless life with a man who wanted nothing more than a willing pair of hands by day, and a willing body at night. Such women did their duty and said nothing, but the truth was there in their eyes for anyone who wished to see. Sturdy women, who lived always with their sadness.

Hetta could not remember being ill. Despite her slight frame she knew the years would broaden her back and strengthen her wrists, and the air of the veld would keep her free from pestilence. She would be one of those sturdy, steadfast women. She would marry Piet Steenkamp, help him on his farm, and bring forth his sons. They were sure to be sons. Piet was a fierce, fire-and-brimstone man, and that kind always fathered male children.

Her thoughts flew back to the Englishman. Had he a wife and sons? Or perhaps there were daughters, with eyes as green as his own and gentle sad smiles. What kind of woman would his wife be? Certainly not one with skin toughened and tanned by the elements, and trained to pull calves from the cow or walk behind a plough. A small pain began to grow in her breast at the thought.

Leaving the oxen to take her home she sat dreaming as dusk gave way to night and the veld became a beautiful

singing place for the beasts of Africa. Darkness did not
worry Hetta. She had a rifle in the wagon and knew how to
use it. But her thoughts took her so far away that she
might easily have been caught unawares.

Englishwomen were all tall and beautiful. She had been
told that by an English friend in Ladysmith. They wore
beautiful white dresses and carried small umbrellas made of
muslin and silk to prevent the sun from touching their
faces. It was most desirable to have white skin—the whiter
it was the more beautiful gentlemen thought it. These
things had stayed with Hetta through her youth and influenced her care for herself. She knew it was vanity, and
vanity was a sin, but it was impossible to forget looking
from her aunt's window and watching for hours the English
ladies strolling past on the arms of their tall, attentive gentlemen. It looked as if, in some way, the women were superior to their husbands.

For a long time the child Hetta had believed this, until
she had overheard a quarrel through an open window that
told her the outward appearance was false. It still fascinated her, however, and she longed to be one of those tall
creatures with pale, pale skin, who smelled of flowers and
wore dresses that showed every speck of dirt and had to be
washed every time they were worn.

She had not dared to tell her aunt she had English
friends, for the Myburghs held themselves aloof from *uitlanders*, but curiosity about other people had led her to
accept overtures from foreign children. From them she had
learned her English, and her tolerance. Not wishing to be
outdone she had worked hard at her lessons, and had an
education beyond many Boer women who had lived all
their lives on their home farms. That, and her generous
nature, was responsible for the unease she felt over the un-
equivocal hatred within the breasts of her grandfather and,
Piet, the man to whom she was promised.

Old Oupa had extra reason to hate the British for they
had killed his son—her own father—at Majuba when she
was still in her mother's womb. The old man swore it was
the shock that brought her forth before her time and lowered her mother's constitution so that she succumbed to a
fever before the year was out.

Piet had no such reasons to add to his hatred, but was
the leader of a ring of young Boers who had sworn to make
the whole of Africa the home of the Dutch and defy any

body of men who tried to make it otherwise. Who were more guilty of that than the British? The pain in her breast increased as she remembered the chestnut-haired British lieutenant saying he knew the Boers hated his people. She was desperate to tell him it was not so—not completely so.

With a start she realized the lights of the farm were in sight. Within half an hour she would be home. Her first thoughts were domestic. Had the black girl remembered to put the stew on to cook at the time she had been told? Would there be water drawn to heat? There was her brother's injured hand to be bathed, and her own hands and face to be washed.

After that she thought of Landerdorp and what she had brought back in the wagon. With absolute certainty she knew the encounter with the Lieutenant must be kept to herself. Her brother, Franz, would understand, but Oupa would be very angry if he knew of it. That she also felt reluctant to share the small incident with anyone decided the question.

Although those inside the house would have heard the wheels on the yard no one came out to greet the girl; she did not expect them. A black servant took charge of unyoking the oxen while Hetta climbed down and stretched like a young animal before walking on to the *stoep* and into the house.

Oupa and Franz were having dinner. They ate with the hunger of men who have worked in the fields all day, and wasted little time over their greetings.

"Did it go well? Have you returned with all we needed?"

"*Ja*, Oupa, it went well. Jacob Meyer had been to the yard where the train brought in supplies only yesterday. I have everything."

"*Ja*, good," was the grunted reply.

"This is not as you usually make it," commented Franz mopping up the stew with a lump of bread. "There is not enough salt."

"I'm sorry. It is hard to tell at the beginning if it will cook well, and I could not rely on Juma. She would have thrown the entire salt jar into the pot if there was no one to tell her how much to add."

The old man looked at his grandson from beneath heavy brows. "If you had not been careless your sister would have been here to cook the stew as you like it. Only a fool puts his hand near a wheel when it is spinning. As she was doing your task, perhaps you should have been set to the cooking pot."

Hetta saw the back of her brother's neck turn red, and felt sorry for him. Franz was twenty—two years older than she—and was much too sensitive. Oupa swore it was because he had been taken to Ladysmith with her on the death of their mother and had not returned to the farm until he was ten, unlike most boys who grew up on the land from the day of their birth. Hetta thought otherwise. As not all women were born the same, so there were men who were gentler than others—men who loved the land for its beauty and the creatures that were upon it.

Oupa thought Franz weak, but Hetta understood. What there was in her brother was in her, too. She smiled at him as she took a can of hot water to her room. Quickly she removed the good white blouse and replaced it with one of blue cotton, washing her face and hands with a tablet of perfumed soap she had smuggled inside in the folds of her skirt. It was pure and white. If Oupa had seen it he would have asked if the usual plain soap were not good enough.

Hurrying back to the kitchen she threw a pinch of salt into the heavy pot on the fire, stirred the contents, tasted from the spoon, then added another slight sprinkling before ladling stew into a bowl for herself. Oupa watched as she took her place at the table.

"So, the train has been in again already?"

She smiled at him. "There is a train everyday."

"Ah—ah," he wagged his head. "What is wrong with a good wagon and a team of oxen?"

"It is too slow," Franz grinned. "The railway brings everything to us within a day."

"It does not," the old man cried, thumping the table. "It brings everything to a depot. We must then go to fetch it. Trains go only where the track is laid. Show me the train that can cross a *drift*, climb a *kopje*, and come into my own yard."

Brother and sister exchanged looks and remained silent. Their grandfather would never become resigned to railways crossing what he regarded as God's chosen land. Those who built them were sinners; those who rode in them blasphemous. He could do nothing about Jacob Meyer and the fact that he used the iron monsters to transport goods from Durban to Johannesburg.

"Landerdorp has changed since I was last there," Hetta

said to turn the subject away from railways. "You did not
tell me of Jan Badenhorst's new foundry, Franz. It is a
great deal larger than the old one."

Franz opened his mouth to speak, but Oupa grunted and
leaned back in his chair. "Nor did he tell you of the English who are making a mockery of a good town. Did you
see them?"

Busy with her meal Hetta said, "I saw them—it is impossible not to do so—but they were not . . ." She broke
off at the sound of a horse arriving in the yard. She knew
who it would be. Without further word she went to the fire
to stir the stew and ladle it generously into a bowl.

Piet Steenkamp entered as she was returning to the
square scrubbed table, and stood for a moment looking at
her before taking his seat by the meal she had placed for
him.

"It is going to be an early winter," he said after greeting
the two men.

"*Ja*, you are right," Oupa agreed getting out his old pipe.
"There is that in the air that tells me we shall have a frost
before long."

Hetta brought Piet a cup of water. He caught her wrist
with a strong grip as she turned away. "You cook a good
stew, Hetta."

Light green eyes blazed up into hers with extra brilliance
tonight. She merely nodded and tried to move away, but he
still held her as he spoke to Franz.

"When do you mean to choose your woman, man? My
house will soon be complete."

Hetta knew what he meant. Until her brother took a
wife, she was needed here to look after her family and
could not marry him. Piet was working with his father, but
had a small piece of land marked out on which he was
building a home for himself and Hetta. His patience was
plain in the way he looked at her and the way his fingers
dug into her wrist.

Franz grinned. "Tell me where there is another young
woman, other than Truus van der Moeuwe, between here
and Durban. I will not take Truus as a wife even for your
sake, my friend."

"Perhaps you should go into Landerdorp before the British steal all our women."

Oupa took the pipe from his mouth and spat on the
floor. "Our women have nothing to do with the redcoats."

Piet said. "Some wear green . . . which makes them less conspicuous, but no less arrogant. Did you not find him arrogant, Hetta?"

She felt their eyes on her. Oupa, brown-faced with a black beard streaked with gray was looking at her with stony eyes. Franz, who had light brown hair like their mother, had blue eyes that rarely showed anger. Now they surveyed her with curiosity as they glanced from her face to Piet's hold on her wrist, and back again to Hetta. Piet's own stare was almost frightening.

In a sudden violent movement he was on his feet looking closely at her face. "I saw you with him—a Myburgh consorting with a British officer. Before God, I would not have believed it if I had not seen it with my own eyes."

Oupa was also on his feet. "Is this true?"

The cosy room, warm from the heat of the stove, gave her courage to face her grandfather. This room bore the touch of her mother's hand and her father's labors—and those of his father before him, who was now prepared to condemn her on the word of a Steenkamp. This farm was the Myburgh heritage, and she was part of it. Until Franz took a woman of his own she was mistress of the house, and did not intend to be held to trial in her own kitchen.

"No, it is not true," she said quietly.

Piet's eyes blazed brighter. "You lie, woman."

Franz was on his feet in an instant. "You are beneath our roof. My sister is a God-fearing girl. She does not lie."

"She is my promised woman. I have a right to chastise her."

Hetta began to tremble. "It is not true."

"You are false before your own family—your grandfather and brother. Before the man who believed you true to your people."

"*Silence!*" Myburgh bellowed, and all three young people turned to look at him. He moved across the room and said to Piet, "You will come here to the book."

The young man did not hesitate. Hetta watched him go to the table covered with their one good cloth where the Bible always lay open. It had been the book of Oupa's father, brought across the sea from Holland, and in time it would go to Franz and his son's son.

She would not rub her wrist though it burned from Piet's fingers; her pride would not let her. Her head tilted higher as Oupa faced Piet and invited him to touch the book. She knew he would do so in complete sincerity. Oupa was taller than Piet and a lot stouter. His flowing beard and hair added to his impressiveness, and Hetta loved him dearly despite his unremitting sternness. Now it was the young man who set her heart thumping. Medium-height, lean, and quick-moving, with a beard and mane of hair as dark as Oupa's, her future husband somehow was the more menacing as he put his hand on the Bible.

"Do you say on the book that the girl lies?"

"I say on the book that she lies."

It did not seem strange to Hetta that he had been asked to prove her guilt rather than she to prove her innocence. It was a man's world in which she lived. Now all three confronted her—Franz shocked, Piet vengeful, Oupa with the wrath of his forbears upon his strong face.

"Am I to bear the weight of your sin? Am I to feel the disgrace of your shame?" The old man referred to the alleged lie, not the meeting with an Englishman.

Still trembling she stood her ground, remembering the Lieutenant with pounding clarity. "No, Oupa, for I have told the truth. I have been accused of consorting with a British officer. That is false. It implies a close friendship—even more."

"Continue!" commanded the old man.

They all still stood as they were—she beside the plate of stew she had set out for Piet, Franz by his chair, Oupa and Piet one each side of the Bible. The atmosphere was tense; even the hissing kettle seemed to blaspheme in the reverent silence.

"I was approached by an Englishman when I left the store, and I said no more than good day in answer. He placed his horse across my path so that I could not leave. Another Englishman in the uniform of an officer did not approve of his behavior and ordered him away." She faced them boldly. "I thanked him, that was all. Would you have me drive away in disregard of an act of kindness?" Expecting no answer she went on, "He was pleased to find I could speak his language and rode beside me through Landerdorp—I did not invite him to do so—and felt some concern for my safety in the coming darkness." A vivid memory of his lean face caused warmth to flood through her body. "He was a stranger in our country and did not know that we ride the veld easily." She looked intently at her grandfather. "That was all. He was, I think, an English gentleman. He would feel concern for anyone in trouble. He rode beside me through the *nek* then returned to his duties. I do not even know his name." Taking a deep breath she asked, "Do you say I should not deny consorting with him?"

The old clock ticked the silent seconds while Johannes Myburgh considered. Then he turned to Piet. "We shall all sit at the table in friendship. The matter is explained, but not excused."

The meal resumed as if it had not been interrupted. Hetta brought tea, then sat, knowing Oupa had yet to speak into the silence. Franz looked at her with slight apprehension in his eyes, plainly wondering what had made her defend her actions quite so tensely. They had so much in common, the handsome boy and his sister.

"Why did you speak the *uitlanders'* tongue to this man?" the patriarch asked heavily.

She looked up from pouring the tea. "He would not otherwise have understood that I was thanking him."

"It was not necessary. Boer women do not speak any language but their own."

Greatly daring she replied, "Are Boer women to be blind to the deeds of a good man because he does not speak Dutch?"

The heavy brows met. "He was an Englishman. There are no good ones."

"They are our enemies," Piet said sharply. "We only wait to collect enough guns and we shall drive them from our country, never to return." He looked around the table with a sense of barely controlled excitement. "I come tonight to tell you of a journey I make tomorrow across the border to see Koos de la Rey. He has great plans. Already he and his supporters have an arsenal of rifles and ammunition from Germany." Leaning forward in his enthusiasm he continued, "Men are gathering all over the Transvaal and Orange Free State—hundreds of them. Soon there will be thousands. We have the winter ahead in which to prepare." Half-rising in his seat he brought his fist down onto the table with a deliberate thump followed by a twisting movement as if crushing a pest beneath it. "With the coming of Spring we shall strike. The British will be crushed into the earth, and we shall plough their bones into the sod as we celebrate our freedom."

Horrified at his venom, Hetta glanced at her brother's

face and saw her own feeling mirrored there. Franz had had English friends in Ladysmith as a child, also.

"We are not at war with the British, Piet," he said now in his conciliatory voice. "We already have freedom. Why should we want to fight?"

"Ach!" Piet turned away and walked the length of the room, too fired with idealism to keep still. "Freedom! What is this freedom? They have their eyes on our gold; we let them come in and take it. But they use it merely as an excuse to add the Transvaal to their empire. They do the same in the Free State with the diamonds at Kimberly. For years they have fought for the right to vote in our states. That is only the beginning. Once we give the franchise they will take bigger and bigger bites until we are swallowed. I tell you, man, the British cannot set foot anywhere without immediately deciding to add it to their vast empire. *Freedom!* You think we shall ever have freedom while they are in Africa?"

Oupa blew a long cloud of smoke. "He speaks the truth. My woman and I made the trek from the Cape to escape them, and they followed us. But," he pointed at Piet with his pipe stem, "they were defeated at Majuba. Eighteen years, and defeat still contains them. The redcoats will not risk such a thing again. They have learned their lesson."

"They will never learn their lesson," was the hissed reply. "Until they cover the *kopjes* with their dead and dying, and run back to their ships, they will go on marching across our land with their imperious boots, making us bend the knee to their decadent rule." He came back to the table and leaned on a chair. "The Lord sent us to this place to create a land in His image. We have fought the wild tribes and the British to find it—now they rob us. Do you think they will stop there?" He looked full at the old man, the respect for his age mixed with the superiority of a younger brain that lived in the future and not the past. "Majuba has not taught them a lesson. In England they are crying still for revenge, and every soldier garrisoned along the length and breadth of this land is only waiting for the word, to rise up and redeem his reputation in the eyes of the world."

Oupa smoked his pipe and thought on the things that had been said. Hetta sat waiting. She believed her grandfather. Piet could not be right with his tales of war. Were they not all free at this moment—free to till the land, read the good book, and smell the sweet air of the veld? In Landerdorp the British soldiers did their normal duties, that was all. The one who had stopped her wanted only to tease her a little—and if they did things to aggravate the Dutch people, perhaps it was because they could not communicate in any other way with men and women who refused even to exchange greetings with them. Warmth flooded through her again as her thoughts went to the handsome officer who seemed so pleased to speak to her. No, she believed her grandfather. Majuba had ended the emnity. The soldiers were not preparing for war. She could not believe they had guns and ammunition stored and waiting for spring to come.

Surprisingly Franz spoke her exact thoughts before Oupa made comment on his deliberations. Hetta wondered at his temerity. Franz loved peace above all things, but she knew he would feel anguish over talk of conflict that would set a man against his former friends.

"The British are not farmers. Why should they want our land? As Oupa says, it is eighteen years since Majuba, and we have lived side by side in peace. We live now in an English state and we are free—always have been free. The English have not tried to take this farm . . . or your farm. Why do we gather rifles against our neighbors? Do we make war on men who have already been defeated at our hands?"

Piet made no secret of his contempt for the gentle dreamer. "Are you a girl that you sit there so blind? Majuba took your father and my uncle—never forget that. It also took hundreds of British—but there are thousands more, and thousands after that. In the memory of your father will you still say the British are our neighbors? What of the Jamieson raid? Was that the act of a neighbor?"

Oupa took his pipe from his mouth. "That was not here in Natal."

Piet was exasperated. The old man had not moved off his farm for ten years. For him, the world was this farm, and the hub of the universe was Landerdorp. His hatred of the British was total and deep-rooted. He would have no dealings with them and drive them from his land with a rifle, if necessary, but that was the extent of his thinking. For him, the British had been defeated by his son's sacrifice. At seventy-five, what he did not see or hear did not bother him.

Hetta had had enough of the conversation that upset her brother and put sad memories into Oupa's head. Many things she had longed to say, but a woman did not join in when men spoke together. All she could do was bring the tension to a close by rising to fetch the Bible. After they had eaten each evening they thanked the Lord for filling their bellies and safeguarding them for another day's labors in His name. Then Oupa read from the book all the beloved words they knew by heart. It was an hour of peace and unity.

She picked up the heavy book in the hope that Piet would join them and drive some of the fire from him. She thought again of the Lieutenant who had ridden beside her that day. Did he know they were gathering rifles in the Transvaal to use against him and his people? A small chill clenched her stomach in a spasm of apprehension. If Piet were right and the *kopjes* would be littered with British dead and dying come the spring, would he be there, still as death with his sad green eyes staring sightlessly at the sun?

Oupa watched her set the Bible before him, then touched her hand in a gesture of affection. He knew why she had done it.

"You have a good heart, Hetta. Sit here at my side and turn the pages."

For Oupa this was the best hour of the day, for the word of the Lord carried him nearer his own good woman and their beloved and much-mourned son whose own wife had died of grief after bearing the girl-child, Hetta. To Franz, the creed of his people told him to till the acres and thrive to build the promised land. Build, not destroy—that was the message. Hetta knew what was in her own heart and those of her family, but as she looked at the face of the man of her future she grew cold. The directive to flourish and prosper had a stronger meaning for him. Not only would he give her sons, he would destroy the sons of any other people that appeared as a threat.

When he had departed and Oupa had gone to his bed, Hetta tidied the room while her brother sat dreaming into the embers. What pictures did he see in them? she wondered.

"So you would not take Truus van der Moeuwe as a wife?" she teased softly.

He came out of his reverie and grinned. "She has a scolding tongue and wields a broom without discrimination. I want a peaceful woman who will cook a stew as good as yours, and smile with me." He raised his eyes to hers as she stood with a cloth in her hands. "It might be some time before I find her, Hetta."

He was asking her a question. It was easy to answer. "It does not matter. I am in no hurry."

He got slowly to his feet and went across to her. "Piet has changed."

"Yes. Do you think it is true what he says?"

"I hope with all my heart it is not . . . but the voice of aggression always shouts louder than the voice of peace."

"The Boers are importing weapons from Germany in vast quantities, yet we can hardly rustle up a rifle between two men," Guy Cuthbertson complained as he reached for the salt to season his breakfast bacon and eggs. "I suppose they do know about it back in the jolly old country."

None of the eight officers sitting around the table seemed inclined to answer, so he went on, "Dash it all, are we going to let them prepare for war and do nothing about it?"

An artillery captain looked up with a pained expression. "It *is* breakfast time, old boy."

Guy scowled and banged the salt back onto the table. Then he turned to Alex who was sitting next to him. "Your regiment might well be renamed the Dozenshire Rifles, for I doubt you have more than twelve between you."

Alex smiled. "A slight exaggeration . . . but I agree with your point. We are hopelessly unprepared."

"For what?" demanded a belligerent voice, not liking the breakfast hour being ruined by conversation on serious topics.

"War, man . . . *war!*" Guy said with characteristic drama. "Don't tell me you were not well aware we would see battle during our spell of duty in this country. It had been coming for months."

A short-sighted infantry subaltern looked up from his plate and peered across the table. "I'm going home shortly. Don't start anything until after the ship has sailed. I'm getting married in July, and she's been waiting two years already."

"Aha!" Guy pounced immediately. "Don't you think she might be prepared to wait a little longer at the prospect of receiving a hero to her bosom?" A wicked gleam came into his eyes. "And think how brave it would make you. Impatience to return to England would make you run through the

Boers with a steel wrist and quivering sword, leaving behind a trail of corpses and bringing a speedy surrender."

"Do you mind!" an aggrieved captain growled. "It's bad manners to continue when it has been pointed out that we are having breakfast."

"It's not done, old chap," Alex drawled under his breath, "tradition and all that!" Then, he gave his companion a wicked smile and said loudly, "Frightfully good bacon this morning, what?"

This remark received silent glares from eight pairs of bleary eyes, until, one by one, chairs began to scrape on the floor as the officers left the table.

"Russell," Captain Beamish said suddenly, "come along to my office right away, will you? Something has come up. Better order your horse to be saddled and water bottles filled."

"But it's Thursday!" The protest was a vocal edition of his immediate thoughts.

"What about Thursday?"

Caught off guard Alex began to invent. "I have ordered an inspection of all quarters, followed by weapon training at eleven o'clock."

"Oh!" The vacuous face of his company commander showed little reaction to this lie. "I'll have to send March, I suppose. Damned nuisance. You didn't tell me you had made all these arrangements."

"I didn't think you'd be interested," Alex replied caustically.

Captain Beamish frowned. "One of these days you'll go too far, Russell. You're only tolerated in the regiment because of your connections and your handiness with a rifle."

"So I am constantly being told. I'm sorry if doing my duty has inconvenienced you but, since you are in the habit of leaving us subalterns to use our initiative, it did not occur to me to ask your approval of something I have been doing since I arrived here."

Characteristically, Beamish retreated, "Very well. Go ahead with your inspection—but instead of weapon training your men will be better employed painting the outhouse beside the mess. I have heard a hint that Rawlings–Turner might be coming up the line shortly, and the only possible room we could give him overlooks that outhouse."

He turned to leave but Alex, very conscious of Guy

Cuthbertson beside him, said, "Isn't that a job for the Sappers?"

"Eh?" Captain Beamish turned in the doorway, irritated by this further spanner in his works. "No . . . too much bloody rigmarole. All that deuced paperwork to be done, and a two-day wait for another lot of papers to come back giving approval. Quicker to do it ourselves. The colonel could arrive at anytime. Besides, it will give your men something to do."

Left alone in the room, Alex and Guy exchanged exasperated looks. "So much for your sappers!"

"Yes," said Guy thoughtfully. "Do you think we are the only two who believe there will be war?"

Alex strolled to the window and stood looking out into the street. It was quiet, still, but before long the wagons would come in and the women would be walking with shopping baskets, their long skirts dragging the dust into straight trails behind them.

Common sense told him it had been ridiculous to create that scene at the thought of missing a possible five-minute chat with a girl. There was no certainty that she would come today. It was all so flimsy and tentative; why had he made so much of it?

"I didn't say I believed there would be war, Guy, but I do think we should take far more heed of what they are doing in the Transvaal and the Free State." He turned away from the window. "Landerdorp is only a handful of miles from both borders. Riflemen would be better employed at target practice than painting an outhouse, in my opinion." He grinned. "Since I had made arrangements to do neither with my men I must now hurriedly order an inspection before collecting some paint brushes from you."

Guy Cuthbertson was a sharp-witted man and caught on immediately.

"Bit desperate to avoid a mission that would take you out of this metropolis, weren't you? Would it have anything to do with the dashing rescue of a damsel in distress last Thursday? I saw you ride off with her. Don't tell me you are trying to undermine the enemy, old chap!"

The words irritated Alex. "Cut it, Guy." He headed for the door. "I think we should get going. The day promises to be hot."

They went their separate ways, and Alex cursed his friend's keen observation. Just because the thought of seeing the Dutch girl had colored his last few days it did not mean Guy should start . . . well, he should not have made the kind of remarks he had!

It took him only a short while to buckle the wide leather belt around his waist, fasten the shoulder straps, and pick up his cap before going out in the sun again. Stepping off the *stoep* he knew it was going to be a blazing day for autumn. Already he was beginning to sweat, the high collar of his jacket clung to damp skin.

The men grumbled over the hastily ordered inspection but put up a good showing. They spent so much time cleaning their kit, if only to pass the time, that sudden turn-outs seldom caught them napping. About the painting, there was open resentment. It was a poor job for a hot day and they were riflemen, not sappers. Alex expressed his sympathy, but rounded off by saying unpleasant things had to be faced and the sooner the better.

"It's orl right fer 'im," said one under his breath. "It'll be the mess and cool drinks now. I'd like to see 'im paint a shed on a flamin' 'ot day like this."

"I'd rather have him than bloody Beamish," was the retort. "Red Russell would paint a shed if he had to. Beamish wouldn't even bloody know what to do with the brush."

"I'd soon tell 'im, mate!"

Alex was, in fact, back in the mess sipping a soda and lime, but only because the window overlooked the street. It had been a sweet momentary encounter—one of life's beautiful bubbles that soon floats away out of reach—yet every detail had stayed vividly in his mind. If she did not come, he would be bitterly disappointed and would never know why. She had cast a brief warmth on his inner chill, held out a hand of friendship he badly needed. Could she, on reflection, have realized he was just another of the hated British?

Then he saw her. Hesitating long enough to enjoy the pleasure of watching her unobserved, he put down his glass, snatched up his cap, and went out across the street to where she had drawn up her wagon. The heat was suffocating between the wooden buildings and shacks that comprised the hamlet of Landerdorp, and the usual smell of horses and oxen, tanned leather, fired metal from the foundry, coarse flour, and saddle polish were all stronger than he had noticed before.

Threading his way between ladies in bonnets and voluminous skirts, who strolled in pairs; ox wagons; and mounted men with urgent business, Alex arrived breathless beside the wagon. Their eyes met immediately. Neither smiled, yet he knew she was as glad to see him in that moment as he was her. It was evident in the deepening bloom on her golden-brown cheeks and the way she bit gently on her lower lip as she nodded a faint greeting.

"Good day, Miss Myburgh. Allow me to assist you." He put a hand beneath her elbow as she stepped from the wagon, then reached onto the seat to take down her basket.

"Thank you, lieutenant."

How sweet and husky her voice sounded, pronouncing the English words. Just standing beside her was exciting. She was taller than he had imagined. But there was a submissive feminine quality about her that had nothing to do with the soft white blouse she wore. It was more the tendrils of hair that escaped the thick glossy braids as they circled her head; the dark lashes that moved up and down as she blinked in the sunshine; and her hands, so capable yet fashioned for gentleness. He fought down an overpowering desire to touch her.

"How fortunate that I happened to come along at this exact moment," he lied keeping hold of the shopping basket. "Perhaps I can help you with your purchases."

She seemed uncertain how to answer, and he felt the urge for physical contact more strongly. At any moment she might float away like the elusive happiness he sought.

"You are very kind, for which I thank you," she said then, "but I must not keep you from your duties. It would not do."

She held out her hand for the basket. He knew the moment was over unless he acted quickly.

"I am not here by a fortunate chance, as it happens. I have been watching for you all morning." He offered the admission in place of the basket and waited for the result.

"I thought you might. I hoped you would not." Her brown eyes saddened, but retained their steady gaze. "My brother and I had English friends in Ladysmith when we were young, but the head of my family cannot change the old ways. I am forbidden to speak your language." She put out her hand again, but he still would not give up the basket.

"Let's use French . . . or German."

She shook her head.

"Latin?" he suggested. "Greek?"

Her color deepened. "You are very determined, lieutenant."

"Yes, aren't I?" he agreed softly.

They stood looking at each other, Alex fighting a losing battle with the warning whispers in his brain. Only now did he realize how much she reminded him of a girl he had lost beside Westminster Bridge years ago.

"How long would it take me to learn Dutch?"

She pulled herself away from the trance she was in. "I am sorry. Perhaps I should tell you this. My father was killed at Majuba by your countrymen. When my mother died of fever a year later Oupa believed the shock killed her and lays the blame at their door, also. His hatred is very great." It took her a moment to add. "He wishes his grandchildren to continue his hatred."

Alex swallowed the pain of rejection and disappointment. "I understand. I am sorry about your father. It must be difficult for you all with a farm to run." He handed back the basket, saluted, and walked away.

The morning was ahead of him, long and empty, and the sun was suddenly unbearable. It cut across his eyes like a knife and made his jacket seem like a tight bandage across his chest. A quick sluice down in his quarters freshened him outwardly, but the inner ache of loneliness seemed intensified in the confinement of his room. An inspection of the outhouse did not improve his mood, for the men were making a terrible job of painting the building and a better one of daubing the ground. They received the brunt of his temper morosely. It was adding insult to injury, in their opinion, but the paint did arrive more exactly where it was intended to go after that.

Unwilling to remain in Landerdorp, Alex decided to make a needless inspection of the outer defenses as an antidote to his depression. Shouting for his horse to be saddled, he went back to his room to change his boots, then emerged again onto the *stoep* feeling a mounting urge to get away into the soothing width of the open country.

Lost to his surroundings he had to pull up short to avoid bumping into a small figure right in his path. The sight of her swamped him with longing. She had come into Landerdorp only a week ago and left behind a hope of release, and sweet communion with a gentle spirit. For seven days he had lived on that hope. The reality of her today had heightened it to a painful degree. He had underestimated her beguiling charm—the huskiness of a voice trained to form the sounds of an alien tongue; the beauty of frank brown eyes; the softness of a mouth he had seen only once curve into a smile; the air of femininity that owed nothing to frailty or false helplessness. She was a woman in an honest acknowledged fashion, and his male spirit answered her honesty.

"Are you off on urgent duty?" she asked looking at his riding boots and the whip in his hand.

"No." He found it difficult to speak. "Is there some way I can help you?"

"I . . . I cannot do what Oupa wishes."

They looked at each other for several seconds, as if the last seven days had been an eternity for both of them. He knew what she was telling him with those words; by coming back to him after sending him away. He knew the cost of defying her own people, and knowing it took his breath away.

"I cannot believe it is sinful to have English friends," she said softly, as if bewitched, and her eyes told him the truth if he had not already known it. It was hard to keep his head in the middle of that sun-baked street.

"I'm glad," he said, at last. "To me, it is more sinful to hate indiscriminately."

"Please?"

He swallowed. "To hate the sons of those who only obeyed orders."

She gave the little nod he was coming to know. "You do not hate *me* because my father took arms against your people."

"I cannot imagine ever doing so."

A breathless pause hung between them as they stood oblivious of anything but each other. They could have been anywhere in the world and it would have been the same.

"Do you have sons, lieutenant?" The question was hesitant, yet hung between them with a suggestion of now-or-never importance.

"I am not married."

It was not exactly a sigh she gave, but her slow relaxation of breath brought a similar response from him.

"You cannot continue calling me Lieutenant. My name is Alex Russell."

"That is nice," she said gently, then asked, "When will you begin your lessons in Dutch?"

"Now, if you will be teacher," he replied instantly.

"You . . . you are very determined, Mr. Russell . . . as I told you before."

"Yes, but I have found my match in you, Miss Myburgh. Do I get my lesson, please?"

Her lips parted slightly. His directness had taken her unawares. "It must be on how to say good-bye. I must leave now."

"May I ride beside you?" The request was eager, almost desperate, daring her to refuse.

"I should like it." It was not shyly said, exactly, but there was a suggestion of bewildered wonder in her answer. "I think only as far as Devil's Leap. It would be best."

"If that is what you wish," he replied.

Next minute he was escorting her to her wagon, helping her into the seat, then striding back for his horse, trying hard not to run with the excitement of a boy. Caution, common sense, and the situation between British and Boers were all forgotten. None of them seemed important set against the joy and warmth of finding this girl who wanted his company . . . if only for the short distance between Landerdorp and Devil's Leap. If those were the boundaries she put on him he would accept them. He would accept anything, rather than lose her altogether.

## CHAPTER SEVEN

In May the situation in South Africa flared brightly again. The Boers in the Transvaal and Orange Free State had been ordered by Pretoria to stand by their arms ready to take the field against the British. In answer, those British troops that should have returned to England on the arrival of relief regiments were retained in the scattered garrisons of Natal and Cape Colony. Both sides were rattling their sabers with deliberation.

The points at issue were the same that had divided the two nations for years. While an uneasy sharing of Southern Africa had existed for a short while, the discovery of gold in one Boer state, and diamonds in the other had sent so many prospectors to settle there they soon outnumbered the Dutch. While the Boers were prepared to let these settlers slave in the mines and pay crippling taxes for the privilege of doing so, they had no intention of allowing them to become full citizens with the right to vote and a voice in the government.

The Boers rightly knew such a grant of franchise would result in losing control of the two states to the British, and they would then have no hold on the area they had settled at great peril and through great hardship. Men like Rhodes had made no secret of the fact that a British Africa was the ultimate aim, and continental countries, in particular Germany who had large interests in Africa itself, were almost as eager as the Boers to prevent such a thing happening. The British Empire was too powerful already. With Africa added to it, where would it stop?

But the British had also settled the country amid great hardship and after several wars with the native tribes—one on behalf of the Boers themselves, who were being threatened with annihilation. They felt they were being treated as inferiors by the people who were doing nothing to claim the wealth beneath the soil. Such minerals would make the country prosperous—a valuable addition to Queen Victoria's empire, as the pioneers were quick to realize. In their opinion, it needed men with insight and commercial experience to govern the two rich states, not a parcel of bearded farmers who still lived in Old Testament times.

The British were imperialists; the Boers were idealists. The two could not live side by side easily.

This time, the issue was over a new law passed by the Boer council for government that directly threatened British business interests in the Transvaal, and investors in London demanded protection of their companies and employees. Rumors were filtering through of Englishmen being attacked by Boer police, of a meeting being mobbed by armed Boers who beat up the protesting *uitlanders* with iron bars and sticks, and of respectable businessmen being arrested on trumped-up charges designed to turn world opinion against Britain.

There were also rumors that the British imagined they

had the right to march into the Boer states to protect their countrymen whenever they felt it necessary, and were planning to do so shortly. Smarting with the knowledge that the Kaiser had already intimated that he would support his Dutch friends in any conflict with his grandmother's people, and that most European countries would side with the Boers in spirit, if not actively, the British government in London was faced with a tricky problem. They could not allow Englishmen to bend their knees to farmers with flowing beards. It was too humiliating. Yet they had no real wish for a war. Their only hope was to send a reliable and tactful man to President Kruger to point out how much more politic it would be for the Boers to make concessions to the *uitlanders* than to risk the might of the British Empire.

Two weeks of talks ended in deadlock. Sir Alfred Milner, gentleman, scholar, statesman, with typical British pride and a great deal of intolerance, could find no common ground with the bluff, determined Paul Kruger. It was after the breakup of these talks that both sides made open preparations for conflict—except that the British did so with characteristic, slightly insulting nonchalance. Certain the Dutchmen would never dare to take the field against such a mighty adversary, they maintained a facade of defense behind which the garrisons continued playing their polo matches, upholding mess traditions, and charming the ladies in their ballrooms. Meantime, the Boers imported guns and rifles from anyone who would sell them, and made their plans.

Hetta was shocked and dismayed to hear Oupa discuss these plans with Franz as they sat over the fire after supper. To her it seemed inexplicable to read the Bible and pray for the Lord's guidance one minute, then speak of killing Englishmen the next.

Even if her heart had not ruled her head she would have cried out against such a war . . . but her heart did rule her every thought. There was not a day in the week when she did not think of Alex Russell, hardly an hour in the day. Thursday was a glowing ember as bright as his hair, in the ashes of the week. Wednesday was unbearable and Friday the same—for opposite reasons. It gave her sweet pain to hold her secret to herself, yet she longed to speak of him in order to bring him near and alive.

Unable to contain the love that burst within her she

would stand in the yard where the wind from the veld blew
back her hair and long skirts as she spoke his name to the
sky and waving branches of the trees behind the house. In
the middle of feeding the poultry her hand would become
stilled in the bowl as some memory of him mastered her.
Then, she would stand dreaming with the noisy hens
around her feet, and corn running gently through her fingers as a smile touched her mouth in response to the image
that filled her mind.

Pumping water from the well took much longer now.
Her rhythmic movement of the handle slowed too often to
allow buckets to fill rapidly, and she stood idly gazing in
the direction of Landerdorp. He was there. What was he
doing at that very moment? Could he possibly know she
was thinking of him? Was he thinking of her?

Every household chore, ever task she had ever done for
years earned more devotion because of her love for a man
cut off from her by the very life she led. He could not share
the simple home and fare, but everything she did well was
because of him and for him. Her upbringing had instilled in
her the part a woman should play in life, and her response
to his sexual challenge was natural, generous, and undenia-
ble. Alex needed something from her and she gave it
gladly.

A Boer girl did not pleasure her man by donning frills
and perfume. Care, devotion, and obedience were the ways
of love their men understood. Failure in anyone met with a
stricture if the marriage was a happy one; a beating, sometimes, if it were not. Yet there were ways a woman could
tease and tantalize as others did with perfumes and soft
dresses. Self-adornment was out of the question, but a
home could be cleaned and brightened, a meal could be
flavored with extra care, and a warm hearth with a pipe
beside it could be an overture to seduction. Hetta did all
this for Oupa and Franz, but it was really her offering to
Alex in her own traditions.

Yes, feminine devotion was something she well understood; politics and imperial pride she did not. For that reason she kept silent about her journeys to Landerdorp. Oupa
would never accept her disobedience and, much as he
loved her, would put the guilt of a nation onto one innocent man. Lieutenant Alex Russell was an Englishman and
one of his country's hated soldiers. To most Boer people
that was enough to condemn him forever. Even Franz, who

did not want to take arms against any man, would disapprove of his sister's passion for a British officer. Despite the new fever that burned in his veins, Franz would still believe Hetta's duty was to Piet Steenkamp, the man who had spoken for her. He would never understand that what she felt for Alex made her deny all else in her life.

To Hetta, her love was a gentle lonely man who made her world sing and had opened her eyes to an emotion so powerful she was engulfed by it. It allowed her no thought of where such a road might take her. Piet was away in the Transvaal, and out of mind, in consequence, and the meetings in Landerdorp had gone too far in personal reaching out to be torn from her week of days. Now, however, the appellation *enemy* was suddenly being added to Englishman, and it frightened her. How could he ever be her enemy . . . or she his?

It was in a mood of apprehension and impatience that she drove into Landerdorp midway through June. The previous evening a neighbor had called at the farm with a new rifle for Franz and told him to see his horses were good and strong for the spring. Her brother had gazed at the rifle as it lay on the table in their room, and Hetta had known his feelings at that moment. He was a man of peace. A gun was no stranger to him, for he shot wild buck and birds for food, but to use bullets on a man, to see a human body lie twitching in the last throes of death would be more than he could stand. At the thought of Alex or Franz falling in such a manner she had gripped the mantel until her knuckles showed white, and her heart ached for the two young men she loved in the world.

Oupa Myburgh had innocently saved his grandson's predicament by exclaiming loudly and vehemently over the age limit of sixty-five that prevented him from taking the field against those who had killed his son; and Hetta noticed it was he who took the rifle from the table after the visitor had gone and examined it with pleasure and excitement.

The oxen had never seemed so slow that day, nor the veld so unending. It was midwinter so the brilliant, clear day had a chill that made her clutch the cloak around her. And yet it seemed she could not feel warm until Alex had reassured her that all she had heard was wrong. Still, in her mind, she could see that rifle lying on her table—the table she scrubbed with loving care—and Franz's face as he looked at it.

The long line of *kopjes* was visible for the last two hours of the journey. She knew he would be waiting and watching for her wagon soon after ten o'clock, as he always did. He had respected her wish not to come beyond the *nek* below Devil's Leap, but she wished he would disobey her rule for just this one day. The need to see him and know her fears were groundless was so strong, she wanted him to gallop toward her now as she crossed the thread of road covering miles and miles of open country.

The cart creaked and lurched at a pace that had her biting her lip with frustration. A gust of wind set her shivering. It came from the northeast—from the Transvaal. The Boer state lay only a few miles away in that direction, and the same distance to the northwest lay the Orange Free State. The men of Landerdorp garrison would be caught in a narrow vee if they were attacked in the spring. By September days and nights would be growing warmer, and the veld would be rich with grazing for bands of roving horsemen and the cattle they would need to keep them alive. *Three months!* It was not long.

He was there in the usual place and urged his horse into a canter the minute she drew near, as if he had held back with the greatest impatience. In a plain jacket and breeches of perfect fit, polished boots that could only have been made by an expert, and with his hair whipped up by the wind that had tanned his skin, he stirred every instinct in her body . . . but he looked so supremely English those instincts froze in sudden fear.

The glowing smile that always betrayed his pleasure at seeing her slowly faded and was replaced by a concern that flooded her with fresh yearning. He brought his horse up to the wagon and turned to accompany her. His usual greeting in newly learned Dutch was put aside.

"Something is wrong," he said sharply. "Is it your family?"

"No . . . yes." She pulled the oxen to a halt, finding it impossible to speak from the swaying seat. He reined in and jumped from the saddle to come to her.

"Are you all right?"

Her nod did nothing to remove the anxiety from his face, yet when she was standing beside him, so near and longing for the relief of his denial, the words inexplicably stuck in her throat. She remembered the neighbor who had brought the rifle, and Oupa cursing the years that made him too old to fight for his freedom from the British. She remembered Franz, who would be forced to do so if this war came. She remembered that her love was an Englishman.

Fearfully she looked up into his face and saw the lines she had come to know—a sweet curve of gentleness around his mouth, a firm honest jawline, a furrow of uncertainty on his brow, and a network of little creases around his eyes where the sun-brightness forced him to narrow them. It was the same as it had always been since that first day.

"You do not look like an enemy," she half-whispered.

The furrow on his brow deepened as he put out a hand and tilted her chin very tenderly with his fingers until it was easy for him to bend his head to her. His mouth was warm against her own, drawing the chill from within her. The kiss was sweet—the sweetest thing she had ever known—and as free as the rolling veld. It took away all her doubts; it made life sing within her. It conquered her.

"It is a strange enemy who would do that," he breathed, moving his fingers from her chin up the line of her cheek to touch the dark lashes over her eyes, then on to the dark clouding of hair beneath the brim of her bonnet, his eyes drinking in all he saw. "I have waited. I told myself at the beginning that you must dictate the pace at which we traveled, but all this time I have suffered from impatience. Now, you come calling me an enemy. What am I to do?"

There was no way to answer except to catch his hand and take it to her mouth to kiss the brown fingers that had caressed her. He disentangled them and gently traced the curve of her mouth before taking the ribbons beneath her chin and pulling them so that her small bonnet fell to the ground. She trembled as he cupped her face between both hands and looked at her with eyes grown dark with emotion.

"I love you, Hetta. I would die rather than hurt you."

This kiss was just as gentle, but it was not enough for her now. Sighing beneath his lips she pressed against him with instinctive desire, knowing only that the ache inside her must be eased. His response was all she needed, and her love soared high as his arms tightened around her slenderness, and the kiss awakened them both to the depth of feeling between them.

For several minutes they were lost in the timeless haven of an emotion that overrode all obstacles, and then he held her away and said unsteadily, "Oh, my love, you are an enchantress of the veld . . . and I shall not explain that for I am certain you will know exactly what I mean."

Dazed and shaken by the past few minutes she could only say softly, "You could speak in your Latin or Greek and I should know very well what you say when you look at me in that way." She touched his mouth lightly with one hand. "I am a proud woman to have the love of such a man."

He seemed completely overcome for a moment or two. "What can any man reply to that? An Englishwoman would leave such words to her lover, but you are all the more beautiful for saying them."

His words broke the moment; reminded her that there were other countries, other cultures. Fear returned to her—fear for him.

"They brought my brother a rifle—to use against your soldiers. They say you will take our land. They call you enemies."

He drew her back against him, and she clung to the rough jacket while he stroked her hair. Please let him tell her it was all a mistake.

"That is how we appear to men like your grandfather."

"He is wrong?" she asked against the tweed. "There will not be war? You do not wish to take our land from us?"

He was so long in answering she pulled away and searched his face. He seemed reluctant to put anything into words.

"Alex, there must be truth between us now, yes?"

He nodded gravely. "I promise that. My dear, your questions are too simple."

Apprehension made her say, "How are they simple? You do not wish to answer, is that the truth?"

"Hush," he murmured brushing her lips with his own. "I will always answer anything you ask, but this is very complicated and difficult to explain to you."

"But you must."

He sighed and gave a rueful smile. "I am not the only one with determination, it seems."

"And great love for you. Do I not deserve to know all you know?"

"You deserve a great deal more," he said heavily.

He picked her up very swiftly and set her on the seat of the wagon and stood facing her with one foot on the wheel, leaning his elbow on his knee. Patiently, choosing his words with care he set before her the situation facing the two nations. She was astonished because it all seemed to concern affairs in Johannesburg, and in no way suggested that the soldiers in Landerdorp were about to take the farm away from Oupa, or even Franz.

"So Oupa is mistaken," she said in relief when he had finished speaking.

"If he thinks we shall march onto his farm, yes . . . but giving the franchise will mean that your people will no longer have sole government of their states. We should be metaphorically taking land."

It was too difficult. "Is that your answer? I do not understand it."

He took her hand and fondled the fingers as they lay in his. "It baffles people with a greater understanding than yours, dearest."

She looked down into his face and knew there was only one question that mattered. "Will there be war?"

"It will never come to that, I am sure."

She looked at him with love in her eyes. "I knew you could never be an enemy."

He shifted uneasily. "Hetta, things are never as straightforward as you seem to think. I am a soldier. Wars are started by politicians or kings, or emperors who are greedy. When it happens, the soldiers on both sides are *ordered* to fight each other. It does not mean they are personal enemies—they are often very good to those who are hurt— but if doing my duty means fighting, I have to do it."

He was trying to tell her something, but she did not want to recognize it and took refuge in another question. "Why did you become a soldier?"

This time the answer was something she could understand. "It was my father's wish."

She gave her little nod. "You once told me he is an important man in England."

"Yes. He is one of those politicians who start wars." It was bitter and brusque. He let go of her hand and turned to lean back against the wagon, staring out across the countryside. "It had been his original ambition for me to follow in his footsteps." He seemed lost in thought for a moment. "My brother would have done so brilliantly."

Hetta watched his profile with loving eyes. Would she ever understand how she had won this man? "I did not

know you had a brother. You have never spoken of him
before."

"He died when he was twelve . . . in the lake at Hallworth. He drowned after saving my life. My father will
never forgive me, I see that at last." He glanced over his
shoulder at her and his eyes were sad again. "Anymore
than your grandfather will forgive the British for killing *his*
son."

What he was suggesting appalled her. She climbed to the
ground beside him. "No, it is not the same. You did not
kill your brother."

He put an arm around her and held her against him.
"Indirectly, I did . . . as I also killed my mother. She died
because I was born."

"But your father planted the seed," she protested. "How
can a man lay such blame on a child?"

"I have asked myself that many times in the past," he
admitted gazing into the distance, "but I have only just
found the answer. When a man loses someone he loves
there is only one way he can go on living. He cannot blame
God, who has His reasons for such things, so it must fall on
someone else. All my life I have been expected to atone,
but I see now it was an impossible task." He rested his
mouth against the dark braids of hair. "Knowing you has
taught me so much. I have discovered a freedom that
makes me humble, yet more complete. I am a new man
here in this country with you."

Not perfectly understanding all he said but recognizing
that he was again pledging his love for her, Hetta felt the
tears well up. A man was a proud, strong creature. To have
this one bare his soul before her was a prize unlooked for
and unexpected. It was more than she could bear.

In the silence he came to stand before her, but she made
no attempt to turn her head away to hide the tears.

"I made a girl cry once before. It was a long time ago,
but I have never forgotten it. Please stop."

She drew in a long quivering breath. "There is only one
way to stop it, Alex."

His response was immediate, fired by the things that had
been said between them. The surging upthrust from within
her was a combination of joy, pain, pride, and surrender,
and they lingered forgetful of time and place, kissing and
speaking of their innermost feelings. To Hetta the experience was heady. She could not guess what it did to Alex.

It was fully half an hour later than usual when they drove beneath Devil's Leap on the way to Landerdorp. Alex, laughing and exultant, had tied his horse to the seat and was driving the wagon with erratic panache. Landerdorp was busy at this hour, and Hetta hoped he could cope with the oxen. They only obeyed commands in Dutch. She mentioned the fact to him but he teased her with, "My dear Miss Myburgh, you would do better to concern yourself with straightening that bonnet. It is all too plain what has delayed you this morning."

She felt the heat flood her cheeks as her hands flew to the bonnet, and memories of their wild kisses and the things they had said to each other made her suddenly nervous now that they were in town. The next minute her worst fears were realized when three people came from a building so lost in conversation that they walked straight into the path of the wagon. Alex pulled on the reins with no success, and she cried a swift command to the oxen.

Her voice caught the attention of the three. The British officer quickly held the two ladies back as the animals plodded to an unwilling halt that brought the wagon alongside them. The women were English, Hetta could tell by the exquisite clothes they wore, and all three looked thunderstruck. Waiting for Alex to speak some word of apology, Hetta suddenly realized there was more in their manner than annoyance.

Swiftly she looked up at the man beside her, and curiosity turned to alarm. He was stiff and remote, his eyes shocked as he stared at them. The younger woman was so white Hetta thought she must be ill. It was as if Alex had gone away from her in a moment.

"We were told you were visiting the guard posts, Russell," said the brisk gray haired man. Hetta recognized authority daring to be defied.

Alex stepped down slowly, like a man who is tired and old, leaving her forgotten in the wagon.

"Yes, sir." He was looking at the pale young woman all the time. "Judith, I cannot believe you are here. It is incredible."

"Yes." That was all she said, and it seemed a great effort to speak.

"We hoped to see you at Ladysmith," said the other woman. "Your letter telling us you were in this place must have arrived after we left England." She smiled at the officer. "Colonel Rawlings–Turner very kindly agreed to accompany us as he was intending to make a visit very shortly."

"I heard you were expected, sir." Alex's voice sounded different. He had become a man she did not know.

All at once the three English people were looking at her, and the older woman said with a pleasant smile, "Will you not introduce us, Alexander?"

He turned to a frozen Hetta and presented her to a Mrs. Davenport and a Miss Burley, beside his Colonel. All she could do was nod in return. Instinct told her they had come to claim Alex. They were English; *his* people. Mrs. Davenport was a grand lady in a dress and coat of blue-gray that had velvet across the collar and beautiful stitching on the bodice. Her velvet hat was unlike anything Hetta had ever seen in size and complication. The smile she gave was gracious, but there was an air of speculation in her bright eyes that was uncomfortable to face.

The young woman was strikingly lovely, yet she felt it would not be easy to get to know her. There was something supremely aloof about the tall slender creature in creamy skirt and jacket trimmed with fur the color of wild buck. Hair that was silver fair was piled in coils beneath a fur hat, and the picture of elegance was completed by creamy gloves. Great beauty was Hetta's first impression. A study of her pale face showed it to be expressionless, and the blue eyes as shocked as Alex's had become.

"Do you live in Landerdorp, Miss Myburgh?" Mrs. Davenport asked pleasantly.

"We have a farm beyond the *kopjes*. I came only for supplies."

"I must say I admire you people," the Colonel put in heartily. "How you make a living from this wild area I do not know."

"It is hard work," she replied through stiff lips. Why did they make her speak with difficulty the language she used so easily with Alex? Could it be because he and the girl were staring at each other like people bewitched; as if no one else was there?

"Hard work . . . yes, I daresay it is." The Colonel looked pointedly at Alex. "Russell, Mrs. Davenport and your fiancée have broken their journey to Johannesburg in order to spend a few days with you. I will now leave them in your hands. I expect to see you all for luncheon in about half an hour." He saluted. "Ladies . . . Miss Myburgh," then strode off leaving a silent group behind him.

Hetta stared at Miss Burley. He was not married, he had said, but she should have known there was a woman in his life. Alex was the kind of man who drew women to his side . . . but this one would never make him happy. Cold, unbending, she would never give him comfort before his hearth, nor in his bed. A terrible pain twisted inside her at the memory of his need out there beyond Devil's Leap so short a while ago . . . and her own.

"It's really dreadfully noisy and dust-ridden here, Alexander," said Mrs. Davenport, "and we have so much to tell you. If you have finished being of assistance to Miss Myburgh I suggest we retire to the Colonel's sitting room, which he has put at our disposal." She nodded coolly to Hetta. "Good-bye. It has been a pleasure to make your acquaintance."

Miss Burley also nodded, but said nothing in parting. Alex saw them begin to move off and turned to look at her. She saw loneliness and pain written there, and a defeat that sat in not unfamiliar lines on a face drawn and haggard.

"Forgive me," he said hoarsely, then turned to untie his horse and join the two ladies who walked ahead.

She sat looking after them until his hair was only a blurred glow in the distance, and the elegant women seemed to shimmer like pale shapes in a sun-soaked vision as they took him away from her.

Judith believed she knew the true and full meaning of humiliation as she walked beside Alex. The back she held so stiff and straight burned from the knowledge that that girl's eyes would be on it. The elegant costume she wore flattered her blonde beauty, yet she had felt a terrible sense of inferiority before a girl in a brown cloak who sat with such dignity in an ox cart. Walking now through the dusty Landerdorp street, to the colonel's quarters, she held her head high, but felt each passerby could see through her expensive exterior to a girl who had degraded herself.

Locked in her prison of shattered pride Judith sat silently as her aunt chatted with Alex of the voyage and train journey from Durban that had given them incredible glimpses of this vast country. Deep within she cried, *"Why did I come here like this?"* He did not want her in England, he wanted her even less out here. It had been there in

every part of him when he saw her. Why had she not
heeded her aunt's words and stayed at home, letting no one
know her true feelings?

Throughout luncheon she was miserably conscious that
Colonel Rawlings–Turner was covering an awkward situation with irritating heartiness. The genial pleasantries to
herself and the undertone of reproof in all he said to Alex
made her humiliation worse because it had been witnessed
by him. Answering automatically she could only think of
the moment when she had turned to see him. In her mind
had been a memory of the last time she had seen him, five
months before, standing at the top of a gangway in great-
coat and cap. That memory had persuaded her it needed
only a confession of love to end his unhappiness; a show of
understanding to win his respect; and her constant presence
at his side to gain his love.

Such thoughts had burned within her, governing every
moment of the long journey. Disappointment at not finding
him in Ladysmith garrison made her determined to persuade the Colonel to escort them to Landerdorp. Pink
flushed her cheeks at the memory of how anxious she must
have seemed to him to reach a man who had sailed away
three months before their wedding with such lack of interest in the parting.

Her arrival in Landerdorp had been fraught with breathless agitation. One look at the dust-ridden, uncivilized hamlet tricked her into believing he would see her with un-
blinded eyes, recognize that neither money nor position,
but only love, would bring a girl half across the world to
him. Her certainty now made her humiliation worse. Far
from being unhappy and restless, longing for England and
for her, he had been neglecting his duty in order to continue the libertine tendencies their engagement was meant
to curb. The shock of seeing him seated so intimately beside a peasant girl in a rough ox cart was still with her. Her
aunt had seen his careless disregard of the ring on her finger, the colonel saw it, and *that girl* saw it! How she must
have laughed. For all her beautiful clothes and superior upbringing, the English lady was forced to chase after a fiancé
who gave his kisses to any pretty girl who caught his eye—
and a Dutch girl, at that! It was unforgivable!

She looked at Alex as he ate his luncheon. He was leaner,
tougher than she remembered, and his face was tanned so

deeply it emphasized the clarity of his eyes. Did she have no pride at all that she could still want him so badly? What was there in a woman that could make the pain of being with a man preferable to that of losing him?

Thank goodness for Aunt Pan. She was bearing the brunt of the conversation, turned attentively now to Colonel Rawlings–Turner—a man who must be a martinet in the officers' mess, but knew how to turn a nice phrase when entertaining the fair sex. Alex was being impossible. Judith had seen him in a bitter resentful mood too many times, but now he was exceeding any previous performance. Not once had he addressed her directly, and he made a point of keeping his eyes on his plate or the person to whom he spoke. All his replies to the Colonel were stonily correct, as though he were surely aware of a reprimand in the offing.

It was the most terrible meal Judith had every endured. The trip to South Africa had been a disastrous mistake. Her determination to confess her real reason for wanting marriage to Alex must be forgotten. Far from flinging herself into his arms with a confession of love, she must keep the secret even closer.

After the meal the colonel excused himself, pausing only to tell Alex he would like a word with him after dinner that evening. Mrs. Davenport immediately announced that she intended to rest for a while, and left Alex no choice but to remain alone with Judith, who half-expected him to plead duty and go. He did not, and then she wished he had, for there seemed no way of breaking the silence left behind by her aunt's departure.

He stood by the window, tall, face drawn in the harsh light from outside as she sat on a cane chair, her back ramrod stiff, her full cream skirt falling gracefully to one side. The smart frogged jacket of her suit clung to her restrictingly, and a fine mist of dampness sat on her brow beneath the swathes of shining ash-blonde hair. Her head thundered with the slow tick of an old clock on the shelf, and she trembled with his continuing silence. Finally, she could stand it no longer.

"After five months you should have something to say, Alex."

He blinked several times as if he had been far away and had to focus on her properly. "In those five months you might have seen fit to tell me you proposed following me here." His voice was hollow, accusing, and she lashed out at his rejection.

"I was not aware that you needed advance warning of your fiancée's arrival . . . but I see now it would have avoided that distasteful scene this morning."

He stiffened considerably. "It was only distasteful because you made it so. I am used to your cold superiority, but must you use it toward everyone you meet?"

"I'm sorry you felt my manner was superior. Perhaps it only appeared that way because of the company you have been keeping. Five months in a primitive place like this must have dulled your appreciation of civilized living." Feeling she had struck a blow he would find hard to parry she was quite unprepared for his reaction.

"My God, even for you that was an insufferably insensitive remark to make about someone you barely acknowledged. Hetta is a person of feeling and courage whose understanding is greater than you could possibly achieve in a lifetime. If you are a product of civilized living, I want none of it."

In a lightning moment of perception, Judith saw it all— saw the anguish she had known herself, the total commitment, the rawness of amputation. It was there in his pain-clouded eyes, it set in rigid lines all through his body, it flashed like a sword's point in every word. The truth shattered her: Alex loved that girl. He *loved* a little Dutch farm girl in homespun clothes!

Her own journey half across the world for his sake now seemed even more humiliating. Promiscuity would have been easier to dismiss than this.

"I think you have no choice in the matter of what you want. Your father decides that, does he not?"

The barb reached its mark. "Was it his idea that you should pursue me across several continents?" he whipped back.

Shaking with self-condemnation she managed to say, "You flatter yourself, Alex. I came only to accompany Aunt Pan on her journey to Johannesburg. We came here as a minor diversion from the true purpose of our visit. It would have seemed most odd for me not to visit my fiancé while in this country. One has to keep up appearances."

"Of course," he said, "by all means let us keep up appearances . . . whatever the truth may be."

"And what does that mean?" she cried, heading for disaster and unable to stop.

"I think I need not put it into words, Judith. You have left me in no doubt of what you want from me."

"It is not true," she said in a voice that had dropped to a near whisper. "You are mistaken."

"I think you made it clear enough," was the savage answer.

Silence stretched between them, a widening gulf. Now was her moment, but how could she seize it when his mind was full of a small girl in a brown cloak who could set him alight with life and laughter? In that split second before Alex had turned to see them all standing in the road, Judith had seen the man she would give anything to know. How could she possibly reach him? Certainly not with a halting expression of love, when he was haunted by a pair of brown eyes and rural charm. The seconds ticked away while the anger left him and bleakness returned. The moment had gone.

"Perhaps you'd kindly leave," she said in a low voice. "It has been a trying day, and I should like to rest for an hour or so."

"By all means." He began moving to the door. "We must both be sparkling at dinner—if only for appearance's sake."

He went out, and she sat down again very abruptly, clenching her hands together tighter and tighter in her grief. It was over. She could not fight him *and* another woman. The small bare room in a wooden building on the edge of the veld seemed so foreign, so hostile. She ached to be back in England. Alex might find it infinitely more attractive here, but she would always feel a stranger in a land of never-ending wildness, a land where the rivers were deep and dangerous, fordable only at *drifts*, and cut into the land with tortuous force. A land bright with perpetual sunshine, where nights were sharp, lonely, and bitterly cold.

Africa frightened her. No, she could never feel happy here, as Alex so obviously did. Neither could she find any kind of understanding of the Boers. Those few she had come across were surly, hostile. The girl with Alex had been fresh and clean with lovely dark eyes that gave her a wild attraction, but she was a Boer—an uneducated farmer's daughter who had been tongue-tied before them all. How could he? *How could he?*

She was sitting in the same chair when Mrs. Davenport

appeared in a flowered wrapper a few minutes later, and Judith hastily dabbed at her cheeks.

"I thought I heard Alexander depart," she said, as if her niece were not there with obvious tears as company. "He has duties to which to attend, no doubt." When Judith made no answer she went on, "It would have been better to let him know you were coming. Do you not agree with me now?"

She stared straight ahead, unable to look her aunt in the eye. "I think it would have made no difference. He . . . *loves* . . . that girl."

"Nonsense," was the immediate answer. "The poor boy is infatuated, that is all."

"*No,* Aunt Pan," Judith insisted sharply. "Alex is not a 'poor boy' he is a very attractive adult man, and he cares enough to protect her from anything I might have to say." She paused and Mrs. Davenport came across to sit beside her. "Aunt Pan, there is no point in going on. I thought it only needed a reunion for him to see the true reason for my journey, but he is too involved with the Dutch girl to care what I am doing, and why. When I spoke about her he flew into a bitter defense of her virtues and qualities—none of which I appear to have."

Mrs. Davenport sighed. "Oh dear, you did not attempt to criticize?"

Hurt and angry Judith jumped from the chair and walked to the window.

"What else could I do? I have never felt so humiliated. Right there in front of Colonel Rawlings–Turner! I thought . . . I thought he was . . ."

"*Wenching* is the word I think you need, my dear," Mrs. Davenport said.

Rounding on her Judith cried, "You are so calm over something that should anger you. Have you any notion of how I felt standing there with that peasant girl looking down at me and knowing Alex held our engagement so cheaply?"

The older woman spoke gently. "I should say we all knew, dear girl. That was when you made your big mistake." She rose and joined her niece beside the window. "The very last thing one should do under such circumstances is to show one's feelings. You are English, and a lady. You should remain dignified and unruffled whatever occurs."

"I know the penalty of being a member of the English upper classes—you have mentioned it before," Judith retorted bitterly. "You are not in love with Alex. How can you know what it was like?"

Mrs. Davenport turned away to look from the window. "I know, Judith. Every woman knows." She seemed to travel to a faraway place that lay beyond the hills in the far distance seen from that window. "Your uncle was a fascinating man—talented, witty, and generous. She was a poetess—bohemian, a member of the demimonde. I suppose she satisfied his excessive desire for adventure—something I could not do with James and Emily clinging to my skirts." Her hands moved on the warm sill in a gesture of resignation. "It was several months before I discovered that they were meeting, but I decided to say nothing. I am certain he guessed I would be a fool not to grow suspicious, but we both pretended to each other. After two years it ended, and we were happier than we had ever been."

"Two years! Oh, Aunt Pan, how did you endure it?" Judith said with emotion.

The other woman turned away from her past. "It nearly broke me . . . but I should have lost him completely otherwise. How much do you want Alexander, Judith?"

The girl sighed and closed her eyes momentarily. "You are telling me that I must act as if that did not happen this morning—as if that girl did not have some claim on him?"

Mrs. Davenport gave a faint smile. "The first priority is to stop thinking of her as that girl. She has a name."

"And she has something that appeals to Alex. Is it likely that he will ever grow fond of me in comparison—the English lady who hides her feelings?"

Putting her arm behind her niece's waist Mrs. Davenport began to lead her across the room. "You will never find out if you give up now. My dear, be sensible. This affair cannot possibly last. She is a little farm girl who answers some need in a lonely young man. What could they have in common? Alexander is a cultured, highly intelligent man with a duty to his father and ancestry. Can you truly see her in his future?"

Judith hesitated and turned to her aunt. "Alex is different. I have no idea what he really feels about his future—or his past. Perhaps we are all wrong—including Sir Chatsworth—and he would find happiness with that . . ." she smiled faintly, ". . . with Miss Myburgh."

"That is defeatist talk. Find the key to Alexander's inner self and you have every hope of winning him . . . but you will never do it with criticism. I have a shrewd suspicion he has had more than enough of that already."

Judith sighed. "I wish I were more like you."

A smile came by way of answer. "When I was twenty-two I was a lot like you, my dear. Learn by my experience, and I shall be happy."

They went up to the room that had been hastily prepared for them. Judith removed the cream costume, the oyster silk blouse, and the corset needed to set off such an elegant outfit. Then, in a wrapper, she lay on the narrow uncomfortable bed, her head full of frowns and sighs, aches and hopes. This tiny South African hamlet seemed unreal after Hallworth and her own home. She seemed unreal in it. The only live vibrant thing was her love for Alex. After five months without him, and even after the events of today, it was stronger than ever. If only she knew how to tell him!

"All the same," Mrs. Davenport said softly, "I think we must get him away from here before it goes any further."

## CHAPTER EIGHT

The officers at Landerdorp entertained the two ladies at dinner that evening. The mess had been hastily decorated for the guests by the addition of flowers and a starched tablecloth, and the menu included several lighter dishes with fluffy jellies to finish.

It was a genial evening, with the young men falling over themselves to attract Judith's attention, and the three senior officers basking in the maturer charm of Mrs. Davenport. If anyone noticed that Lieutenant Russell was subdued it was thought natural, under the circumstances. His fiancée was a beauty; what man would not resent having to share her company with a dozen or so contestants for her smiles?

Alex was happy to let his fellow officers entertain Judith.

He still felt too shattered over the events of the day to think straight. Leaving England had been his first step to living again. Arrival in South Africa, with its enormous distances, its endless bright sunshine, and unconventional pioneering spirit had been a giant stride. Meeting Hetta, loving her and being loved in return, had removed the ghostly weights that had held his life down in England. Gradually he had become at peace with himself—had regained his self-respect. Her simple philosophies had made him understand so much he had fought against in the past. The blessed freedom he enjoyed at Landerdorp, knowing she would be there every Thursday had been so complete, all else had been pushed to the back of his mind.

Today he had told her what she must have known already, and her response had been the most exciting he had ever experienced. To a man very well acquainted with the pleasures of women, Hetta had been an utter and a heady surprise. Her replies to his kisses were almost wanton, the pliancy of her body in his arms innocently inviting. She was a bewildering mixture of harlot and virgin, surrendering eagerly to his demands—so eagerly he had been hard put to keep the situation under control. It had taken him a little while to realize she was a stranger to ritual teasing and dalliance. The harsh life of the trek-farmers left no time for flirtation, so Hetta had answered his touch with the honesty of a woman with a man. Out there, on the veld below Devil's Leap that morning, he had never wanted a woman as much, or resisted the impulse with such determination.

Now, he closed his eyes momentarily against the exquisite memory, then let out his breath slowly as reality rushed back. How would he ever forget Hetta's face as he abandoned her? How could he ever estimate the extent of her hurt? Judith had looked superbly beautiful—and utterly disdainful, with that untouchable quality he so disliked. Judith could have saved the situation so easily, but she had stood like a frozen madonna, pale and remote, looking at Hetta with marble features. All at once, his freedom had slipped away from him. The regiment and Judith—his father's two restraints on him—had claimed him back. All the old ghosts had risen up to join forces with them, reminding him that his money was all held by Sir Chatsworth until he married Judith Burley, that he was his father's heir and Miles's proxy. Having robbed his brother of the right to Hallworth and the family honor, he must compensate with his own life—his own *living* life. How could he explain such a debt to Hetta?

It was after nine-thirty when he knocked on the colonel's door and entered. Colonel Rawlings–Turner was a widower with two daughters well married, and was one of those military men whom age hardly seemed to touch in passing. Affectionately known as "old Bawling–Sterner" because of his tendency to intimidate subordinates with stentorian tones and thick frowning brows, he was nevertheless a just and intelligent commander of the Downshire Rifles. Alex might have liked him if he had not always regarded him as an agent of his father.

Looking at him now, Alex knew this interview was not going to be easy. All his old resentment rose up at this suggestion of disciplining naughty boys. It must have shown in his face.

"I am well aware of your contempt for our traditions, Mr. Russell, but no army is efficient without discipline," the colonel said by way of introduction. "As you expect your men to obey you, so I expect diligence from my officers. I also expect them to behave like gentlemen of whom the regiment can be proud."

Alex said nothing, sickening memories of the subaltern's trial during the musketry course occupying his thoughts. It was as if England had suddenly been transferred to this wonderful wild spot.

"That disgraceful affair this morning is one I hope never to experience again. Quite apart from the affront to your fiancée, I do not expect my officers to indulge in liaisons that so blatantly offend the standing of the regiment in a foreign country."

Alex stiffened even more. "I cannot see how the regiment is concerned in my friendship with Miss Myburgh, sir."

"Can you not, sir?" the colonel shouted. "Then allow me to enlighten you. Any man with intelligence can see a war with these people is practically unavoidable. The situation is touchy—very touchy indeed. They are watching us for the slightest signs of imperialism, and interpreting any move we make as arrogant contempt for their way of life. The position of the army is important right now, in particular. We have to give an appearance of strength without aggression. The Boers have to be made aware of how formidable a force they would be taking on." He brought his brows together and gathered his breath for a vocal blast. "What kind of impression do you imagine they receive when they see British officers rollicking through the streets on an ox wagon with one of their womenfolk? I sent you to this outpost to curb your wilder tendencies. I did not dream you would be so brainless as to force your attentions on Dutch girls. What the hell do you think will be the outcome?"

Silence fell and went on so long the colonel was disconcerted.

"Well . . . have you nothing to say?" he barked.

Alex spoke with dangerous quietness. "Miss Myburgh is a highly respectable and virtuous young woman. She is supremely aware of the situation between her people and ours and would do no more to worsen it than I would. Our friendship—it is not a liaison, I wish to point out—was designed to improve understanding between us."

"Hmph! I have no doubt what that understanding was. You are an engaged man, Mr. Russell."

"My engagement, sir, is my own affair."

"No, it is not!" the colonel roared. "If there is a scandal it reflects on the regiment."

Alex lost his temper. "Then I'll leave the damned regiment! There is not a member of it who will not rejoice to see me go."

The colonel drew in his breath, but his voice was considerably softer as he said, "You are coming dangerously close to insubordination. I suggest you take hold of yourself a minute."

Alex stared across the bare comfortless room and saw the man through aching eyes. It had been a bastard of a day. He knew he could not leave the regiment. The army and Judith—those were the two conditions of his inheritance. If he repudiated either . . .

"The real reason I wanted to see you, lieutenant, was to ask if you had a valid reason for not inspecting the outlying guard posts this morning, as you informed Captain Beamish you would do."

Alex shook his head. "No, sir."

Colonel Rawlings–Turner took to striding back and forth—the usual procedure he adopted when conducting weighty military matters. The fact that he had no office in Landerdorp and had to deal with this extraordinary case in makeshift quarters did not help matters.

"You are aware of the seriousness of that admission, I

suppose?" he asked without expecting a reply. "At best, it
was plain neglect of duty but, with a state of emergency
such as we are experiencing at the moment, it was gross
negligence that could have endangered your men's lives."

Alex was beginning to sway with fatigue. "Isn't that a bit
dramatic, sir?"

The colonel halted in mid-pace. "Damn you, Russell,
you are here to defend British settlers and their interests!
The Boers are arming rapidly, and Landerdorp is in a dangerously vulnerable position, equidistant from both borders.
If they had launched a surprise attack this morning your
company would have been minus an officer and completely
misled as to his whereabouts. Imagining you to be with the
guards, Captain Beamish could well have left your men to
aid your retreat."

It was preposterous! The old boy was getting out his
war-horse and romping over an imaginary battlefield. Alex
began to feel that the entire day was a hideous fantasy, but
the colonel's next words made it disastrously real.

"From what I have seen, discipline is extremely lax in
Landerdorp, and you have taken advantage of the fact. In
view of that I am sending you back to Ladysmith. I've already telegraphed for a relieving officer to come up on the
train tomorrow. You will hand over to him and take the
return train."

It was irrevocable. As an alternative he could have been
court-martialed. For a wild moment Alex thought of forcing such a course, telling the colonel he had no intention of
going back to Ladysmith, and suggesting a good destination
for the old man himself. Then, the old sense of inevitability
invaded him. His jaw had grown so rigid it was difficult to
move it when he tried to speak.

"Is . . . that all, sir?"

The other man nodded with brisk satisfaction. "That is
the end of the official wigging. Consider yourself out of my
office now and in my home." He waved a hand. "Take a
seat, Alexander."

"I've had rather a long day, if you don't mind, sir," he
said stiffly.

"Oh . . . sit down, boy, for heaven's sake. You're a soldier. You must expect long days."

Swallowing hard, Alex sat down. It had been difficult
enough to remain polite under the demands of rank; now
they were relaxed he could not imagine how he would hold

his tongue. To be posted back to Ladysmith was a blow. He longed to be alone to collect his thoughts.

The colonel shouted for his servant who brought whiskey and two glasses. It steadied Alex a bit and gave him something to do while the Colonel looked at him shrewdly.

"Bit of a setback being sent back to Ladysmith, eh?"

"Yes."

"Mrs. Davenport and Miss Burley are going down on the train tomorrow. I thought you'd like to accompany them—spend a little more time with your fiancée before she continues to Johannesburg." The colonel tossed back the whiskey and poured himself another. "She has traveled a long way, and who knows when she will see you again?"

"Yes, sir."

A heavy silence fell. The colonel refilled Alex's glass. "I have been soldiering for twenty-eight years. Been in India, China, the Sudan—more time abroad than at home," he said casually. "Never known outpost duty in India, have you? Hellish country. Malaria, dysentery, cholera—a fellow can get the shakes and be down in the cemetery within four hours." He shook his head. "Hellish country, not a doubt of it. And deuced lonely. Sometimes there's only one other fellow, and if you don't happen to get on with him . . ." He wagged his head again. "China's not much better. They have something in common, though. The women are extremely lovely." He shot a look at Alex and pursed his lips. "We all go through it, you know. Lose our heads and think we have found the idyllic life in some exotic pin dot on the map. Truth is, we only find it charming because we know the call of duty will prevent our growing disillusioned with time."

Alex gulped his whiskey and burned with anger. Did he think he was a headmaster talking to some adolescent schoolboy with a passion for the gardener's daughter? To hell with his cosy chat!

The colonel seemed disappointed when Alex did not respond. He leaned back, a slight frown furrowing his brow. "Of course, native girls are a different thing altogether. This young woman is of European stock, which makes the whole business more complicated. The fact that we are very likely to be fighting her people before long makes it downright dangerous to continue the lies . . . the friendship. Use your sense, man and admit I am right."

Alex twisted his mouth. "If we are already regarding them as enemies what hope is there of avoiding a war?"

"None whatever," was the quick reply. "Take my word, Alexander, they will not be satisfied until we are face to face holding rifles. Their leaders have been determined on it for a long time. Whatever reasons one might give for the present tense situation do not cover the fact that this had to come. We cannot both rule South Africa—even side by side. Sooner or later one of us must take over, they know that as well as we do. Negotiations do not seem to be getting anywhere. Rifles will settle it once and for all. There *will* be a war."

He was so authoritative that Alex began to listen seriously to what he had to say. This morning he had assured Hetta it would not come to conflict. Had it been only this morning?

"Are you certain of this, sir?"

"Yes." He held out a polished box. "Cigar? No? Well, I shall. In my opinion it finishes off a pleasant evening." He lit a cigar and puffed several times to establish the smoking pleasure of it, then waved it toward the window. "Landerdorp is practically Boer country with its population almost one-hundred-percent Dutch. So close to both borders it forms a vital railway link with the two Boer states and offers a prize to Boer raiders from either side. Now do you see what I am trying to drive home to you? In such an event, its people could be killing your men—even you, if you stayed here."

Alex thought of the rifle given to her brother that had alarmed her so much, and of her grandfather's undying hatred of the British. Yes, her menfolk would fight against the English, his own men, himself. And what if he, not knowing, took her brother's life?

It was impossible to sit still. The night outside the window was pitch black, lit only by the primitive lamps hanging above the doors of the building he was in, and the stables nearby. Out there, somewhere beyond Devil's Leap, was a farmhouse and the girl he loved. There was no way to explain to her why he had to leave for he had no idea where the farm lay, nor what it was called. He could not say good-bye. He could not tell her he had meant everything he had said that morning. He could not repeat that he had believed it true when he denied a coming war. What were her thoughts at this moment? Did she stare from a window as he did, longing for him and longing for him to know? What would she think of him when Thursday came and she found he had gone?

"Soldering is a lonely profession at times." The colonel broke into his thoughts, making him turn back into the room. "But our first duty is to our country. Because of that I left my wife and daughters, to whom I was devoted, and sweated out long years in primitive places."

"Why?" challenged Alex harshly.

"Why? Oh . . . I don't know," the colonel mused. "Perhaps I believed in the empire. Perhaps I had the fire of youth in my blood then, and looked upon my profession as crusading against the forces of evil in the world." He gave a soft laugh and squinted against the smoke of his cigar. "Now I am old enough to see things as they really are . . . and I haven't changed one jot." He got up and stretched slowly. "I suppose it all boils down to a belief in the old country and all its glorious past."

Alex walked across the room and put his glass on the table. "You sound just like my father."

"If I were, I should have brought you up a damned sight better."

It was such an astonishing reply, Alex was halted in the midst of turning away.

"You have been fighting the regiment since the day you joined it. The men accept you, but your fellow officers do not. You have gone out of your way to sneer at our traditions and the pride they have in this regiment. I understand they reacted in the time-honored manner with very unfortunate results—oh yes, I heard about that. I hope the next time they decide you have gone too far they will choose a method that will crush your bloody insufferable patronage."

Gone was the friendly adviser and back was the irate colonel. "Your father made one big mistake, Russell. A damn good hiding would have done more for your soul than all his sermonizing about obligations to your dead brother." He poked his cigar stub in Alex's direction. "I don't give a tinker's cuss for what you owe to young Miles . . . or any of your valiant ancestors. I do care, however, about a man who hasn't the sense to see that he is throwing away the best chance he has ever had to make something of his life.

"You are an individualist," he went on. "Contrary to

public belief, such men make much better officers than the
endless succession of descendants from one of Wellington's
staff officers. In an emergency it is the individualist who
will act while the others are busily conferring."

Completely nonplussed Alex stared at the fierce mili-
tarian as he drew nearer.

"I accepted you into the regiment at your father's request in order to make a man of you, as he put it. However, I soon discovered you were a man already—a man
who had been duped into thinking he was a callow youth. I
also discovered I had one of the most promising subalterns
I had seen for years."

Reaching Alex he looked him in the eye with a burning
glance. "Why do you think I have let you get away with
your contemptuous attitude for so long? Why do you think
I have not had you court-martialed several times already? I
had hoped the first would be knocked out of you by your
fellows. Unfortunately, that lake affair frightened the life
out of them. As for the second, I did not want to lose the
regiment a valuable officer. I am determined you will stay
with the Downshires because I want you—not because
your father is an acquaintance of mine. And remember
this," he tapped Alex's chest with a hard finger, "I am also
an individualist, and can fight every bit as hard as you. We
shall see who emerges the winner."

The cigar had burned down to a tiny end, and the Colonel strode to the table to put it in an ashtray. "All right,
Mr. Russell, clear off to bed. It has been a long day."

"A soldier must expect long days, as you said, sir. Good
night."

Alex clattered down the stairs and into the night, feeling
like a man who has hit a brick wall. The groom on duty at
the stables was asleep, but a sharp nudge in his ribs from
Alex's foot soon brought him awake.

"Oh . . . sorry, Mr. Russell. Must've jest dropped orf."

"If it comes to war, you might just drop off never to
wake again one of these days," was the dry reply. "Saddle
up Muskrat for me, will you?"

"Wot . . . now, sir?"

"Now."

"Yes, right away." He walked up between the stalls.
"You goin' dressed like that, sir? Must be urgent. Is it a
vital dispatch?"

"You read too many books, Meakins. I can't sleep, that's all."

"Oh yes, I see what you mean, sir." The man vanished into a stall and used its protection to venture, "She's a very charmin' lady, your feeancé. We couldn't 'elp noticin', being that there's not many English ladies in Landerdorp."

Alex leaned on a stall and stroked the flanks of a beautiful chestnut. The warm smell of horses and hay took him back to a time when he had watched a foal being delivered in the stables at Hallworth. He fancied Miles had been with him.

"I'm going back to Ladysmith tomorrow. There's a relief officer coming up on the morning train."

Meakins led Muskrat down the dimly lit gangway past the slumbering beasts until he reached Alex. "Sorry about that, Mr. Russell. We'll miss you."

"Yes," he answered slowly. "I shall miss . . . Landerdorp."

Ladysmith was an important town, a rail junction connecting the port of Durban with the northern part of South Africa. Supplies and passengers came in by sea and passed through Ladysmith where the railway line branched to the diamond state to the west, and the gold state to the east.

Because of its importance a military barracks had been established about two miles from the center of the town, its neat rows of single-storied huts known locally as Tin Town. Ladysmith barracks lay along the left bank of the Klip River on an open plain bordered by a long range of hills that fronted a higher range beyond. It was a desolate exposed spot, frequently swept by dust storms, pounded by noon temperatures that soared over a hundred degrees in the summer, and plunged into icy extremes at night.

But the beauty of the veld vistas provided every form of dramatic natural effect, magnificent sunrises and breathtaking sunsets, and the *kopjes* astonished watchers with the variety of colors to be seen on their slopes, from early morning rose to dusk purple.

Compared with places like Landerdorp it was civilized, but a far cry from the towns the British soldiers knew as home. The streets were earth that became thick churned mud after heavy rainstorms that swept across the veld from time to time.

Murchison Street, the main thoroughfare, was lined with

a hodge-podge of buildings. The two-storied hotel had a first-floor veranda that overhung the street to provide a covered entrance for visitors. There were bungalow stores of varying kinds before another two-storied facade rose up to break the line. Mostly of brick, the designs were certainly individual to suit the pocket or fancy of the owner, rather than the distinction of the town.

Private residences were mostly bungalows set among trees and surrounded by white-post fences, and it was here the mainly English population lived. The few Dutch residents clustered together, also. They had lived side by side for years, and life in Ladysmith continued much as it had for years. But now, one or two of the Boers had begun avoiding English acquaintances.

Alex escorted Mrs. Davenport and Judith to the hotel, then returned to arrange for his baggage and horses to be taken down to the barracks where the major part of his regiment had remained while his own company had been on outpost duty at Landerdorp.

Judith was thankful that the journey was over. The route had taken them through miles and miles of uninteresting and uninhabited country. Alex had been polite and solicitous, but the bleakness of his expression and the length of time he spent looking back at Landerdorp as the train pulled away, left Judith in no doubt of his feelings.

She could not believe her aunt responsible for his being sent back to Ladysmith, yet dared not ask if she had prevailed upon the Colonel for fear the answer would be yes. Loving Alex as she did, some inner sense told her tearing him away from the Dutch girl in this manner was not likely to make him forget her.

During the next two weeks she had no cause to think otherwise. Their relationship was the same as it had always been, except some of the fight seemed to have gone out of him and he had grown introspective. With a garrison full of lonely officers it was inevitable that Judith should be very popular. Alex did not seem worried. He gave his permission with unflattering readiness when his fellows applied to him to take Miss Burley riding, or for a carriage drive. At the garrison's midsummer ball (midwinter in Ladysmith, but immaterial to the British) Judith was besieged by partners. She hardly saw Alex all evening.

As the day of their departure to Johannesburg neared, Judith had to acknowledge that the venture had failed. In

England it had seemed that she only had to get to him to put right all that had gone wrong over their engagement, but the Alex of her imagination always did the right things . . . and another girl had reached him first.

The day before their departure, Judith went riding with Lieutenant Neil Forrester. Her aunt greeted her return with, "My dear, you will never guess what has so fortunately occurred."

Judith smiled. "Then I will not attempt to do so." She drew off her gloves and unpinned the provocatively masculine hat that matched her dark-red riding habit.

"You look extremely fetching in red, Judith. Why don't you wear it more often?"

"I have always felt blue was my best color." She walked across to join her aunt on the veranda.

"A *cool* color!" Mrs. Davenport observed somewhat dryly. "Perhaps you should reconsider."

The girl sighed inwardly. She knew her aunt was referring in a roundabout way to her lack of success with Alex. "I cannot think my preference for blue in anyway affects the way Alex regards me, Aunt Pan. That Dutch girl wore the most unattractive clothes, yet he still can't get her out of his mind—I know he can't."

"If he has nothing strong enough to push her out, of course he will think only of her."

A wagon rumbled past in the street below and Judith watched it reflectively. Just how had she caught his restless spirit? Had it been her simplicity?

"If I have not achieved it with my presence I certainly shan't with my absence."

Mrs. Davenport rocked gently in her chair, her brown velvet dress changing color as the planes of light touched the pile of the material. It was a warm brown that flattered the golden lights still bright in her hair, and Judith wondered once more how her uncle could have been unfaithful to such a vivid woman. Men were incomprehensible.

"Your absence will not be necessary, my dear girl. The greatest stroke of luck—you will hardly believe it."

A passing group of cavalrymen created such a din and kicked up such a dust with their hooves that the ladies waved their handkerchiefs before their faces and found themselves coughing.

"What a *dreadful* place this is," Mrs. Davenport complained. "Do you suppose Johannesburg is any better?"

"I doubt it," Judith replied getting to her feet. "This entire country is a hundred years behind the times, in my opinion. Do let's go inside before we choke to death, or before this veranda collapses from the shaking of the earth. I see the Army is approaching with one of those great guns they are so fond of hauling along Murchison Street for no apparent reason."

Mrs. Davenport rose and followed her niece inside. "Between ourselves, it is more or less the only one they have. Colonel Rawlings–Turner confided to me that they are 'pulling a fast one'—I think that was the expression he used. It is to give the impression that the artillery contingent is greater than it truly is." She rang a bell on the wall. "I think we'll have some tea, shall we?" Settling herself in a chair she added sotto voce, "It is really for the benefit of any Dutch spies."

"Dutch spies! Whatever do you mean? And how is it the Colonel has told you so much about the artillery?"

Mrs. Davenport smiled serenely. "He has called on me once or twice since he arrived back from Landerdorp. Unfortunately, you have been out with one of your admirers. He has been the instrument of your good fortune."

It was all too mysterious for Judith. She sat gracefully, sweeping the red skirt to one side in a natural movement, and waited for her aunt to continue.

"Mr. and Mrs. Besant—the lawyer and his wife—have to visit Johannesburg for several weeks and, since her husband will be engaged in business such a lot of the time, Mrs. Besant is rather anxious to have female company during her stay." Her dainty hands spread in a gesture of explanation. "The colonel suggested it was foolish to drag you all the way up there to spend the time with two matrons when you would have a much better time here, so Mrs. Besant mentioned the fact to her sister, who will welcome you as a guest in her house while we are away."

"But I hardly know Mrs. Besant's sister," Judith protested, carried away by all the arranging by all kinds of people that had gone on without any reference to the person most concerned.

"You will have ample time to remedy that during the month we are away."

"Month?"

"Yes, a month," Mrs. Davenport repeated firmly, and looked very seriously at her niece. "Judith, make the most of that month. When a man has just lost one woman he is most vulnerable to the ploys of another. If you do not do something soon you will lose him altogether. With you back in England he will very likely fall head over heels in love with the next pretty face he sees . . . or . . ."

"Or what, Aunt Pan?" Judith asked tautly.

"Or war will come and catch him up in its filthy grasp."

The two women sat looking at each other for a moment, then Mrs. Davenport said, "The colonel has also to go to Johannesburg to investigate the situation there with a group of senior businessmen. There is reason to believe soldiers from European countries are arriving to join the Boers. It looks most serious, my dear."

Judith felt again the clutch of fear that had gripped her at the docks, when she had seen the guns and ammunition being loaded onto the ship at Southampton.

"Did the colonel say that?"

"Yes." The older woman hesitated then added, "He also reassured me that it is perfectly possible for a couple to be married by the Army chaplain in the Ladysmith garrison church. As Alexander's wife you could remain here. You should have been married in March; there is no reason why he should not agree to the ceremony in September, instead."

"I'll never do it," Judith cried. "It is hard enough even to hold his attention during a conversation."

"I'm not surprised," was the reply. "Most men prefer cuddles to conversation. I suggest you consider that during the coming weeks—and wear red. It's a warm color. When I return from Johannesburg I expect to find Alexander ready to go to the altar as soon as it can be arranged."

It was then that the rain decided to lash down on Ladysmith for almost a week. However, Alex rode up from Tin Town to honor his acceptance of a dinner invitation from Mrs. Besant's sister and vowed it had been worth struggling through the mud when he greeted the ladies. The compliment wore a bit thin when he sat at the table exchanging polite but distant conversation and seeming not to notice the very pretty rose gown worn by his fiancée.

During the second week the sun shone and there was a winter picnic. Alex escorted Judith and joined the general lightheartedness, but she noticed that he drank rather too freely. Although she saw him several times during that

week it was always in company with no opportunity for
"cuddles instead of conversation."

At the beginning of the third week the speeding of time
made her grow desperate. They never had a moment
alone, so she determined to create one. Alex had lent her
one of his horses during her stay in Ladysmith, so it was an
easy matter to send a message down to the barracks ex-
pressing her concern over the animal's lack of spirit. Once
the deed was done she sat with a thudding heart, certain he
would send a veterinary officer in his stead. What could
she possibly do then?

But he came almost at once, and she could not help a
bitter thought that it was only the fear of his horse being ill
that prompted such a response. He would have pleaded the
demands of duty if she had merely asked him to call on
her.

She received him in the parlor, her hostess tactfully finding tasks to occupy her in other parts of the bungalow, and
he came straight to the point.

"Good morning, Judith. It was good of you to let me
know about Fidelio. I have just had a look at her, and she
seems quite well. What gave you cause for concern?"

He appeared not to notice how well the warm amber silk
dress suited her fair coloring, nor the smooth coils of
newly washed hair over which she had spent so much time.
All he had on his mind was the wretched horse!

Swallowing her disappointment she said as evenly as possible, "I did not mean to alarm you so much that you
feared for her safety, Alex. It was simply a feeling I had.
She usually greets me with a whinny and tossing head. This
morning she stood silent and bowed."

He shook his head. "Probably a little tired after that long
hack yesterday. It was frightfully hot all day."

To her horror it seemed that he was about to leave
again, so she said quickly, "I had a letter from Aunt Pan
this morning. It is full of interesting information about Johannesburg, besides some amusing anecdotes on people she
has encountered."

He lingered near the doorway. "Really? How is her mine
manager? Has he really been arrested?"

"Wait. I'll fetch the letter. You are sure to find it entertaining." Hurriedly, she left the room, relief flooding
through her at finding a way of keeping him there.

When she came back he was standing at the window

staring out at the distant *kopjes*. He did not even know he was no longer alone until she touched his arm, and he came back from his spiritual journey to look down at her face. It was the most intimate moment they had shared since the New Year's Eve ball, when he had told her the regiment was sailing at the end of that month. Now it was there she was fearful of shattering it—like a spun-glass bauble on a Christmas tree that hangs from a delicate thread until a careless movement dashes it to the ground.

"Is that the letter?" he asked, about to move away.

She held his arm and halted him. "Alex, we don't seem to have had much time alone, have we?"

His eyebrows furrowed into a frown. "I have been busy. My second-in-command seems to have had numerous duties waiting for my return. Whenever there is anything to be done, I am selected to do it. I think I know why."

She drew in her breath. "So it's genuine duty?"

His mouth twisted. "Oh yes, it's genuine, I assure you."

"I'm sorry. Something gave me the impression you were deliberately avoiding me."

He leaned back against the wall and she felt again that overpowering physical reaction he always created in her. *Cuddles instead of conversation.* Why did he not feel the urge to take her in his arms? She knew she had never looked better, yet he stood watching her with expressionless eyes and a polite mask of a face.

"Why should you think that?"

"You must agree no one would call you attentive, Alex. Your friends seek my company more often than you do—especially Lieutenant Forrester," she added with quick artfulness.

"So I have noticed. If you remember, I recommended him as an eminently suitable husband for you sometime ago."

"You were recommended to me first," she replied swiftly, then realized such talk would do her no good. "Please . . . don't quarrel with me, Alex. This is the first chance we have had to talk things over since I arrived in South Africa."

"You said what was most to the point at Landerdorp."

"Would . . . would you please explain that?" It was not going as she had hoped. He was saying all the wrong things.

"After your admirable performance as the outraged English lady, it must have been easy to give another to Colonel Rawlings-Turner." The relaxed manner had gone. He was suddenly tense and angry, standing to his full height and accusing her with every inch of it. "Did you think I would not know you had a hand in my leaving Landerdorp?"

She opened her mouth to deny it, then closed it again. Her aunt had made it plain she thought Alex should be separated from that girl; her aunt could charm the colonel. Put the two together, and Alex was right. Guilt made her defensive when she should have pleaded.

"Would you deny I had every right to such an action? We are engaged. We would have been married by now, if the regiment had remained in England. Surely I am entitled to your respect of the ring on my finger."

"By God, Judith, you want it all ways, don't you? You can make your rules, but I am allowed none of my own."

Desperately trying to recover ground she said, "The rules you speak of . . . I . . . I think you misunderstood. Perhaps you don't know me as well as you think you do."

"Does anybody know you . . . except my father?" he challenged. "I thought I did. I remembered you as a well-bred girl, extremely pretty but with natural generosity beneath the callous facade of most girls just discovering their own attractions. I told my father you would be affronted at his proposal. I said it was an insult to approach a girl like you as if he were a marriage broker. I protested—said that in my opinion only one kind of woman would accept his proposition." The bite in his words grew stronger. "But he was right: You are that kind of woman. All you want is a wealthy protective *accessory*!"

She had forgotten she was dueling with a champion. "You accepted that explanation?" she cried. "Did it never occur to you that there might be other reasons for what I did?" It was an attempt at an overture, but he had no ear for her music—the song of the veld was so strong in him.

"It was certainly not through any feelings for me. We had not met for five years and you walked off with my friend on that occasion. As for the reasons why you accepted, I think you have made them plain enough." The contempt in his voice iced every word. "The rules of this marriage can be regulated to your satisfaction. Where any other husband would demand, I shall only have to rattle the handle of your bedroom door to have you appealing to my father to bring me into line by turning the thumbscrew a little more. My name and wealth are there to protect your future, and my colonel will control my behavior so that you are free from scandal. Finally, there is that coat of cool morality you wear to keep away anyone or anything in the least disturbing. No, Judith, you are a cold, calculating, selfish, and very beautiful shell. I doubt there is a *you* to know."

Slowly she turned from him to stare from the window, unable to face what was there in his eyes. He had just peeled off her skin, and the flesh beneath was agonized by the sudden exposure. The contest was over.

"Do you believe you know *her*?" she asked through the thickness in her throat. There was an interval during which she wondered what his expression was like. If only his reflection would confront her in the pane of glass before her.

"Yes." It came at last. She had mentioned no name, yet he had known to whom she referred. Swinging around once more she saw it all in his expression—the softness of memory, the light of happiness in recall.

"And what does she want from you?"

"I think only my love. She has been taught it is better to give than receive."

"We are all taught that, Alex," she told him with the greatest difficulty. "Your ideas on what I was hoping to receive were wildly inaccurate . . . but I also know how to give." She drew off the diamond ring and held it out. "You suggested I should do this five months ago."

He did not move. "What about the breach of promise case?"

"It . . . it seems you never really promised anything."

He held her eyes for a moment, and there was a strange mixture of gladness, disbelief, and puzzlement in them.

"Take it, Alex."

There was a slow shake of his head. "I suggest you return it to my father. He gave it to you; I merely paid the price."

She stood for a long time after he had gone, looking at the ring in her hand. There were no tears. Ladies of her class hid their feelings and carried on as usual. She knew now that was wrong where she was concerned. Alex had been reaching out a hand for years, waiting for someone to take it. Pride, fear of being hurt, love that was selfish, had led her to ignore the hand, and it had been left to a little Dutch farm girl to curl warm fingers around his.

The ring dropped onto the lid of the piano, and she turned to look from the window once more. The veld stretched out forever, like her empty and featureless future.

## CHAPTER NINE

At the start of September Hetta knew that Alex had been wrong. War was a certainty. Piet was back at the Myburgh farm boasting a commission as field cornet of a commando of Boers in northern Natal who wished to support their brethren in the other states. All through the winter months loyal Dutchmen had been leaving their women and trekking north to the Transvaal or Orange Free State. Others who could not or would not leave their farms pledged their loyalty by vowing their readiness to rise up in revolt against the English rulers just as soon as the Boer armies swept into Natal and Cape Colony.

Above the Boer inhabitants of the Landerdorp area the banner of freedom rippled. Barns and outhouses hid rounds of ammunition for rifles, and the strips of dried meat known as *biltong* that every man carried on excursions into the veld were stored, ready for the great drive down into Natal from both borders. Horses were tended as never before, and repairs that had been awaiting a spare half day were tackled between the heavy demands of the farm. If the men were going off to fight, they must leave their women to see to the crops, the cattle, and the vegetable patch. It needed only one bad year and they would be finished. It was a perpetual struggle.

Apart from this, the women had to run the home, bring up their children, bake the bread, spin yarn for clothes, and stitch it into garments. Without their menfolk life would be harder than ever. All Boer women could handle a rifle from an early age, but it would avail them little if their servants turned against them when attacked by one of the bands of vicious natives that roamed the veld raping and murdering white women and children.

Hetta had always felt secure, for she had two men at the
farm and devoted, trusted servants. Others were different.
Jacob Steenkamp often flogged his natives, and Piet followed his example. Hetta suspected it would not be easy
for the woman left behind when those two went to war
together, as they fully intended.

On an evening in the first week of September, when
spring was hovering on the front doorstep, Piet arrived at
the farm in great haste. Those inside the house heard him
cursing old Johnny, who would have gone to take his
horse, before he burst into the room like a god of war, with
green eyes wild and hair flowing from beneath his hat. He
looked a formidable figure, and Oupa greeted him warmly.
With a dish of springbok and potatoes before him he began
speaking of his plans.

"Our brothers are flocking to us. They bring horses and
guns—guns that have reached them through South-west
Africa—guns the British cannot blockade. We have troops
coming from Germany and France, and a whole regiment
of Irish who hate the English as much as we do." He nodded at Oupa. "The Landerdorp commando is already a
hundred strong, and there are more arriving everyday. We
shall be grateful to elders like you who can provide us with
food and shelter." He turned to Franz. "We gather next
week at Leni Cronje's farm. We can travel together."

There was an unexpected silence as Franz struggled with
himself. He had paled, and his eyes sought a resting place
with nervous speed. At length, they met Hetta's, and she
signaled her sympathy. In her heart she knew he was lost,
but prayed he would fight bravely.

"I do not wish to be a member of your . . .
*commando*," he told Piet in a hoarse voice, then cleared his
throat. "I am a farmer, that is all. I till this land my grandparents chose, and raise good cattle. In the spring there is
much work to be done. I am a farmer. I have no quarrel
with the British."

Piet's chest swelled visibly but he kept his anger under
control, for the moment. "They killed your father," he said.

"And he killed many another man's father before he
died. For what—so that their sons could do it all again?"
Franz had found his voice, and now, feelings locked inside
him for a long while, came forth. "My father left the farm
in the hands of his own father when he went to war. I
cannot do that. Oupa is an old man. If I die, who will have

this farm? I have no sons yet, and my sister is to be your woman. You speak very heady language, man. You cry battle for our freedom and land, but of what use will victory be if there are no young men left to work the land we have won?"

"You doubt our skill as fighting men?"

He shook his head sadly. "There is no stronger arm than the one that fights to defend its own. But the British are renowed soldiers. They have conquered half the world."

"*Ja!*" shouted Piet. "That is just it. They now want the other half." He struggled to keep his control over himself. "So, you are a coward—a girl?"

Franz flinched, and Hetta could not bear his hurt any longer. "This farm has suffered from the loss of our father. Is all my brother's labor to be sacrificed and the land he loves returned to the wild?"

She knew Oupa would not approve of such a speech in the middle of a discussion between men, but it was born of her great dread of the coming conflict. Oupa frowned—she saw it from the corner of her eye—but Piet swung around on her immediately.

"You know nothing. You make Franz more of a girl by your defense. He must speak his own words."

He began turning away, but she burned inside and could not leave it at that.

"I know—I do know. There is conflict in Johannesburg, that is all. It is the gold. They do not want our farms."

"Silence!" Oupa said heavily, but Piet stared at her with blazing aggression until his attention was taken by Franz.

"I have no quarrel with the British," he repeated. "Is a man a coward when he follows the word of the Good Book?"

"The word is that we shall prosper," Piet said with heavy accusation.

"And shall we do that by dying in hundreds before the British guns?" was the soft-spoken question.

"Better that than be trampled beneath their imperial marching boots." Piet stood up, restless beneath the fire of his spirit. "They think us ignorant peasants. They think they only have to threaten and we shall tremble before them. *They are wrong!* We have fled before them for over a hundred years. Now is the time to stop and make a stand against their greed and arrogance." He turned on the unhappy boy at the table. "You have no quarrel with them because you stay here on your land and dream of the promised greatness of our people. You should cross the borders; hear what your kinsmen speak of. The British indulge the black people beyond foolishness and take their case against ours; they walk across land we fought bitterly for, as if they have conquered it; they plot in London for an Africa beneath the British flag—an Africa where they rule supreme. Do you still say you have no quarrel with them? Will you still say it when they take your farm and build their cities on this land? Will you sit and watch while they increase their numbers and play their childish games with ball and stick on horseback? Will you not care when their spoiled and pampered women stare at your sister, and turn away when she passes . . ." his voice grew steely, ". . . or when their white-skinned men make play with her?"

Franz got to his feet quickly, angrier than Hetta had ever seen him.

"I have the heart of any Boer man. As God is my witness, I shall fight my enemies and protect my own with all my strength—but I am a man of peace. I do not *seek* enemies."

"You will never find peace with the British, son of my son," Oupa said gravely, holding the attention of all in the room with the blackness of his expression and the authority in his tone. "You will avenge your father; it is your inheritance. You will uphold the word of the Bible and drive these men from our land. You will join with your people when they take arms against the redcoats."

Franz stood breathing deeply, shocked and upset. Hetta ached for him, and the fear deep inside caught at her stomach. She must have made some sound, for Oupa turned his lowering brows on her.

"Have both my kin softness in their bellies? Your mother was a good woman with a strong body and a stout heart. She was killed by the British just as surely as your father. Where is her spirit in you?"

Hetta remained silent, terrified she would give herself away even more than she had by admitting she knew about the trouble in Johannesburg. Oupa would beat her if he knew she had continued to defy him in speaking the English tongue to an enemy. She remembered Alex saying that kings ordered their soldiers to fight each other but it did not mean they were personal enemies. Her brother would be like that. Each time his bullet brought a man down, Franz would die a little with him.

Looking at him she compared his features with Piet's. Piet was a true man of this wild country. He had its savage distances in his eyes, and its restlessness in his spirit. He was strong-faced and as uncompromising as the veld itself. He saw the harshness of sun-baked country as something to break, not respect. The beautiful creatures upon it were mere sources of food to men like Piet Steenkamp, and the bright flowers that bloomed so miraculously after rain were trampled underfoot without a thought. Like Franz, Piet was a dreamer, but he dreamed of far different things—and his emotions were strong, running deep within his angry soul.

Her legs grew weak. Most Boer men were like Piet, not Franz. They would fight the British to the last man. The *kopjes* would run with their blood and the bones of British soldiers would be scattered across the veld—just as Piet had promised. It was inevitable.

"Speak, girl!" Oupa commanded, bringing her back to the present. "Where is your mother's spirit?"

What could she say? "I pray I shall find it when the time comes."

The answer did not please him, and he said hoarsely, "We must all pray. Let us do so now."

It was over. Oupa had pulled away the farm from beneath his grandson's feet by putting the obligation of vengeance on a man who felt no aggression within his soul. And he had shown too plainly that he was deeply disappointed in his kin, and thought their visitor a truer man of their cause. Hetta felt ashamed that he should have found them lacking, and prayed for help in the coming days.

It was late when Piet departed, and he looked pointedly at Hetta after saying his farewells to the two men. "A cup of milk would send me on my way satisfied," he told her. "It is a long ride."

She gave a little nod and went to the churn, then followed him outside with a fast-beating heart. He was standing by his horse, waiting for her. In the darkness all she could see of him were two light eyes and a dark shape against the night sky. A shiver passed over her.

"Are you afraid?" he asked probingly.

"The night is cold after the warm house. Why should I be afraid?"

"How is it that you know so much about things they do not understand?" He gripped her wrist as she held out the cup to him. "What do you know of the trouble in Johannesburg? Who can have told you about it?"

She swallowed hard. "You forget I now go into Landerdorp each week. I hear talk there. Those who come in on the railway speak the word."

"You discuss such things with them . . . in English?"

"I . . . I listen when they talk among themselves."

*"Englishmen?"*

"Sometimes . . . but Dutch folk mostly." An attempt to pull her hand away succeeded only in making him tighten his grip. "I know very little."

"Enough to speak into the things men are discussing. Why have you kept it a secret from them?"

"I have no secret," she breathed, disliking his nearness and the gleam of his wild eyes so close to her face. Could he possibly know or guess about Alex? He had been away in the Transvaal during that time.

"The red-haired officer—he has spoken to you of this?"

It was a trap she neatly avoided. "Englishmen do not speak Dutch, so how could he have done?" Then she fell right into another. "And he has now left Landerdorp."

Her wrist was twisted so that she gasped. "So you have been seeing him?"

"It was because I had not seen him that I guessed he had gone. He no longer walked with the others." She edged backward to try to ease the pressure on her arm.

"You are my promised woman, Hetta Myburgh," he said across the chill night air, "but I want no traitorous creature who casts her eyes at *uitlanders*." He spat at her feet. "They are worthless; they are our enemies."

"I know what they are," she said, trying to hold on to her dignity.

"I know what they are not," Piet said. "They are not *men*. They dress in pretty coats—like a woman—and their skin is soft and white, untouched by the sun. Even their smell is like a woman—perfume as sickly as the pale creatures who wear it. They cannot even grow hair upon their chins. Is that a sign of manhood?" He jerked her wrist and made her bite her lip for fear of gasping. "Let them wear their fancy coats with bright buttons, and trot out on their sleek horses, but we shall bring them to their knees and tread them beneath our feet. There is not one among them who can ride for a day across the veld and not lose himself. They will die of sun and thirst while we watch them; they will drown in our rivers; their great guns will sink in the mire and their glossy horses will thin into skeletons without the strength to carry their burdens." He was shaking with emotion. Hetta could feel its trembling power through the hand that held her.

"They want this land of ours; let them try to take it. They will not heed our words, but they cannot ignore the word of the veld. It is written that this land shall be ours. Let not any man attempt to take it from us or the wrath of God will be mighty." He threw her aside with a violent gesture. "And any who consort with them shall feel it also, mark that, woman."

He mounted and rode away without any further word, leaving Hetta holding the hand that had grown numb from his grip and staring into the darkness. Sky was everywhere. Apart from the little house behind her and the outbuildings, it reached down to the earth wherever she looked. It took four hours to reach Landerdorp in a cart; two and a half to the Steenkamp farm. Beyond that was the Transvaal border. In the opposite direction lay a vast stretch of country thrown up into *kopjes* and scored by rivers—harsh land with few hamlets, land that offered no hospitality to travelers until a track ran down to Ladysmith.

It was in this direction that she looked as her cheeks grew wet with tears. The cold night swam around her as she moved to the corner of the house, as if ten feet would take her nearer and into his thoughts. For a moment she closed her eyes, so that the wet lashes met and shook off the trembling drops that hung on them.

For two months she had lived with the anguish of that day. Out there beneath Devil's Leap she had pledged herself to a man whose eyes held ghosts of sadness that denied the happiness in his smile. She had loved a gentle man with tenderness in his touch and honesty in his words. During those short weeks she had seen him come alive and known it was because of her. That morning he had bared his soul so that she could see his weaknesses as well as his strength. He had offered the truth along with his love in a way no other man she knew would, and she had loved him the more because of it.

Now, she was haunted by a haughty beautiful creature in clothes trimmed with fur, who wore on her hand a ring that flashed in the sun. A lady, like those English ladies she remembered from her childhood in Ladysmith, who wore pale skirts that trailed in the dust as if it were not there. She had had the most lovely features Hetta had ever seen, but they had been frozen, like the statue at the end of Landerdorp.

There had never been a woman in Hetta's life since her aunt in Ladysmith—nothing to equip her for what she felt toward the girl who had taken Alex away. It ruled her days. In everything she did, it was there like a constant pain deep in her stomach. It clawed into her whenever she thought of blue eyes as cold as morning ice or a mouth that would give only petrified kisses. There had been no spoken word, no smile of greeting, she had simply stood there between the other two . . . but he had gone with her.

Landerdorp had been an empty place that next Thursday. She had told herself he would be waiting in the usual place beneath Devil's Leap. Long after the cart had passed through the *nek*, and was creaking its way along the track leading to the town she had gone on looking for him.

She had lingered in the stores, her pulse leaping at every sight of a dark green cap, until she had been approached by an officer in the usual khaki uniform whom she did not at first recognize. It was only when he smiled that she knew him as the one who had tried to prevent her leaving on the day she had first met Alex. Lieutenant Russell had gone back to Ladysmith, he told her, but he was most willing to step into his shoes.

Hetta had looked up into the handsome smiling face while a terrible cold weight expanded in her chest until something had to be done to release it. Her voice had grown strangely harsh when she told him, in Dutch, that she needed help from no one, then turned and walked away.

Standing there at the corner of her house Hetta hugged herself—not against the chill of the night, but the chill of loss. Somewhere along the way, since that first day at the end of March, she had lost herself. Somewhere along the way she had become bewitched.

The anguish grew too strong and she bit on her clenched fist to prevent a moan of despair. For him she had defied Oupa and all he had taught her; for him she had refused to follow the dictates of her own people—had risked discovery and condemnation by her family. For him she had opened her mind and her heart to embrace a belief much wider than those around her. All this she had done for him—an Englishman.

How easy it was to see the truth now—and yet how hard. With eyes no longer blinded by willfulness she recognized what had been on the faces of the handsome officer and the three beside her ox cart that day—arrogance. She saw now that it must have been in the eyes of all the soldiers, if only she had known. The British looked down on the Boers from the saddles of their thoroughbred horses and from the upward tilt of their proudly held heads.

Alex had had that same quality, and she had been captivated by it. He had caught at her breast with his strong face, his dark chestnut hair, and muscular limbs; he had captured her soul with haunted eyes that softened and blurred with pleasure whenever they met; he had broken her mind with a deep voice that spoke of things sweet to her ear; he had weakened her stomach with his deference, with careful words in Dutch that she had taught him.

On that last day he had told her of a love she had lit in him, of a new life he felt since their first meeting. He had spoken of gratitude and thankfulness. He had held her hard against his body and drawn out her love with kisses that had taught her the secret of suffering and endeavor between a man and woman. Then, he had left her—for a tall remote creature with silver hair. He had stepped down from the wagon and walked away forever, leaving her with the truth of her own sinfulness.

For two months she had borne the guilt every time she looked at her beloved grandfather and brother. How could she have dared to defy and question their teachings, set herself up in opposition to the revered head of the family? Oupa was right. She did not have her mother's spirit, and she was ashamed.

An Englishman had told her there would not be a war, but he had lied. An Englishman had spoken the words of friendship, then the words of love. They had also been lies. He had walked away with no backward glance, and she knew now what he was—what they all were. She also knew why Oupa had said they would find no peace with the British.

She leaned against the wall, staring into the darkness hanging over the veld. There would be war. Soon men would be fighting out there where the vultures hovered and waited for death. The still clear air would ring with shots, and it would be men who twitched and fell with staring eyes in faces paled by fading life, not animals needed for food. Her kinsmen would ride bravely out for freedom and justice, and Franz would be with them. A knife twisted inside her at the thought of his danger.

The knife twisted even more, bringing a gasp of pain. *The kopjes will run with their blood and the bones of the British will be scattered across the veld.* Would *he* be there among them, lying alone and broken on some hillside, green eyes sightless and burned from their sockets by the sun of a land that was not his?

*"Alex."* She breathed his name on a mist of vapor that floated on the cold air, then vanished away, as he had done. The tears began to gather again on the cheeks he had covered with his kisses, and she thought of the days ahead. He was a soldier who would be ordered to fight, and she would never know if he lay dying as she tilled the land or washed the clothes.

She turned against the wall and tried to find comfort in the ancient stalwart stone. He had deceived her in every word he had spoken; he had deserted her. He had gone with his chosen woman as if all else had never been . . . so why did she find such anguish in every minute of the day? Why did she toss and turn at night while her body burned for his touch? Why was she filled with every moment they had spent together until it seemed she could carry the burden no longer? Clenching her hands against the wall in an effort to ease it, she acknowledged the answer that was so difficult to face. It was because she could not forget his face as he prepared to leave her. Something in his expression told her the ghosts of his past had reclaimed him.

"Hetta! The lamp is burning low. Come before darkness accompanies you to bed."

Franz stood in the doorway, a slender shadow against the light from the lamp he held. She took a last look in the direction of Ladysmith, then wiped her cheeks with her apron before going inside.

"You have grown cold," her brother said gently.

"Yes. It is a coldness that will not easily go."

They walked side by side toward the doors of their rooms, wanting to reach out to each other in mutual unhappiness, yet holding back. She lit her candle from the flame, then looked at the familiar face yellowed and illuminated by the lantern he held.

"It is sometimes difficult to see the ways of the Lord, I think," she ventured. "But He decides and we must accept."

Her brother's expression grew bleak. "Some find it easier than others, my sister. Good night."

Once in her room Hetta began to pray, not only for her family and the farm, and for the food and the crops, but for her mother's spirit that Oupa wished so badly that she should have. She prayed for Franz and for herself—for strength; for the courage to endure what must be endured. The war would come, and she would never see Alex again. He belonged with his own people, and she with hers.

The news was black. The British government issued orders for ten thousand reinforcements in South Africa, half of them regiments from India because of its nearness to Natal. The men of Ladysmith garrison laughed nervously. They had heard the Boers were at least fifty thousand strong—almost three times what their number would be after reinforcements arrived. If the war began before that it would be five to one against them.

British soldiers always rose to a challenge, but there was something about Africa that gave them pause to think. It was a country with a will of its own. Those old soldiers who had fought the Zulus spoke of " a bloody awful feeling that every crest of a hill, every rock and bush hid black woolly heads" and those who remembered Majuba vowed they would never fight uphill again no matter what the officers said. The silly fools could rush up waving their swords, if they liked, but they would go up alone this time.

Others, the "death or glory" faction, whooped it up in the mess every night to relieve their impatience; while some guiltily welcomed the chance of quick promotion in dead comrade's shoes to help with the burden of a growing family's bills back in England. And then there were the thinking men who doubted the wisdom of allowing a war to develop. Officers of the Royal Engineers who had been occupied since July in trying to survey the area, shook their heads in despair. The only maps they could possibly supply were more than half guesswork. Their equipment had been inefficient; the time given laughable. To survey a country such as southern Africa would take years for a well-organized topographical team. They had had neither the time nor the manpower. How an army on the march would fare they dreaded to think. In view of this, garrison commanders set about interviewing and hiring local black people as guides.

Artillerymen wished there were someway of saying "abracadabra" and doubling the numbers of their guns and limbers; cavalry captains scoured local stables for remounts; and infantry rankers looked gloomily at the endless veld.

In view of all this drama Judith was near despair when Mrs. Davenport arrived back from Johannesburg to report that in the Transvaal a panicked evacuation was already underway, with the Dutch openly spitting at the feet of the fleeing *uitlanders* and jeering as the trains pulled from the stations. Mrs. Davenport had been acutely disturbed, and the Colonel's apparent gravity over the situation alarmed her even more.

The journey had been cramped and exhausting, under the circumstances, with temperatures well above the eighties, and Judith felt concern over her aunt's appearance.

"My dear girl, a short rest in a darkened room followed by a pot of tea is all I need," Mrs. Davenport assured her, but this, in Judith's opinion, did not produce the expected result.

She sat with her aunt in the cool of early evening and dreaded the inevitable question that would oblige her to tell of the broken engagement. But Mrs. Davenport was full of the present situation, recalling heatedly what she had seen and heard in Johannesburg. "The British" she concluded, "would make a better job of running this country than anyone else. We always do. The Dutch are only simple folk."

"Yes," Judith agreed absently, thinking of a girl in an ox cart who had won Alex with her simplicity.

The older woman sighed. "Simple they might be, but there is no doubt of the nasty attitude they are taking against us. I think I have never felt so uncomfortable as on that journey, Judith. Women and children alike stared at us with dark eyes full of some emotion I shudder to name. I know it's foolish, but I was really glad of the Colonel's presence. I know men have fought since time immemorial but, looking at these women, I was almost persuaded they would fight also. You might think that a shocking observation, my dear, but you did not see them." She smiled suddenly. "Thank heaven Alexander is out of that affair at Landerdorp. It might have caused a diplomatic incident."

The moment had come, and Judith had to know the answer, however painful it might be. "Aunt Pan, did you say anything to Colonel Rawlings—Turner about sending Alex back to Ladysmith?"

The fair eyebrows rose. "I had no need. The minute I began speaking on the subject he assured me it was not necessary. He has faith in Alexander and believes he has a great future once he finds himself. He was not prepared to endanger it by leaving him exposed to temptations of that nature." A smile played around her lips. "I am pleased to say he believes you could play a large part in bringing about the change."

Judith took a deep breath. "Then I am sorry. I broke the engagement three days ago."

Mrs. Davenport sat perfectly still for a few moments, then said, "I do not believe it. What possessed you to do such a thing?"

"It was the only thing I could do."

"I see." But she did not, and Judith was unprepared for what came next. She rose and walked wearily to the window where the sound of tramping boots told Judith there were yet more soldiers marching through the street below. "Then, all that talk of dying for love of him was so much dramatic silliness such as your mother indulges in, was it?"

"Aunt Pan, it takes two to make a success of marriage— a man and a woman. Not a woman and her aunt," Judith said in a shaking voice. "As you have often pointed out, Alex is a complex person who fights any attempt to manipulate him. He had little enough opinion of me before. Now he hates me for causing him to be sent back to Ladysmith. Diplomatic incident or not, he loves that girl."

"As he has probably loved more than one before now. My dear Judith, young men of Alexander's class do not marry farm girls."

"And I do not marry a man who longs all the time for another woman."

"I despair of you, I really do," Mrs. Davenport cried. "I have seen young men at your feet in the past. You are very beautiful. I left you here with the express purpose of making him forget all other women. Where on earth did you go wrong?"

"By accepting his proposal in the first place," Judith said

with growing heat. "He thought me cold and unfeeling from the start."

"Then you must have allowed him to think it."

"It was on your advice that I did so," Judith accused.

Her aunt stared at her. "On my advice?"

"You left me in no doubt of the way ladies of the English upper classes should behave. Calm and dignified, you said."

"And did I not berate you for the way you handled that meeting at Landerdorp? Calmness and dignity can be warm qualities, you know."

"Not when one feels humiliated and sick with disappointment," said Judith bitterly.

"But this!" her aunt exclaimed with her hands to her temples. "My main purpose in making this journey to South Africa was to help you gain your heart's desire. Now, I find the *desperate love* of which you spoke fades before the first reverse."

"This is not the first reverse," was the taut answer. "All the way along I have met with the greatest opposition from him. Aunt Pan, you did not see his face when he spoke of her."

"A good thing I did not, for I should have given him my opinion of such folly. I shall do so as soon as possible, and when I have finished with him that ring will be back on your finger."

"Alex returned to Landerdorp today," Judith told her quietly. "In view of the emergency the garrison there had to be strengthened. The second-in-command knew Alex was familiar with the area, so he was the natural choice. Mr. Forrester told me this morning."

"Oh!" Mrs. Davenport sat down very abruptly. "So that is that. You have lost him!" For a few moments she gazed into space, then looked up at her niece with color spots flying in her cheeks. "And what do you propose doing now? Your mother will never forgive you, nor will Chatsworth. Gossip will have it that you jilted a young man on the eve of battle; you will be branded heartless. To think you have thrown away all we worked for in a moment of . . . oh dear, I should never have gone away and left you here alone."

"I am glad you did," was the warm reply. "For too long I have relied on you for help and advice. It is time I began running my own life. You accuse my love of fading before the first reverse, but that is quite wrong. It was because of my love for him that I set him free from a duty Sir Chatsworth forced on him. It was the hardest thing I have ever done, but it gained, at least, some small respect from him, which I never had before."

"I see." It was a remote phrase, as if the older woman had gone far away in her thoughts.

Judith knelt down before her aunt, who looked suddenly old. "Dear Aunt Pan, I shall be eternally grateful to you for making it possible for me to come here."

Slowly Mrs. Davenport came back to the present and looked at the hand holding hers. There was tiredness and regret in her voice as she said, "Perhaps I expected too much of you."

"No," said Judith gently. "I think you did not expect enough."

They were to take the train to Durban. The Colonel had telegraphed to book a passage on a ship leaving the following week, and he advised them to get down to the port as soon as possible. Mrs. Davenport seemed calm, but Judith sensed undercurrents of emotion. For herself, the stunned empty feeling that had been with her since taking off Alex's ring was worsened by what her stand had done to the relationship between herself and her aunt. A terrible dread filled her each time she thought of the preparations for war that were going on all around her. Alex would be part of it and she suffered the fears of all women who loved a soldier. On the afternoon prior to their departure Neil Forrester called to escort Judith on a ride along the outskirts of the town. Mrs. Davenport had retired with a headache, and Judith felt one behind her own eyes as she set off with the young man Alex had recommended as a suitable husband. He had the kind of looks one often found on the faces of old Etonians—the stamp of breeding and confidence—and his manners were easy. After Alex, he was relaxing company, and Judith had been grateful for his daily visits that took her mind off a future she had no wish to face until she landed in England.

He looked at the sky as they trotted along the main street. "No sign of rain, yet this heavy heat suggests a storm in the offing, wouldn't you say?"

She smiled. "I am not as familiar with this country as you are, Mr. Forrester, so I shall accept your word on the subject. I must say I would welcome a storm if it would bring a breeze or a lower temperature." They fell silent for a while, then she said, "It will seem very strange to find winter awaiting us on our return."

"Yes. England seems a long way off, sometimes."

She looked at him curiously. "You sound a little reminiscent. Do you miss your home?"

"A great deal. The beeches around the old house must look glorious right now. September is a golden month in the Cotsworlds." He let his gaze travel over the blue *kopjes* in the distance. "A far cry from this desolate country."

"Alex finds it . . ." she caught herself up, then realized the sentence had gone too far to stop without giving the very impression she was trying to avoid. "Alex finds it fascinating."

Neil avoided her eyes. "Well, he would. Alex is that sort of fellow. He has always disliked any form of restriction. I suppose these lonely aspects suggest freedom." He grew slightly embarrassed. "I don't really know; it's only a guess. I mean, I don't know him all that well."

"But you are a friend of his, aren't you?"

He avoided a direct answer. "He is not easy to get to know." He must have felt it inadequate because he added defensively, "There's no finer shot in the regiment, and I pity anyone who faces him when he has a sword in his hand."

"He was a foils champion at seventeen, I am told."

"Ah, that would explain it."

They could think of nothing to follow that, and talk of Alex seemed to put up a screen between them until they reached a shady stretch along the banks of the Klip River, where Neil suggested they sit for a while out of the sun. Judith sat on the rug he spread for her, and the young officer sat beside her with one knee bent, leaning on his left arm. With his right hand he flicked at the grass with his riding whip in a nervous manner, then he cleared his throat.

"Forgive me if I am out of place, but is it . . . I mean, what is the situation between you and Alex? He said . . . well, he said you had thought better of it . . . and you no longer wear his ring. On the other hand, you do talk about him rather a lot." He turned to look at her. She had seen that expression on the faces of young men before. "The thing is I shall miss you most frightfully when you leave . . .

and I was going to ask your permission to write to you. That is . . . if the engagement is really off, I mean."

What could she say—that it was all over except for a longing tearing sadness every time she thought of him? That talking about him created the false impression that he was still part of her life? That only now did she realize how empty her future would be without the hope of ever winning his love?

"I should be pleased to receive letters from you," she told him, thinking it might be one way of hearing news of Alex. "In return, I will write and describe the autumn beeches."

He looked relieved and delighted. "I say, that's splendid! I shan't mind your going half as much now."

Steering away from personal feelings Judith told him, "The ship we are joining is coming from India with several cavalry regiments, according to Colonel Rawlings–Turner. It all sounds very ominous."

"Don't worry," Neil said airily. "These people would never take us on—they wouldn't stand a chance. I mean, a lot of farmers against the finest army in the world!" He shifted restlessly, unhappy at the change of topic. "The whole thing is a big test. They are bristling their beards, and we are standing on our dignity. When the moment comes they'll back down—certain to. Besides, we don't want to fight them. There's not a man in the regiment who would be happy about shooting civilians, because that's all they are."

Judith spoke without thinking once more. "Alex says they have a great number of rifles and ammunition. That doesn't sound like civilians."

Neil sighed. "Alex looks at things in a different light from anyone else in the regiment. He has never been impressed with our history of battle honors."

"Perhaps the Boers have never learned of them in order to be impressed," she suggested. "And they do have the guns."

"Yes, they have guns, but they only shoot animals, you know. What good would that be against a solid square or a cavalry charge?" At that point he seemed to remember that he was talking to a girl and gave an apologetic smile. "Sorry. Hardly the right topic for a time like this. I would much rather talk about you."

"That would be most uninteresting," she murmured.

"Not to me. Judith, I . . . I would like to find out as much as possible so that I can think about you after you have left. As a matter of fact, I have always thought you the most marvelous girl I ever met, but being engaged to someone else put rather a limit on . . . I mean, a fellow can't very well . . ." He trailed off and swiped at the grass with the whip. "What I am trying to say is, you look absolutely beautiful sitting there with the sun shining through the trees."

For a silly ridiculous reason tears welled up in her eyes. How could she appear so different in two men's eyes? Alex was right, once more. This man was part of the backbone of Britain with old-fashioned ideas about the relationship between men and women. He would make some girl a wonderful husband.

"Thank you," she said softly. "I'm sure you'll learn all you want to know about me through my letters. The written word is supposed to reveal things about the writer that would normally stay hidden."

He broke into a rueful grin. "Oh lord, that is sure to spoil my chances."

The tearful feeling increased. He was really very nice, and the afternoon had suddenly taken on a tight-throated, young-men-off-to-war quality. The reality of returning to England burst upon her, and with it the knowledge that part of her would remain here in Ladysmith. A strange kind of familiarity with the dust-ridden South African town had crept up on her unaware, and she knew now she would miss the creaking carts, the jumble of buildings, the uniforms, the brilliant clear skies, and the sense of sweeping space wherever one looked. All at once, the thought that it would still be here, that Neil would still ride up from Tin Town, that Alex would be isolated in Landerdorp, made her departure something she dreaded. After this, the house in Richmond would seem over-pretty; her life there dull and frustrating. Africa, she realized, had won her over.

They returned to the hotel at four, and Judith asked Neil to tea. He accepted eagerly and waited while she went upstairs to change and collect her aunt. Mrs. Davenport, still in a silk wrapper, was sitting at the dressing table putting the finishing touches to her hair.

"Oh dear," she exclaimed when Judith told her Neil was downstairs. "I have ordered tea to be brought here."

"Has your headache not gone?"

"Not really, and I do have rather an uncomfortable pain in my chest. It was that pork we had for luncheon. There is an R in the month. I had forgotten."

Judith smiled fondly. "I shouldn't think that applies in South Africa. The seasons are in reverse."

"Yes, I suppose so," she agreed, then before her niece's shocked eyes, slowly doubled up and slipped to the floor where she lay ashen-faced and frighteningly still.

"Aunt Pan?" Judith knelt beside her. Panic flared for a moment, but the need for action rose above it. Gathering up the skirt of her habit she hurried down the stairs. Neil rose to his feet, the smile on his face dying as she approached.

"Come quickly. My aunt has collapsed."

He took her outstretched hand and strode toward the stairs. "How bad is it?"

The words jerked out of her. "She is still breathing, but she looks gravely ill. Oh Neil, what a terrible thing to happen! I'm so afraid for her."

It took but one look for Neil to decide that only a qualified man should touch the afflicted woman, and the local doctor was sent for immediately. Judith felt part of a nightmare as Neil did his best to comfort and console her, while her aunt lay on the floor as if already in the hands of death. The doctor ordered her outside when he arrived and joined her half an hour later in the saloon where Neil had taken her.

"Your aunt has suffered a fairly severe stroke," he told her gently but firmly. "With intensive care and treatment she will recover, but it will take a long time."

Neil was marvelous, as was Colonel Rawlings–Turner, who arranged for Judith to return to the house of Mrs. Besant's sister, where she had stayed during Mrs. Davenport's visit to Johannesburg. The lady was a widow who welcomed company, and agreed with the colonel that a young woman should not be left alone after a shock such as she had received that day.

Neil escorted her there, then supervised the packing of the two ladies' things and arranged the transport of them to the bungalow on the outskirts of town. He settled the hotel bill and telegraphed to cancel the passages on the liner bound for England.

Judith was too shocked to think of all the consequences. Only later when she blew out her lamp and the darkness brought a modicum of clear thought, did she realize what the doctor had said: A long time—several months, at least. That meant that Christmas would almost certainly be spent in Ladysmith.

## CHAPTER TEN

Surely there was no place in the world where it could rain so hard for so long, Alex thought as he went out onto the *stoep* outside his quarters, knowing he could no longer delay going into the downpour. As he fastened his dark green weather cloak he reflected that it would avail him little in the deluge. The minute he stepped into the street the mud would rise almost to the top of his boots, and his khaki breeches would be soaked through. The small green forage cap would be no protection, and runnels would course down his face onto his neck and through the high collar of the cloak to saturate the tunic so that it clung uncomfortably to him for most of the morning. That had been the pattern for almost a week.

Letting out a sigh, he stepped off the wooden staging and sank into the mud so that he could make his way to the railway yard to relieve Lieutenant March from his spell of night duty. The man would be glad of his breakfast and would not mind turning out in such weather with that welcome meal at the end of it. For Alex there was only the prospect of dismal hours of waiting, and watching the rain.

Struggling through the slippery dragging mud, he bent his head against the driving sheets of rain, only to shield his eyes from it not in the hope of keeping any drier. Already, his knees and lower thighs were wet where the cloak had blown open. He consoled himself with the fact that today he would, at least, be under cover. Yesterday and the previous Thursday on outlying guard duty there had only been the limited shelter of rocky outcrops, and a short spell under the tarpaulin of the gun emplacements when he visited the artillery officer in charge.

He had hated that duty for another reason altogether, and he acknowledged it yet again as he passed through the empty street where the stores no longer stood open. The longing for Hetta grew even worse when he was out on the *kopjes* with the veld tormenting him with its never-ending distances that hid her somewhere beyond his reach. When she had left him at Devil's Leap the veld had swallowed her up until the ox wagon had appeared in the distance a week later. Where she had spent the intervening seven days had been a complete mystery to him.

He paused to pull his foot from a tenacious patch of mud, and looked at the distant rail yard with slitted eyes. Only another two hundred yards.

In that distance he would pass the spot where he had first seen her, sitting with such dignity while Guy Cuthbertson tormented her. He swallowed back the tight lump that seized his throat every time he thought of the morning he had walked away, leaving her sitting with that same dignity. As always the familiar tide of aching pain rose slowly in his stomach and washed over the whole of his body. He threw himself with great vigor into reaching the rail yard, heaving his feet from the mud and heading into the rain defiantly—but nothing would remove it. He had learned that lesson through the long lonely days.

He had been back in Landerdorp four weeks and he wanted her more and more as the days passed. The place had changed while he had been in Ladysmith. The carts had rolled in less often as the time went by, and not at all now. Only those stores run by English sympathizers or impartial and determined traders remained open. The Dutch storekeepers had closed their premises and melted away in the night. He had watched for her, but she had not come on any day during those four weeks. The chasm between Boers and British had grown too wide.

He had only Guy's account of meeting her soon after that dreadful day on which to ponder. It was no consolation to be told she had spat a whole tirade of Dutch at him, turned on her heel, and walked away like an outraged virgin when he offered to take Alex's place. Alex had railed at him for his behavior and Guy had been speculatively silent on the subject ever since.

Alex was all churned up inside these days. The relief and freedom he had felt the minute Judith took off that meaningless diamond ring had died upon his return to Landerdorp. His love would remain out of reach, believing God-knew-what of him. She had been his so short awhile: the bubble had burst so soon.

Now a state of war existed. The Boers had invaded Natal a little under a week ago. That they had precipitated the war was unarguable. They had presented the British with an ultimatum that was not only unacceptable, but almost insulting to a nation with an empire second to none, for it demanded that all troops lining the borders should be with-drawn, all reinforcements that had arrived should leave the country immediately, and all those on their way should turn around in midocean.

The demands guaranteed Britain's refusal, and the Boers were delighted to launch their well-planned and long-prepared offensive. The British were shocked into a war they did not want and for which they were ill-prepared. Many had no real heart for it, since they could not help a sneaking support for the Dutch cause. The Boers were Eu-ropeans not a lot different from themselves. They were not even soldiers in the accepted sense.

However, their martial prowess was dismayingly effec-tive, Alex reflected as he entered the wooden hut used as a guard post in the railway yard.

"You're late! Sergeant Cutler and his men arrived five minutes ago," Clarkson March informed him, rising from his chair with a yawn. "I'd think you might make an effort when a fellow has been awake all night."

Alex smiled, knowing March well enough to be sure he had slept like a top. "Enjoy your breakfast when you get it. It might be your last for some time."

"Eh? What's that supposed to mean?"

Alex threw off his dripping cloak and unhooked the col-lar of his sodden khaki-drill tunic. "News came through this morning that Newcastle has been taken by Joubert, and another Boer force several thousand strong is on its way to Dundee. A galloper came in half dead with exhaus-tion just after dawn to tell us the telegraph line to Newcas-tle has been cut, and the railway is in Boer hands as far as Pinter's Nek." He walked across the hut leaving deposits of mud on the floor. "You know what that means, don't you?"

"We are next," said the blond Lieutenant.

Alex nodded. "We are all on standby."

March's face flushed with excitement. "I wrote to the

Guv'nor saying I hoped to see some action soon. God, I hope Johnny Boer is not turned back by our fellows at Dundee before we get a chance to cross swords with them."

"Our fellows at Dundee" had every intention of turning Johnny Boer back, of course. It was an important military base on a branch line from the main Ladysmith track that shot off northeast at a place called Glencoe, and therefore essential to defend successfully. There were nearly four thousand British soldiers and vast amounts of supplies at Dundee, but as an advanced post it was in a most vulnerable position, close against the Transvaal border.

With the fall of Newcastle, a small outpost on the main rail line to the west, Dundee was in danger of being sandwiched by the advance of another force from that direction, but even with that knowledge, they were caught unawares when the Boers occupied a hill overlooking their camp during darkness and hauled several field guns into position for dropping shells right into the town. Come morning, the British had their first lesson on the kind of people they were up against as, happily secure behind rocks on the hill, the Boers used their excellent marksmanship to pick off anyone who moved across the open ground in the camp below. Farmers of the veld they might be, but few men had straighter aim and better sight than those born to the necessity of hunting fleet-footed animals for meat.

Against this situation the British soldiers, weighted down by official military procedure and commanders who had no experience against sharp-shooting enemies, were ordered to capture the hill. In their inimitable way they obeyed the order without question, and began marching up the hill in straight lines with no cover or protection other than the supporting fire of those regiments behind them. The Boers, beautifully hidden behind rocks, mowed down the lines of advancing khaki-clad soldiers with no danger of being hit themselves. Picking off the officers with unerring aim, they soon created confusion among the ranks that pressed on up the hill over the bodies of their dead comrades.

To add to the confusion, British artillery that had been kept in reserve until almost too late, began shelling former Boer positions that had since been occupied by their own troops, and efforts to signal the gunners proved negative. As a result, both opponents retreated down their own side of the hill, and a ludicrous impasse was reached.

The battle at Dundee was to last three days during

which the hill was retaken, but at terrible cost in British lives. The Boers always retreated or surrendered rather than die, and their losses were negligible. The end was sad but, perhaps, inevitable. Although the taking of the hill could be called a victory for the British, it was an empty one. The Boers were still there in full force hidden in the *kopjes*, while the British numbers had been drastically reduced by casualties and the deplorable capture, due to bad leadership, of over two hundred cavalrymen who were separated from the main force and surrounded.

At the end of the third day, when a second request for reinforcements from Ladysmith was refused with an order to fall back on the garrison town, Dundee was surrendered quietly and secretly. The survivors marched out under cover of darkness, cutting the telegraph lines as they went. The following morning the Boers attacked the tented camp and found only doctors and wounded there. They lost no time in breaking open the storehouses and helping themselves to a bounty of supplies their enemies could ill-afford to lose.

Unaware of what was happening at Dundee, the tiny garrison at Landerdorp watched and waited for signs of an enemy force coming straight down the line from Newcastle. All morning Alex waited for outlying piquets to come galloping in with news of large bodies of horsemen approaching from the north, but it remained quiet. He handed over to Sergeant Major Turnbull just before afternoon and went squelching back to his quarters for some lunch.

During the afternoon the rain ceased, and they increased their vigilance as the sun baked the mud into a crust and set them all sweating. Alex sat by the window with his jacket unfastened at the neck and his Sam Browne belt lying on a chair beside him, complete with sword and pistol in its holster. The weapons of war, he thought, as he looked at them. He had never killed a man and wondered how he would feel when the time came. Did every soldier dread being a coward when put to the test? It was easier for rankers—they were always surrounded by their fellows—but an officer was out there all alone with the world looking on to condemn his actions.

He moved uneasily on his chair. Some men he knew were thirsting for action. They came from families with a long record of gallant service; they had been brought up to the sound of sabers rattling and bugle calls that stirred the

blood. They would rush forward without a thought, reck-
less with courage and conviction. With him it was different.
He was an unwilling soldier, aloof from traditions and immune to the call to arms that thrilled his fellows. There was
no hatred of the Boer people within him; each enemy
would be a man with a wife, children, and a plot of land to
defend. How could he bring to an end the life of such a
man?

Deep inside him another reason lurked. In vain he tried
to ignore it. As he gazed out at the steam rising in the
empty street, at the vapor lifting from the tin roofs of
shacks, at the track winding up to Devil's Leap, he had to
acknowledge that he would look at each enemy face and
think of Hetta. Somewhere there was a man who was her
brother. Suppose it should be he who was run through by
the sword on that chair! What if a bullet from his own
pistol should be the cause of a dark-haired girl crying with
grief somewhere out there on the veld? His mind ran on.
There would be a girl, a woman, a child thrown into
spasms of sorrow every time he killed an enemy. There
would be a farm without a man to run it; another undying
fount of hatred against the British.

He turned and stared at the store where he had fought so
hard not to surrender a shopping basket to a girl struggling
with her own conscience. What of his own possible death?
So far, he had done very little good with his life. Would it
matter if it ended shortly? Perhaps he had half died standing on Westminster Bridge that day. Certainly, after that he
had fought life with heavy weapons—or had it been his
father he had fought? He considered the problem for several minutes and reached no answer. It didn't matter. His
father had won.

He shook himself mentally. It was not like him to be so
damned fanciful. It persisted, however. His father would
regret his death only because he could not fulfill the legacy
Miles had left him. To die in action might gain the old
man's approval in some small measure, at last, and if he
died saving another man's life it might almost raise him to
his brother's level. A smile twisted his mouth. If he *were*
killed it was sure to be in some ignominious way—kicked
on the skull by a fright-maddened horse, perhaps.

His expression grew more sour. His fellow officers would
hardly raise a memorial to his memory—rotters were not
commemorated in stone nor missed at the mess table.

There was Judith Burley, of course. She would grieve no end . . . over the fact that she was not entitled to all his worldly goods as his widow. His eyes narrowed as a picture of her pure fair beauty blotted out the tin huts and mud road. She could have any man she chose—was probably weighing them all up right now back in England. He still could not understand why she had gone to all that trouble to pursue him out here, unless she hoped to get him in front of the army chaplain. Surely he was not that much of a matrimonial prize! There were wealthier men by the score even in his own regiment.

He mused on. Aunt Pan might shed a tear or two; Aunt Alicia would shed many, all for dramatic effect and self-indulgent emotion.

The vista of Landerdorp came back again with the onset of pain. What of Hetta? She had loved him once. If she did not now hate him; if she did not think him a liar and philanderer; if she could think of him as himself and not an enemy, would she feel sadness at his going? Maybe, but she would never know of it. He felt a sweat break out over his body. There must be someone who would grieve for him!

*"Boo!"* said a voice right in his ear, and Guy Cuthbertson laughed when Alex jerked involuntarily and flung out a hand toward the belt on the chair. "Caught you napping then, old boy," he said heartily. "Thank your lucky stars I'm not a Dutchman or you would have had your throat slit by now."

Alex's heart was thumping as he voiced his anger. "By God, I suppose you'll grow up one day, Guy."

"If I do not die a gallant death on the battlefield," was the smooth answer. "You look upset, old fellow. Must learn to be more alert, you know."

"Cut it," he said tautly. "Your humor can be a little wearing."

"Sorry . . . sorry," Guy said, his hands in the air. "I forgot you had a wench in the enemy's camp."

Alex was on his feet instantly and had the other man by the neck of his tunic. "If you don't know when to keep quiet I shall soon teach you, you bastard."

Looking shaken, Guy apologized with great speed, straightening his crumpled tunic self-consciously when Alex let him go. He cleared his throat noisily. "Got carried away, you know," he said by way of explanation. "Actually, I came to ask you to drink a sundowner with me. It looks as if the attack is off for today. It'll be dusk in half an hour, and no one in his right mind launches out against the enemy at that time of the day. Early hours of the morning is the correct military procedure, you know," he added attempting a faint smile. "Well, what about that drink?"

Alex stood stiffly, not yet out of his sudden anger, but Guy stood his ground and gradually the anger petered out into a mood of resignation. "Yes . . . all right," Alex said quietly.

They went to their tiny mess and were soon deep in a discussion of polo. The war was forgotten. It had not reached them yet.

They came just before dawn, as Guy predicted, but took the small force at Landerdorp by complete surprise. With piquets and guards reinforced in the northern facing heights, those not on duty were given orders to sleep by their rifles, fully dressed.

Alex lay on his bed with his boots beside it and the sword belt hooked over a chair back. Too restless to sleep, he spent half the night listening for the sound of piquets galloping in, or distant shots to warn of the enemy's approach, but all seemed peculiarly quiet. He dozed, but not for long, and was just deciding to take off his tunic in the hope of relaxing enough to sleep soundly when his heart leaped into quickness brought on by the unmistakable rattle of musketry outside in the street.

Instinctively, and with a drying throat, he rolled to his feet, reaching for the Sam Browne and clipping it around his waist as he poked his feet into his boots with more haste than success. Hopping to steady himself while he tugged them on, his brain worked feverishly. The firing sounded as if it were coming from the south—up the line from Ladysmith. They must have circled the small depot and come in from that direction, knowing the concentration of defense would be to the north where they were known to be advancing. That meant they must have been in the hills all night!

Snatching up his pith helmet he ran out into the street. There was nothing in his mind at that moment but anger that no one had thought of such a maneuver. Captain Beamish and the other two commanders at Landerdorp—including Guy Cuthbertson—had assumed the Boers, having captured the railway at Newcastle, would follow it down during their advance. It was a standard tactic when crossing unknown and featureless country. A railway track was the best map in the world to the next town, and insured easy access for supplies and reinforcements.

*"Stupid bloody fools!"* Alex swore to himself, and included himself in the epithet. This enemy had no need to follow a railway in country they knew like the backs of their hands—and their supplies were dotted all over the veld in the farms of their brethren.

A slight frost had stiffened the mud enough to make it traversable as he ran to the huts that accommodated his men. The darkness was rapidly fading and heightened the drama being played out in a gray mist. Now that he was in the open, the firing seemed all around him, designed, he realized, to throw the defenders into total confusion.

It was succeeding. From the buildings nearby came the shouts of N.C.O.s as they did their best to organize the men, their tense voices several tones higher than usual.

As he rounded the corner by the stables Alex nearly ran headlong into a charge of horses as the cavalry rushed out shouting and yelling their normal blood-curdling battle tactics, as if they were already fighting the enemy. Lights from the stables flooded out into the street, illuminating the scene and making it appear completely unreal. The horses remaining in the stable neighed nervously, not liking the continued captivity when their companions were racing like the wind.

Nearing the men's quarters, Alex increased his pace. Khaki-clad men were tumbling onto the street, still scrambling into their equipment; Sergeant Turnbull was lashing them with his tongue.

"Get them down to the rail yard double quick," cried Alex. "The stores are vital."

As he spoke there was a whizzing noise he knew very well, followed by several more. Sergeant Turnbull dropped to the ground and lay motionless, and the men froze into a tableau of shock as they looked at him.

"Fall in these men," Alex ordered a corporal who stood as transfixed as they. His voice was hoarse, honed by his own stunned witnessing of instant death. "Take them down at the double. Move, man . . . *move!*"

He ran on, confident he would be obeyed, his brain pounding with the implication of all he saw. The Boers were closer than he imagined. The light piquets on the south boundary must have been surprised and killed, or taken prisoner. How strong a force was it? Could they be driven back now they had come so far?

The rail yard was even in worse confusion. Lieutenant March was desperately forming his guard into a defensive line that would cover the approach to the station and store-sheds. He did no more than nod when Alex shouted that his men were on their way. Their arrival coincided with that of Captain Beamish who, in typical style, had stopped to collect his horse. The Commander immediately broke up his subaltern's defenses and ordered Clarkson March and Alex to take their men in opposite directions along the line.

"Surely it would be better to concentrate our strength and defend the stores," Alex protested.

"Our purpose is to prevent them getting this far," snapped the captain. "Get going."

Much against his better judgment, Alex signaled his men to follow him up the line as far as the signal box where they would set up their defenses. The rattle of rifle fire seemed to have decreased, but there was still shouting and confusion in the yard.

They moved silently, a single file of wide-eyed, unbelieving men. Occasionally, a stone rattled beneath their boots as they made their cautious way beside the railway track out into the open veld, rifles at the ready. Alex drew his sword. He found his heart pounding his chest and his knees growing weak as they neared the signal box. Dawn was lifting and he swallowed nervously as he imagined shapes that were not there. The green grass was discernible against the gray now, and it was only a moment later that he thought he could make out the base of the signal box.

In the act of turning to indicate extra caution to his men, a sharp stab of alarm robbed him of breath and brought him to a frozen standstill. As from the very earth itself, there rose up along the right side of the cutting a long line of men. They were bearded, dressed in drab coats and breeches, with slouch hats, and each had a rifle pointing at them.

"Sir . . . look."

Alex turned to find another line to his left. There must have been over a hundred and fifty, all told—odds of five to one against them. If they fired there would not be an Englishman alive after the first volley.

A silent confrontation began and lasted in deadly pantomime until Alex was certain they were not all to be slaughtered.

"What do we do, sir?" the corporal asked from the side of his mouth, not daring to move more than a muscle.

Alex was away on a lake somewhere with a gnarled hand beckoning to him from the black nightmare of water, and he returned with the memory half holding him.

"We surrender, corporal," he said expressionlessly, and with slow movements, reversed his sword, offering the hilt in the direction of the Boers. One by one the soldiers let their rifles drop, then watched with set faces as the bearded men came forward.

The only place large enough to keep so many prisoners in a hamlet like Landerdorp was the stockyard. The officers were separated from the men by imprisonment in the barred area reserved for the fully grown and aggressive bulls. It had appeared to amuse the Boers—some of whom the British soldiers recognized as former tradesmen or visiting farmers—for they laughed and exchanged guttural comments as the officers were waved into the cage with a flourish of slouch hats.

Captain Beamish had been killed making a foolhardy solo charge at a group of Boers looting the storesheds, and Guy Cuthbertson had a hand wound. Apart from Sergeant Turnbull and a rifleman who had died making a gallant effort to close the yard gates before the advancing enemy, there were only four slightly wounded prisoners. The remainder of the garrison were in the stockyard, unblemished, and half of them had not fired a shot.

The day grew hot and the afternoon was sweltering. During that time others were brought in to join their fellow prisoners. The northern pickets, not knowing Landerdorp had already been taken, fought bravely, then fell back straight into the arms of waiting Boer forces. When evening fell several soldiers were taken under guard to prepare a meal, and it was served in tin canteens to officers and soldiers alike, a spoon being the only implement with which to eat it.

Alex tasted none of it. The officers were all the same—silent and separate in their thoughts—men who had been broken by the events of a mere dawn hour. But none was as near utter despair as Alex.

All day he stood leaning against the iron rails, looking out toward Devil's Leap. The whole of his life tormented him. God alone knew why He had let Miles save a small eight-year-old boy before taking him into His care. If one had to be lost why had it been Miles? His father had said more than once. Why had he been left with an impossible legacy? He had tried—dear God he had tried—but he was a failure at being Miles's successor. And when he had broken out in defiance, he had failed again. How well he remembered that afternoon in his father's study when he was presented with the ultimatum. The army and marriage, or bankruptcy and the curse of a vengeful parent. He might have accepted the discipline of the army if he could have married a girl he loved. Alison had been cast out of his life and a cool virtuous lady of suitable birth had been thrust at him instead.

Even Judith Burley might have been tolerable if he could have courted her. No man could remain immune to her beauty, and there had been times when he had dreamed up ways of breaking her barriers of purity—had planned to force her surrender in his arms—but the excitement went out of such schemes when he remembered why she had jumped at the prospect of their marriage. A girl who was willing to take a man she hardly knew in return for money and position was probably unseduceable.

His hands gripped the rails as a vision of Hetta's golden-skinned face pushed him deeper under the weight of his failures. He loved her; he had found a new life and confidence in the reflection of her loving warmth. For eight weeks he had been a man freed from shackles; a man infinitely worth saving from a watery grave. He had been full of giving and she had been eager to receive from him, and give in return. At last, at long, long last, there had been someone who wanted Alex Russell, not a copy of Miles, or a bank balance.

They had snatched her away from him: Judith, the Colonel, and his father's demand for penance, but he had returned to Landerdorp full of determination. He would resign from the regiment, take a job on the railways until he had earned enough to marry Hetta. He would settle in South Africa . . . and to hell with his father and England!

His head bowed under a fresh spasm of hopelessness until his forehead rested against the hands gripping the rails. He had been far too late! The demons of greed and intolerance had risen suddenly and snatched her out of his reach once more—too far for him ever to get her back, too far for him ever to remove the pain that had been on her face as he had walked away.

For a long while he stood riding out the torture of memory before present recollection came thundering in. Only yesterday he had considered the implications of impending battle, but none had been anywhere near the truth. The Downshires were a proud regiment and, in some surprising and inexplicable way, he had also felt that pride as he tumbled from his bed that morning. Now, a bare two weeks after the start of the war, he was a prisoner. He had not fought a desperate battle before being taken. His body was completely unscathed; his uniform neat and unsullied by mud or the sweat of endeavor. The sword he had offered them was a virgin weapon; the pistol had not fired a single shot.

His grip on the rails tightened painfully as he admitted to himself there had been a moment out there on the railway line when the voice of the Devil had whispered to him that he needed only to run at the enemy to end it all. He was a born loser; what was the point of fighting for life any longer?

Putting back his head with a soft groan he gradually returned to sane thought, and it was then he became aware of a man leaning against the wooden stockade several yards away watching him intently. He was plainly the leader of the commando of Boers for he wore something approaching a uniform, but he wore it with a farmer's soft hat and his black hair, like his beard, flowed freely. Light green eyes watched him with fierce contempt and, for some unaccountable reason, Alex felt that glare of hatred was meant, not for the others, but for him alone.

Hetta nearly dropped the bread she was taking from the oven in her joy at hearing Franz's voice shouting for Johnny. Franz and Piet had been away for over a month—four weeks of worry with no way of knowing what was happening or if they would ever return. She rushed out to greet them and was given a one-armed hug by her brother, who looked pale and tense.

"God has been with us," he assured her.

"God is always with us," Piet added harshly. "He showed us the time to rise up against our enemies, and the time was exactly right." His hand fell on Hetta's shoulder with a heavy grip that dug into her flesh. "They are run-

ning from us. They flee in disorder, or beg for mercy." He
laughed and it had an exultant ring to it.

"It is over?" Hetta asked incredulously of her brother,
who gave a weary smile and shook his head.

"Landerdorp is ours," Piet told her. "We took it four
days ago."

"When was it not ours?" It was all beyond Hetta's comprehension—all too far away from the farm for there to be
any feeling of triumph over his words. All she knew was
that she had missed Franz more than she had thought possible. He sagged with weariness—something that alarmed
her. He was as strong as an ox and worked unceasingly on
the farm without showing more than the usual slow easing
of muscles at the end of a hard day. What had happened to
reduce him to a man with hollowed eyes and a dying fire
within his frame?

She took his arm. "Come, I have supper enough for two
more. Tonight we have meat in plenty." She gave a quick
nod. "*Ja*, I went out with the rifle this morning."

He allowed her to coax him into the house even though
his eyes were scanning the distant crops and grazing cattle.
"Does it go well?" he asked anxiously.

"It goes very well," she assured him, but said nothing of
how hard life was now there was only a young woman and
an old man to do everything, nothing of the maggot that
was eating the maize crop on the south corner, and nothing
of the few head of cattle that had been milked from the
herd by native thieves who knew through their own inexplicable intelligence which farms were now without a master.

Oupa had heard the voices and came stumping in from
the barn where a cow was struggling to give birth to twin
calves that would not let themselves be born. He wasted little
time in greetings. No one would guess from his expression
that he was thankful to see the two men. There was an immediate crisis on hand, and he was a farmer first and fore-
most. Hetta noticed with a little tug at her stomach how the
life flowed back into Franz as he took off his coat and laid
aside his rifle with quick and gentle hands, to follow Oupa
into the barn. Her two men went out together, bonded by
love of the land, and it was like it had always been before.
She turned from the doorway and went to her oven again.
Piet was completely forgotten until he said, "That is all he
thinks about—a beast and its spawn."

There was contempt in his tone, and it spoiled her pres-

ent happiness of her brother's return. The loaves were hot
and burned her fingers, the small tingling shock added heat
to her words.

"He is a farmer. The loss of three animals would be a
sorrow to him." Turning with the cloth in her hands, and
the heat of the fire blooming in her cheeks she went on, "It
has not been easy for those left on the farms. The tribes
have been stealing cattle in the darkness, and many young
plants have been washed out of the earth by the rains. We
have not eaten meat for two weeks. You are lucky to come
today when I have taken out a gun."

He leaned back half sitting on the table. "The old man is
here for that. Many women are alone on their farms. They
do not complain."

"Have you spoken with them all?" she cried. "Oupa has
age sitting upon him more and more. He says the buck are
quicker, but it is he who is slower. There is much to do at
this time of the year. A farm needs someone young and
strong."

Slowly he studied her from head to foot in a way that
told her of hidden thoughts within him. "You are young
and strong. You have a fine body—the body of a true Boer
woman."

She turned back to her loaves, but he came up behind
her and took her shoulders in his hands.

"The body of my promised woman," he breathed in her
ear, and his hands slid beneath her arm to wander slowly
and comprehensively over her breasts and flat stomach; his
right leg moved to press against her thigh.

She stood breathless and perfectly still, completely un-
warned against the deep drenching anguish the traveling
fingers unlocked within her. It had been there for a long time
waiting to be released—ever since a day in June when the
sweet heady overture had been played by gentle and loving
fingers. Since that day she had been unable to forget the
full symphony that was to come, and the elusive but sono-
rous rhythm had tormented her continuously.

Now, it rose above her consciousness to whirl her into a
throbbing limbo. She closed her eyes, the better to lose herself in this newly discovered music of womanhood, and
when he began opening the buttons of her brown dress she
could not help giving a shiver of eagerness as she leaned
back against him.

"Riding the veld gives me a great need for a woman,"

said the voice in her ear. "You are ripe for entering a man's bed. I have seen it for some time. You have a fire within you that many a woman never finds. There is that in your eyes that tells a man he may demand whatever he will, and still receive more."

His hand on her bare skin was rough. She gasped with the shock of a stinging pain as he gripped the tip of her breast with iron fingers. Her eyes flew open and the symphony died, ruined by the insensitivity of the conductor. As a crashing discord breaks the spell of a listening audience, so her body was suddenly revulsed by its own quivering subjugation, and she spun around, drawing away from him against the arched wall of the recess that housed the iron range.

He leaned upon an arm outstretched against the wall and studied the curves of her breasts. She made no attempt to draw her dress together across the under-bodice, loath to give up the erotic freedom she had glimpsed, yet crying out against him who had given it.

"*Ja*, you have much to give," he said again. "It is there in the way you walk and move. You are a proud woman, Hetta, and that is a challenge. One day soon you will be mine in the eyes of God, but for now you must serve me in a different way—serve me and our cause." He walked back to the table, caught up in another passion, and she slowly fastened her dress with shaking fingers, the ache inside her intensified.

The following morning found her riding the old black horse toward Landerdorp. She had not been there for two months, not since the Dutch traders moved out to join the farmers with all their supplies, and the nearer she drew the more reluctant was her progress toward the scene of her sweetest and bitterest memories.

It was a long ride, made agonizing by the war she was waging with herself. All night she had lain with prayers on her lips, but the dawn had not brought the heart's ease for which she hoped. A year ago her path had been simple and lined with contentment. She had had the farm where her duties were clear-cut; Oupa and Franz as beloved companions; a man of her own with a new farm, when the time came. Everything had changed. The farm had become a taskmaster that was never satisfied; Franz was separated from them; and Piet had become a man she did not know with a flame burning him so fiercely he was consumed by it.

She gripped the reins to give vent to the rush of heat such thoughts brought her. When she had arisen to light the range this morning, and draw water from the well, she saw Piet's departure from the hut of the native servant girl. He had, indeed, great need of a woman, she realized. But it did not help her understand her own response to know where he had gone after caressing her as he had.

She might tell herself it had been the sudden arrival of a strong young man straight from danger, but in her inner soul she knew the searing delight of his hands upon her had been due to her yearning for another day, another passion. It made her ashamed, yet the shame seemed to be for the touch of the man who had been there rather than for the dreams of the one who had not.

As she neared Devil's Leap the truth rose above subterfuge and increased the turmoil that had lived inside her since the day Alex went off with his pale fiancée. Yesterday her body had responded to something he had lit inside her out here in this very spot. She drew in her breath. Did God send temptation in such crushing form to every woman? Did He test His suppliants so severely every time? And did He always make the penance so strict and long-lasting?

To compensate for her sin she had worked doubly hard, had heeded Oupa's every word, had baked bread and dried meat for the men who would come to the farm for food and rest during the fighting, as Boer women were doing in farmsteads dotted all over South Africa. It was because she had sinned that she was doing this today, although she felt it was wrong.

Telling herself she was no judge of right and wrong, she rode beneath Devil's Leap, remembering Alex's assurance that there would be no war. Now that it was happening, no one appeared to think it was wrong. What she was about to do must be regarded in the same light, she told herself, and urged her horse forward in order to get it over quickly.

The first sight of the rail yard dismayed her. The huge metal engines were there, but standing neglected with none of the hissing steam flying from around the wheels and little chimney on top; the large sheds stood open and were busy with Boer men; the rails criss-crossed over dusty ground; the big circular plate that turned engines around flung back a reflected glare from the blazing sun; but her sensitive soul cried out against the mass of khaki-clad men filling the cattle enclosures. There was something throat-catching about the soldiers who stood listlessly beneath the growing heat of the morning sun, or sat beneath the tin roofs sunk in thought. Used to seeing them walking smartly about the street, or riding their huge horses with an erect-ness born of pride, it brought home the humility of defeat and the actuality of the war to a girl from a distant farm who had heard words but no gunfire.

Instinctively drawing rein at the large wooden gates, she slid from the saddle and tied her horse to a post. At that point, she found she could go no further, even though she spotted other women further along doing what Piet had sent her to do, and showing no reluctance. Swallowing hard she told herself these dejected men were the enemy, but still she held back. It was not in her nature to be cruel. How could she further torment men who were already beaten, by taking away any hope they might still have?

It was then that she caught sight of a small group of officers separated from the rest in the bull cage and recog-nized the handsome face. She would know that face any-where, the face that had looked at her with insolent famil-iarity as he kept holding the reins of her ox wagon just out of reach.

It gave her courage to go forward. He saw her and straightened instinctively, pulling his tunic into smarter lines. She smiled, trying to ignore the thick bandage around his hand.

"Good morning," she said in her best English and caught the attention of them all immediately. "It is not of-ten we see so many of you gentlemen together . . . and in such a place."

"I see you have remembered your English," the hand-some one said caustically. "Like all your sisters, you are happy to talk to us now that you are so well protected." He rested a hand on the bar.

It was harder than she thought, but she fought to keep smiling. "You will be moving to Pretoria soon. The railway is in our hands from the border to . . . to . . ." Her words died and the smile swam on a tide of pain as she caught sight of the chestnut hair of a man in the corner who was looking at her with the stillness of shock.

It was all there for her to see—the humiliation and despair—just as it had been the moment before he walked away from her, only this time it was etched deeper into the lines of his face and right at the back of his eyes. All Piet's careful instructions left her mind as she realized why he had sent her here. *Oh no . . . no,* she cried deep inside her as her eyes held his, and the other officers blurred into a shadow of khaki.

Slowly, feeling her way like a blind person, she drew nearer him as the pain of the meeting grew. Why was she doing this when she should walk away, as he had done? They were face to face with the bars between them. There were no words as each searched the other's face. The moment of their parting still hung between them in a breathless barrier of anguish and love defeated.

She saw the dark shadow on his chin, and the creased tunic worn bare of weapons. It made his loss of pride more acute, somehow. She knew now why he had called her questions too simple. It was not merely a matter of who owned a veld farm. It was pride and bitterness; deep hatred and distrust; greed and intolerance. It had been well within his understanding, but beyond hers. She saw it all now and knew she was part of what he was suffering at that moment. The cold truth beat against her with wounding blows. *Forgive me,* he had said that day, and God knew she had not . . . until now.

His hands gripped the rails as if they were the one steady thing in the world, and she knew the ghosts of his past had returned to him. If she failed him, he would be lost. Hardly knowing what she was doing, her hand moved slowly until it gripped the rail beside his.

"You came back," she whispered. "Why?"

For a long moment she believed he would not find the words to answer for his lips moved without any sound. At last he said with difficulty, "Because I could never be your enemy. I told you that."

Her hand moved fractionally closer to his, and soon they were touching each other. Immediately the contact set them both alight so that their fingers curled tightly intertwined through the heavy bars.

"But I have to be yours," she said brokenly. "Your army is defeated and trapped in Ladysmith under siege. I was sent to tell you."

He fought against the blow by taking a long inward

breath, then letting it out slowly. "Who . . . who sent you?"

With everything within her crying out against the words she forced herself to say, "My people . . . the Boers . . . your enemies."

# PART TWO

# CHAPTER ELEVEN

Judith watched the train get up steam and nose its way from the little station at Ladysmith, along the line that soon broke out into open veld. It was a peculiarly stirring moment—one she felt certain would remain with her the rest of her life—and the now empty track before the platform emphasized the drama of the departure.

She stood in the shade thrown by the station roof and watched the long snake of carriages as they curled away from Ladysmith on their slow journey to Intombi, a few miles down the track to the south. The clack and rumble of wheels, the hiss of steam, the slamming doors and urgent voices were gone now, leaving behind a sweet listening silence that was heavy with finality.

The slight movement of air caused by the train's departure died, there was only slumbering bee-buzzing heat that settled everywhere with relentless strength and brought dampness back to Judith's forehead. She absently pushed up her thick hair as she continued watching the train, now well out into the open, a perfect target for the Boer guns.

Narrowing her eyes against the sun she cast them over the horseshoe of hills around the besieged town. They were up there, in force, yet out of sight. It looked so peaceful and innocent, yet for the past two days, puffs of smoke all along the skyline had heralded the whine of shells that had rained on the town with deadly intent. Today there was an armistice, by arrangement with General Joubert, while all the sick and wounded along with any civilians who wished were installed in the train destined for a neutral camp outside the town. Tomorrow the bombardment would begin again.

"You should have gone with them," said a voice behind her. "I wish I could have persuaded you to go."

She turned with a smile to the young officer. "You would have done better to use your persuasive powers on the Boers, Neil. What opinion would you hold of a girl who would abandon an elderly lady under such circumstances?"

His bosom swelled. "Nothing would alter the opinion I have held of you since the day we met—except, perhaps, the discovery that you are very courageous."

"Nonsense," she replied softly, starting to move off the platform toward the street. "If you are referring to the fact that I did not take advantage of the opportunity to leave on that train, you must also take into account a great number of women—some with children—who have also remained in Ladysmith because they could not bear to leave someone they loved."

Neil fell into step beside her as they left the shade of the station and began walking up the dusty street. "But they have taken up daytime residence in the holes their husbands have dug for them in the river bank. You have remained beside your aunt in imminent danger from the shells."

"I have little choice," she pointed out. "Aunt Pan cannot possibly be moved, especially to lie in an earth-lined hole during daylight hours."

She glanced up at him as they walked—a slender man with a golden tan on his well-bred face with its clipped moustache. He was not wearing the distinctive rifle-green of his father's day, but he was still every inch a general's son in the now familiar khaki with only a green-and-black flash on the side on his sun helmet to distinguish him as an officer of the Downshires.

"You are exposed to all kinds of danger, Neil—all day and night. Isn't that even more courageous?"

He smiled—always a gentle attraction to add to his overall appeal. "Not in the least. I am a soldier doing my normal duty."

She looked away from him and up ahead at the street that now had several large holes in it. Men were busily filling them in during the armistice.

"Alex would say you were being frightfully noble in the jolly old traditions of the regiment," she said slowly.

There was hesitation from her companion, then he replied, "Yes, I suppose he would . . . although captivity might alter his outlook somewhat."

She looked at him quickly. "Do you know for certain yet?"

He shook his head. "The Boers have been asked for a list

of all their prisoners, and the names of any casualties in the engagement. Until they decide to send in a message, we can get no reliable information." He returned the salute of a passing rifleman. "Native messengers have come in with reports so widely variant we can't really believe any of them." He put his hand beneath her elbow to guide her around a pile of debris caused by one of the previous day's shells. "We know some of the native runners have been sent by the Boers with false information to mislead and depress us."

She turned with a shocked expression. "That is terrible! We are speaking of men's lives."

He smiled again at her concern. "It's not 'playing the game,' as we know it—but such ruses are used only by individual commanders of small groups. The senior men and generals like Joubert stick much more rigidly to the accepted codes of warfare. Don't worry, Judith, in time we shall be given accurate details of the surrender of Landerdorp."

Silence fell between them, as it always did when Alex had been mentioned, and Judith drifted away on a tide of private thoughts. The past ten days had been a bizarre nightmare. No sooner had she understood her aunt's illness than war had been declared, and her life had become one of witness to frightening events beyond anything she could ever have imagined.

In an appallingly short time it had been plain the British troops were no match for the civilian farmers. In their ordinary drab clothes that merged so well with the colors of the veld, they rode across country they knew intimately and, using the cover of rocks, fired individually and with deadly accuracy upon the concentrated ranks of British soldiers who followed the rules of battle with rigid faithfulness. The Dutch marksmen picked off the officers first, then relied on the confusion of leaderless troops to do the rest. The tactic worked without fail.

The Boers had swept into Natal like a plague—deadly but unseen—and boasted that they would be in Durban by Christmas. Once that great port had been lost the British would have no way of bringing in supplies and reinforcements, other than Cape Town, and with Natal commanded by the Boers, their countrymen in Cape Colony would take arms against their British rulers in support of the cause.

Durban had to be protected at all costs; reinforcements

by the thousand were on their way. With those two facts
before him, Sir George White, commander of Ladysmith
garrison, decided to withdraw all his outpost troops to the
town and make his stand there.

As Judith progressed along the street she remembered
vividly looking from her window early one morning to find
the wide red dustway filled with marching men, ox wagons
laden with equipment, mule carts full of ammunition, gun
limbers, ambulances, and boxes marked with a red cross,
Lancers and Hussars on their splendid horses, remounts
roped in long lines, pack ponies, Indian stretcher bearers
and grooms, and the inevitable long tail of camp followers.
The garrison was moving in from Tin Town, leaving the
hutted barracks deserted on the exposed plain at the foot of
the Boer-held hills, their movement raising a choking red
dust that penetrated the bungalows lining the street, laying
a coating over furniture and floors.

Fear for Alex's safety had sent Judith through the town
during the heat of day in the hope of seeing an officer of
the Downshires who could give her news but she had found
only pandemonium—orders, counterorders, bellows, brays,
curses, marching boots, short tempers, clash of personalities, and the inevitable jam of vehicles. Against this had
been the scramble for exodus on the last train going south,
a crowd of frightened residents with all the belongings they
could carry, trying to force their way to the station against
the stream of military.

Looking back, she realized her fear was a purely antici-
patory emotion. Those chilling preparations for meeting the
enemy had filled her with a dread that froze her senses for
several days, yet once the Boers were there on the threshold and the imagined danger became real, she had found a
calmness unhoped for. A sense of inevitability governed her
now. She had lost Alex despite her love for him; Aunt Pan
had been struck down right on the eve of war. That Providence had decided to take a hand in her life Judith did not
doubt. It was useless to make her own plans any longer.
Fear left her—even when the shells whined overhead and
thumped into the ground with deadly regularity. Caring for
her aunt gave her enough occupation, and thoughts of Alex
overrode thoughts of her own safety.

She wondered if he would feel anxiety if he knew her
true whereabouts. She was sure he imagined her to be
safely back in England long ago. Half of her wished he

could suffer the knowledge of her danger, and the other half feared he would not even care. If he were really still alive.

A new surge of pain made her miss her step, and Neil's hand was at her elbow immediately. She looked up and saw that he had been watching her.

"You really shouldn't come out in this heat," he chided. "Caring for Mrs. Davenport must be exhausting enough in itself."

"Yes . . . but I felt I should offer my help with the children this morning. They don't understand why they have to leave their papa—especially when some of their friends are staying. It's a terrible thing when war is brought to the feet of children."

"I couldn't agree more, and I have no respect for the men who have allowed their families to remain in Ladysmith. In their shoes, I would on no account expose them to such danger."

Judith slowed her steps as they approached the bungalow she now rented for herself and her aunt. "Neil, you are the most conventional person I know, and I understand your sentiments . . . but have you considered things from the women's viewpoint? I know if it were I who had to choose between safety and possible widowhood, as against sharing danger with the one I loved until the end, there would be no hesitation."

They stopped at the gate and faced each other. "War is something from which women and children should be protected, and it is up to their menfolk to see that they are."

"So you would order your wife away in such a situation, despite her tears and pleas to be allowed to remain with you?" she teased gently.

"Most definitely."

She studied his face with a smile flitting across her mouth. "How well Alex summed you up." He flushed, and she went on, hastily, "It was very complimentary, I assure you. He said men like you were the backbone of England."

Neil gave a grunt of disparagement. "Such words from a man like Alex are not meant as a compliment, Judith."

Remembering the context in which they had been said, her own color came up and, to cover it, she said, "Will you come in for tea? Aunt Pan will be delighted to see you."

"I should get back . . . but I daresay it will be all right to take another half hour over the journey." He laughed self-consciously. "Can't let Mrs. Davenport down, can I?"

Whatever excuse he used to salve his conscience, he looked profoundly guilty when Colonel Rawlings–Turner arrived and caught him chatting to the two ladies over teacups.

"Good morning, sir," he began, rising to his feet. "I was just . . ."

"Leaving?" the colonel queried lightly. "That's all right, Mr. Forrester. I will excuse you."

There was no alternative but to go, and Judith gave the young man an understanding smile as he made his farewells. Then, she turned to the colonel.

"Mr. Forrester was here at my invitation. My aunt welcomes company to liven the hot weary hours . . . and he has been of such great service to us during this very worrying time."

Rawlings–Turner nodded. "Yes, an excellent young fellow, I agree." He looked pointedly at the tray. "Did I interrupt your morning refreshment?"

"Ring for another cup for the colonel, dear," Mrs. Davenport said. Her voice had lost its ring of determination. "I had flattered myself that his call was prompted by solicitude, but I see now it is because we serve the best tea of anyone left in town."

Judith rang the bell.

"Now, ma'am," the colonel said, "you know that is not so. In fact, I have made it abundantly clear that you should have left on that train this morning."

"Yes, my dear man, but I am not one of your subordinates who has to obey your every command."

"Oh, come," he protested. "That is a little strong."

"Poor Mr. Forrester had not even finished his biscuit," she continued blithely. "When he is liable to face the guns of the enemy at any moment, surely a few minutes spent in the pleasant civilities of life are excusable. Is it not up to those ladies who remain to provide comfort and a reminder of gentility in the harshness of war to those gallantly defending the town?"

"No, ma'am," he told her firmly. "Ladies should be out of such a situation completely. We have quite enough to worry us, as it is."

The cup and saucer were brought, and Judith used the diversion to intervene. "Mr. Forrester is of the same opinion, colonel," she told him as she handed him the tea, "but we are in the unhappy position of having no choice. If the doctor forbids moving my aunt at this stage, we are obliged to trust in the protection of the military."

He cleared his throat noisily. "Yes . . . er . . . as to that, I cannot help feeling the doctor is a little too susceptible to persuasion at times."

Mrs. Davenport raised her eyebrows delicately. "My dear sir, you are not suggesting that I am upon this couch from choice, I trust?"

"No, no . . . dear lady . . . I would certainly suggest no such thing," the colonel put in. "It was merely . . ."

"Will you have a biscuit, colonel?" Judith asked, taking pity on him.

"Er . . . no . . . *yes*," he amended. "Thank you, Miss Burley." He looked relieved and bit into the biscuit as if giving vent to his feelings. "Nice, these," he blustered, studying the gingersnap. "One of my favorites."

"It was the last packet in the store. Mr. Avignon was expecting supplies at anytime. I suppose they will not reach him now."

"Oh, yes. It shouldn't be too long before we are back to normal again. There's a relief column marching up under the command of General Buller, which must get here within the week. He's a clever and experienced soldier who will soon put an end to all this."

"Within the week?" questioned Mrs. Davenport. "Why are you making such a fuss over our staying here? From the way you spoke, I imagined you anticipated a long siege."

Judith jumped in before he could reply to such provocation. "Those in England will be glad to hear it. I'm sure my own mama is in a state of extreme anxiety over our predicament. I managed to get a letter out on the last train, but it could not be very reassuring."

He sipped his tea. "Pity. We are able to send out urgent messages by native runners at night, but cannot really put any dependence on their reaching their destination. Unreliable fellows at the best of times. Personal letters, I am afraid, will have to wait until Buller gets here." He lowered his cup and saucer onto the table and looked up under thick brows. "One thing that did come in today will interest you both. Isn't young Russell some kind of relative, besides being . . ." he realized his error and mumbled instead, ". . . a friend of the family?"

"You have the official list of prisoners?" Judith asked breathlessly.

"Yes. The Boers sent it in to us this morning. His name is on it. There was no mention of any wounds."

"Thank heaven," she murmured wanting immediately to be alone in her relief.

"They are being transferred to Pretoria today, where camps have been prepared. The message expresses an apology for the conditions in which they were kept at Landerdorp and makes the rather caustic comment that they had not expected to capture so many in a small outpost."

The finer points of the Boer message did not bother Judith. She was too grateful. But when the colonel had taken his leave the happy state did not remain with her long.

"You were rather hard on the poor colonel," she said to her aunt.

"Nonsense! That man is well able to withstand any comments I might make to his detriment, and if he believes I am taken in by what he says he is a great deal more foolish than I take him for."

Judith went to sit on the footstool beside the velvet couch where Mrs. Davenport spent her days. She was recovering slowly—more slowly than Judith had hoped—and the doctor blamed it on her indefatigable spirit. Someone like Judith's mother would have progressed more quickly because she enjoyed being ill. Mrs. Davenport fought against it and burned with frustration over her compulsion to sit or lie about day after day. At this moment there were blobs of color in her cheeks—witnesses to her encounter with Colonel Rawlings–Turner—but her face was hollowed and the bright eyes dimmed by remnants of shock. Judith had discovered that like most people who had been healthy all their lives, this self-assured, vivid, and intelligent woman was terrified by illness.

"Dear Aunt Pan," Judith said taking up the limp hand from the throwover quilt, "whatever do you mean by being *taken in* by what he said?"

The elderly lady looked straight. "He does not believe for one moment that this . . . this Buller man will be here inside a week. If that were so, the sick and wounded would never have been sent out today neither would the doctors have transported tons of equipment and medicines to a place that will only be in use for three or four days."

Judith was taken aback. "It was because of the shelling. Neil said . . ."

"That young man will say anything to make you happy. It is a general failing in military men—they rarely tell the truth of a situation to women. If the story is true, those guns in the hills will be firing in the opposite direction in a day or two and Ladysmith will be quite safe. Why are they taking out the women and children, in that case? Answer me that, my girl."

"You are imagining things," Judith said to cover her own sudden doubts. "The hospital camp will be used as a permanent medical base. You are reading far too much into something we know little about."

Mrs. Davenport looked from her pillows with accusing eyes. "Not you, too, Judith."

Confusion swept over the girl. She wanted to believe the colonel, but there was truth in what had just been said. Neil had been very definite in his wish that she should leave. Would he have been if rescue were just a day or two away? Restless, she stood and went to the piano beside the large curtained window.

"Shall I play to you? Let's not wonder over what the colonel did or did not mean. It is their job to worry about the situation. As you told him, it is our job to provide a modicum of gentility in the midst of the harshness of war." She began sorting through the music. "For me, it is enough to know Alex is safe."

"Behind bars?" Mrs. Davenport asked. "Poor boy!"

Judith's hands stilled. "Poor boy? Why do you say that? He could have been killed."

"Yes, but to a man like Alexander imprisonment might be unendurable—the last straw. I cannot see him accepting it, my dear."

It was raining again, and the British prisoners were restrained in their sleeping quarters instead of the rail yard. Although Alex thought Landerdorp had a wild rural appeal beneath blue skies, even he had to admit that sheeting rain from leaden clouds gave the hamlet an end-of-the-world desolation.

It was two days since Hetta had come with the news of the British humiliation and the sieges of Kimberley, Mafeking, and Ladysmith. His own regiment was trapped in that last garrison town, and his particular company of it was

behind bars along with him. It seemed incredible. Ever
since his father had enlisted him in the Downshires he had
had regimental pride and honor forced down his throat.
Now that this had happened, he felt angry—not for himself, but for all those of his fellows who held tradition and
esprit de corps so dear.

Hetta had told him very little of the situation after the
initial news of Ladysmith. There was too much between
them for the meeting to be anything but wrought with emotion. For Alex, it had been a matter of history repeating
itself. He had been toppled into the dust before Alison's
eyes: before this girl whom he loved with greater depth,
the fall had been even more agonizing. Like Alison, she
had been unable to bear it and walked away without a
backward look.

It was there the similarity ended, however. Hetta had
gone out of his life knowing his love had been genuine and
his failure not of his own making. Having been given that
heaven-sent chance to vindicate himself, something in him
throbbed to take up the fight once more. For the sake of a
slender girl who had defied family and traditions to love
him, he must walk tall again.

He stood by his window watching the rain. It hit the tin
roofs with a continuous roar before rushing in great eddies
down the metallic slopes to slap onto the reddish mud below. Although it was barely noon, a pall hung over Landerdorp like approaching night. At the corner of the *stoep* two
Boer guards were gazing unemotionally at the scene, as he
would at a March downpour on the paddock at Hallworth.
This was their home as England was to him. For a moment
it smote him that he would fight just as desperately if foreign boots tramped over his acres, then pushed the notion
aside. To succeed he must be single-minded.

"Bloody awful weather for a trip up-country," Guy
Cuthbertson commented from the doorway, then strolled in
to stand beside Alex watching the rain. "Do you think
there's a chance they might postpone it?"

"I'm not going," Alex said unemotionally.

"Oh? Why are they keeping *you* here?"

"They're not. I'm going to have a crack at getting to our
lines."

Guy took a long breath. "You'll be shot . . . in the
back, old son."

Alex turned with swift anger. "Better that than walk meekly into a Pretoria prison camp."

The other man pursed his lips and stared at the rain. "How do you fancy being mauled by a lion; savaged by hunting dogs; charged by a wild buffalo? Then, there is slow death by starvation, thirst, and sunstroke—madness brought on by finding oneself lost on the veld. And if you fancy that a trifle dramatic, consider plain old blisters on the feet, my dear fellow. A bullet in the back would be preferable to any of those, I should think . . . but a prison camp sounds by far the most sensible choice to me." He rocked back and forth on the balls of his feet in a few moments' silence. "It's out of the question. Without transport one wouldn't have a hope. Even with it the chances are slight, but worth a gamble, I suppose."

"I am prepared to take it," Alex told him. "The only problem is how to get away from Landerdorp without being seen."

"That's easy. As officer in charge of the railway yard I know the place intimately. There's a small storeroom off the engine shed where I was allowed to keep spare equipment. Since it had nothing to do with the civilian authorities they have probably forgotten all about it. The key is in my room." He turned speculatively to Alex. "One could hide in there quite easily until nightfall. It's . . . er . . . big enough for two, old chap." He paused to watch Alex's reaction, then went on, "The only problem is transport once we get away."

Alex grinned. "That's easy! Under the *stoep* of my company office are some bicycles. Several of my men had them sent up from Durban. They wouldn't object if we borrowed a couple, under the circumstances."

Guy looked pained. "*Bicycles!* Is that the best you can come up with?"

"It's better than blisters on the feet."

"Don't you believe it. The blisters come in a far worse place," said Guy gloomily.

When the moment came it was unbelievably easy. In the driving rain no one noticed two men slip from the marching column as it passed the engine shed, and they were soon safely in the tiny room hidden beneath strings of musty bunting once used to festoon the station at its official opening. They stayed there for four hours unable to converse because of the thunder of rain on the tin roof.

It grew dark early, and they made their way through the hamlet until they reached the former company office of the Downshires detachment. The bicycles made a noise as they were dragged out but, as the military had quit the outpost, the lamps on the corners of the huts were unlit. Nothing disturbed the excellent cover of darkness.

Stealth was nearly unnecessary. Landerdorp appeared almost deserted now that the prisoners had been marched out. Those Boers who had been guarding the soldiers had melted away to farms dotted all over the veld, leaving just a few former residents to occupy the tiny rail depot.

Pushing the bicycles with great difficulty through the mud they followed the track uphill to Devil's Leap, but there their familiarity with the terrain ended. They soon realized it would be fatal to wander in the darkness in the hope of following the track south. Stumbling over a cluster of rocks, they propped the bicycles together, threw their cloaks over the machines, and crept beneath the frail shelter they afforded.

It was the most uncomfortable night Alex had ever spent, and dawn found them both drenched to the skin and shivering convulsively from the bitter cold of the nighttime veld. The rain had stopped and a mist heralded the coming heat of day. Alex looked at it in dismay. In this obscurity, they could easily ride back into Landerdorp without knowing it. He voiced his thoughts to Guy, who tapped his pocket with a grin.

"A compass, my dear Alex, is standard equipment for an engineer officer. How do you imagine you fellows ever get anywhere if it were not for us?" But Alex was not entirely relieved. They walked for some minutes due south in the hope of coming upon the track which would allow them to mount the bicycles. It was an eerie experience, Alex thought, and full of hazards. At anytime without warning they could walk into a group of enemy horsemen or hostile animals. Luckily they found the track quickly and pushed the bicycles onto it.

"The exercise might warm us up," Alex grunted through chattering teeth.

"Can't think why we brought all this damned water with us," Guy complained. "Dying of thirst appears most unlikely in weather like this."

Each man had four water bottles slung around him—three commandeered from fellow officers—and their bulk hampered them on the rough cart track. It was hard going for two weary stiff-muscled men who were drenched to the skin and shivering.

By eight o'clock the mist had cleared to reveal a typical South African midsummer day. Heat hovered five or six feet above the ground in a shimmering silver layer that played tricks on a person's eyes as it softened long distances into nearness and put imaginary rocks or trees just ahead. The sky had become the luminous blue, and mile upon mile of undulating scrubland fell away from them in every direction until the distant horizon rose in blue ranges to prove how hilly was that particular area of Natal. Behind them were the *kopjes* curving around Landerdorp and ahead, beyond the far-off ranges, lay the garrison of Ladysmith.

Now that the mist had cleared to reveal the clarity of day Alex realized what a mission he had set himself. Two figures moving across this terrain could be seen for miles away, and horsemen at the gallop could overtake bicyclists in a drastically short time. There was no cover—just never-ending plains dotted with rocks and bushes where beasts ran and birds circled high, high above, waiting with beady eyes for the sight of a still, lifeless form putrifying in the brassy heat.

They were soon glad of the water Guy had cursed and they ate a little of the fruit they had managed to bring in their pockets. They exchanged little conversation. The blazing heat had dried the khaki upon their bodies and the rough-dried material rubbed as they pedaled, raising red patches on their skin that grew more and more painful as time went on. The unaccustomed action of cycling set up protests in their muscles, and the stony uneven track jarred through arms and shoulders. But it was the sun that defeated them finally.

By midday the temperature was over a hundred, and both men were exhausted. Alex was finding it difficult to see at all. The harsh inhospitable land threw back the heat coming from above, until it seemed to scorch his eyes into the need to close. Every time he reopened them he was blinded by sweat that ran down his forehead from the crown of his helmet. As he put up his arm to wipe it away the wheel of his bicycle hit a stone, and he fell with a heavy thud.

"That settles it," came Guy's voice in a tone that suggested he was not far off complete collapse himself. "We have to rest until the sun goes down."

Alex got wearily to his feet and looked through squinting eyes at the barrenness around him. "There's no damned shade for miles!"

"It'll have to be the cloaks again. It'll be one way of drying them."

They certainly dried, but the two men lying in the limited shade they afforded had to suffer the humidity created beneath the steaming serge. They discussed the need for keeping a watch, but since all their weapons had been taken by the Boers there seemed little point. If they could not defend themselves the only alternative was to evade capture, and on bicycles it was a vain hope.

Guy looked at the dark steaming cloaks above their heads as they lay on the grass and murmured, "My father always maintains that the Lord looks after his own, especially the British. Let's hope he's right."

The sweat was swamping Alex and the heat accentuating the pulse that pounded in his temples. "I have always found the Lord unpredictable," he said, more to himself than his companion, and drifted off on a tide of remembrances that took his mind hundreds of miles from where his body lay on isolated veld.

It was late afternoon when he awoke, with a tongue swollen by dehydration and clothes that stuck to him. When he tried to move, his aching body protested violently and pain stabbed his head.

"Oh God!" he groaned, and heard a grunt beside him.

"Shake hands with a fellow sufferer." There was a short pause, then, "I'm not so certain this was a good idea, Alex. If we ever reach our own lines we shall be no good to them."

"We'll worry about that when we get there," was his reply. He forced himself to sit up. "Go easy on that water, Guy. It's essential to drink in short sips in temperatures like this. I read it somewhere in one of those infernal manuals."

"Written by a man who has never felt thirsty in his life no doubt."

Alex got painfully to his feet and put on his helmet,

trying to find a place under his chin where the strap felt comfortable. "I think we should go on. I'd like time to find shelter for the night. Those hills don't look too far off. There might be an overhang, or even a cave of some kind . . . and if I am not mistaken, there is another storm in the offing."

Progress was slow, laborious, and painful. In two hours they seemed no nearer the hills and there was no way of telling how far they had traveled. The featureless veld provided no landmarks to men unused to it.

The storm overtook them with the usual fury and once more they were forced to push the bicycles against rolling sheets of rain that beat so hard against their faces they had to turn down their heads for protection. Darkness caught them still exposed to the wild weather with no prospect of anything other than spending another night like the one they had already suffered. With the night came a sudden dramatic drop in temperature.

Lashed by rain, shivering continuously despite the heat that remained in his body from the daytime temperature, and aching in every limb, Alex had to acknowledge the truth of Guy's words. If they were not caught by Boers, they would be in no state to fight when they reached their army—if they ever reached it. Unable to move at night for fear of wandering off course, yet restricted by the heat of full day, they could progress only slowly, and if they did not get enough food inside them their strength would diminish daily.

His spirits reached rock bottom. There was also something about the insistent beating of wetness against his face that forced his eyes closed and had him fighting for breath. The vast blackness put a whisper of dread in his stomach— as if it had all happened before, long, long ago . . . with terrible results.

The feeling grew, and with it, the premonition of disaster so that, when the ground began to rise and he saw the shimmer of light through his rain-filled vision, he homed to it without hesitation.

"By God, what a piece of good fortune," Guy shouted against the elements. "I think we have come across a farm, with the most perfect sense of timing. Let's hope they're English . . . or neutral Boers."

"Whatever they are, I'm going to occupy one of their barns for a while," Alex said grimly. "With luck, they

won't even know they played host to us. We can be away
before dawn."

It took another half hour to reach what had seemed so
near, and both men stumbled into the large stone barn with
gratitude and relief. Engulfed by the smell of hay, apples,
and leather, they breathed again. Alex threw off his helmet,
cloak, and water bottles before sinking wearily onto the great
mound of hay, unutterably glad to be under shelter of some
kind. He was vaguely aware of Guy flopping down somewhere near him and heard grunts as his companion unslung
the water bottles from around his neck. Making a mental
note to fill them before leaving the farm, he unhooked his
collar, fell back, and closed his eyes. Even the discomfort
of soaking wet breeches and boots that had grown painfully
tight was insignificant against the need for rest.

"I could go for a nice steak right now," came Guy's
voice in the darkness, ". . . or a filet mignon."

"Direct your thoughts more along the lines of a few apples," Alex murmured. "That's all you are likely to get."

"I'm in no shape to climb bloody apple trees."

"No need. They're stored in here somewhere. I recognize
the smell."

Indeed, the familiar scent of maturing apples had taken
Alex back in time to his youth at Hallworth with a memory of trays of yellow-green apples filling racks in the long
room above the coach house. There was someone with
him—his brother almost certainly—and they filled their
pockets with the fruit in great daring. Funny how he had
so many childhood memories in which Miles was a shadowy figure. Try as he might, he was never able to get a
clear picture of the boy who had shared his early childhood.

Inevitably, his thoughts veered back to the night he had
been dragged into the lake by his fellow subalterns and,
germinated by the heavy rain on his face and the complete
blackness of the open veld, the familiar half-memory hung
in his mind on the brink of recall.

There was a great black void everywhere, voices calling
his name—in fear, not friendship—and a giant figure in a
black cloak that menaced him in some way. The recollection of the hay trolley and hands pushing him toward black
shining water set him up from his lying position to sit with
his head in his hands, the wetness of his hair lying cold

against his fingers. It must be weariness and hunger bringing the old ghosts back at a time like this.

Mentally shaking himself he was about to lie back again when it seemed as if he had floated into the fantasy of the past. There, a few yards, away was a lantern bobbing in the darkness. For a crazy moment he almost expected to see the giant figure with a cruel yellow devil's face. He must have made some kind of exclamation, for the lantern stopped moving and, in its faint light, he could make out a shape in flowing cloak.

With his heart thudding from the shock of past and present merging, he got to his feet and walked slowly toward the circle of light like a man in a daze. The soft yellow glow decreased its aura as he drew near, undazzling his eyes enough to see behind it.

She looked much as she had that first day—soft dark hair braided around her head, sweet lips slightly apart, and apprehension widening brown eyes of immense beauty. In the warmth of the lantern light she shone out of the darkness like truth in the midst of eternal doubts.

"Dear God in heaven," he breathed unsteadily. "From the whole vast wilderness out there, I am lead straight to you!"

## CHAPTER TWELVE

Hetta stared at the beloved face while her body melted with shock. She had left him broken and defeated behind bars, the memory of his pain racking her every living moment since. He could not be here, standing before her in her own barn, tall and free, with everything he had once said there in his eyes again.

She began to tremble, and the lantern shook its light across the beaten earth floor. In an instant, his hand closed over hers to steady it, but the physical contact increased her trembling while she continued to gaze at him, all her longings made flesh and blood. He moved almost against her and, as if in a trance, her other hand moved up to cover his. He completed the union and held her imprisoned in a firm clasp.

In the flickering light his hair was aglow like the pelts of the large roan stags that ran beneath the sun on the veld, and his eyes were full of leaping golden desire. Her heart leaped, too. It was useless to deny that this man would be within her unto eternity.

"Who is it, Alex?" The low voice broke into her stunned joy at the meeting, and she stiffened as something moved in the hay and another man appeared in the pool of light thrown by the lantern. He was also in the familiar khaki uniform, and she knew him immediately.

"By God, it's the little Boer beauty from Landerdorp!" said the smooth tongue. "Can she be trusted, do you think?"

She tried to pull her hands free, but Alex held them firmly as he said over his shoulder, "Keep out of this. It's a hell of a situation." Then he said to her, "They moved the others to Pretoria. Lieutenant Cuthbertson and I escaped. We are on our way to join our troops."

Sense was returning to her very quickly now that the shock of seeing him had passed. Piet would be roaring with anger that this particular man had slipped away from him. That he had come to the Myburgh farm was a disaster. Suddenly, she was frightened.

"If my grandfather knows you are here he will shoot you." A nod emphasized her fear. "Yes, he will kill any Englishman he sees." Thinking of Oupa in the house who might come out into the yard she tugged her hands away from her lover's grip and asked, "Where are your horses? If they are seen . . ."

He took her shoulders gently as he explained, "There are no horses. All we have are bicycles which are in the corner of the barn. We escaped yesterday, and we have been out on the veld ever since." He swept her with an intense glance. "I would never have come here if I had known. Do you believe that?"

She nodded, torn by anguish. Piet had said: There is not one among them who can ride for a day across the veld and not lose himself. They will die of sun and thirst while we watch them; they will drown in our rivers. Their bones will be scattered all over the *kopjes*.

"You will never reach Ladysmith," she told him desperately. "A Boer man with a good horse and a rifle could do so easily. It is better for you to return to Landerdorp."

"No, Hetta, you know I can't do that." He took a deep breath. "We'll leave right away."

Only now did she notice the dark patches on his uniform that showed how the rain had drenched him, and the mud caked on boots that had always been so highly polished. He wore the black leather belt, but the sword sling was minus the weapon, and there was no pistol, either. Her heart contracted. With no horse, no means of defense, she could not send him out onto the nighttime veld. He would surely die! Yet, how could she return to the house with this knowledge within her?

Tormented, she surrendered to those voices a woman listens to when love brushes aside all else in the world.

"The Lord sent you: I cannot turn you away. It is His wish that you shelter here." Then, remembering the other one, added, "But *he* must leave. A Myburgh cannot shelter the enemy."

There was the barest silence before the man said, "We are both the enemy."

It hurt her; it cut through the reborn quivering desire within her like cold steel. She wanted to cry out, "No . . . *never!*" Finding Alex here, in the one place she thought he could never be, had ripped off the layers with which she had tried to subdue what she felt for him.

One morning on the open veld he had approached passion with gentle hands, and left her throbbing for fulfillment. Another woman had taken him away; anger and jealousy had driven desire deep beneath their black folds. Then, at Landerdorp, a love that shone above passion had bled, pain intermingling in a bond that had sent her hurrying from the sight of his humiliation with wet cheeks.

This moment was different. He stood before her a free man again, and dormant longings quickened with life. His strong body was wearied by the harshness of the veld; his clothes were drenched by the African rain, crumpled and dirty; there was a dark shadow around his chin; and he smelled of scrubland, clean air, and the honest sweat of endeavor. Here, in her own barn, surrounded by sweet hay and barrels of apples, he was her man come home to rest after an absence of too long.

*He was her man.* Whatever else he was did not matter. The hands that touched her just now should be taking her melting body with pride and possession. They should move over her skin with searching caresses, touch her breasts with tender but insistent demand. His mouth should be upon her lips, her throat, her body, telling of the length of time he had waited. The breath caught in her throat. She yearned to be crushed beneath his weight, with the hay all around them, and the soaring, breathless, throbbing surrender within her. Yet, she could only stand before him knowing her own weakness.

"Well?" asked the smooth confident voice of Alex's companion, and she heard herself say, "Until it is light . . . and then you must go." She turned away. "I will bring food if it is possible."

"Hetta!" Alex was behind her holding her arms so that she was against him. He continued in faltering Dutch that brought her to the edge of tears. "I want nothing that will harm you. You are my life . . . my only love. I think we should leave."

For a moment she let her head rest against his chest while the bitter sweetness of his words coursed through her. "I thought I would never see you again." She spoke slowly so that he would understand. "It must be the will of God that sent you here."

He laid his cheek against the top of her head, and his voice was low as he said, "My dear, the Lord is sometimes careless."

"No." She was sure, and he must be also. "You came out of the wilderness to my door. On the veld a man has to be guided by his knowledge, but if he has none he is guided by the Almighty. His love is my love." Forcing herself to walk away from his arms she went to the door of the barn. "Stay quietly, and I will return when I can," she told him in English, and went out into the rain forgetting the apples she had gone to collect.

It was warm and bright inside the kitchen. She closed the door behind her, leaning back against it while her heartbeat still thudded through her breast. Oupa was in his chair working on a pair of boots, pushing the thread through pieces of hide with an awl. The familiar figure, pipe in mouth, intent on his task might not have been there.

*You are my life, my only love.* Alex had said those words as he held her close against him. The knowledge that he was here, only a few yards from her, filled her mind and every nerve. He was her man. Why was he not in her kitchen, before her hearth, while she gave him food for his body and solace for his inner hunger? Her love was mere pain if she could not show it.

"Does it rain still?" Oupa asked without looking up.

"*Ja,* it rains. From the west it comes."

"Ach," he grunted, "so it will for several days. Pray for your brother that the Almighty provides shelter this night." Attracted by her stillness he looked at her. "Have you some affliction that you stand there?"

It was kindly said, but set her heart racing in a new pattern. Only now did she realize the full danger of what she was doing. "The warmth after the night is great, that is all."

The old man studied her shrewdly. "It has been hard work with your brother away at the war . . . but it was so for your mother when my son went to fight the redcoats." His hands dropped to his lap and lay idly with the leather as he gazed reminiscently into the fire. "She had your brother suckling and you already in the womb. They took him at her time of greatest need. I rode out to avenge him, but they were already finished."

She forced herself to walk to the great range where the pots were swinging above the fire. They had killed a bullock that day and she was busy preserving the meat that had been cut into joints by the black servants. The heat of the fire added to the fever possessing her.

"They say I am too old. You know that is what they are saying?"

"*Ja,* Oupa." It came from her throat thick with apprehension.

"If they take my son's son, they will all see that Johannes Myburgh holds vengeance dear. He will take up his gun against the enemy until this land has seen the last of them. They will see he is not too old!"

It was a theme the patriach pursued all too often. Now, in a complete turmoil of thoughts and emotions Hetta stirred the contents of the pots with automatic movements.

"The rain will flatten the maize. Already we have lost the young shoots in the south corner." She heard the abstract note in her voice, but continued desperately, "It will not be a good year."

"There have been worse," was the impassive answer. "No man can stop the rain. God tests our strength with adversity. The weak fall by the wayside; the strong continue in His sight."

It was as if the old man knew—as if he were testing her own strength. The heat of the fire in the range burned her hands and face; steam and smoke swirled around her like the deeper corners of hell. Turning away from such torment, Hetta walked quickly to the cupboard that glowed with the polish of loving care, and took dishes from the shelves with hands that shook. Laying the table for supper became a feverish task to occupy her limbs, but it did not ease the longings and doubts, the ecstasy and guilt that battled within her. She flinched when Oupa suddenly reached out and took her hand as she passed, but he patted it gently and smiled with moist eyes.

"You are a good woman, Hetta . . . *ja,* a good woman." He patted her hand again, then let his slip from her fingers to fall heavily in his lap with a suggestion of weariness. "Perhaps they are right, and Johannes Myburgh *is* too old."

"No, Oupa," she said huskily.

"A man is old when he lives all the time in what he imagines is the truth: When the years that have faded appear richer than they were, and those that have gone to their Maker take on virtues they never had."

Hetta grew still. She had never seen her grandfather so . . . so *humble*. It added to her apprehension.

"Your father begat a son in his own likeness, for he was also a man of peace. I have turned him into a giant because of his sacrifice." His forehead creased into a frown as he said, "I loved him as Abraham loved his son, yet I sent him to fight against his will, as I have sent my grandson, for the sake of our people—because the Lord has promised us this land. But I have held up before your brother a false image. My son was no more than a gentle dreamer who rode unwillingly from his farm and kin." He sighed heavily. "We are all but the vassals of the Lord. Some serve His purpose very quickly and are gathered to Him; others labor on for long years in His sight, until He is pleased to take them into His care."

Hetta sank onto her knees beside him in overwhelming affection and looked up into a face that showed his years more clearly than before.

"Why are you saying all this to me?" she whispered.

He passed a hand over a beard that was growing grayer.

"There comes a time when words must be said, and that time is now." For a moment he stroked the piece of leather in his lap with weather-worn hands, as if reluctant to broach what he must say. "A man is more a father to a son than to a daughter. I pray your brother returns before it is too late."

"Too late?" she repeated bemused.

"The maize is springing and ready to yield forth, like our young men. God has sent rain to flatten the shoots before the time of fulfillment. It was the same in the year of Majuba, but this time it is worse. Before the rains end, a whole field will be barren. It is a sign."

Unable to answer the terrible thing he was suggesting, Hetta took his hand, swamped by the new fear he had planted. He was old and wise; he saw signs in many things—and he was seldom wrong."

"Lay aside your work," she begged. "Supper is almost ready."

He might not have heard her. "This afternoon I watched as lightning struck down the old boabob. That tree was my age when I came here. We have grown together and watched over this land. The time is nigh, child, and I must say this to you, also. Your mother was a good and true woman to my son, as I have always said, but without him she lived alone. When he died, none of those remaining held any claim to her—even the child she carried within her. She followed her man to the grave within the year, and it was by her own will. The strength of her love led her to abandon all else for its sake." He put up his hand to touch her hair. "You have your father's gentleness, but also her independence. The burden of your inheritance is great. I pray you will bear it in the sight of God, and not the devil."

Their eyes held for a long time while Hetta felt that burden already pressing her down, further down. When the door opened she turned her head expecting to see the servants, and it was several seconds before reality invaded her swirling thoughts and the color drained from her cheeks.

"Piet!" she whispered in shock, and froze as he came further into the room followed by her brother and half a dozen more of the Landerdorp Commando.

If Hetta had known agony of mind before, it doubled during the next hour. The arrival of eight hungry, drenched, and weary men demanded much activity from her but, while she threw logs on the fire, flavored the stew, set extra plates upon the table, and pulled rawhide boots from sixteen feet, the spinning of her head and the sickness in her stomach grew.

The quiet farmhouse had come alive with noise. Clattering buckets outside told of old Johnny feeding the horses. Inside the kitchen, the young men laughed and ate with gusto, demanding more when the plates were empty. They spoke with bravado, clapping each other on the shoulder, and bragging of the way they had intimidated the British.

"I tell you, man, I never saw men quicker to hand over their rifles than these *rooineks*," laughed one.

"They did not look like empire builders when they marched off to Pretoria in the rain. Eh, Franz?" Piet prompted harshly.

"They looked very far from their homeland," was the strange reply.

Piet turned away from him to shout, "Hetta!"

She jumped and dropped the plate she had been filling with stew. It splashed on the cloth rug and across her apron, leaving a brown stain against pale calico—like blood that had dried beneath the merciless sun. Pushing the lurid thought from her mind, she looked up quickly to find Piet's eyes on her. Nervously she bent to pick up the pieces only to see two feet clad in thick socks arrive before her and halt.

"You look disturbed," Piet said as she rose to meet his scrutiny. "I have never seen you so clumsy."

"The . . . the meat was hot. It fell on my hand and burned it."

"I think it is for a different reason." He took hold of her hand turning it over and back for signs of a burn mark he knew would not be there.

"You are wrong," she managed to say and began turning away from him, but he took her arm and held her where she was.

"I am never wrong."

"Let us eat first," complained a boy of barely seventeen who was reveling in his sudden jump into manhood. "There will be time for courtship when we are all sleeping."

There was general laughter, but Piet snapped at his boy-soldier, "You will be given the cradle, Boetie. It is the best place for you."

A louder shout of laughter greeted that, and the lad turned red. Hetta used the moment to her advantage and fetched a fresh plate from the dresser, a renewed wave of despair filling her. What had Piet meant? Did he already know two of the prisoners had escaped? Could he possibly suspect they were here?

Several times during the next quarter of an hour she caught Piet watching her. Her hands grew clammy with fear. Oupa appeared to have forgotten his hour of confession. With the arrival of the warriors he had regained his old choleric spirit and avidly joined in the warlike conversation.

Only Franz sat quietly while his eyes rested on the familiar things around him. The old dresser brought from Holland by his great grandparents; the rocking chair used by the woman of the house; the pipe rack he had carved as a boy for Oupa; the set of rugs woven by his mother; the skin of a crocodile shot by the trek leader as it attacked the girl who was the promised wife of young Johannes Myburgh; and, last, the Bible that would be his, his son's, and his son's son's.

Hetta met his eyes, but could not smile. The whole evening had become a nightmare. Even when her brother rose from the table and went to her, she met his fond inquiries with the wide eyes of fear. Lost in himself, Franz could only imagine it was the farm that was causing his sister such anxiety, and asked eager questions of crops and livestock.

Hetta answered him, feeling desperately weak. The name "Ladysmith" caught her attention, and she heard Piet declare that he and his men were heading to join the siege.

"We shall stay tonight in your barn, and move on tomorrow," he concluded.

"The barn?" echoed Hetta in such forced tones everyone turned to look at her. "No . . . it . . . there is room in the house. It is warmer. Not . . . not the barn." The phrases were jerked out, each second she took over saying them seemed like an hour.

Franz looked at her with surprise. "The barn is warm and comfortable compared with thornbrush and bitter winds. We have spent too many nights in such a manner not to enjoy the blessings of hay and a roof above our heads." He cast a look around his home. "It will not do to sleep in a house. We might decide never to leave it again."

Piet seized on the remark. "What man would choose to stay at home when he could be out chasing the British into the sea at Durban? And if we do not move out tomorrow we shall be too late even to see the fall of Ladysmith." He turned to impress the next statement on the old man. "There are twelve thousand troops in Ladysmith, guns and ammunition. When it falls they will have lost the war. We can cut off Buller's relieving force in open veld without supplies and force their surrender. By Christmas we shall be masters of our own land."

Oupa thought for a moment. "Twelve thousand is a large number."

"*Ja,* it is a large number," Piet agreed impatiently, "but we are in the hills surrounding Ladysmith, and our guns are bombarding the town everyday. They cannot break out without being slaughtered. It will be surrender, or a choice between starvation and being blown to pieces." He grinned. "From what we saw of the *rooineks* at Landerdorp, they will be quick enough to surrender."

While such talk flowed between the menfolk, Hetta was conscious only of the compelling need to get Alex out of her barn before he was trapped. That these men eating her food before her fire would kill him was in no doubt. They were hot-blooded and roaring for retribution but, even if others took a merciful line, Piet would never give a second chance to the one man he would enjoy killing. It might be a bullet in the head or, more likely and more satisfying to the assailant, a stab in the heart with a skinning knife.

The sickness in her stomach increased, and the walls began to shimmer like folds of cloth. It was hot in the room, and thick with the smoke of the fire and numerous pipes. Their voices were loud and their clothes and bodies gave off the strong smell of sweat and horses. Unobtrusive in the presence of so many large aggressive males, she edged her way toward the door, feeling the need for solitude and fresh air before faintness could prevent her from reaching the barn.

So ill did she feel, it was necessary to stand for a minute or so in sheeting rain to clear her head and dispel the nausea. Then, she was running across the yard to haul open the door while the veld wind wrapped her skirt around her legs and sent her apron up to whip across her face.

Without a lantern the interior was black. She stood inside wiping the wetness from her face, and listened. Silence.

"Alex," she called softly, but there was no response—not even the rustle of hay. "Alex."

Had he gone—gone out into the storm as he had threatened? She smelled the nearness of hay and reached for it as a support. It was all so clear to her now. He had escaped for her sake—because imprisonment had brought him down in her eyes. He would go on for the same reason. And he would die. Out there on the veld he would surely die. The strain and emotion of the evening became too much. Digging her fingers into the sweet spiky hay she gave herself up to tears. *They will die of heat and thirst . . . they will drown in our rivers . . . their bones will be scattered over the kopjes.* Piet was right.

Had God guided him here only to torment her before sending him on? Was He testing her strength, as Oupa claimed He did? If so, she was failing the test. Without Alex her life would be meaningless—as her mother's had been after Majuba. How well she suddenly understood that unknown woman who had counted her children and life as nothing without her man beside her. She cried then, for a life she had not yet lived which had gone before its birth.

Light surrounded her and she spun round to find Piet standing with a lantern just a few feet away. The sight of him brought revulsion to fill her throat and stiffen her body. Well, he was too late; the quarry had gone.

"What are you doing here?" he asked harshly.

"A woman has to prepare what comfort she can for those who seek hospitality."

"Without a lantern?" he mocked, and drew nearer. "I think it is comfort of a different kind that you seek tonight." He stood close and his glance ran over her. "Any man can see it. Tonight you hold your body like a rippling banner of pride. Your mouth is full and eager, and the fire of urgency burns in your eyes." His hand went out to curl around her neck. "We should have been man and wife by now. I have seen you ripen over the past weeks. You have been ready for a man long since." A faint smile crossed his face. "Tonight, it is plain you can wait no longer . . . and neither can I." His hand traveled down her body to rest on her thigh. "You came out here knowing I would follow."

In a quick movement he set the lantern on the floor and reached for her. She angled her head so that his mouth found her neck just below her ear, but nothing could prevent the strong hold he had on her. It was the final shock of the evening, and her cheeks grew wet again where they had begun to dry. Her gift for Alex would be snatched by callous fingers and spoiled forever.

Piet eased her slowly backward until there was no choice but to fall against the hay with his weight upon her. She put back her head and moaned a protest.

An exultant laugh broke from him. "You mean to drive me hard? Then you shall see what a man you have."

His hands began fumbling with the buttons of her bodice, but she rolled away. This time she would not let him touch her as he had before. With another laugh he flung himself after her, and it was at that moment that she heard a faint sound, way above them in the loft. Her very breathing seemed to cease, but Piet was too far on the road to seduction to sense the fear in her. And why should he heed a faint scuffling that could be made by a rat? He did not know two men were here earlier that evening.

His breath was upon her face and his thick beard scratched against her skin. There was a terrible decision to make and it must be made now. Alex must be witnessing all this from his hiding place above . . . and so must the other man she hated. What must she do?

The bodice of her dress was open now, and her body quivered at the touch of Piet's hands. Staring up into the dimness above her she cried out silently to Alex to turn away from what he saw and close his ears to what he heard.

"You have a man to be proud of, Hetta Myburgh." Piet was breathing heavily. His hand seized her breast. "Now you will find out it is true, eh? You saw him—the Englishman in his cage?"

"*Ja*, I saw him," she said slowly.

"I, Piet Steenkamp, took his sword with my own hand. He trembled as I took it—trembled like a girl." He gave a spasm of laughter that shook her own body. "They are fit only for dancing and games. They are not men."

His hand was feverishly trying to bare her body, but the straps of her under-bodice became entangled on the buttons, and he gave up for the moment. Instead, he covered her shoulder and throat with sharp bites. Each one brought a gasp that increased the cry growing within her.

"You have been wayward, woman, but it has taught you

a lesson you will never forget," he panted, attempting once more to pull off the bodice. "It is good that you have fire within you, but I am here to quench it. Piet Steenkamp's woman will be of some consequence when this is all over and the British are gone. We shall be married, and Franz must look to his own future." The bodice tore beneath his impatience, and he grew more aggressive. "But when a woman looks as you do tonight, there is no waiting for such things."

They struggled. The more domineering Piet became, the more Hetta resisted. Forgotten was the need to lull his suspicions of any noise in the loft; hammering in her head was the anguish of knowing Alex would see her humiliation.

Piet was strong, but it was tempered by the confidence of her willing submission and he was enjoying the prolongation of final victory. Hetta threw herself from side to side, clawing at the hay and finding it falling away from her grip in a shining landslide.

Dust was rising and filling her throat and nostrils. The hay scratched her skin. Perspiration was beginning to spring up on her body as they slithered together across their shifting bed. The lurid events of the evening swam across her mind in a series of nightmare impressions. Alex appearing from the darkness like a ghost; a field of maize falling like young men beneath a rain of bullets; her father, looking like Franz, lying covered in blood on a hillside; khaki soldiers flying up in fragmented pieces inside Ladysmith.

The cry within her gathered into a wave that crashed and broke from her throat, and in that moment she was freed by a collapse of hay that took Piet to the floor away from her. In a single movement she was up and running toward the door, clutching her bodice across her shivering body. Piet was after her with a roar of laughter, and had caught at her skirt when brightness washed over them and brought them to a standstill.

The men of the Landerdorp commando understood the needs of their leader, but had not expected him to use the barn when the girl had a bed in the house. They covered the moment with laughter that took no account of Hetta's feelings, then pressed into the barn out of the rain and prepared to make themselves comfortable for the night.

Hetta ran into the blessed darkness feeling the rain like the baptism of purity on her skin. Reaching her room she

closed the door and leaned against it, fighting for breath.
Then panic sent her to the big carved chest that held bed
linen. She pushed and heaved at it until it stood against her
lockless door. Only then did she fall on the bed and weep
the tears that heralded a sleepless, anguished night.

Piet was eager to rendezvous with the scattered sections
of his commando. He called for the horses shortly before
dawn. Hetta gave the men breakfast when they came into
her kitchen with pale-colored chips of hay sticking to their
clothes. They were men of the land. Sleep had come easily
despite their makeshift bed, and each was refreshed and
clear-eyed. Apart from a bluff greeting, no word was spoken to the girl who put plates before them. All talk was of
getting to Ladysmith before it was too late.

When they rode off Franz only held back, and swept his
acres with a lingering glance. Once he looked back at his
family, then he urged his mount forward in pursuit of his
comrades. Hetta knew the reason. In Oupa's eyes there was
only pride; in her own was regret. The understanding and
sympathy between them had been lost somewhere in the
past weeks. Their kinship had been halted by love and war.
Neither was the same person now.

Piet had taken his leave of her as though the night before
had never happened. He was fired with the present passion,
and all his thoughts were of a battle ahead. A promise that
he would be back was all he gave her, from the saddle of
his horse, and she watched his distant figure with no emotion.

Although she had kept her eyes on the old clock ticking
in the corner, when Oupa eventually took his horse for an
inspection of the damage done by the night's storm, it was
an effort to fill the skillet with porridge, wrap bread, and
meat in a cloth, and approach the barn. At the door her
courage nearly failed her, but she had to face him, if he
were still there—and something told her he would be.

Signs of occupation were all too apparent. The piled hay
had been dragged down and spread over the floor in thick
layers. It would have to be forked back into the high stack
or there would be no room for storing the beets and cane.
As she stepped across it there was a rustling noise from
above, and the dark-haired officer dropped from the rafters
into the soft carpet below. Steadying himself, he grinned at
her.

"You had me worried when I heard those horses gallop in last night. I thought you had called your friends in." He nodded at the skillet. "That smells good . . . or don't I get any?"

Hetta heard none of the last sentence. Alex had lowered himself slowly and dropped to the ground a little behind his companion. Even in the dimness of the barn she could see something of what he was feeling in his eyes. His pain and joy had always betrayed him to her by etching themselves on his face, and it was there in vivid evidence as he drew nearer. He was bruised by what he had witnessed. His eyes asked questions. They accused and apologized at the same time.

"There is very little time," she forced herself to say. "Eat. I will return in ten minutes when I have set the servants to their tasks."

Knowing she was running from him, avoiding what would have to be said between them, she turned and headed for the door, aware that Alex was staring at her while the other man squatted eagerly by the skillet.

He overtook her almost immediately and barred her way, knowing they were hidden from view of the yard outside, and from his companion by the piles of hay. A second day's growth around his jaw gave him a satanic look, and there was none of his usual gentleness in his manner.

"What does he mean to you?" he began harshly. "Did he have the right to . . . ? What did you expect me to do?" He gripped her arms and shook her a little. There was a wildness about him that made her tremble. "Have you any idea what it was like up there . . . watching . . . ?" He could not put it into words. "I couldn't be sure . . . Are you his . . . does he expect you to marry him?" He shook her again. "Does he?"

At her silence he slowly relaxed his grip and his arms fell helplessly to his sides. "I see. You came to Landerdorp because he sent you." His voice had gone flat and distant. "Why didn't he kill me that day? It would have been absurdly easy."

She threw herself against him, pulling his head down so that she could stop his words with her mouth. She wanted to drown in his strength, submit to his anger, forget the world in his arms. In a short while he would be gone forever. It was imperative she make him believe the truth.

Her hands moved against his shoulders in spasms of possession, then fastened in the thick hair that grew in unruly fashion against his neck, while her lips sought punishment from his. When his arms pulled her up against him in fierce anguish she reveled in the melting of her bones that allowed her to arch against him as if their bodies were one.

While he found relief from the jealous impotency of the previous night in slowly subduing the force of her challenge, she beat with rhythmic fists on the solid width of his back, hitting out at his anger with the rage of her humiliation in her hands.

It took only a short time before her rage was spent. Yielding, drugged by his kisses, she caressed his face and body with supple hands. He spoke her name in husky tones between small kisses that covered her face and throat, then pulled her back into a passionate embrace that left her lips bruised.

"I love you," she whispered against his mouth. "From that first day I loved you."

He buried his face in her shoulder while his hands stroked her dark braids. "Last night . . . dear God, I was about to come between you. He spoke of marriage, and I held back." His head came up and she saw the pain in his eyes. "Why didn't you tell me about him?"

Now that the thing was fought between them she could speak calmly. "You are to marry Miss Burley."

He took a deep breath. "That is over. She has returned to England."

The wonder of what he was saying swam through her. He had done it because of her, she knew.

"This man . . . he knows about us?"

She shook her head. "He would have killed you that day."

"You are bound to marry him?"

Again she shook her head. "No. He has changed . . . and I love you."

He kissed her again with savage swiftness, and there was a different kind of anger in his voice when he said, "When this is over, I will come for you. Believe that, and wait for me."

The short ecstatic moment collapsed before her, and reality rushed in. There was a whole world between now and the future.

"You must go," she told him softly. "Every moment you stay is dangerous."

He took her hands up to his mouth and kissed them. "Hetta, you have given me a reason for being alive. Before you came I was nothing. When I come back it will be to take you away with me . . . as my wife."

"Eat quickly," she told him desperately, afraid such words would make it impossible to say good-bye when the time came. "I will give the servants tasks that will keep them from the house. Then, you must leave."

She was a Boer woman, brought up to accept that her man would spend days away from her yet, when Alex struck out into the veld that promised merciless days ahead, Hetta returned to the house with her loss heavy upon her. Inside, she rested her cheek against the cool wood of the door frame while she gazed at two specks in the dancing distance.

"*Tot siens,*" she whispered, knowing she would never see him again.

## CHAPTER THIRTEEN

It was dusk and the shelling had ceased for the day. Over the beleaguered town hung the strange silence that heightened normal sounds. Voices were clear in the still air; bricks rang against each other with sharp regularity as debris was cleared; laughing children free to run in the streets again were treated to parental rebukes in voices made shrill from tension; returning guards tramped back from lookout posts, the sound of their boots audible long before and after they had passed; bugle calls, melancholy but comforting, rang out over the town announcing that the military were still masters of their garrison at the end of yet another day.

No sooner had darkness screened the streets than others were on the move. They came slowly, bearing their burdens wrapped in simple brown blankets; small parties of grim-faced soldiers with reversed rifles said farewell to men who had been laughing and vital at sunrise. They made their way to the cemetery below the hill by the light of a dim lantern reflecting, perhaps, that a tiny piece of metal might lie between their own life and death tomorrow.

For these poor souls there were no flag-draped coffins, black plumed horses, or rumbling wheels of gun carriages. There was not even a last volley over the grave— ammunition was too valuable. A brown blanket, a hole in the earth, and a white wooden cross sufficed for those who had wasted away through illness, or those who had gallantly rushed the enemy guns and destroyed themselves along with the weapons. Either way, the garrison was being reduced slowly and tragically.

To those trapped inside Ladysmith, Buller's relief column had at first meant high hopes. Now, two days before Christmas, hope was nearly gone.

Ten days ago a heliograph message from the relief column had raised a cheer with the information that Buller was a mere fifteen miles from Ladysmith and was launching an attack on Colenso which would clear the way straight through to the besieged town. On December 15 British guns could be heard in the distance—a sound that was sweet music in Ladysmith. On December 17 the sun flashed on the metal signaling plate to relay the news that Buller had retreated again after a battle of horror at Colenso leaving over a thousand British casualties.

General Sir George White, commander of Ladysmith garrison, published the news of defeat to the hopeful inhabitants. He said nothing of General Buller's recommendation that the garrison should fire away all its remaining ammunition and surrender to the Boers. Sir George had a stouter heart than his would-be rescuer and promptly ignored the recommendation. He then sat down to draw up a revised table of rationing for his remaining supplies, and discussed with his staff the forthcoming Christmas party for the two hundred and fifty children in his charge. Not only did they plan for the young ones, but mule races and a sports meeting were quickly organized for the troops, and a dance in the evening for the military and civilians alike.

The holding of Ladysmith was vital. The final outcome of the war could depend on the fate of that small town, and the British were determined to stay. Even in their most depressing moments practically everyone of the inhabitants would fiercely resist the suggestion to wave the white flag. The odd one or two civilians who were glorying in the profit to be made from exorbitant prices for their goods, would doubtless cry surrender if the danger to their own skins became too great—or if the merchandise ran out! But, in the main, the longer the siege went on, the stronger grew the determination not to give the Boers Ladysmith.

Judith stood on the *stoep* in the fast-gathering darkness, gazing unemotionally at the hills in the distance. Long Tom, the gun that caused such havoc with its deadly range, no longer gave forth puffs of smoke that announced the imminent arrival of a shell. The Indian signaler who stood on a knoll to wave a warning flag on sight of the smoke had gone to his dinner and rest until the gun began again precisely on time the next morning.

She imagined the scene up there in the hills. The Boers in their drab clothes and slouch hats would be lighting fires to cook their own dinners and, after eating, would sit around laughing and smoking their pipes as if they had not been dealing out death and destruction all day. She sighed. Perhaps it was easier to kill at long distances, without seeing the angel of death garnering his harvest.

As if echoing her thoughts, the first of the burial parties appeared and wended its way toward her. The stretcher bearers went up to the hill with sweat darkening their khaki jackets, but they would return with their collars turned up. At midsummer the temperature was over a hundred by day, near freezing at night.

Judith pressed her forehead against the supporting pillar and remembered an afternoon at Richmond when she had watched a green and springlike scene from her window. The Judith Burley of that day had longed for adventure, for a man of idealistic substance, and for an escape from a house of women. At that moment Sir Chatsworth Russell had arrived to offer his son on a silver salver.

She dreamed. How far Judith Burley had traveled since then; how many lessons had been learned! Alex had taught her that life was more than whipped cream on top of a trifle; war had shown her human nature without its social coating. How easy it was now to see herself as Alex had seen her, and how clearly she recognized what he had sought and found only in a little Dutch farm girl.

The droop-shouldered troops passed with the corpse, and she shivered. Thank God Alex was safe in Pretoria and not likely to become one of the blanket-shrouded shapes on a twilight journey.

"Judith," called a weary voice from within, and she turned and went inside.

Mrs. Davenport was busily gathering together the things that had been designed to occupy her all day, and which lay scattered across her cotton quilt. She looked up when her niece entered.

"I think I shall retire now. Mr. Forrester will be here shortly, and I have no wish to treat him to the spectacle of an elderly invalid who cannot even move from one bed to another without being supported and propelled by someone else."

"Don't be foolish, Aunt Pan. Neil knows you have had a stroke—gracious, it was he who sent for the doctor. There is not the least likelihood of his thinking you are a tiresome creature who languishes in ill-health."

"The thought had not crossed my mind," was the answering lie. "I am sure the poor boy sees enough of genuine sickness to wish to find me giving an exhibition of helplessness."

Judith knew it was futile to pursue the subject, and tried to ask lightly which of the things her aunt wanted taken to her bedroom.

"None of them."

"None?"

"Judith," said her aunt fixing her with a stern eye, "of what use is it to write letters that cannot be sent; how can one read when flies swarm all over the book and one's hands; and is there any point in starting a tapestry when one knows there will not be enough wool to finish it?"

There was only one answer, but Judith would not give it. In her ceaseless battle to ease her aunt's frustration she told lies, wracked her brains for fresh distractions, and fought to remain even-tempered. With her mother it had been easier—soothing fingers on the brow, a bottle of smelling salts, a darkened room, and her silent presence had been all that was needed. Her aunt, on the other hand, did not want to be ill—resented and chafed at the compulsion to be inactive—and would accept sympathy from nobody.

Amidst all the other difficulties Judith was often tried to her limit, and without Neil Forrester would have found refuge in tears more than once.

"What shall you do while I am away?" she asked patiently. "The evening will seem long unless you find some occupation."

They began the slow progress from chaise longue to bed that depressed them both with its unavoidable reality of illness.

"My dear girl, I shall spend an hour appreciating the blessed silence, as usual, then Colonel Rawlings–Turner has promised to call after dinner for a little chat."

"That is extremely good of him," commented Judith a little caustically. "Since you invariably quarrel with him, I can only applaud his stout determination in continuing to try to cheer you."

"Cheer *me!*" exclaimed Mrs. Davenport, pausing at the doorway to muster her strength. "It is patently obvious you have no grasp of the situation whatsoever. There is no greater blessing to a military commander facing a troublesome problem than a whipping boy." She looked up at Judith. "Do you know he is known as 'old Bawling–Sterner'?"

"Yes. Neil told me."

"Mr. Forrester and his fellow subalterns might receive a lash of his tongue now and again, but there are rules and regulations governing what he can say or do to them. In me, however, he has the perfect victim. All his annoyance and frustration is put into a tirade that I answer at my peril. He can accuse whomsoever he wishes, rail against decisions, demolish reputations, and all in the confidence that his words will reach no other ears than mine." Her eyes had grown brighter. "I cannot walk away from him, neither can I go around the town spreading gossip. No, Judith, he has the perfect captive whipping boy. The poor man comes for me to cheer *him*."

"I see," said Judith bemused. "Then why does he invariably leave with bristling moustache and a red face?"

A smile that held an echo of her old self broke through. "You should know by now that men of strong character fight against being soothed from their anger. They grow stubborn. The only solution is to let them feel justification for their bad mood by turning their resentment from the real cause to oneself. That way they relax their major concern in order to enjoy the luxury of dealing with an impossible woman in the age-old manner. Never treat a man like a child, Judith, unless he has a trifling indisposition. One can soothe to the utmost in that circumstance. At all other times, he must be allowed to believe himself a tower of strength."

Neil arrived soon after Mrs. Davenport had been settled comfortably, and before Judith was ready. She hurried to greet him.

"Is it that late? The clock must be slow."

He looked grave, as he did these days. "No, I am early. We shall have to cancel the concert. The hall was damaged by a shell this morning and one wall is down. Everyone is frightfully disappointed, as you can imagine."

Suddenly, an empty evening stretched before herself and several hundred siege-weary people. "Couldn't we cover that one wall with a tarpaulin?"

"Ye–es, there'd be no problem there," he agreed thoughtfully. "Some sappers are already clearing the debris. Unfortunately, the piano was damaged." He spread his hands. "I'm sorry, Judith, even an angel like you can't give a piano recital without an instrument."

"Oh, Neil, I can't disappoint all those people," she said in dismay. "There must be something we can do."

He smiled through his weariness. "I've got a banjo, but my playing is more likely to drive them to surrender than entertain them."

Judith had been thinking quickly. "Mrs. Bywaters has a piano. Could you arrange for it to be moved from her house to the hall?"

"You are surely not thinking of . . . Judith, old Bywaters is not the least interested in the morale of the people here. He is charging fourteen-and-six for a dozen eggs when everyone else sells at thirteen shillings. His only interest is in fleecing people of their every penny. The only reason he does not want the Boers to have Ladysmith is because they would be getting it for nothing."

She smiled and put a hand on his arm. "The piano belongs to Mrs. Bywaters, and she is on the school committee with me. Away from her husband she is a different person altogether. You should see her with the children." Already she was turning toward her bedroom. "I'll fetch a wrap. Come with me to her house. I guarantee she'll lend the piano." Over her shoulder she added, "Your job is to keep Scrooge Bywaters talking while I speak to his wife. Once she has given her consent, he will hardly defy six burly soldiers who turn up to collect it. And it will serve him well if we leave him to take the piano back himself."

"We can't do that," said Neil. "It is the policy of the

military to pay for or return anything that is commandeered."

The words halted her in the doorway, and she looked
back at the young man bearing the scars of his recent brav-
ery. "You are an exceptionally nice person, Neil," she told
him softly. "Alex was quite right."

The quick flush of pleasure faded immediately. "Isn't he
always!" he replied a trifle hollowly.

By January 15, old Mr. Bywaters was charging thirty
shillings for his eggs, and the numbers dying from dysentery and enteric fever had multiplied alarmingly. In the big
neutral hospital base at Intombi supplies were running
short, and beds were scarce. The residents of Ladysmith had
even been asked to hand in all their spare spoons for use in
the hospital, and the Boers had asked the British for qui-
nine—and got it.

Rations for the garrison had been further reduced, and
the military authorities began plans for commandeering all
livestock and produce owned by civilians in order to stop
the hoarding and exorbitant prices. The cattle had all been
slaughtered and there would be a Hobson's choice of trek-
ox or horse unless Buller arrived within the week.

Christmas had passed in as merry a manner as possible,
with the Boers sending in a shell charged with Christmas
pudding as their contribution to the festive season. "Father
Christmas" had sweltered in traditional garb, as if the ba-
rometer did not show 103°F in the shade, and several
young maidens had received proposals during the dance
from lads fired by the urgency of life that promised to be
short. Queen Victoria telegraphed an inspiring seasonal
message to all her troops, and the thrill of heralding in the
twentieth century in such a unique situation proved diversion enough for several days.

Then, spirits crashed, and the future seemed hopeless.
The year 1900 would see them all in their graves: what lay
ahead but starvation and defeat? In every direction there
was sickness and death. The women were driven to distraction over the welfare of their children; husbands worried
and feared for their wives. Soldiers grieved over their comrades; officers frowned over their diminishing companies.

The shelling went on with never a letup, both sides pouring ammunition at each other during the prescribed hours
of combat. On the Sabbath it was peaceful, the Boers' reli-

gious scruples forbidding them to kill on that holy day. Ladysmith was beginning to look a shambles, and more and more families were driven to living in caves or holes in the banks of the Klip River. People bathed in it, women knelt beside it while they did their washing, the natives used it as a latrine. It was the town's only water supply. One weatherbeaten old soldier coined the macaber phrase: Klip River wine—the drink with body in it. It was tragically true, as many a white cross proved.

If there was anyone still stoically cheerful against these odds, there were regular dust storms that covered the whole town with gritty red clouds, blinding people and sending beasts crazy . . . and there were flies in swarms . . . and mosquitoes in hundreds! Of course, there was Buller's relief column for any who felt optimistic against all those odds, but rumor had it he had gone back to Durban for reinforcements.

Since there had been no sunshine to send heliograph messages for over a week, there was no way of knowing where he was and, as there had been no sound of British guns since Colenso, it was supposed the column had gone away. Even so, the military went about their duties as always, and nobody mentioned surrender. Although supplies of ammunition were dangerously low they would go on firing at the enemy—as long as someone was left to fire the guns.

On that day in January Judith left the little tin-roofed market with her rations in a basket, and began her return to the bungalow. It was not far, but the burning pitiless heat made even a short walk an ordeal. Her spirits were already low. The ration had been reduced again to half a pound of tinned meat, half a pound of biscuit, and only one-sixth of an ounce of tea.

Her basket was ridiculously large for such meager parcels. The basket would not be needed at all by the following week. For the moment, it gave her and the other women the comforting illusion that they were doing their daily marketing. It was one of the silly pretenses indulged in to keep up morale.

Another was the matter of dress. Despite the sweltering temperatures, the dust and gunsmoke, the overhead scream of shells, and the gaunt weary men in the streets, the daily visit to the market was prepared for with as much care as usual. Judith, totally unused to buying her own provisions or budgeting a weekly account, had learned the hard way how to recognize a bargain, and which vegetables were the freshest.

Where dress was concerned she was no exception, although she had one problem the other ladies did not share. Having arrived in South Africa in midwinter for a stay of no more than two months, the clothes she possessed were thick and designed to combat the clear chill of July and August. Fortunately, she had persuaded an Indian tailor to make her two cotton dresses before supplies were cut off, but the remainder of her dresses were the best English cloth or silk for evenings.

Today she wore the skirt of her cream costume with a white muslin blouse. The top had started out crisp and fresh, but now clung to her with limp discomfort. She longed to tear the high-frilled collar away from her throat, push up the sleeves that sheathed her arms, and take off the petticoat that wrapped itself around her legs as she walked. So strong was the urge, a fresh wave of heat broke over her at the need to resist it. Everything about life in this dilapidated and uncivilized town suddenly seemed ridiculous. She had been in Ladysmith so long she had become blinded to the things around her. In a flash she saw the place as she had first seen it—raw, unhygienic, and half a century behind the times.

Homesickness engulfed her: bitter anger against her aunt who had forced her to stay here when she could have left, and self-criticism of the pointless life she was living. Why not tear open her blouse and push up her sleeves, go out minus a petticoat to give shape to her skirt? Who would care? Who would think it shocking in this godforsaken town?

Her feverish glance took in the scene around her. Broken buildings; torn roads; gaunt women; soldiers in shabby khaki, with bleary eyes and the haunting of death upon them; starved horses who would grace the cooking pot before long; a few mongrel dogs who might join them; and, most distressing of all, thin, silent children dragging on their mothers' skirts with a listlessness that suggested there had never been the capacity for laughter and playfulness within them.

Something grew inside her and began to expand to painful proportions. Her feet slowed, and she stood looking into the shopping basket as if mesmerized. She had done this yesterday, and the day before . . . and the day before that. She had eaten the same tasteless meat and hard biscuit day after dragging day. It was not the amount of food, it was the deadly sameness of it. If only the half a pound were of something different.

Her hands tightened around the handle of the basket, as the heat and the noise and the hopelessness swam around her. So tightly did her teeth clamp together, they set up an ache in her jaw.

"Good morning, Miss Burley. We are looking forward to the concert tonight."

She stared at the passing judge as if he were an apparition, then her attention was taken by a horseman who was waving as he approached. Rooted to the spot she kept her eyes on him with only abstract attention, until the familiar scream of an approaching shell brought her back to some semblance of rational thought.

With great alacrity the man threw himself from the saddle and ducked, the shell passing over his horse and landing harmlessly in the road with a great explosion of dust and splinters. Judith found herself coughing and choking from the flying clouds of grit but looked up when Neil emerged from the gloom leading his horse. He looked white and strained.

"You shouldn't be out when they are shelling."

She stared at him. "You are."

"That's no argument. We have to be out." He tried to smile, but was not very successful. "Besides, I have a charmed life, it seems."

She indicated the basket. "The rations have to be collected."

"I could do that for you."

"No. The other women do it." She wiped her dusty face with a damp hand. "You have too much to do already."

He took the basket from unresisting fingers. "I still have time to walk you home." He offered his arm, and she took it just as if they were in Park Lane instead of a filthy shroud of red dust in a beleaguered town in the center of a wild underdeveloped country.

The fullness in her breast began to subside. Her skirt swayed from side to side as she walked like a fashionable Englishwoman, and her back grew straight in the tight-fitting muslin blouse.

"Have you just come off duty?" she asked calmly.

He nodded. "Another quiet night. If it weren't for the shells I'd almost believe they had gone away."

"Like General Buller?"

Her caustic question simply made him thoughtful. "You should go to Intombi, you know. Mrs. Davenport is sufficiently recovered to make the journey."

"She will not go . . . insists that the hospital is meant for soldiers and not silly females who should know better. In any case, I'm no invalid. I have no right to be there." They walked for a moment in silence, and she kept her eyes on the distant hills. "I'm a coward, Neil. They are crying out for help with the sick, but I would be useless. I couldn't face the pain and the blood." She gave a nostalgic smile. "Alex once said I had been protected from anything unpleasant and knew very little about life. It's true. I am a very poor creature."

He was angry. "What nonsense! And how like Alex to throw out disparagement whenever possible. A hospital is no place for a lady, Judith. Nobody would expect someone like you to expose herself to the sights to be seen there. Your aunt is burden enough for anyone, I should imagine. It's my opinion you have been an angel of patience and sacrifice these past three months."

"Oh, hardly that. She's my aunt, after all."

"And a most exacting patient. Mrs. Davenport is an admirable lady, but . . . well, I have to say it . . . she would try the patience of a saint. To withstand it day after day needs a very special person."

The pressure inside her vanished completely, and her head no longer drooped. In that moment she was a girl on the arm of a gallant young man, walking through the sunlit streets with the promise of youth strong in her breast.

They reached the bungalow, and Neil turned to face her. "I wish you would go to Intombi. There would be others to care for your aunt, and I would not worry over you. There's so much danger here."

She looked up at a face that still bore the signs of fever. He had been ill for three days, but had pulled himself out of it.

"It's more dangerous for you."

"I'm a soldier. We thrive on danger."

Her glance rested on the scar on his neck where a Boer bullet had grazed it during a night operation over a month ago. A party had crept from Ladysmith to blow up some

Boer guns that had been finding excellent range, and Neil had apparently taken a very great risk to drive off several of the enemy who were pinning down some of his men in open country. The Colonel had told the ladies of the exploit, but Neil had not even mentioned it to Judith.

"Will you come in for a cup of tea?" At his hesitation she smiled. "I always make some at this time of the day, and we can manage an extra cup for our friends. Who, more than you, earns that title?"

"There's nothing I'd like better, but I'm hardly in a fit state to . . ."

She tucked her arm through his and began persuading him up the path.

"Don't be foolish. If we took such things into account, visiting would be at a complete end these days."

Smiling he allowed her to lead him to the *stoep* but, once inside, he took up the subject of Intombi once more.

"You're wasting your time, Neil," she told him firmly. "Aunt Pan refuses to go, I'm glad to say."

"Then let me find a safer place for you down by the river," he begged, taking her hand and looking earnestly into her upturned face. The loud thump of an exploding shell and the accompanying rattle of windows was an ally to his cause. "You're in constant danger here."

"Even if I wished for it, it couldn't be done," she told him. "My aunt might manage one journey to Intombi, but moving her morning and night is out of the question."

He took her other hand and stroked it gently with his thumb. The gesture comforted her immeasurably. It was such a relief to have him there to lean on for a while, standing tall and masculine in the middle of the parlor.

"Judith, I am very concerned for your safety," he said with warm gentleness, "but also for your health. You cannot keep up this pace without being ill. Nursing your aunt, piano lessons for the children, committee meetings and piano recitals—mostly those. It is in the evenings when you should be able to relax. The audience certainly does, but the performer exhausts herself."

An understanding smile curved her lips. "But it is an exhaustion that brings satisfaction." It was easy to slip into a reminiscent mood from there, and it might have been to another man that she spoke.

"I have led a sheltered life in the past. I'm neither full of charm and wit, nor abounding in compassion that overrides timidity. My one talent is as a pianist. Since I cannot be an angel of mercy in the field hospital, do not deprive me of what little good I can do."

Neil's eyes glowed darkly and he moved fractionally nearer. "You do not hear what is being said about you. Ask anyone in Ladysmith and he will be full of praise for the way you set an example with your courage and spirit. Your calmness and cool serenity is an inspiration to the other women, and it is only because you contrive to walk through the streets like an English lady strolling through Hyde Park that they try to copy you." He drew her gently into his arms. "I don't want to hear anymore about compassion and bandages. You are the bravest and most wonderful girl I have ever met."

The flat broadness of his chest was there to lean on; the leather shoulder straps and raised buttons that pressed against her suggested strength; and his arms enclosed her with comfort and protection. Her body and soul cried out for relief from the burden she was carrying alone. His praise and admiration revived her bruised spirits; tenderness soothed her past unhappiness.

He bent his head to hers, but his lips hovered above hers for several moments, as if waiting for signs of a refusal. When none came he took the kiss swiftly, then repeated it more comprehensively. Judith sighed. They stayed together drawing comfort from the nearness until forced apart by the entrance of the maid with tea.

It was not until he stood to say good-bye to Mrs. Davenport, then followed Judith out onto the *stoep* that he put into words what had been in his eyes throughout the visit.

"I must be the happiest man in Ladysmith . . . or anywhere, for that matter." He took her hand and kissed each finger very gently. "Since you refuse to leave, trust me to protect you."

"There is no one I would trust more," she replied softly, and as he rode off was smitten with a strange pang of wistfulness that remained with her all day.

Soon after four the maid announced Colonel Rawlings–Turner, and the gentleman strode in in a manner quite unsuited to a visit to two ladies.

"Good day, Miss Burley," he nodded to Judith, then approached Mrs. Davenport who rested tranquilly against the cushions on the chaise longue. "Ma'am, I have come to register the very strongest protest. This time you have really gone too far!"

He had been so angry when he entered he had forgotten to hand his helmet to the waiting maid. Now, he looked round for a place to put it, found none, and held it behind his back to prevent himself waving it around.

"How nice of you to call, colonel," Mrs. Davenport said with a smile. "Will you have some tea?"

"Oh no, ma'am, you cannot treat me to an innocence that suggests you do not know very well why I am here. For the past two weeks you have seen fit to interfere with the running of my regiment, but . . ."

"The running of your regiment? My dear colonel, I have never heard anything so absurd."

He bristled. "Have you not? What about a certain bottle of liniment that gave Captain Johns such a painful rash he was unable to ride his horse for a week?"

She smiled with angelic atonement. "One was not to know the poor man had such a sensitive skin. I have sworn by it for years."

"And the penny lending library to raise funds for Rifleman Goodenough?"

Mrs. Davenport appeared hurt at this being spoken of in such a context. "My dear sir, he lost all his money when a shell landed in his tent."

"My dear ma'am," he grated, "that man lost his money at cards. He is an inveterate gambler."

The lady was equal to the occasion. "Then I do feel you should take steps to cure him of the tendency. Have you not the authority to order compulsory savings for those of your men who have a family to support?"

The colonel gave out a sound something between a groan and a gurgle and Judith saw the helmet behind his back wave up and down in agitated fashion.

"I cannot believe you did not know you should have obtained my permission before occupying four of my men in the construction of a roundabout in your garden for use by the children."

"You should have seen the pleasure it gave them to do it. They were all family men, and the task enabled them to forget the horrors around them for a while." She fixed him with a clear eye. "Mr. Forrester gave his permission, you know."

"Ha!" snorted the colonel, "Mr. Forrester is a good deal

too susceptible, and I suggest you often take advantage of the fact. However, this time he was sensible enough to query the authority for this . . . this latest outrage."

"Oh . . . what *outrage*?" was the untroubled query.

Judith heard all this with astonishment, and sympathized wholeheartedly with the military man. She had been so occupied with her own activities she had done no more than note that her aunt complained less since Christmas, but it had not occurred to her that Mrs. Davenport had found pleasing tasks for her frustrated and organizing nature. Poor Neil had probably come in for censure as a result of all this. She grew angry. He was so well-mannered and obliging; women like her aunt would exploit him to the full. It was most unfair.

The colonel had taken from his pocket a sheet of paper covered by handwriting and thrust it at the invalid. "I think you are the author of these notices circulating Ladysmith."

"Indeed, yes. The doctor has been telling me how some people are hiding all kinds of articles and foodstuffs that are desperately needed in the field hospitals, hoping to sell it at a premium in a week or so. By advertising the fact to everyone in the town I expect to shame them into giving them up." She pointed at the paper. "You will see I have not asked for their entire stock, just one item per person given as a contribution to my charity appeal." She smiled. "I'm quite pleased with the wording. I think it will touch the conscience of the most miserly of our citizens, and the door-to-door collection will ensure a wish not to lose face by refusing."

"Mrs. Davenport, are you really so cut off from reality here that you are not aware that the military authorities are in full control of food and supplies in Ladysmith? Within the next few days steps will be taken to commandeer all remaining stocks at basic prices. A collection such as you suggest is illegal under the present regulations and in direct competition with the supply officer."

"I see," she returned crisply. "So my action has sparked off a decision to put an end to this disgraceful hoarding of things needed for the sick. I am delighted."

Colonel Rawlings–Turner grew purple and had to mop his brow with a large handkerchief. "The supply officer is following normal siege procedure. Your . . . your . . . *action* has not influenced his conduct in anyway whatsoever. He is, in fact, blissfully ignorant of this." He flapped the paper before her. "I, unfortunately, am not, and have been made to look extremely foolish before one of my subalterns as a result. Let me make it quite clear here and now that I forbid—I *absolutely* forbid—your using my men for a house-to-house collection . . . or for anything else! Since Mr. Forrester detailed four men to construct a roundabout in your garden, you have been giving them all kinds of occupations which they have performed in the belief that their officer is prepared to allow it."

"But I have asked them to do nothing that is difficult or exhausting. My little tasks have been light relief for them."

"Light relief! *Light relief!*" The colonel was infuriated. "Those men are soldiers. They have duties to perform in defense of this garrison. Our numbers are growing less each day, and survival depends on every man being at his post when needed." His agitation prevented his standing still any longer, and his long legs strode about the room taking him back and forth very swiftly. "At this moment, ma'am, I should be consulting strength returns and duty rosters in my quarters. Instead, I am wasting valuable time over a matter which is really quite unforgiveable. I cannot stress . . ."

He was cut short by the entry of the maid to announce that a soldier was outside wishing to see the colonel urgently. Caught up in the air, he demanded testily of the rifleman standing in the doorway to state his business. The man retained a wooden expression, and stood to attention with his helmet neatly beneath his arm.

"Sorry, sir, but your quarters 'as jest been struck by a shell. They're gone, colonel."

"Gone?"

"Nothin' but a pile o' bricks, sir. The adjutant's bin cut about a bit, but no one else is injured."

It took a moment for the colonel to collect his thoughts but, even then, he sounded abstracted. "Thank you, Piper. I'll be there directly."

"Yessir."

The soldier went, and the silence was broken by a faint voice saying, "Dear me, I hope Captain Merriman is not too badly hurt. What a terrible thing to have happened."

Judith and the colonel turned simultaneously, and the girl was surprised to see that her aunt had gone white and was looking at them with over-large eyes.

"I cannot help thinking how very providential it was that

my little scheme caused you to be here when it happened, instead of working on those duty rosters." The calmness, the pretended innocence had gone. She was a frightened woman.

"Yes," said the colonel slowly. "Yes . . . indeed." With a conscious effort he pulled himself together and bowed to the invalid. "You must excuse me, ma'am. There will be documents . . . papers . . ." He turned to Judith. "I'll see myself out."

"I am sorry," Judith said, shaken herself. "Give Captain Merriman our wishes for a speedy recovery. I trust you will manage to recover everything safely." As an afterthought she added, "We should be pleased to hear the outcome if you care to call this evening after dinner."

"Thank you. Yes, I should like to . . . er, excuse me, ladies."

It was only after he had left that Judith remembered that she was giving a recital that evening and mentioned it to her aunt.

"No matter. I shall be here," was the soft answer. "Poor man. What a lucky escape."

Judith was roused. "You can say 'poor man' when you have been driving him to distraction all this time? I knew nothing of these schemes you've been organizing. It really was inconsiderate of you to trade on Neil's good nature. He has obviously received a wigging from the Colonel because of it."

Mrs. Davenport wrinkled her nose. "A *wigging*? Really, dear, you have been adopting the strangest words since the Boers surrounded us. Is it ladylike?"

"I do not care one way or the other. I believe it is possible to be too ladylike . . . or so I have been told. Now, what about poor Neil?"

"Mr. Forrester is sure to survive any *wigging* he receives and reach the top of a profession that is in his blood. I am very fond of him."

"Then why did you use his men without asking his permission? It's not like you to behave that way."

Mrs. Davenport patted the chair beside her and Judith went to sit on it.

"We have one advantage over men, my dear," she began. "When things become too much for us we can break into tears and earn comfort and sympathy. They, poor things, have to be strong and manly throughout all adversity. Those four riflemen have enjoyed doing things for me because it made them feel a sense of normality—of life going on as usual. A roundabout for the children was as far from defending a besieged town as they could get, and it drew them nearer to their own families at home, in some curious way. I saw it in their faces, Judith. The colonel is a slightly different case, however. He needs to ease his tension and cannot do so in the same way as his men. Colonels are lonely men, because there are not many of them about . . . in any one situation, that is. My exploits have given him ample opportunity to rid himself of the burden on his nervous system." A curious brightness filled her eyes. "Mr. Forrester has his devotion to you to keep him going. I like to think I have done what little I could to ease the worries of his colonel." She smiled a little wanly. "And all my schemes *were* designed to help the community."

The piano recital that evening gave Judith little pleasure for once. The hall had been finally demolished several days before. Tonight, the concert was given in the granary. Perhaps it was the unfamiliar surroundings, or the events of a long sweltering day, that made Judith's fingers feel leaden.

An hour on the piano stool made her back ache, and the flickering lantern light on the sheets of music made her strain her eyes to read the notes. Unhappy with her own performance, she took no pleasure from the applause. It seemed to her she had chosen particularly melancholy or nostalgic pieces, and a cloak of depression settled over her as she collected her music at the end of her performance.

The audience vanished quickly into the night, leaving only herself and Neil. She looked up from her task to where he was waiting a few yards away.

"I'll only be a moment. Some of this music is so worn I'm afraid of tearing the pages. There's no chance of replacing it."

His boots rang on the concrete floor as he walked to her. "Judith, I have something to tell you."

She looked up again quickly at the strange note in his voice. "Yes . . . what is it? You look . . . I don't know . . . almost angry."

He stood gazing at her for a while, and something about him reminded her of her aunt's words earlier that day. Something was inside him bursting to come out. The strain of the past months showed in his face and there was a depth of near desperation in his dark eyes.

"Neil, what is it?" she asked growing still.

"I waited until now to tell you. I had a feeling it would be better to do so. The fact is, we received a heliograph message late this afternoon informing us that one of the regiment's officers reported as being taken prisoner by the Boers has escaped and joined the relief column. It's Alex. He is now with Buller on his way to Ladysmith."

It was too much. She had believed him safe until the end of the war. To hide her tears she turned away, staring at the wall that blurred and shimmered.

"Don't," whispered Neil, putting his arms around her and pulling her back against him. "Please don't."

## CHAPTER FOURTEEN

Alex swayed in the saddle as he stared at the long khaki line in front of him. Did any man, apart from those who lived upon it, appreciate the true power and scale of the veld? He had seen it from the windows of a train, had watched for an ox wagon to emerge from its distances every Thursday, had crossed it slowly and painfully with Guy such a short time ago, and yet saw it again with renewed awe.

There was no greater leveler than God's wilderness when a man was put upon it to prove himself. He had emerged from that journey with Guy, humbled, yet more at peace within himself than he could remember. For days he had defied the sun, the vastness with the knowledge that he was not master of his own fate. Hetta's simple belief that he was being guided by the Almighty had taken root.

When he continued to survive through the fortunate chance of coming upon an English farmer who lent them horses, fed them, and guided them to Buller's headquarters, Alex felt the influence of Divine guidance more strongly than ever. As a result, his thoughts these days dwelt more

and more on his brother Miles, as he wondered if there had
been a reason for the sacrifice of that young life to save his
own. With a battle ahead, it was a powerful thought.

The marching column ahead came to a halt again. Alex
saw the ranks concentrate then expand before standing still
like a dark glistening serpent reaching out across the brown
surface. Urging his horse slowly onward he rode alongside
the stationary men, struck by the grimness of what he saw.
The tiny outpost of Landerdorp had been no center of endeavor, nor had Ladysmith Tin Town, he realized now.
For the first time since his father had enlisted him in the
Downshires he could see the true meaning of soldiering.

Riding with General Buller's relief column he was in
company with some thirty-two thousand men—more soldiers gathered together than he had ever seen at one
time—and the whole multitude with its accompanying
stores and wagons straggled for seventeen miles across the
sodden rain-swept shelterless plains.

It had rained continuously for four days and nights, and
he had forgotten what it was like to be dry . . . as had
every man in the column. Now, at two P.M., it was dark
with lowering clouds yet the heat of afternoon assailed
them as they sweltered in weather cloaks or oilskins. The
khaki sun helmets, turned putty gray with saturation, had
the virtue of protecting the face from the deluge, but the
overhanging brim at the back designed to shade a man's
neck from the noon sun merely channeled a rivulet to soak
through onto his back and chafed shoulders that carried
heavy packs.

If the sky was leaden then everything beneath it was
equally somber. The distant hills were no more than
blurred humps that melted into the funereal draperies of
cloud above them, and the surrounding plain lay flat and
ominous before him. To march for long across any part
that was not marked with a track would surely take the
traveler over the edge into the underworld. With imagination, a man could see the rim dangerously near and tempt-
ing.

Even with a track to follow, the destination held little
attraction. The relentless rain had softened the earth, and
marching boots, plodding hooves, wagon wheels, and heavy
gun carriages had turned it into brown sludgy liquid. It
sucked greedily at everything it touched; it rose up to fill
boots and drag at weary feet. It gurgled and shifted beneath

horses' hooves, sending them crashing down to deposit their riders heavily time and time again. It was unresistant to the rolling wheels that sank above their axles in the filthy stream, and it frothed and bubbled as oxen trampled it.

Another ammunition wagon had bogged down and caused the halt. Alex sat his horse watching the attempts to pull it free and felt a tide of anger wash over him. From what he had heard of the affair at Colenso it was the army's very cumbersomeness that had contributed to the defeat. To Boers hiding in the hills with a rifle, a speedy horse, and simple rations, all fears of a surprise attack vanished at sight of a column of uniformed men with all the paraphernalia of supplies, ammunition, forage, rations, field kitchens, medical equipment, observation balloons, signaling apparatus, pontoons for bridges, poles and wires for the field telegraph, farriers and blacksmiths, native grooms and stretcher bearers, naval guns and sailor crews, and as many as fifteen thousand oxen. From the surrounding hills they knew so well, the enemy could watch the snail's pace approach of the British and build their defenses at leisure.

Alex watched the long span of oxen heaving and struggling. The wagon was sinking lower beneath the slime as their frenzied hooves loosened the mud. Then he looked around him. Soldiers, hunch-shouldered and resigned, stood regarding a scene they had seen too often. Efforts had been made to march round the obstacle, but without much enthusiasm. They welcomed any excuse for a halt, even though it was impossible to sit down or seek respite from the driving rain. One or two still had enough vigor to offer crude and useless advice on how to solve the problem, but the majority watched with a hopeless patience.

Not so with the officers. They dashed about, their horses sending brown liquid streams flying from their hooves, and shouted urgent words to the native drivers of the teams, certain it needed only a firm voice of command to achieve the impossible. At last one of the newly arrived traction engines was brought forward with a noisy roar, and succeeded where eighty oxen had failed. The gigantic trail of men and vehicles moved off once more, winding across enemy-free territory toward the River Tugela which had to be crossed if they were to reach Ladysmith.

Since Alex's own regiment was shut up in the town they were headed to relieve, he was used whenever there was a

need for another officer. It was not to his liking, for it
meant he was given duties everyone tried to avoid. But he
had a more serious objection to not being given a regular
command.

The earlier battles of the war had taken a terrible toll of
officers, who were so easily distinguishable by their uniforms and swords. To counteract the Boers' habit of picking
off officers as targets and leaving no commanders for the
companies of troops, general orders had been issued for all
ranks to dress alike, and for swords to be abandoned in
favor of rifles with bayonets. Without insignia of rank and
the customary sword, officers could only be recognized by
those who knew them—and Alex was unknown to nearly
everyone. In the forthcoming battle how would he ever persuade men to follow him?

The column moved inexorably forward like a great
floundering snake watched by hidden eyes in the hills rearing up along the far banks of the Tugela. By the time they
were near enough to make out the enemy through field
glasses, it was apparent they had reinforced their positions
in preparation, and General Buller was forced to split his
column in order to keep the Boers guessing.

The rain stopped after the fifth day, but the continuous
deluge had swelled the Tugela into a fast-flowing treacherous barricade that eddied in brown fathomless swirls. An
African rain could increase a river's depth by as much as
twelve feet overnight, and even the men of the country
were unwilling to cross without careful reconnaissance. The
natural fords could be deceptive after flooding, so pontoon
bridges were decided upon.

Guy Cuthbertson, who had been gladly absorbed into
the royal engineers detachment, voiced his opinion to Alex
as they stood surveying the gigantic camp that had mush-
roomed around them on arrival.

"God only knows how long it will take to get this lot
across the river. He surely does not intend that we drag it
over the hills, lock, stock, and barrel." He grinned. "From
what I remember of Ladysmith it will never all fit in."

Alex assumed a drawl. "It's tradition, old chap. What
Wellington did, we must all copy."

Guy raised his eyebrows. "You've never had much time
for the military system, have you?"

"Not a great deal . . . and when I witness what I have
seen these past six days I think I'm justified. It's absolutely

absurd to move around like an Indian maharajah and his entourage. You saw those men at the farm. All they had was a horse, a rifle, dried meat, and comfortable clothes. It is people like them that are holding us all up to ridicule in this war. You only have to remember Landerdorp, Guy. They appeared out of nowhere, in silence, and caught us napping. We tramp up to them in great lumbering columns, blowing bugles and clattering pots and pans. It's ludicrous."

Guy grinned. "Wellington did it."

"Wellington was fighting an enemy that did exactly the same. They even exchanged pleasantries over breakfast before blowing each other to pieces. We might still be frightfully good sorts, but the Boers are not. They are sensible and fight only to win."

"Oh come, that's a little hard. From what I hear of Colenso our lads fought desperately hard to win."

"I know they did . . . but why load themselves down with every disadvantage to do it?"

"They didn't. Someone did it for them."

Alex looked at the formidable battleground ahead. Across the tortuous Tugela lay a green and exposed plain encircled by very high hills, one hiding another so that it was impossible to tell the depth of the range or the space between them. It could be one long range with saddles between the peaks, or there could be a series of unscalable hills with a valley twisting between. One thing was plain: To get to Ladysmith they would have to capture one of the two massive heights that dominated the range at each end.

At the moment, the Boers were in full occupation of the hills, in the perfect position to mow down soldiers crossing bridges and the open plain at the foot of the range. It looked like suicide for any attacking force.

Turning to Guy, Alex said, "The only hope, as far as I can see, is to cross under cover of darkness and launch a surprise attack where they least expect it." He indicated the double bridge reaching out over the Tugela. "We'll never do it with a column seventeen miles long."

Guy tried to find excuses. "We've got to get the guns over, old boy. It doesn't mean . . ."

"Let's hope it doesn't," Alex finished grimly.

But it did.

On the morning of January 17, the main force, under Sir Charles Warren, began crossing the pontoons in broad day-

light, and the great tail of wagons, guns, and meat on the
hoof clattered across, too. Apart from a few desultory
shots, the Boers did nothing to prevent it. Why should
they? It was easier to wait until the khaki hordes came
clambering up the slopes, presenting perfect targets. Those
who were not killed then would be driven back in disorder
with the treacherous Tugela between them and safety. It
would be Colenso all over again.

Alex was restless all morning, watching the streams of
men and vehicles swaying over the boat bridges exposed to
view of those in the hills. It was his first real approach to
battle, so he waited uneasily for the sound of heavy guns
and the shells that would send men and equipment rocket-
ing into the air as the bridges flew apart. He did not understand the delay. Those who had been at Colenso, who were
old hands at fighting the Boers, knew they would hold their
fire until the very last moment. To Alex, it seemed inexplicable to let such masses of troops go unmolested when
completely defenseless. A few shells on the bridges could
cause utter chaos and retreat.

His tension lifted when he received orders to assist with
the remounts that were to cross with the cavalry a mile
further downstream. He gladly ordered his horse to be saddled and joined the men who had been rounding up the
spare horses. It was good to have something to do at last.

No one hurried. The cavalrymen joked among themselves, or talked of polo, tent-pegging, and steeplechases
until Alex had to admit a grudging admiration for a breed
that had always earned his derision. It was not done to
show the slightest concern when danger loomed. He began
to understand why the colors of so many British regiments
were emblazoned with battle honors. Fleetingly he recalled
returning from a nightmare to hear Neil Forrester saying,
"You see, we don't like rotters in the regiment."

Funny that that memory should come to him as he was
riding beside the river. He had been so intent on his companions the swirl of water had slid past on his right without
commanding his attention. Looking at it now, the familiar
pricking along the back of his neck started, and his hands
on the reins grew clammy. He would be glad when the
bridge was crossed.

With an effort he turned away and forced himself to look
at the grass that was lush and faintly steaming in the heat
of sun after the rains. It created an unreality of haze, as if

one were looking at a paradise garden through an ancient window, cobweb-laced and forgotten. Small hovering birds of iridescent green took his attention, and he drifted away from his surroundings on a daydream. Such a peaceful sun-drenched scene wooed a man into a romantic mood, and he swayed with the motion of his horse, lost in a study of the sweeter pastimes of living creatures.

The grasses were aquiver with vivid butterflies disturbed by the horses' progress, who moved on to fresh resting places before them, and down by the water a kingfisher did the same with sweeping flights, skimming the water. The semblance of normality so charmed him, he was taken unawares when the line halted. The remounts were mustered at the head of the column, and Alex rode forward to discover the reason for it.

There was a Hussar captain in command—he looked no more than a boy who had not yet been in South Africa long enough to acquire a tan—and he studied a scrap of paper in his hand.

"According to this sketch map," he began, "it would appear the *drift* is roughly here." He gave a self-conscious laugh. "If I've made a mistake you'll soon find out." He swung his horse to face the rushing water.

Alex reeled. Nobody had spoken of a ford to him. He had thought there was another bridge—a pontoon. He would have refused the command . . . lied. His brain spun; his body went through spasms of shock. The oily-smooth whorls that raced past his gaze reduced him to a terror no thought of battle could ever do. Pain flared in his chest with violent suddenness, limiting his breathing. He felt his face sprout sweat, and a roaring in his ears grew so loud it hurt his head.

The young cavalry captain was well out into the water and struggling to keep on a straight course. The horse he rode held its head high with fear. With a swift glance over his shoulder he was waving his arm.

"Come on. It's lovely once you're in!"

The man beside Alex growled, "I suppose that's his idea of a joke. Here goes, then."

As his companion moved forward, a great wave of dizziness swept over Alex, and he gasped for enough air to counteract it. The pain in his chest grew worse, and the river with the men in it blurred and tilted.

"No," he cried on a racked breath and instinctively tried

to urge his horse backward up the bank, away from the
yellowish brown water. All rational thought had left him.
He would fight anyone in order to get away from what he
knew awaited him beneath the surface. Panic took hold as
his hands yanked on the reins to turn his mount's head. But
there was a whole company of cavalry behind him who
were pressing down the bank ready to cross. There was no
room to turn, and his horse preferred to stay with the herd
than fight its way back through its companions.

Slewing sideways Alex was pressed down to the brink of
the water, fighting like a maniac. With the roar in his ears
and all sane thought gone, he was vaguely aware of a man
near him shouting angrily. The next minute, there was the
crack of a whip, and his horse plunged into the river,
whites of eyes rolling and snorts of fright coming from its
nostrils.

It was icy cold and went through his clothes to lap right
up his legs in a series of sinister snatches. All around him
riderless horses were struggling and plunging, setting up a
turbulence of frothy foam as they fought the pull of the
powerful current. Those just ahead of him were being
dragged downstream, horses neighing with fear as the submerged foothold vanished beneath their hooves. Men were
shouting to each other, and above it all was the din of rushing water.

Alex's leg was pinned between his own horse and another beside him. It was then the voices started. *There's
something around my legs. Get me out, Alex.* All this had
happened somewhere before.

With fierce strength he struck the neighboring horse
across the nose, caring nothing for the fate of the beast and
knowing only that there were things below the water that
must not be allowed to pull him under. The water level had
reached his waist and the pull was so strong it was difficult
to stay in the saddle. He clung on with hands that clamped
an iron hold on the pommel. A branch raced past just
ahead. It looked like a gnarled hand. *The housemaid has
been here for a hundred years.* Dear God, they meant to
get him this time!

There was a lurch and he was suddenly moving sideways
away from the sleek-skinned jostling animals. The bank
was getting further away. Beneath him the horse struggled
and kicked until, pulled by something he could not fight,
Alex found himself separated from his mount.

The water closed around him and over his head. It was silent down there and things touched him. With a great burst of sound his head broke through to the world of the living.

It was useless to struggle. They had caught up with him at last. No wonder his brother had been so much in his thoughts lately. He had been calling to him. He heard Miles's voice quite clearly. *She was wronged, you know. Her hand comes up through the water trying to hold onto something.* The world receded, but the voices would not stop now. *We might see the hand come out of the water . . . the body was tangled in the reeds . . . it's been there a hundred years.*

The housemaid was waiting for him when the sky exploded in a silver flash above him. Her hand clutched him—a bony skeletal hand that seized him around his neck and tried to drag him down with her for another hundred years. Terror beset him and he fought like a demon, but the harder he fought the stronger grew the grip. Helpless, swept along, he kicked out and touched her body that grew closer to his.

"Help me. Get me out!" It could not possibly be the housemaid. The voice was deep and terrified, as Miles's had been. His hands were locked around Alex's neck, dragging him down and refusing to let go.

"Help me. Get me out of here."

Water bubbled up to Alex's nostrils, then subsided. He spluttered and choked, fighting desperately to free himself. He must get to the punt. Miles was bigger than he was and stronger. The only way to save him was to get the punt. The sun was hot, but the lake was icy cold. He wished they had not disobeyed father. It was a long way to the boat, but he must go on. *Alex, help me.*

The punt was enormous, looming above him in the water, and it was a hard struggle to pull himself over the top and into it. He must reach Miles. Somehow he must get the punt over there. The pole had gone when his brother fell in, so he must paddle with his hands. But he was such a small boy, and the punt was so wide. One side only—he could paddle on one side. It was turning in circles, going nowhere. *Alex, I can't move. There's something around my legs. Get me out. Get me out.*

He was crying, sobbing with desperation. He was saying prayers: God, please help me. His arms were sore, his body was aching, but the punt just went round in circles. Suddenly, he looked up and Miles had disappeared. He wanted to scream, but no sound came. His brother had been pulled beneath the water by the housemaid. He was sick, but no one came to comfort him. He was alone in the dark, like a naughty boy who will not say he is sorry. He wanted to tell them, but his mouth would not move—would not tell them he had done his best to save his brother. He had tried, he really and truly had.

*If God had to take one, why did he choose Miles?* His father asked that and walked away. The next day he ordered them to put him in the lake with Miles and the housemaid. They had held him there wanting him to disappear. It frightened him. There were terrible things beneath the water. He kicked and bit them, but they were stronger and took him back the following day. He must go with Miles. They did not want him any longer. But he wanted them. He fought and fought to get out of the lake. He was still fighting.

"Steady, steady," came a kindly voice. "Take hold of this, old chap." A hand clasped his firmly, and pulled him to where his feet touched solid ground. They were reaching out for him, welcoming him back, drawing him out of the water and back to life. He still clasped Miles by his shirt in a tight grip, and they had to pry his fingers open to carry his brother off. They were glad about what he had done. The voices were friendly, using terms of companionship.

Half staggering, half leaning on them, he felt himself climbing the bank, and the threshing of water and whinnying of horses was back in his ears. They let him lie on the warm grass to recover, then attended the other one.

"Cardew can't swim, apparently," someone drawled. "Some damned fool should have warned us before he crossed. This Rifle chap kept him afloat. Perkins has drowned, I believe. Hell of a country, this. No maps, and bloody rivers that flood to three times their depth! As far as I'm concerned, the Boers are welcome to it."

Rustling sounded beside Alex, and a hand fell on his shoulder. "How is it with you now, old chap?"

"Everything is fine . . . absolutely fine," he murmured thankfully, and the wronged housemaid disappeared forever, along with the ghost of a boy he had tried to save.

# CHAPTER FIFTEEN

Where any other enemy would have come streaming down from the hills upon those exposed on the plain, the Dutch preferred to fight safely hidden from sight. It was not that they were cowards, but they liked to live to fight again another day. They would lay down their lives for their country, but only if there was really no alternative. The British who made outstandingly courageous advances under murderous fire, or who galloped through heavy shellfire to bring in their guns, earned their admiration but were regarded as fools for throwing away their lives so willingly.

The Boers were vastly outnumbered but sat tight knowing a good marksman behind a rock could hold off ten times his own number advancing uphill in straight rows with no cover. Sooner or later the British would start moving. Until then, the burghers were happy to smoke their pipes and wait. Each day that passed meant the weakening of Ladysmith garrison. Their two attempts to attack the town had been miserable failures. To their annoyance, the garrison did not appear as anxious to surrender as they had imagined. However, all the time the relief force played games with wagons over bridges, the people of Ladysmith were suffering and their resolution growing weaker.

Playing games with wagons over bridges was about right. Having spent two days sizing up the situation, General Warren, acting on reports from his various subordinates, decided that the Boers had closed up the original route through to Ladysmith and another would have to be taken. This involved the capture of a low ridge and crossing the plain around the foot of the massive Spion Kop. Since wagons would be unable to cross that particular track, it was proposed that they should all recross the Tugela while men advanced with four days' provisions in their packs. But advance where? No one seemed sure.

For several more days small skirmishes and minor oper-
ations were successfully made—at one stage the cavalry
captured control of a direct route through to Ladysmith.
Instead of following it up, Buller, who disliked the cavalry
commander, ordered the mounted men back to guard the
cattle. The chance was lost. In other places all around that
block of hills vantage points were being won, only to be
surrendered on orders to fall back on the main force.

It was already January 23, and they were all sitting
along the banks of the river as if they were on a picnic
outing.

They also wanted a victory for the sake of those at
home, who must feel the British Army was taking a beating
at the hands of the farmers. Attempts by the relieving
forces marching on the other two besieged towns of Kimberley and Mafeking were also failing quite disastrously,
the casualties running into thousands. Soon the British public must be given something to cheer, something to restore
their faith in their sons and husbands who were fighting on
their behalf. A glorious victory had never been wanted
quite so badly by army and country alike.

General Buller and General Warren, disliking each other
intensely, met head on in a clash of personalities on January 23, and took a step that neither wanted, neither had
intended taking, and which was the result of temper clouding judgment. Buller charged Warren with unnecessary in-
activity, to which the subordinate man replied with his
hastily contrived plan to cross the ridge with men only.
Testy to a degree Buller pointed out that the huge height of
Spion Kop overlooked this route and asked if Warren intended capturing the hill also. Warren snapped that of
course he intended capturing it, and the fatal decision was
made. Buller left with an order to attack Spion Kop that
night or retreat over the river.

Thus, the troops were committed to assaulting a hill of
unknown features and height, a hill of doubtful strategic
importance, an objective that had been in no plan of cam-
paign until that morning. The regimental officers, feeling it
was better to attack something than do nothing at all, took
their orders calmly despite the fact that there were no maps
or sketches of Spion Kop, nor any local guide to lead them
up the rocky sides. The companies selected for the assault
were warned, and spirits began to rise. Ladysmith, here we
come was the general cry.

* * *

Alex leaned against a tree and stared into total darkness. There was nothing so black as an African night when moon and stars were hidden by clouds. The only way of telling there were nearly two thousand men surrounding him was by the rustle of grass or cracking twig as someone shifted nervously; by the occasional cough quickly smothered; by the rattle of a rifle butt against the stony ground as a soldier shifted his weight onto another foot. There was also the smell of sweat, khaki, leather boots, and the whiff of smoke from cigarettes extinguished just a few moments ago. Less obvious, but there just the same, was the aroma of scented soap and macassar oil where the officers had prepared for the night's work. Why did a man dress with as much care for a battle as for a ball? Alex wondered. He had shaved only an hour ago and stood in the gully at the foot of Spion Kop as immaculate as if going on parade. Bloody ridiculous, he mused, and a quick thought of Neil Forrester came into his mind. Was he growing as traditional as that son of the regiment?

A hand touched his arm. "Who are you?" came the whisper.

"Russell . . . in temporary command of C company."

"Right, move off, Russell. Don't lag or you'll lose your way. Absolute silence, and watch out for Boer pickets. See you at the top."

"Right," Alex replied having no idea who the speaker was. He tapped the body next to his. "Sergeant Cutler?"

"Yessir," came the low affirmative.

"Good. Pass the word back. We're off."

"Right, sir. We're off."

The silence was suddenly filled with the swishing sound of rhythmic feet passing through long dew-laden grass, and Alex soon found just how wet it was. The inside of his boots grew uncomfortable and his breeches clung to his legs. The discomfort was increased by a chill drizzle of rain, but no one dared slacken the pace for fear of falling behind the company ahead.

It was easy going across the plain, but the ground began to slope upward after an hour and Alex supposed they were then on the lower slopes of the hill. Thankfully the rain ceased, but it was still as black as hell everywhere. He felt sweat breaking on his forehead. It was damned unnerving playing a game of silent blindman's buff on a hillside. Ev-

ery step he took could take him over the edge. He only had
the faint trace of the man ahead to rely on . . . and so
had every man. That their leader had no knowledge of the
route was a disturbing thought; yet, minute by minute,
hour by hour, they were all going up to meet what lay at
the top.

All at once he thumped into something ahead, and a
voice snarled softly, "Watch what you're bloody doing!
We've halted, that's what."

Alex made no answer. There was a medley of groans and
grunts, as the message was passed to the back. He sat
against a rocky wall and revived all his misgivings about
the night's operation. They should never have put an unknown officer in charge of troops at such a crucial time,
even though their own subaltern had gone down with fever.
In accordance with present regulations, there was nothing
to mark him as an officer, and his men had seen him for
the first time at dusk when the light played tricks with a
person's sight. In the midst of battle could he possibly hold
his adopted company together; would any man obey his
orders instantly?

A jab in the ribs and a hoarse voice advising him they
were on the move again brought a halt to such thoughts,
but a long climb with no verbal or visual distractions left a
man open to reflection. He had doubts—fears, even. Landerdorp had been nothing, but what lay ahead tonight
would be vastly different, he felt sure. His throat was dry.
His hands, so skillful with a rifle, would have to use that
skill against a living human target for the first time. He was
full of excited apprehension . . . but so must be every
man with him.

He let out a long sigh of release. He could be afraid, he
could fail, he could join the ranks of his fellows in the living of his life. No longer need he be humiliated by his own
fallibility. There was no more need to strive for impossible
perfection, to stand apologizing for his own inadequacies.
Nothing would ever change the belief of his father that
Miles died courageously saving his young brother, but the
truth was now his and that was all that mattered. The
ghosts, the guilt had gone during that revelation in the
Tugela—and with it his fear of the water. There was nothing beneath the surface that could harm him now.

He was free as he had never been before. He owed no
man anything except his fellowship and whatever happened

in the minutes ahead, it would be to his own conscience and nothing else that he must look.

The path steepened and the surface grew stony. Boots began to slip on pebbles, and strange rattles and scraping noises broke the silence. All around Alex was the sigh of heavy breathing, and the smell of sweat. A great clatter, an involuntary cry, "Oh Christ!" The cascade of stones growing fainter in hollow depth, and an angry barrack-square whisper of "Shut up!"

His own armpits were growing damper: an ache filled his legs. The next halt was a long one—too long. The whole damned force was lost. Was that it? What if the leader had walked clean off the path and plunged to the bottom? Would they all be forced to turn around and go back the way they had come . . . and which way was that? Alex shook his head to stay awake. They had been climbing for hours and all kinds of fantasy thoughts invaded unoccupied minds. God, if they could only see something!

They were off again. Round and round, twisting and turning, climbing even steeper rocky paths. Another hour passed. Three more halts and three advances. They must soon be at the top. What a laugh if their leader had fallen from the path and they were now following a Boer who was leading them straight into the arms of his comrades! What he would give for a drink!

The path vanished and the only way to move was on all fours, feeling for hand and footholds in the sharp uneven rock. Two thousand men imitating apes in the pitch darkness—apes in full marching order with nailed boots, heavy packs, rifles, and ammunition. It was madness. The fool in front had better be climbing up the right hill!

Suddenly, it grew colder. A chill wind began and Alex shivered. Vegetation had ceased; he was climbing across a bare surface. No sooner had he guessed the summit had been reached than those ahead stopped and whispered back that Boer sentries were ahead. Then came the whispered command rippling back through the immobile ranks. "Fix bayonets!"

The bayonet; a weapon that filled the Boer with dread. He preferred a distant bullet or shell. Alex took the long sharp piece of steel and fitted it to the end of his rifle with a soft click. *Will I find the courage and inhumanity to stick this into a man's flesh?* he wondered. His heart was thudding, and it traveled up into his ears like the sound of the big drum in the regimental band.

"Advance! Make no noise," came the whispered word, and he turned to pass it on to whomever was behind him.

Holding his rifle steady he walked slowly forward into the unknown hoping nobody would bayonet him in the back by mistake. There was an exposed feeling about the atmosphere now, and wind whistled desolately around him.

"Halt! Lie down." A rattle of weapons; a rustle of clothing. This was it. The Boers were so near their voices could be heard in the night.

Now they were advancing several yards at a time on hands and knees, not certain quite where the sentries were in that cloak of darkness. It was enough to stretch a man's nerves to their tightest pitch when, at the rear, a loud clatter of shovels being dropped set everything happening at once.

"*Wie's daar?*" came a sharp cry, and an explosion of bangs and flashes followed by the patter of rain—except that it was not rain but bullets, Alex realized quickly. He had dropped flat, as had everyone else on the command. Another fusilade rent the air.

From the front came a loud command in English. "Charge! Come on men, remember Majuba."

The air was suddenly filled with shrieking—the sounds of battle lust that adds hysteria to the human voice. The blackness was dotted with yellow lights. Distant shots sounded like the first heavy storm drops on a broad leaf. Men were running up ahead. Commands were flying in two languages. An agonized moan, then silence.

It was all over. Caution was forgotten as unseen men laughed with relief. They told each other what fine fellows they were. The fear, the battle nerves were forgotten. They had crept up on Johnny Boer and routed him. It had been a complete and utter surprise to the enemy. Spion Kop had been taken. Now it was straight on to Ladysmith.

Alex left them to their jubilation. When they gave three cheers to tell those who were below on the plain that the objective had been secured, he did not join in. It was over, and all he had done was climb a hill. Feeling his way to a clear patch he sat down, heavy with anticlimax. Something told him there was a hollow ring to this victory. If the hill had been occupied by only a handful of Boers, had it been worth the taking?

Dawn broke soon afterward and brought the usual thick mist. The Royal Engineers—those men who had dropped their shovels and raised the alarm—set to work building fortifications. Now that the British had taken Spion Kop they must be prepared to hold it. The bare plateau provided no natural cover so work was started on digging trenches on the crest which would command the slopes down which the Boers had run.

It was not easy. After eighteen inches the picks hit solid rock, and the only thing to do was build a breastwork of stones for those who would have to lie in the shallow trenches. Sandbags were called for, but it was discovered that they had been left below. It was a grave mistake. Even with the piled stones as protection a man had no more than three feet behind which to hide.

While the engineers dug and constructed, the remainder took the opportunity to eat some of their rations, collect water from the tins that had been carried up, and snatch some sleep. Alex saw his men assembled, made certain they knew who he was, then followed suit. He lay restless on the hard ground, thinking over the night's events and wondering if they had all been a little melodramatic. Two thousand men had crept and climbed for seven hours, and there could not have been more than several dozen Boers up here. His mouth twisted. Some fine victory! His final thought before drifting off to sleep was whether the view when the mist cleared would be reward enough for such a stiff climb.

A great roaring in his ears brought him instantly awake to a nightmare. The mist had gone leaving the brilliance Africa can produce in an instant, and his dazzled eyes tried to take in and understand what he saw. The air was full of an incomprehensible fury that pounded his ears and shook his body. Earth and dust were flying up in sudden mushrooms, and the ground just ahead of him was moving as if a million worms were trying to push up from beneath the surface.

On each side of him men were rising up from sleep with oaths on their lips, grabbing for their rifles as their stunned brains fought to translate the scene before them. The terrible truth got through to Alex as he struggled to his feet.

The view he had wished to see was there before him, and revealed that the British were not on the crest of Spion Kop, as they had thought. Soaring above them were peaks on either side that commanded the entire plateau. From these the Boers were pouring shells and bullets down on them at point-blank range. He and his fellow countrymen were caught in a ghastly arena, and those manning the useless trenches were turning into a red-splattered mass.

"Dear God in heaven," he breathed through stiff lips, and deep inside a new kind of anger exploded. Even as he watched, those in the trenches were jerking and falling sideways in grotesque conformity one after the other. In a fury he snatched his rifle to his shoulder and tried to sight the enemy, but all that betrayed their presence was a momentary glint of sun on steel, or a puff of smoke.

A shout went up. "They're coming!"

Swarming up the side of the hill came a horde of drab-suited Boers, running from rock to rock, each man advancing at his own pace and firing from behind cover. Those left alive in the trenches found the downward angle too steep for firing flat, but the minute a head or arm appeared over the breastwork a Boer bullet whistled and found its mark.

Alex was breathing heavily from the need for action, and he looked wildly around for the major to whom he was answerable. It was pointless. Men were running hither and thither at anyone's command, and it was impossible to recognize a face in the confusion of flying rock and shell splinters. Another glance showed him the Boers were gaining ground up the slope, and he moved.

"To the trenches," he yelled to his men. "Throw out the dead and fire at will."

He began to run out onto the open ground, crouching instinctively. The worms pushing up were really bullets smacking into the ground, he discovered, when Sergeant Cutler gave a scream and convulsed beside him. The air was thick with steel and men were falling all around him. Useless to order them to take cover, for there was none, and to lie flat would get them all shot in the back. Keep racing on for the vague protection of the trenches.

Two feet away Alex was thrown flat by the force of an exploding shell, and slithered doubled up against a man taking aim with his rifle. The soldier turned angrily, but his expression turned to one of pleading before he collapsed face downward. There was a neat red hole in the back of the man's head that froze Alex's hand as it moved to help him. There was no time for anything but attack. He tugged the dead man away from the breastwork of stones so that he could take his place.

"Look out, they're coming again," someone yelled, and Alex saw the ragged line of men rise up along the incline and disappear again, further forward behind fresh cover. Quick as a flash he had sighted a bearded face and fired, but before he could check the result someone clouted him on his arm and he turned to see who it was.

His neighbor grinned nervously. "You've bin 'it, mate." He leaned forward. "There on your . . ." It was never finished. His face vanished in a crimson flower that splashed across Alex's eyes. When he wiped the blood away the man lay still, and blood was oozing from his own arm. In the next few seconds two more men on his right cried out and fell dead, while another dropped his rifle and doubled up in agony. Gripping his gun with shaking hands Alex swung around and fired at the peak, knowing that he was driven to make a token return of their fire. He achieved nothing. They were hidden in perfect positions for firing straight into the khaki-clad figures. The British trenches were death traps.

Suddenly, to his left a figure rose up, waving his rifle like a sword. "Come on, lads. Chaaarge!" he cried, running toward the rocks that hid the enemy. He died immediately and so did those loyal enough to follow their officer, falling one after the other and writhing under the rain of death that followed them. Incredibly another rose to take his place, then another when the second fell. They all went the same way; young, gallant, and headstrong.

The ground ahead was piled with bodies, and the sight must have given the attackers reason for hesitation for they stayed where they were for a while. But the Boers had manhandled a heavy gun onto one of the overlooking peaks, and the trapped British began to be bombarded with heavy shells that blew men into fragments and demolished piled supplies.

An hour passed, and the sun rose on a midsummer's day. Alex lay bathed in sweat as the plateau became a griddle. The wound in his arm ached dully and the heat beat down on his back as he sprawled on his stomach taking potshots at anything that moved down on the slope. He had brought down one Boer and thought he had hit two others, but all around him the trench was being filled with dead men, emptied by living ones who were soon dead themselves. There was no order to retreat, so once a soldier reached the trench he was there until an officer, or an angel, released him.

The big Boer gun had found its range and the air was constantly filled with deadly shrapnel. Alex constantly wiped the grit from his eyes, and choked on the clouded air. He looked around for water, and an old soldier who had just jumped in beside him said, "Water? You'll be lucky, son. They left it all at the bottom of the hill . . . along with the sandbags, the heliograph, the field telephone, and the bloody guns." Just as he finished speaking something thumped against Alex's helmet, and the wag added, "But we got our hats, ain't we? What more could you ask?"

Eleven o'clock and Alex's throat was as dry as dust. No one spoke any longer. The sun was high making the rock throw back stifling heat on those pinned down on Spion Kop. Added to the ceaseless bombardment were the torments of heat and thirst. The smell of death increased. Flies buzzed noisily over open flesh. Circling *aasvogels* had appeared from nowhere to blacken the sky. The cry was for water, but who could give it when the little remaining had been commandeered by the doctor in the tiny field hospital beside some mimosas?

Movement below. The Boers were renewing their attempt to recapture the plateau. Yard by yard they advanced, despite the British rifle fire, and Alex realized the trench would be overrun if something were not done. Since bullets did not stop them, bayonets might. The attempt must be made. Swiftly passing the word along on either side he prepared to get up and charge with cold steel. His soldiers rose up as one when he got to his feet and began a crouching run across open ground.

He was hit immediately just below the other wound in his arm, but he ran on through the whining whistling rain of bullets in an air of unreality until he saw the rocks disintegrate into running men who scrambled and slithered down the slope. He raised his rifle to fire, but his finger never pulled the trigger. The ground before him rose up in a solid wall of chunks in a fine dust curtain, and a tremendous punch in the stomach sent him crashing backward.

The world became strangely silent. Alex opened his eyes to find the pandemonium of battle all around him still, but it was as quiet as the climb the night before had been. Men keeled over with no sound coming from their gaping mouths, and earth flew up in clouds without any warning or noise. While the phenomenon lasted he made no attempt to move, but sound returned, at first distantly, then into a full-scale symphony of war.

He rolled over, and immediately a sharp smack hit the ground a foot away. Someone had him in his sights. He tried again, but a hot knife ran over his leg leaving a trickle of sticky wetness. A third attempt brought another bullet whistling into the ground between his outstretched arms. Desperately he swept the scene with a ground-level glance and saw the outer trench to his left. Pausing only long enough to gather his thoughts he scrambled up and began a lurching run that brought all hell let loose.

His helmet was punched from his head, and his left sleeve was ripped by flying metal before a violent tearing pain in his thigh told him a bullet had found its mark and buried itself deep into his flesh. But he reached the trench before collapsing with his hands around the wound. For a while he lay gasping, riding tides of pain that rolled down to his foot and up to his brain, then he twisted to look at it. One glance was enough. Blood was rushing out with dangerous speed and had to be staunched quickly. Grunting and struggling he unwound the puttees from a nearby corpse and wound the coarse material tightly around his own leg. The effort took a lot out of him, and he felt dizziness hit his brain.

For a while he lay as if drugged, until he realized the sun was blazing down upon his bare head. All the warnings about sunstroke worried him, but his limbs did not coordinate with his thoughts anymore. The two wounds in his arms were open and messy, giving pain similar to a gouging knife, and the desire for water was becoming an obsession. If he could only crawl to . . . no, they would pick him off immediately. Nobody moved out here and lived!

The sun rose to its zenith, and he began to feel very ill. Sweat ran into his eyes; it stood out on his upper lip. Reaching for it with his tongue he found the salty warmness no relief. The longing for a drink became a craving. He tried calling for water, but it was a mere cracked croak. The pandemonium of battle echoed louder and louder in his head until he was forced to cover his ears with his hands. The noise in his head went on just the same. With a groan he rolled onto his side, but lay on his wounded arm and was forced back to face the sun once more.

At that moment, giants of men began rushing past and over him, rearing up into the brassy sky like long brown shadows as their legs strode past, careless of where he lay. They were shouting like madmen. Then, one was on the ground only a few feet away, looking straight at him while blood gushed out of a hole beside his right eye. It had once been the other eye, Alex realized. The man's hand reached out, but turned into a bloody mess of bones and pulp.

"For God's sake, help me," came the plea, but Alex forgot all else when something crashed down across his legs and forced a cry from his own lips that heralded a crimson darkness for a while. When it subsided he became vaguely aware that the heavy weight was the major he had looked for earlier. The man's head was twisted at an angle and his bright blue eyes gazed up at the beauty of a South African hill without seeing the mimosas or spiky aloes that covered it.

It was when another man fell across his chest and lay still that Alex realized he might die before the battle was won. It was impossible to move. The sun would either send him crazy, or he would perish for want of water. Unless his countrymen took Spion Kop soon he would not survive. The desperate thought drove him to seek out the living, and he reached out a hand to the man who had asked for his help. It was too late.

The battle went on while the sun passed its height and began its downward path. Even with the dead major's helmet to protect him Alex found his mind wandering. During his rational periods he saw the reenactment of his own forward dash to repulse the Boers many times over, and the plateau was gradually becoming covered with piles of khaki. Those the Boer bullets did not finish off were being tormented by heat and thirst and pain.

There seemed no plan to the battle . . . each man was fighting his own war out there. Some were copying the Boers and ensuring they lived to fight another day; too many rushed forward to bayonet as many as they could before dying themselves. Some officers were leading suicidal charges, while some of their fellows were taking advantage of a plain uniform to hang back from command. At one time, some British and Boers were waving white handkerchiefs, neither sure who was surrendering to whom.

Before slipping into another period of unconsciousness

Alex had time to wonder at the tenacity of his colleagues. They were pinned down in a boiling cauldron of rock from which there was no relief, yet they would not give it up. They were dying in hundreds, but the Boers were no nearer retaking Spion Kop than they had ever been.

By late afternoon he was growing delirious and crying aloud for water. His legs were being stabbed by burning knives of pain, and his dreams persuaded him the surgeon was already there sawing them off. He tried to protest, but his tongue was swollen to fill his mouth, and his throat burned like his legs.

Throughout his agony he was aware that the battle for the hill was still raging. Incredibly, after seven hours of slaughter, they still would not give it up. But, added to the thud of exploding shells, the clatter of musketry, and the bugle calls was a growing chorus of misery as the piles of wounded screamed, moaned, and begged for water. Their agony was doubled by a sun that took the temperature well over a hundred.

Another fantasy of rushing giants; terrible voices howling, and boots thudding past his ears, then a final weight crashed across him and set him silently screaming for release from this burial alive. His flesh was a raging inferno, daggers were in his limbs and throat. Soon, he heard them coming. They would take the suffocating weight off his legs and pour cool water down his throat. But they passed him by and rode into the yard of the farm. Hetta came out and they carried her to the barn, tearing at her clothes with greedy hands.

He tried to run, but they were holding him down on a hay trolley and taking him to his father. There he stood in a black cloak, but Alex was not afraid. He shouted at his father, telling him he knew the truth, and the tall figure collapsed and fell with a hole where one eye should have been. It frightened him and he turned for comfort to Hetta, but a tall pale girl stood there with a skin that was marble cold to his touch. He turned from her, but someone was barring his way—an elderly soldier with a native girl beside him. *We shall see who emerges the winner, Mr. Russell. You cannot have a Dutch girl. She is the enemy.* He began to struggle to reach Hetta. She was waiting for him to go back for her. He must get there before they destroyed her in the barn.

He struggled for a long time and through many corridors

of fantasy, but eventually the ghosts fled and he felt cool
air on his face. It was dark, and the guns had stopped.
Way, way above him stars twinkled in hundreds, thrown
across the sky by the hand of a celestial sower. He could
not think where he was until a strange sound around him
grew and grew into a chorus of frightening and terrible
voices. Was he in hell with the damned?

For a long time he lay believing this, until it was possible
to distinguish words he knew. *Water . . . help me . . .
give me something, for God's sake . . . help me, please
help me . . . water . . . water . . . are you there, Jack?
. . . Get a doctor, I need a doctor . . . water . . . don't
worry, Mary . . . I can't stand this pain . . . water . . .
please give me something, I can't stand anymore.*

Everything came back in a rush—the night climb, the
bullets, the screams, the heat, and the agony. Spion Kop,
the hill men died for in the hundreds. He lay as if outside
his body, gazing at those bright pinpoints so far above him,
and knew how an eight-year-old boy had felt during another night long ago. He was alone. The armies had gone,
leaving Spion Kop to the dead and dying.

## CHAPTER SIXTEEN

For a whole week the two Englishwomen occupying the
white bungalow on the outskirts of Ladysmith vowed nothing
would induce them to eat horse, but they came to it in the
end. Strangely, in the midst of death and disease, heat and
destruction, it was that first meal of horsemeat that sent
Judith to her room sobbing uncontrollably. It seemed, to
her, the ultimate degradation to herself and to the beautiful
creatures that were being shot daily, but the alternative was
starvation for them both.

The strongest of the cavalry horses were being maintained as long as possible, but there was no fodder for them
and they had been turned loose to graze on what little grass
was available on the nearby slopes. The poor animals stood

around in forlorn groups, not understanding such treatment. They wandered off after being shooed by natives, but returned at dusk to cluster around the closed gate, looking for their usual food and grooming by friendly hands. The cavalrymen, tall and burly though they might be, often had a glint in their eyes as they were forced to turn away from a plaintive neigh or nuzzling head. There was no way of explaining the situation to an old and trusty friend.

The horse, who had served man in a multitude of ways, was now saving lives in Ladysmith. A young inventive lieutenant had constructed an apparatus in one of the rail sheds that compounded horse flesh into a tasty and sustaining essence immediately patented as "chevril." This alone was the savior of many during that terrible month of February, when all hope appeared gone.

On February 8, the heliograph flashed in the sun to relay the news of the relief of Mafeking, and eight days later jubilantly signaled that the Kimberley siege had been broken. The whole of Britain was undoubtedly going wild over the news but, to those still trapped in Ladysmith, it was the final conviction that they were to be left to their fate. Buller's relief column was mentioned at the speaker's peril and, among the military, there was another subject made taboo. The man who spoke of food other than chevril, or a drink other than Klip River water was made to put money in a collecting box, then forcibly ejected from the tent. It was no more uncomfortable outside than in, for the heat under canvas was stifling and the flies swarmed in whatever one did, but it was the sense of disloyalty attached to being pitched out that bowed the offender's shoulders. To mention a beef sandwich and a glass of cold beer among starving men was tantamount to treachery.

Unspoken, but in everyone's mind, was the prospect of surrender. The horses would not last forever, neither would the ammunition. Mules and baggage oxen were dropping dead along the streets as they valiantly tried to continue their work; soldiers wore torn ragged uniforms and boots that were falling apart. Medical supplies had been exhausted for two weeks. The town was overgrown and falling down around them, and the inhabitants were gaunt, swollen-eyed people who felt betrayed.

Rumor had it Buller had cut his losses and diverted to Bloemfontein, deciding that Ladysmith was not worth the cost of anymore of his men's lives. There had been a terri-

ble battle on Spion Kop that took well over a thousand
British casualties, but it had gained nothing and the entire
column of men and wagons had retreated over the Tugela.
On February 5, the neighboring hill of Vaal Krantz was
seized but, three days later, Buller withdrew his men across
the Tugela yet again. Nothing had been heard of them since.

Judith looked at the calendar. She had not ticked off any
of the days in the year 1900, but counted them, nevertheless. Today was the hundredth day of the siege. One hundred
days since the last train had left for Durban and all contact
with the rest of the world had been broken. But the tiny
world of Ladysmith had taught her more than she had ever
learned in all that expanse outside.

Sometimes she stood gazing at the hills wondering how
she would fare when she crossed them again. In all these
weeks she had thought only fleetingly of her mother. If . . .
*when* . . . she returned to England she could not possibly live under the same roof with such a selfish, ineffectual
woman, yet what else was there?

An unmarried woman did not set up an establishment
alone unless she wished to advertise herself as a courtesan.
The nursing profession was considered quite respectable
these days, but she knew her own weakness in that direction.

Piano lessons might give her enough to live on, but she
had no wish to be patronized by the wives of the wealthy
tradesmen who brought their untalented children to be
turned into geniuses. Besides, piano lessons would not satisfy the woman she had become, would not ease or compensate for the knowledge that she had thrown away the
dearest thing in her life.

She leaned back in her chair and closed her eyes. The
scene was the library at Hallworth and Alex bent over her
hand looking up at her with a message in his eyes she was
too innocent to read.

If he should do it again she would understand it well.
Slowly reaching out her hand to the leather ring box on the
table, she took the solitaire from its pad of velvet. Its clear
beauty still attracted her as much as when she had chosen
it, but it was only a ring—an inanimate representation of
wealth. How could she have been insensitive enough to
imagine it gave her the right to a man who was under the
pressure of honor and duty? How could she have been so
selfishly immature? When Sir Chatsworth came to her of-

fering his son, trussed up and ready for the altar, silver spoon in mouth, how could she have ignored the inference in such a proposition?

With her new knowledge of human pride, passion, and endurance she realized what her ridiculous acceptance had done to Alex, and to herself. She constantly punished herself with memories and lived with the agony of fearing it was too late. Since the night Neil had told her of Alex's escape she had known he could be killed. There had been fearful battles and hundreds had died out there on the veld. More than a thousand, she knew, had died in a terrible battle at Spion Kop, before General Buller had retreated across the Tugela. Had Alex been one of those casualties? Casualty lists were sent to England, not into besieged towns. He could have been dead for weeks, shot down or blown to pieces while she played a sonata . . . and the loneliness would be within him forever. For a while he had found help from a small girl with dark braids, but the fortunes of war had put an end to their love.

She dropped the ring onto the table and went out onto the *stoep* looking at the Boer-held hills for any sign of activity. It was something everyone did a dozen or more times a day. When and if relief came, it would be over those hills. Today there was nothing different about them. There were the usual puffs of smoke—not as many now that the Boers were confident of starving the garrison out—and the occasional shell thumped down, shaking the bungalow ominously.

She brushed at the flies that were trying to settle on her face and turned away. If God were merciful enough to bring her face-to-face with Alex again, she would be so different. No matter where or under what conditions, she asked only to be given the opportunity to reach out a hand to him. The chances of his taking it were remote, but she could at least say good-bye to him with her conscience eased. If he were never to come back, if she had already said her last good-bye to him, how could she ever live with herself?

Within the next three days the activity Judith had looked for was in some evidence, although no one in Ladysmith dared believe his eyes and ears. Those on outpost duty reported movement of Boer camps and concentration of numbers on the hills that faced the Tugela. Could Buller and his relief column still be trying to get through? Yes,

Buller appeared to have crossed the river yet again, judging by the rumble of distant guns and the layer of smoke that drifted from beyond the hills.

The atmosphere inside Ladysmith was explosive. Optimism was clamped down, yet eyes kept traveling to the plain where a relieving force would come marching. People went about tight-lipped, fearful of saying one word that would tempt Providence. No one commented on the fact that no shells had landed in Ladysmith that day. Were they all being directed at the British on the other side of the hill?

Everyone wondered, but no one spoke the question aloud. Yet, beneath the surface it was there—the certainty that it was now or never. All Ladysmith throbbed with the hope that had been dashed so often. If Buller was not coming, if he was coming and was defeated again, if the Boers tried to capture the town before he arrived—it would be the end. Do not speak of it, do not look for the marching column, do not let up for one minute. Just pray!

Judith was sitting on the *stoep* hoping in vain for a breeze, when a tall figure turned in at the gate and made his way up the path. She still had not grown accustomed to the colonel arriving on foot. He looked worn and thin, as everyone did, but had not lost the upright stance and military bearing that gave him such distinction.

"Please don't let me disturb you, Miss Burley," he said as she began to rise. "I was passing and thought I would inquire about your aunt."

"That's very kind, colonel." She stood just the same, pushing her hair off her forehead as she did so. "To go anywhere in this heat is an effort. Aunt Pan will be very grateful for your consideration."

He took off his helmet and tucked it neatly under his arm. Judith noticed the little dots of perspiration running along in a line beneath the red mark on his forehead where the crown had fitted tightly. It made him suddenly very human, and she smiled warmly.

"You have been very good to us while we have been in South Africa. I shall never be able to thank you enough for all you have done."

He brushed his dark moustache with two quick jerky movements, a habit Judith had often observed in him. "My dear young lady, anyone of us would have done the same, you know that. I think we all have a lot to thank you for

with regard to keeping up our morale. Your talent as a
pianist has never been put to better use, I'm sure . . . but
I fear it has taken toll of your strength. You do not look at
all well, my dear. Shouldn't you be resting?"

She shook her head. "Not at this time of day. It is hot in
my room. Here, it's sometimes possible to catch a breeze."

He nodded then asked, "How is Mrs. Davenport?"

"Making great progress. Life is very strange, isn't it? The
lack of food that has brought general weakness to everyone
has forced her to take the rest she so badly needed. In
consequence, she walked across the room this morning
without any help from me at all."

"Splendid!"

"Yes." Judith fell quiet a moment, then asked, "Is there
any likelihood the siege will be lifted? Her recovery will be
short-lived if she grows too weak."

Surprisingly he put a kindly hand on her shoulder and
patted it. "The real reason for my visit is to break the good
news. We have just received a helio message. The relief
column will be here by tomorrow evening."

It hurt like a physical pain at the back of her throat.
Tomorrow evening! Her hands twisted the cloth of her
skirt with the need to express the fear his words had
aroused. If they marched in tomorrow and he was not
there, how would she stand the loss, the permanent emptiness? The thought of freedom again; good things to eat and
drink; the luxury of fresh clothes and scented soap; the end
of a siege—all those would be nothing if Alex had been left
beneath the earth of some far hillside.

The constriction in her throat grew worse. "Is it . . . is
it really likely this time? There have been so many
days . . ."

"They are less than ten miles away and have finally captured the hills overlooking the Tugela. There's no doubt,
this time."

When he went inside to see Mrs. Davenport, Judith remained on the *stoep*. She needed to be alone with her
thoughts for a moment. Tomorrow evening! It sounded an
eternity away.

She walked to the corner of the *stoep* which gave her a
view of the main street in the distance. She had ridden
along there with him as his fiancée. Now she had no claim
on him. Was there something wrong with her; was she
completely contrary?

Where almost any young woman would be proud of the devotion of a man like Neil Forrester, she dreamed of an evening in the rose garden of Hallworth when the sun lit chestnut hair with fire; of a pursuit on a staircase with kisses that were meant as a punishment. When she was offered a cherishing nature and a smile that made other hearts flutter, it was inexplicable that she should yearn for angry contempt in green eyes, a mouth that never smiled, and a strength designed only to break her. Why, when he had shown so very clearly his opinion of her, did she hold him still in her heart?

Closing her eyes against sudden tears she heard again the Colonel. *They're less than ten miles away.* It was pointless to deny it; when that column came through the streets of Ladysmith she would search for just one face. If it were not there she would remain besieged forever.

When she felt calmer Judith went to the parlor. The door was ajar. Just outside, she stopped dead at the astonishing sight of Colonel Rawlings–Turner patting Mrs. Davenport's hand. There was something more than gentlemanly concern in his eyes as he looked down at her.

"There now, dear ma'am, if I had thought it would affect you so badly I would have left your niece to tell you. It has not yet been made generally known, but the word will go out very shortly."

Mrs. Davenport lifted tear-filled eyes to his. "Forgive me. I am not generally so foolish. It is just that I cannot believe it will be over tomorrow. So many have died, and you have all been so courageous. I do not know how you have managed to keep our spirits up through these dreadful weeks."

The colonel gave a throaty noise that was lost somewhere between a laugh and a cough. "Not at all. I fear I have been something of a grouch at times. I believe I . . . hem . . . vented my temper upon you. Unforgivable of me. Unforgivable!"

Mrs. Davenport gave a rainbow smile through her tears. "Nonsense! I understood only too well your difficulties and was glad to do what little I could to ease them. We all have had to help each other. I do not know what I should have done without your visits. To someone who is used to doing everything for herself it was difficult to rely so much on others."

Before Judith's fascinated gaze the blustery regimental man took her aunt's other hand and held them both in his as he edged slightly along the seat.

"Forgive my saying this, but it has often seemed to me that you should not have to do everything for yourself. A woman needs someone to whom she can turn, someone who will take her problems upon his shoulders, someone who will protect her. Mrs. Davenport . . . *Pansy* . . . you have been alone too long."

"Yes . . . yes, I have," she said softly.

The colonel's arm went around her shoulders, and her head rested gently on his sleeve. "My dear, we have both survived a partner, and our children have flown the roost. My poor dear wife was left alone for long years while I served the regiment in distant countries. I loved her very much and I have been lonely since she went. After this affair is finished it will probably be a comfortable desk job before retirement. There would be no long partings, I promise. My house in the Cotswolds is extremely comfortable, and I have always planned to raise sheep." He patted her hand again. "How does it appeal to you?"

Mrs. Davenport lifted her head to gaze wide-eyed at him. "Reginald, you are not just asking me to take my money out of Transvaal gold and invest in your sheep, are you?"

He swallowed noisily. "No, damn it, I am asking you to marry me."

Judith saw the old sparkle in her aunt's blue eyes for just that moment. "In that case, the answer is Yes," she repiled.

Utterly bemused, Judith turned away and returned to her room. Her aunt would not need her at the moment—would not need her anymore. When she returned to Richmond there would be just herself and her mother.

On February 22, the relief column did not march into Ladysmith as expected. The British troops were still desperately trying to fight their way through the hills around which all roads to the besieged town meandered. It was the same old story: the khaki-clad thousands were held off by the few in the hills. With no maps, no idea of the contours of the deceptive *kopjes*, all they could do was capture each hill as they went along—a slow and slaughterous business for exhausted dispirited men.

It was not until six days later that the Boers remaining in the hills and those around Ladysmith realized they would have to give up their siege and retreat. From early morning there was a great trek of men and wagons across the veld, moving north away from the British, as their ancestors had done.

But the terrible disappointment of the previous week had completely broken the spirits of the occupants of a shattered and encircled town, and the supply officer had worked out an even more drastic system of rationing that would hold out through March, if necessary. After that he had drawn a line across his chart. It would be relief or surrender when April dawned.

The advance squadron of cavalry approached Ladysmith and was challenged by the outlying sentries.

"Halt! Who goes there?"

"The Ladysmith relief column."

"Advance Ladysmith relief column. We've never been so bloody glad to see anyone in our lives!"

The cavalrymen were appalled at what they saw—silent, emaciated people in ragged clothes; an empty town, overgrown and half-destroyed; and animals that were no more than skin-covered skeletons. They had to shake their heads over requests for food and promise that it was on its way, but the small amounts of chocolate, biscuits, and tobacco they carried in their saddlebags were shared out as fairly as possible among a lucky few.

But the majority of the inhabitants of Ladysmith could not raise enthusiasm over this tiny advance party. All they did was stare at their smart uniforms, well-fed constitutions, and glossy horses. One wild-looking private was seen to nod at the leading horse and say, "Last us another week, that will."

It reflected the general feeling. The new arrivals were simply so many more mouths to feed. They had brought nothing to alleviate hunger or pain, and who could put any faith in their assertions that Buller was only just behind them? There had been so many hopes shattered, so many eyes that had seen the phantom khaki ranks approaching, so many crises that had been faced, the survivors of the siege could not celebrate for fear the rest of the column would not come after all.

But come they did. Supplies began rolling into the town

during the next two days and, by the time General Buller made his official, carefully planned entry on the third day, Ladysmith was already a changed place. The city turned out to cheer its gallant rescuer. For that day it was forgotten that he had taken three months and lost seven thousand men to get there.

The garrison turned out in force to line the street through which the column would march and, although uniforms were ragged, boots sometimes nonexistent, and faces yellow with the remnants of fever, the soldiers stood as staunchly as if they were the Guards at the Queen's birthday parade.

The sun blazed down upon two rows of khaki helmets, one on each side of the dusty road. The band was in position, instruments dazzling in the glare and music at the ready, prepared to puff and blow to the best of their ability for their comrades who had fought through to save them from surrender.

Civilians, still unused to living in their homes after the holes in the river bank, gathered to see the procession go past, holding children up to see "Uncle Buller who had brought them all nice things to eat." The children were often sick from the unusual richness of their new diet, women began to cry, men found they had to blow their noses rather hard, and the troops gazed at the smart, ruddy-cheeked relief force wondering if they had ever looked that way themselves. Altogether, it was an emotional occasion, with the men of Buller's army finding themselves choked at the sight of so many pathetic figures, and such a heartfelt welcome.

Judith went to see them pass against her aunt's wishes. She had waited a long time for this moment. Not even the fact that she was barely on her feet after a short sharp attack of fever could keep her away. Neil was on parade, but he found a spot for her in the shade of an overhanging roof before joining his company at the side of the road. He was disapproving, but she guessed he knew why nothing would keep her from scanning those faces as they marched past.

The big drum banged, the bugles rang out, and boots began to thump on the dust as the first ranks appeared to the accompaniment of cheers. On and on they came, miles of smartly dressed men in perfect step, swinging along with a slight swagger, rifles over their shoulders. Regiment fol-

lowed regiment—names that had been associated with past
glories—and the Ladysmith garrison saluted everyone as it
passed. Dust rose over the entire scene making them appear as the phantom ranks so often seen in the past, but
Judith put a handkerchief to her mouth and stayed on,
watching for a mounted officer with the Downshires flash
on the side of his helmet.

Despite her single purpose, from deep inside her came a
fullness of pride, at the sight of her countrymen flowing
into the town. To her, they represented a strength, a soli-
darity that was unshakable, and the tears she tried to hold
back soaked into the handkerchief.

The relief column came in, and General Buller rode his
horse dramatically toward General White, who sat his
horse, waiting to greet his liberator. The two men came
alongside and shook each other by the hand, a staff officer
called for three cheers for Sir Redvers Buller. Helmets rose
in unison. *Hurray! Hurray! Hurray!* Ladysmith was offi-
cially free.

The crowds began to disperse, but Judith remained
where she was. There was still hope. She told herself the
dust had made it difficult to see faces clearly; the waving
arms and shifting crowds had hidden her view so often.
There was still hope. All the time she sat there the parade
would not be over, the marching ranks would not all have
passed.

Neil came to her as soon as he had dismissed his men,
and persuaded her to her feet. She took his arm and allowed him to lead her along the road so recently filled with
triumphant troops. Her legs seemed weaker than when she
set out, and the day had suddenly grown as bleak as winter
in England.

People milled about reluctant to lose any part of the extraordinary day. Judith was crossing a busy street, Neil at
her side, when she heard a soldier say, "Gawd bless my
soul, isn't that old Russell coming in with them wagons?
He must have nine lives, straight, he must!"

Everything within her stopped, but she could not bring
herself to turn around. Neil did so quite sharply, then
breathed, "They're right, Judith. It *is* him."

Gripping his arm tightly she angled her head and saw
Alex wave farewell to those with the wagons, then walk his
horse across to his own regiment. He smiled at their greet-

ings and told them they must watch their step now he was back. Then, he lifted his glance and spotted Neil.

As he approached, the months of weariness and squalor faded away. Judith forgot her faded dress, the sunken pallid face, the arms that had grown so thin. She gave no thought to hair that was dull and twisted into a knot, shoulders that drooped, and a mouth that was pale and tight. She was back at Hallworth where a man had looked at her from beneath his lashes and offered a challenge she could not resist.

Alex dismounted with difficulty, one leg appearing rather stiff, but he shook hands with Neil enthusiastically, telling him it was good to be back with his own regiment. She looked at him hungrily, while her heartbeat hurt her with its thudding, and sang in her ears.

His face was deeply brown and marked with echoes of something that had not been there before. The green eyes, though glowing with pleasure now, seemed deeper set, as if they had witnessed some awesome secret. His voice held an assurance that was somehow gentler than before, when anger had added an edge of bravado. He had been away from her for so long, they had said many things to each other in anger, but she knew yet again there would never be any other man who possessed her so fully as the one before her now.

He finished a sentence and turned slightly as his horse fretted at the reins. The movement brought his glance to meet hers, and he gave a polite nod.

"Hello, Alex," she said softly.

He looked puzzled, then began to really study her.

"Miss Burley has been ill," Neil explained with obvious awkwardness.

Slowly the many shades of shock passed over Alex's face. "Judith! My God, have you been through all *this*? I thought you were in England."

"And I thought you were . . ." The street and all the people tilted, then darkness blotted out everything. Alex caught her before she dropped to the ground.

The glory of autumn lay over the Myburgh farm that March day, and Hetta stood for a moment gazing across the ripened fields. Their land stretched away in the distance, peaceful and abundant. Despite the rain that had spoiled young shoots the harvest was good. The Lord had

sent the sun with the storms—a combination of might that
made Africa so formidable yet compelling.

She arched back with her hand on her spine, a tiny figure on a wide arc of maize-covered land. The world could
have been hers. All around her the sky met the earth in a
merging of indigo and gold with nothing to break it but the
house and barns, and the cattle moving slowly as they
grazed. On days like this it was possible to see the smudge
of purple over by Landerdorp, and it was in that direction
she gazed now, pulling the strands of wind blown hair from
her eyes.

He had promised to come for her when the war was
over. How could she live on those words? It was almost a
year ago that she had looked up from her wagon to see that
strong clean face, and a reflection of her own enchantment
in sad eyes. Some women would be content with any man
who would give her a home to care for and children to
cling to her skirts. She was like her mother. One man alone
could hold her; without him, the world was lost.

In that year she had seen Alex happy and strong with
her. She had witnessed the world from which he had come
when an English girl took him away. She had been sent to
discover what her own people had done to him but, worse
of all, she had suffered the anguish of denying him her
house and sending him into the wilderness without any of
the things vital to a man on the veld. All those things had
happened between them, and she could never forget.

Alex had been young and very strong; gentle and a lover
of the country of South Africa. He had been godfearing, a
good man who loved and honored her. Such a man would
have made a fine husband and fathered many children.
Oupa and Franz would have been proud to have him in the
family; neighbors would have respected him and marveled
that little Hetta Myburgh should capture the attentions of
someone so commanding. But he had been a stranger in
her world, an outsider, and nothing else was of any account. One sight of his uniform, or the sound of his voice,
and they would have killed him—shot him down before
her eyes even as she cried out that she loved him. Yet he
would have been the same man inside. Was hatred really so
blind?

Devil's Leap was there afar off in the blue *kopjes*. One
day he had ridden so joyously to meet her; then she had
seen him broken and behind bars. What had happened in

between? She looked down at the heads of the maize she had been cutting. The shoots had come up, the stalks had yellowed, and the fruits had been yielded, measures of time passing. In her house and on the land there was nothing different. The silence was broken only by the good farm sounds; bellowing cattle, the clatter of pails, the rhythmic swish of the scythe, and the noisy babbling conversation of the natives. The sky was as clear, the storms were as awesome, and the stars hung over the nighttime veld with the serenity she had always known.

All she knew of war was the arrival of the Landerdorp Commando without any warning, and their departure again. They spoke of men dying in hundreds, of women and children starving in Ladysmith, of guns and shells but, mostly, of the enemy. They roared loudly of freedom from the oppressor.

She turned slowly, sweeping the encircling horizon with her glance. Since she had been ten her home had been here with Oupa. It was the same now as it had always been. They farmed the land and raised cattle. They followed the Good Book and the ways of their forbears. Was that not freedom? Had any man told them they could not do what they had done all their lives? She thought of the black people. They had known the chains that took away freedom. Then she thought of the cattle yard in Landerdorp, and men in cages—white men. What was this war . . . and *why* was it? No one had been able to give her a good reason yet—not even Alex.

It was four months since she had walked into her barn and found him there. She remembered so clearly the lantern throwing its glow over his tall figure, the rain-darkened tunic, and shadowed jaw that had made him look like a man of the country. The pain of the memory shook her so violently weakness invaded every part of her body. Her gaze dropped to the stubble at her feet, a living thing cut off in the prime of its beauty. A symbol. Suddenly, there was only herself in the world. So bereft, so terrible was the sensation she sank onto her knees while the shock passed over her, leaving her skin cold and clammy.

"Alex," she whispered against the back of her hand. "*Alex!*"

The stubble was sharp against her knees, but she was lost to all sensations but one. Driven by that she reached out and gathered the tall uncut stalks to her breast in a great armful so that the nodding heads touched caressingly against her face and hair, as he had done with gentle fingers. She sighed with the memory and slowly reached out to encompass a greater and less pliant mass that she pulled against herself with urgent arms.

So she had held him while he had expressed all the anger and possessiveness he had felt on seeing her with Piet, and she relived the joy of it now with her head thrown back and her throat throbbing with the echo of his kisses. Unable to contain what was within her she let the maize yield beneath her weight and sank to the ground, rolling onto her back with a gasp of anguish for what would never be.

Piet was right. There was a great fire within her, consuming her body, whispering of sublime and utter exaltation, but it was Alex who had lit it. Moaning softly to herself she turned her head from side to side, while her arms reached out above her to seize the stalks in a frenzied grip. The sun beat down, drying her tears as they ran over her temples, and the fire raged unmercifully. *Help me. Help me!* It was not to God she prayed, but to the memory of a man who had captured her and never taken his prize.

For a long time she lay in the grip of physical longing, learning the pain of all those who had loved and lost. Gradually, as the sun started its downward path, she grew calmer. Dusk came early on the veld and now it brought an autumn chill, but the afternoon had left her with a listlessness that did not allow brisk work in the fields to counteract the drop in temperature.

The light was already fading to that vivid clarity of color and distance brought about by the sun just below the horizon, when she saw a horseman coming up the track from the south . . . south, where Ladysmith lay. He came slowly, wearily, as if uncertain, and she began to shake.

*I will come back for you.* Was it possible that he had lived out there, after all . . . that he had reached safety with only a bicycle, and the meat she had given him wrapped in a cloth? Had the Lord guided him where other men failed? Had He sent him back to her?

She began moving forward across the field, pushing aside the tall maize that lay in her path. *"Alex,"* she whispered, her eyes glued on the distant figure, and her steps began to quicken. Faster and faster her feet went until she was running with great leaping strides through the sea of maize. The urgent desire returned to her body as she raced toward

the house, holding her skirt high and gasping in the air
with a mixture of sobs and laughter. The freshening wind
rushed past her face and caught at her tangled hair. She
put back her head to revel in it.

Past the house and over the cobbled yard flew her feet,
scattering chickens in squawking flurries, then out onto the
track that had hardened into rigid ruts beneath the sun.
Jumping and hopping over the uneven earth, she flung herself forward to the moment of reunion, until a slight rise
brought her a clearer view of the figure who approached.

Her running slowed to a walk, then died completely
leaving her standing on a grassy hump hugging herself
against the coldness of oncoming night while her brother
drew near. They exchanged no word, but she saw in his
eyes a copy of her own disillusionment and defeat. They
had grown apart; she because of her secret love, and he
because of what they had made him do.

She turned and walked beside his horse, the emptiness
inside her too strong to ask why he was alone or to notice
that his hands on the reins shook with fatigue. They
reached the yard, and old Johnnie ambled out to take the
horse, grinning at his young master and telling him it was
good to see him back where he belonged. Franz merely laid
a hand on the black man's shoulder before walking into the
kitchen and putting his rifle on the table. Hetta followed
him in and automatically went to stoke the fire in the
range, then she turned to find him sprawling in a chair,
looking at her with bloodshot eyes.

"It is over, sister. We have lost."

She stood for some moments trying to understand.
"What is it that we have lost?"

"Ladysmith has been relieved," he went on in a tired
voice. "They have broken through and are sweeping into
the Transvaal. It is over. The war has been lost."

"Will they take our farm now?" she asked apprehen-
sively.

He looked at her with a frown, trying to puzzle out what
she was asking. "Our farm?"

"Will they . . . the British . . . take our farm from
us?"

"Why should they? No, of course they will not take our
farm. We are all returning to work them again. The land
has suffered since we have been away, and all for nothing.
It was a mad dream carried by men like Piet."

"Where is Piet?"

"Who knows? He has real madness, that one. I think it will never go now. We have all returned to our farms and families, but there are a few who still breathe smoke and fire. They speak of David and Goliath but this is one giant who cannot be beaten, and they will not see it."

She watched him and knew he had seen and done things she could not understand. He spoke of giants and madness, he said they would not lose the farm. Oupa was out hunting. Now was the time for asking questions that could never be asked again. If she were to grow, to live in the future, she must know what Franz knew . . . what Alex knew.

"Shall we no longer be free?" Then, when he gazed at her in incomprehension, "Why did you take your rifle against other white men? You had English friends in Ladysmith once, as I did."

He looked suddenly ill and drawn. "I had no wish to go to war, you know that. I am a farmer and use a gun against animals for food or protection—that is all!" A long sigh escaped him. "Oupa is an old man. I owe him everything. His pride would have been broken if I had refused to go. It would have been the end of him. It was my obligation to avenge the death of our father." He put his head in his hands. "Now there will be sons in England who must do the same. It will never end, I tell you."

For a moment the old feeling flared. Alone in the kitchen, brother and sister grew close again, as if the ties of childhood reached out to reclaim them. Hetta went to kneel beside him and her hand covered his gently.

"You have killed Englishmen?"

When he raised his head she saw a death mask that shocked and frightened her, but she had turned the key that unlocked the door of conscience. He spoke as if in a confessional, as if a partition hid her from his sight.

"The sun came out and they were there below us on a plateau—no one knows how many. They did not know we were in the peaks above them. One after another they fell, but more and more came until there were rows of piled khaki on the ground. They had no shade, no cover, no big guns. It was like a leopard is in a pit trap with the hunter at the brink firing down at him. The sun burned them as they lay on the bare rock; they grew crazy with thirst. Doctors could not reach the wounded, water carriers had empty tins. They screamed with pain, moaned for water, keeled over from the sun . . . but they would not go." His eyes grew wild, his hands began to shake. "The dead were in great heaps; the wounded were buried beneath the dead, but *they would not go!* Hour after hour they suffered, and more came up to replace them and die. It was madness; it was inhuman!"

He turned to stare sightlessly at her as his voice began to rise. "It was like taking out a hundred guns against antelope. They fell as easily and fell twitching in their death agonies—but they were not antelope, they were men. I tried to stop it, drive them away. If they had only gone I should not have had to do it. I thought they would see it was hopeless." His hand went up slowly as if holding a gun. "I took aim, pulled the trigger, and a man was dead. I thought they would run back, but it was as if they wanted to die. It made me angry. They knew I had to pull the trigger. *Ja*, they knew I had to do it," he repeated hotly.

Hetta was frozen beside him. Franz's words had revealed a chasm of incomprehensible depth. She dreaded to look down into it.

Franz took her wrist in a fierce clasp and shook it. "What is there in a man that makes him give away his life so easily? You do not know the answer, hey?" He brought his other hand up to point a shaking finger at her. "You would say he was a fool. You would say he did not know what he was doing. *Ja*, that is what I thought, what I said . . . what they all said." He shook his head. "We are all wrong. For a man to do what they did he must have that in him that we cannot begin to comprehend. Those who are blind see only a fool. I cannot yet understand it, but I know it is something so big it will only come to us in time."

She could do no more than clasp his hands and listen, hoping to find some light in what he was telling her, but he had returned to his trancelike reminiscence.

"All day they stayed on that hell plateau no matter what we did, and it was then we realized there was nothing more we could do. When it grew dark we left the peaks and retreated to the valley leaving the hill to the enemy." A frown creased his forehead and he passed a hand across his eyes as if trying to wipe away something he still saw there. "Some of us went up at dawn with a flag of truce to collect our casualties. There . . . there was no one there but the dead and dying."

Hetta was afraid of what he was saying, afraid to hear anymore, but it was something that had been locked inside him and must come out.

"I think the Almighty must have wept that day, for many of us did. The British came with a flag of truce almost immediately, and it was then we all learned the truth. While we had been retreating down our side of the hill, they had been doing the same on their side. When the hill was theirs, at last, they went, unaware of their victory. All those men piled upon each other had died for nothing, had suffered a whole day for no purpose. Their army was going away, back across the river, leaving just a medical team to collect any who were still alive up there." He gripped her fingers. "We both buried our dead, the British simply piling earth over their trenches. Then they went, leaving Spion Kop in our hands. One day of slaughter and madness that will live with me forever. It will never let me forget the price of vengeance." His eyes were back in the present once more and looked brokenly into hers. "Has it brought back the father we never knew? Has it made Oupa a man of pride? Do you think *I* am more of a man because of it? I tell you, I am prouder, more manly, and nearer to God when I cut the grain I have grown by these hands. If I take up my gun against any man again may the Lord strike me down. I already have the vengeance of too many sons upon my head."

## CHAPTER SEVENTEEN

The harvest was all gathered in: There had been three bull calves. Life on the farm was good again. The family was reunited, and if there was now something in each of them that could not be spoken, it drew them closer in their search for consolation. Franz worked hard, and the thin

face filled out with the contentment he found once more,
but there were times when his hands hesitated to take up
his rifle, and moments of distance when he became still in
the midst of activity.

Oupa still castigated his grandson and played the patriarch, but his words held less fire and increasing weariness. Brother and sister caught the old man watching them
and were disturbed by the passages he chose to read from
the Bible each evening. He spoke often of signs from above,
and read God's word into small events of the day. Not
once did he mention the British.

Hetta had her family complete once more, and the daily
tasks lessened now Franz was back. Autumn was going
into winter and she was a year older. At twenty she should
be seriously preparing for marriage. One day Piet would
ride in and speak to Oupa about claiming his wife. He was
impatient, and they would listen to him. Every time she
thought of it agitation beset her. Countless times, she raised
her eyes to the distant track leading from Ladysmith.

The war was over, Franz said. The British were in Ladysmith and the Boers had gone home. If Alex were alive he
would come for her. If the track remained empty, she
would know he was lost. But how long should she wait
before giving up hope?

As the days lengthened into weeks she longed for him
with increasing heaviness and told herself duty might keep
him from doing what he most wanted. Anything could
postpone his journey—anything but that which she most
dreaded. Franz had spoken of something within those men
that he still did not understand. Was it there in Alex, also?
She could not forget that afternoon in the maize field and
her body had been lit with the same awareness ever since.
He *would* come . . . and he would claim what was his.

In her everyday pattern she was supremely conscious of
the things her world contained. Her hands moved caressingly over smooth polished wood, feeling the satin coolness
with pleasure. When she milked the cows, her cheek often
rested against the warm hide that provided a physical contact with something warm and alive, and when tying her
apron strings she pulled them tighter, finding the pressure
around her waist some little relief for her aching senses.

But it was at night that her longing for Alex took hold of
her so strongly. When she let down her hair she did it for

him, imagining his hands wandering through the dark
strands, brushing them against his skin. Unbuttoning her
bodice and letting her petticoat drop to the ground, she
stepped from them into phantom waiting arms, then lay in
her bed telling him silently that she would wait, wait, wait
for him. Meanwhile her body remained a prisoner.

When a horseman eventually rode in from the south it
was not Alex but Piet Steenkamp. Hetta saw him from the
milking shed and remained hidden while he dismounted
and walked out to the forge where Oupa was shoeing a
horse. It was early May and already a noticeable winter
chill was present night and morning, yet Hetta found the
shed stifling from that moment.

What was she to do? It had been agreed between Oupa
and Piet that Hetta should be his wife when the farm was
ready. They had expected Franz to find a good woman
before that time, but he had not found the girl to suit his
gentle nature. Piet would not wait—she knew that to her
cost—and had every right to arrange with the Predikant
to conduct the marriage service.

Oupa had agreed two years ago, and she had said nothing against it. The Steenkamps were good farmers—they
had more land than the Myburghs—and Piet had been a
strong, determined young man. He had grown more determined—stronger than she liked—and there was fear when
she looked at him. Then she had met Alex. She could not
give them that reason for refusing. . . . There was no
reason they would accept from a woman who had been
promised to a man by her grandfather. For a long time she
stood leaning against the stall knowing it was her duty to
go and prepare food for her menfolk, but unable to move.

They came in from the yard just as she was taking bread
from the oven. It was immediately apparent that Piet had
come on a vastly different errand from the one she
dreaded. He gave her a sweeping look but only a short
spoken greeting. All three men were tense, particularly
Franz who had plainly only just ridden in from inspecting
the cattle.

"I have had much to occupy me," he said shortly as he
followed the other two in. "There are those who are anxious to make up for their absence. The farms have suffered.
We have to work hard before winter arrives. *Ja*, of course I
saw you ride in. If you had something of great importance

to say to me it was for you to come out to me." He put out his foot for Hetta to pull off his boot. "Do not expect a man to leave his work before the day is ended at this time of year."

"You left your true work two months ago," Piet said harshly. Franz turned with his other foot held out while the speaker went on, "You were not the only one with no stomach for battle. One small reverse and you all ran like springbok before the lion."

Hetta pulled off the second boot, and her brother hopped backward a few steps to keep his balance, then grabbed the back of a chair. "And were you not there leading us when we ran?"

"There are times when it is necessary to run, but it is a wise man who knows when to stop." He walked around the table to stand before Franz. "You deserted the commando."

"There was no commando left. It is over, Piet. We are all back where we are most needed."

Piet's fist slammed onto the table. "The commando needs you now more than ever."

"It is over." Franz looked weary and unhappy.

"It is not over. The lion roars most when it is wounded. *Think*, man. They kept Ladysmith, but how many men it took to do it—a thousand for every hundred of ours. They buried their dead in piles; their hospitals are overflowing. Pretoria is full of their prisoners."

Oupa sat heavily in his chair and looked from one young man to the other, frowning. "Is this so, Franz?"

Hetta's brother turned. "It was . . . but there are thousands more coming from England, from India, and from all over the Empire. What is one thousand among fifty thousand . . . a hundred thousand?" He clutched his hair in distress. "It *is* over. They come like a great tide. It has now swept up to Pretoria and their prisoners have been released." His glance swung to Piet for a moment. "I met Kobi Prinsloo in Landerdorp yesterday. Even he agrees we cannot stop them now. For a wounded lion it moves very well, eh?"

"The redcoats are in Pretoria?" Oupa asked, as if he could not believe it.

Franz pulled out his chair and slumped into it. "They no longer wear red coats," he explained once more, sounding impatient with an old man who lived in the past. "But we now have half a million more of them than we had before. The war was a mistake. It has taken our men and given us nothing."

"Does he speak the truth?" Oupa asked of Piet.

"It has given us the chance to tell the world of our cause, to show the British as the oppressors they are. I tell you we have never been so strong. We have made fools of them. The mighty lion against the tiny springbok . . . but they shall all see the true courage of the springbok. De Wet and de la Rey will never surrender while there is an Englishman on our soil. The war is only over in the breasts of the feeble. Is Franz Myburgh to be counted among them?"

Franz turned an angry red. "Feeble, is it? Can any man who defended Spion Kop be called that?"

Piet strode to him and seized his shoulder. "You were splendid then. You will be splendid again."

Hetta had been listening and watching so intently she had forgotten Oupa's boots. His impatient slapping on the leather made her hurry forward and sink onto her knees to take his foot upon her lap. Forgotten were her fears of Piet's demand for her, replaced by an even more terrible dread. The war was not over, after all. They were going out to fight the British again and wanted to take her brother with them. It was so painful a thought she could not keep silent.

"Franz has done his duty. He has avenged our father. He is needed on the farm." It was paid as a plea to her grandfather, but he was still frowning at Franz.

"Three days ago I took the gun out to shoot buck, and I saw a lion. *Ja,* a big male lion, with its pelt red in the evening sun. It was old, an outcast from the pride, and the buck leaped around it with no fear." He raised his head and looked up at Piet. "The saliva ran from its jaws and its thin body craved food. But the buck would not be caught. I believe this red lion is the one of which you speak, Piet Steenkamp."

"They no longer wear red coats," cried Hetta, not liking what her grandfather was saying.

"Did you kill the beast so that it did not suffer?"

Oupa looked at Franz. "The Lord decides such things."

The young man flung himself from his chair and walked about the room in his thick socks. "The Lord has decided that we should return to our land. To go on fighting is against His will." He flung out a hand to Piet. "What can we do? Did you not see it as I did? There is something inside those men. They will never go."

"If we sit and do nothing they will never go," Piet snapped.

Franz exploded. "What can we do? If everyone of them could be killed there is another half a million to take their place."

Piet moved up and stared straight into his eyes. "Even the British cannot go on forever. You say the Lord has told you to return to your farm? To de la Rey and de Wet, He has spoken different words. He has told them the British have to eat and sleep. He has told them they need ammunition and medicine. Above all, He has told them the British burn in the sun, fall from exhaustion on the veld, and have to march everywhere in great numbers. That has shown them what we must do."

Franz stayed silent, knowing Piet would not be stopped until he had said it all. Oupa was intent on the speaker, leaving his foot in Hetta's lap unheeded. She sat back on her heels, all her hopes, her dreams being destroyed moment by moment. For three months she had believed the hatred ended—that Alex might still come.

"What must we do?" she heard herself ask. All heads turned to her.

Piet moved across and took her arm to raise her to her feet. Then, he walked her slowly toward Franz, speaking deliberately and passionately a few inches from her face.

"We must blow up their supply trains and ambush their wagons. We must creep up on them in the night, so that they are afraid to sleep. We must leap from place to place like the springbok, so that they wander in the veld trying to catch us until they fall exhausted." He reached Franz and looked at him. "That is what the Lord has told them . . . and He tells me the same."

"No!" Franz looked determined and still very angry. "You are listening to the wrong voice. It is written that we shall build and prosper on this chosen land. We cannot do that if we follow men like you. The springbok may leap as much as he wishes before the old lion, but he will be eventually caught by the young one."

Piet flung Hetta aside in a sudden violent gesture. "You will let the British destroy us?"

"They will not destroy us; we shall destroy ourselves." It

was said in a desperate attempt to reach someone who
could see nothing beyond his own madness. "Can you blow
up every piece of ammunition and food? Can you attack
every night and stay awake yourself? Can you wander the
veld forever? They will not give up and we shall suffer
more than they. It is over, I tell you."

Suddenly, they were two young stags preparing to fight
to the death, antlers lowered and hooves pawing the
ground.

"I am Field Cornet of Landerdorp Commando. We fight
on," Piet challenged.

"I am no longer a member of Landerdorp Commando."

"You are the only man who is not." The antlers crashed.
"Every man has left his farm again at my call."

"I will not." They disentangled again and faced each
other. "I will not leave an old man and a girl to do my
work."

"The man is old, but experienced. The girl is strong.
They will manage."

"This farm is my birthright."

The antlers clashed again. "They killed your father for
defending it."

Struggling to disentangle, Franz said, "He had a son to
take his place. I have none yet."

The challenger slid clear but charged again immediately, taking the other unawares. "It is as well. He would
not be proud of his father."

"I did all I had to do."

"You must do more."

"It is useless. We cannot win."

"They *must* not win. Will you have that on your conscience?"

A last desperate crash of horn against horn. "Will you
have the death of more men on yours?"

"Better that than the death of a whole people." They
were inextricably caught now, and the weaker was being
dragged along by the victor, flanks heaving with defeat.
"We ride tonight from the Grobelaar farm. Come, we shall
eat and then be on our way."

Piet indicated the chair Franz had occupied a short time
ago, and he stared at it before dropping onto the seat.
Hetta saw his face and cried out.

"No . . . no!" She turned and went to her grandfather,

gripping his arms in pleading. "It will break him to go back again."

The old man looked at her with glassy eyes. "God has spoken to him. It is meant."

The argument was ended, but Hetta suffered defeat as silently as her brother. He ate what she had prepared then collected his things. There was just a brief moment as he left when their eyes met, and he said something very strange to her unheard by the others. Oupa blessed him and smiled approval of his action, yet there was moistness in his eyes as he turned back indoors.

Hetta remained at the door a long time after the two men had ridden off. Piet had told her he would be back soon for shelter and rest, but it was her brother's words that haunted her and put such sorrow in her heart. *If you ever have sons tell them kindly of me.*

Ladysmith had made an incredible recovery. Houses and shops had gone up again within a matter of days, gardens were cleared and replanted. Pots of paint came out to whiten fences; holes in the roads were filled in; school began again; and the market was filled with produce. Civilian men looked to their occupations with an eye to the future once more; women thronged the streets in their new dresses and shawls, and gossip ran rife. With the advent of thousands more in the military garrison there was a rush of scandals, romances, and broken hearts. To the women of Ladysmith the men of the relief column were dashing heroes.

Sir Redvers Buller remained where he was for ten weeks, while General Roberts out from England with massive reinforcements, marched straight on to Bloemfontein sweeping the Boers north. But it was already clear there were small bands of them still in Natal, bent on harassing the enemy at every opportunity. Knowing such enormous numbers of troops had to rely on stores and supplies that must be carried all over the country by the railway from Durban and Cape Town, the roving commandos concentrated on wagon convoys and the railways. It was through these they could hit the British hardest.

The railway was on Judith's mind as she walked through the town one May morning, but it was not supplies for the troops that had prompted the thought. A letter had arrived from her mother begging her to return to England at once, as anxiety and worry over the siege had made her ill. There was a lot more about leaving her aunt in the care of the "person" with whom she had so ill-advisedly formed an alliance, and looking to her first duty as a daughter. There was also a dramatic reference to the broken engagement about which she had only just heard, concluding with advice to her daughter to remove herself from the vicinity before she did her reputation irreparable harm. How this was to happen there was no clue.

If she really believed Mrs. Burley urgently needed her presence Judith could have made her return on one of the many homeward bound liners, but the letter only firmed her opinion that the lady was indulging in one of her periodic bouts of self-pity. And Judith had every wish to stay exactly where she was. Her aunt was making it possible by her determination to remain with the colonel until she was recovered enough to marry him. The army chaplain would perform the ceremony, and Judith could not help thinking of her own plans to get Alex before him.

She was so deep in thought as she walked, that she nearly collided with someone who was just leaving a shop, only his swift action avoided it. Judith stumbled backward, startled, then grew weak as he took her arms to steady her.

"Alex! I was thinking about . . ." Confusion rushed over her. "It's difficult to grow used to so much activity. The place has been quiet for so long."

"Yes," he said, then asked, "How are you, Judith?"

"Fine."

"And Aunt Pan?"

"Stronger everyday. Though her left leg will always drag, of course."

"I'm sorry to hear that. I should have called to see her again long before this . . . but you know how it is."

She studied his face carefully. "You have been busy. Do they still give you every duty under the sun?"

He gave a grunt of a laugh. "Not anymore. I have a valid excuse."

"Of course. How is your leg?"

"The stiffness is going. I can walk with much more ease these days."

"I'm glad."

Suddenly, there seemed nothing more to say, and Judith knew he was about to walk away. The providential meeting must not be wasted. Here was the perfect opportunity, away from her aunt and his fellow officers, to try to mend the breach between them.

"Our conversation sounds like a medical bulletin," she said quickly, "and there are so many things I want to know. Must you dash away?"

"Well . . . I . . ."

"Surely you can spare fifteen minutes? Neil always manages it, and I know the colonel is safely occupied. He was drinking tea with Aunt Pan when I left. It's amazing how often his duties take him past our door now."

He smiled at that, and it was like the sun breaking out through winter clouds. *I love him so much, how is it he cannot see it?* Since he had arrived in Ladysmith she had seen him a fair number of times, but never alone like this. He no longer seemed aggressive, but wariness had taken its place. She knew one false step would put him back on the attack.

"Our redoubtable colonel has met his match in Aunt Pan—a determined and vivacious lady, to say the least." Alex's comment explained his smile. "The officers are taking advantage of the romance to disconcert the old boy in every way possible," he said, "To his credit, the colonel is taking it like a man."

"How unkind of them," she declared; she would discuss anything that would keep him beside her. "But it's very cheering to know their spirits are so high again. And they are looking so much better than they did."

His eyebrows went up. "Back to the medical bulletin?"

Her laugh was breathless and caught at her throat. "Sorry. I promise not to refer to such things again."

Somewhat unwillingly he looked along the street. "How far are you going?"

"To the school," she lied quickly, knowing it was the furthest point from where they now stood. Before he could change his mind she began moving along the covered path outside the shops. "They have reopened it and I promised to call in one morning."

He made no attempt to offer his arm, so they walked apart, he taking her elbow to assist her down steps, then dropping his hand again.

"Where is your horse?" she asked.

"In the stables. I was told to walk as much as possible, and now that it has grown cooler it's quite pleasant."

"You have not decided that bicycling is more to your

taste?" It was said in a half-teasing, half-daring manner, but he shot her a look that took her breath away.

"What do you know of that?"

"Only what everyone knows," was her swift reply. "An escapade like that is bound to attract interest, and you know what a place this is for gossip."

"Yes." He drew in a long breath. "I think bicycles will never rate highly with me. One gets a long way in a long time, and with the maximum effort."

"And the maximum determination, I should imagine. Everyone was astonished when they flashed the message that you had joined the relief column. They said it was practically impossible for two men to cover such a distance on bicycles."

"It is," he said curtly. "We had help."

They turned a corner and waited for a cart to pass before crossing the road. "Neil said something about an English farmer lending you horses, and giving food and rifles. How lucky that you came across him."

"That's right." He kept his eyes on the road ahead.

Judith talked fast, afraid any break in the conversation would give him the excuse to salute and plead duty elsewhere. "Why did you do it, Alex? You have always hated the regiment . . . being a soldier."

He still studied the distance. "I hated being a prisoner even more."

"Aunt Pan said you would."

His eyes met hers then. "Did she? How well she understands."

Venturing even further she went on, "Neil says you took part in a terrible battle that gave you such injuries they wanted to send you home. For a man who wanted no part of the army you are strangely reluctant to seize your opportunities to leave."

He offered no answer, merely screwed up his eyes against the sun as if trying to puzzle it out himself. Suddenly, he seemed distant from her. She tried again.

"Was it as terrible as Neil suggests?"

He gave her a quick look. The frown still creased his face. "Spion Kop? Yes, it was."

With unspoken consent they had stopped, and the dusty streets with the bustle of normality were forgotten. Judith watched his face as he spoke and saw revealed emotions he had hidden since coming back to life on a starlit hill.

"It is something I shall never forget. I had not realized the speed of death until that day. It cut into sentences so that they were never completed; it left smiles on some faces, and surprise on others. An exploding shell took as many as six or seven men in an instant—six or seven who were quick with life and intelligence one moment, broken piles of khaki the next."

He spoke so intently she almost felt his sense of shock. The planes and shadows that had been on his face when she saw him ride in with the relief column were stronger than ever now. He was a man who had broken from his inner prison and she longed to share his freedom.

"I had not realized the slowness of death either," he continued. He seemed to have forgotten who she was. "For a whole day and a night some lay there before its mercy released them." He grew reflective. "Life becomes desperately dear when it is about to be taken away . . . and falseness dissolves to leave only the truth about oneself. I was lucky: Others discovered it too late." At that moment he came back from that distant hill and was again the man who stood before her. The frown deepened. "No man could go back to England after Spion Kop and remember only that of this country. He would never be free of it."

Spellbound by the man she was discovering Judith was as lost to the present as he, until a group of horsemen passed and sent choking dust flying to lodge in her throat. She began to cough and Alex, seeing a seat nearby beneath some trees, guided her to it for the shade and fresh air it afforded.

"Forgive me," she said, looking up with eyes moist from the coughing spell. "One would think I should be used to it after all this time."

He looked concerned. "It was thoughtless of me to keep you standing there while I spoke of such things. I'm sorry, Judith."

"Don't be," she replied softly. "I did ask for an explanation, if you remember."

"Yes, of course." He put a booted foot on the seat, leaning on his leg while he took off his helmet and wiped his forehead with the back of his wrist. "Did I say it was cooler? In England we would call this a devilish hot day." He looked down at her reflectively. "It's spring at home. I suppose Manners is busy rolling the lawns at Hallworth."

"And the lilacs are purple and white by the river at

Richmond. It seems such a very long time since I saw them."

"It is a long time." The frown returned to his brow. "You should go go back, Judith. Aunt Pan has the Colonel to look after her. There's nothing to keep you here now."

Like heavy boots marching through the first clump of hesitant fragile snowdrops, his words crushed the delicate blossoming of hope that had pushed through as they spoke that morning. For a while she had believed . . .

"No woman should have to endure what you went through," he continued. "Especially one of your type."

"Aunt Pan endured a serious illness at the same time," she pointed out through lips grown stiff.

"Aunt Pan is different." He stared at the lining of his helmet. "It was very disturbing to come across you the way I did. You had booked passage for England when I left. I had no idea you had not sailed."

"Why should you? I only knew your whereabouts because the rest of your regiment was here and had to be informed." She heard the chill in her voice but seemed powerless to banish it.

"I had not realized a person could change beyond all recognition in so short a time. It was something of a shock when I realized who you were."

"I'm sorry. It was foolish of me to faint right into your arms. You must have thought me very poor-spirited."

His head came up quickly. "No . . . not at all. It simply made me angry. Sieges are damnable. Women should not be brought into wars."

Through her unhappiness she managed a faint smile. "You are beginning to sound like Neil."

He gave her a strange sad smile. "God forbid!" Straightening up he slid his boot off the seat and settled his helmet back on his head. "He appears to have been a tremendous support to you through all the hard times. If you remember, I always recommended him as eminently suitable."

"Yes, you did," she replied bleakly.

He offered his arm and she had no option but to take it. They were still half a mile from the school, and she wished she had chosen a closer destination. Every minute spent with him now only mocked at her hopes and dreams. He had just told her with the greatest clarity that she had no place in his life . . . or any chance of it. All she could do was hold onto her dignity and give no sign of the blow he had dealt her. After all he had been through the last thing he would want was a tense scene with a woman he could not shake off.

"I suppose I should book my passage soon," she said as calmly as she could. "With the war virtually over the ships will shortly be full of troops going home. You might be back in England within a few months of my arrival."

"I'm not going back," he said. "Once the peace agreement is signed I intend to resign from the regiment and settle in South Africa."

*"Settle?"* she repeated, thunderstruck.

"Hetta and I will be married and I shall find work with the railways. It is a profession that has always appealed to me . . . and I like it here. There's nothing for me in England."

Judith only continued walking because her feet were in some kind of rhythm, and because he was holding her arm. He had not just defeated her, he had driven her into the ground, never to rise again.

Yet, when they reached the school her head was high as she said good-bye to him and added the conventional phrase about calling whenever he wished.

"Thank you," he said. "But it might not be for a while. We're running an armored truck up the line to Glencoe tomorrow. The Boers have been attacking supply trains. We're going to see if we can put a stop to it."

He saluted and walked away, limping still. She turned from him toward the hills, feeling she could never travel far enough to forget that moment.

The rail yard was bustling, as the armored supply train prepared for departure. Extra cars were being shunted onto those that had come up from Durban, and men were shouting at the top of their voices to counteract the blast of steam and clanking metal. Beside the train a Light Infantry company and one of the Downshire Rifles were receiving their orders before clambering into the armored cars. These were two ordinary flat cars reinforced with boiler-plates slit by loopholes for rifles.

Alex looked at his men. They did not seem overjoyed, and he sympathized. The trucks were not ideal. Firing through narrow slits was always limiting—especially against men on horses, who could move freely and quickly, and the open roof left them vulnerable to sun and storms—

and to Boer riflemen who might be sighting down on them from any hill.

When the train began to move, they were nearly all jerked from their feet.

Alex steadied himself and leaned against a corner of the car, gazing through the tiny opening, his thoughts running wild. The nearness of sweating uniformed men in the cramped space brought back visions and sounds that would live with him forever. He did not need to close his eyes to conjure them up; without warning they superimposed themselves on whatever surrounded him and refused to go until something broke the barrier of recollection. At first, he had fought them, but as he had recovered he had seen the inhumanity of Spion Kop with senses grown acute and comprehending. The remembered suffering made him more tolerant; the ease with which life ended had shown him it should be valued and used with thought.

He had seen the full range of life that day—heroism and cowardice; rashness and fear; self-preservation and sacrifice. Up on that plateau he had learned what kind of man he really was—he, Alex Russell. He moved restlessly as anger bubbled through him—anger for all those lost years when his father had extracted a penance he had had no need to serve; the days when the old man had stripped him of his identity, made him don the hair shirt. He knew it was impossible ever to forgive or forget.

A flooded *drift* had given him back his right to individuality, and Spion Kop had taught him more than most men learn in a lifetime. The desperate need to begin again had kept him going during that nightmare of eternity beneath the stars; the dread message of the dead around him had kept him sane enough to fight from joining them. When they had come with stretchers in the morning, it had been the newly born Alex Russell who had found the strength to move a hand to show that he was alive beneath that pile of corpses.

Once on the stretcher, safe from the shades of mortality his tenacity had begun slipping away, but even through the fever and pain some subconscious drive had insured his survival. A strong constitution had won the battle with fever; the pure veld air and the skill of doctors had healed his wounds. It had taken time and his own fortitude to recover. They had recommended his return to England, but he had

applied with great desperation to remain in Africa and the
shortage of fighting men had been in his favor.

As he stood in the armored car swaying with the motion
of the wheels he thought of Judith the previous day questioning his wish to remain when he had had the strongest
of excuses to shake off something he professed to despise.
He could not have told her it was not only Hetta who kept
him here, but a surprising new feeling of kinship with his
fellow men that made him wish to see the war through to
its conclusion.

During the hell of Spion Kop he had glimpsed what he
had previously decried—tradition, esprit de corps, and
comradeship. Men had put their trust and lives in his
hands. It had uncovered in him a pride he had never suspected and would shy from putting into words. Where
Spion Kop had broken the minds of some, it had strengthened his.

At last he saw himself as a man other than a shadow of
Miles. In heat of battle he had been strong. Men heard his
voice and followed. He was as good a son of the regiment
as anyone. Looking around him at the men lurching within
the confines of the moving train he felt the sharp pleasur-
able pang of responsibility move inside him once more and
knew he would not fail them.

The phantoms of Spion Kop filtered away as he squinted
through the slit. The train was approaching Landerdorp,
and he throbbed with awareness. The spirit, the sweet
memory of Hetta was all around him as they drew closer.
Already, the line of purple *kopjes* put a smudgy barrier
across the sky. Yet he knew that over the flat-topped hills,
through the *nek* below Devil's Leap there opened out another stretch of flat yellow-brown grassland.

The war would be over in a few weeks, and he would
ride out across that plain as he had promised. Ever since
the moment Hetta had stood outside the bull cage he had
longed to drive the picture from her mind by taking her
body with his own—proving his pride and manhood in a
way she would never forget. At her farm he had been a
prisoner still—trapped in her barn by his uniform—but
soon he would claim her as a free man.

They were past Landerdorp and running out toward the
hills. Alex realized with a shock that the Myburgh farm
could not be far from where they were at that moment.
What was she doing right now? Did she feel his nearness—

a sudden awareness, a quick breathlessness that would pass leaving her wondering? He concentrated hard, foolishly hoping she would receive some kind of message, then the ground began to rise cutting off his view. He was just straightening up when there was a tremendous clamor of screaming steel before buffers began slamming against each other like exploding shells, followed by splintering wood and escaping steam so shrill it hurt one's ears.

The men in the armored car were hurled to the side of the car, slamming into each other. Alex hit the metal sideways. He felt a stinging pain in his cheekbone as he slid down between two riflemen and, for a moment, he was dazed. But a new sound distinguished itself—one he recognized immediately—and it told him the complete story. They had been ambushed; there were Boers up ahead exchanging fire with those in the front truck.

He shouted above the noise for his men to get to their posts, then scrambled to his feet. The slit gave him no clue, for the view was restricted. Finding a foothold on the metal rivets, he pulled himself up until it was possible to look from the top of the truck toward the front of the train.

It did not help. They were on a bend, and the engine and lead cars were out of sight beyond the jutting curve of a bank. Telling his sergeant to take over, he climbed out and dropped to the ground. Behind him the straight track ran through endless peaceful veld: just ahead round a bend leading through the hills, a battle was going on.

Running from car to car he reached the bend. The engine had run off the rails, slewing sideways across the track, and the tender had overrun the engine so that it stood on end, coal spilling everywhere. The armored car and the two following ones had derailed and tipped sideways in a terrible pile of twisted metal, light field guns, and split boxes. The men of the Light Infantry company were trapped and trying to hold off a large group of Boers who were closer than they would have been if they had known the train was manned.

It was clear they intended to loot the train for rifles and ammunition. It was also clear there must be some wounded and dead in the leading car, and that they would not be able to hold off their attackers for long. With the car on its side they had very little protection from those above them on the bank.

The Boers had been taken by surprise by the armed es-

cort. Alex guessed it had not occurred to them there might
be more at the end of the train, out of their sight. He returned to his men, warned them of the need for surprise,
then led them along the track, hugging the train and indicating the various forms of cover that were available to
them.

Slowly and carefully he positioned them all without giving away their presence. When he gave the order to fire,
the Boers were taken by surprise. Two or three fell immediately—Alex accounting for one himself—and several
were plainly wounded as they retreated to some trees. For
half an hour or more there was a sharp exchange of rifle
fire until the bearded men galloped off.

There were hills—the features Boers liked best—and
they retreated only that far. Alex used the interval to advance his men and discover the plight of the Light Infantry.
It was bad. Seven had been killed in the derailment and
two more were crushed to death by the guns that had
tipped from the adjoining wagon. Several were dying from
bullet wounds, and fourteen had been hit less seriously but
needed attention.

One of these was the officer in charge, a captain who
had a bullet wound in his left arm. He told Alex of a man
trapped by a gun on his legs and a rescue was soon organized. He was brought out but both legs were broken and he
was in agony. The two officers held a conference and
reached the same conclusion.

As long as they remained under cover of the train they
were safe, but the minute any man showed himself he became a target for the Boers' unerring aim. There were no
horses, so messengers could not go for assistance even if they
could get away unseen. Two men had tried climbing the telegraph pole alongside the track, but had rushed back amid a
hail of bullets. One of them had died a mere ten feet from
safety. Alex pointed out that the Boers would almost certainly have cut the lines.

They took stock of their chances. There was an endless
supply of ammunition on the train, and the cars supplied
fair cover. From experience they knew the Boers would not
rush them; they could play a waiting game in the hills. But
the British soldiers had only one day's rations and one water bottle.

"We can only sit here like hens in a coop," the captain
concluded heavily. "When the train doesn't arrive they'll

send out another engine, guessing what has happened—but it might be too late for some of these men. If they don't receive attention soon some of them are going to die."

"What about yourself?" Alex asked, nodding at the blood-covered sleeve. "That binding I put around there is not going to last long."

"It's nothing to worry about. The bullet didn't lodge in there, I'm glad to say." He nodded at the badly wounded lying in the shade of the truck. "It's them I feel sorry for. The poor devils are going to suffer before the end."

"Yes." Alex felt again the torment of pain and thirst and the weight of dead men across him. "We must be sure to incur no further casualties. I'm certain they're just after the supplies on the train. To men operating as they do, prisoners would only be a nuisance, extra mouths to feed. They need ammunition, rifles, food—anything they can lay their hands on. Their object is to kill or wound us. If we sit tight they can't do that, neither can they come down for the things they want. I think they'll give up."

The captain looked skeptical. "They don't have to waste bullets on us. If they wait long enough in those hills we'll all die of thirst."

He shook his head. "Men take a long time to die that way—longer than you'd think, believe me. The Boers will cut their losses. There'll be another train, another day. If we lose no more men they are outnumbered two to one here."

The captain recognized the assurance in Alex's voice and nodded. "All right. We'll hang on until they send up another engine, or the Boers go. Better hope one or the other happens before too long."

From noon until four P.M. they stayed beneath the train in silence broken only by the occasional ping of a bullet striking metal, and by the soft groans of the wounded. Water bottles emptied alarmingly soon, and several men urged an attack.

Finally, at five P.M. when dusk was not far off, Alex took off his helmet, put it on the end of his rifle, and held it aloft. There was silence. He told several men to do the same along the length of the wagons. Still silence.

"They've gone," he declared.

"Just because they didn't shoot at those damned helmets it doesn't mean they are no longer there," the captain protested, wincing from the pain in his arm.

Alex pointed behind them to where the great blinding red sun was setting. "They would be looking right into that if they were still in the hills. Is it likely they would stay where they could see nothing? If I thought they would, I'd advise an assault on the hills at once. They'd never see us coming. As it is, we haven't heard a shot for over an hour. I'd stake my money they've abandoned this train."

The men began to crawl out and stretch their cramped limbs. The two officers climbed the embankment and, by the light of dying day, surveyed the area through field glasses. After a moment, the captain tapped Alex on the shoulder.

"Looks like some kind of farm over there, old chap."

Alex swung his head round to the extreme right and saw through the twin lenses the barn where he and Guy Cuthbertson had hidden.

"Yes . . . it is," he said woodenly, taking the glasses from his eyes as if by doing so the farm would vanish.

"What a stroke of luck," the captain went on. "We'll get horses and send a couple of men back to Landerdorp. An engine can come up with a team of navvies to clear this mess up."

Alex had grown cold and tight inside. "I don't think we should . . ."

"Thank God, we can get some help for the wounded. Godfrey and Davis are delirious, and the others need water and bandages."

He began walking away and Alex followed him, conscious of the blood seeping through the other officer's bound arm. He slithered down the steep embankment, his mind in a turmoil. How could he let them go to Hetta's farm—fifty odd armed men who would commandeer horses and food at rifle point? He caught the captain's sleeve, and the man turned.

"Look, I . . . actually, I know that farm. When I escaped from Landerdorp another fellow and I sheltered there. I . . . well, I know the people."

"Good. English, are they?"

"No."

The other man looked hard at him. "Who are they, then?"

"The Myburghs . . . a . . . young girl and her grandfather."

"Friendly? I suppose so, since they sheltered you."

Alex was growing angry. "Miss Myburgh did it out of humanity. The old man would have killed us if he had known."

"Mmmm. Have to sort him out, in that case."

Alex held him back when he would have walked on. "I don't think we should go there."

"We have no choice, man, surely you can see that?"

He had to say it then. "The farm is used by Boers as a base. We might walk right into their hands."

"Right. We'll send scouts ahead and approach with caution." He gave Alex another long hard look. "Up until now you have been making all the right decisions. We have men here who need urgent help. If you have reasons of your own for keeping away from that farm, forget them. I'm in command, and this is my decision. Get your men ready to leave."

They made improvised stretchers from the split boxes and set off across the veld, silent and weary. It was a trudge Alex made in misery. What if he had been exchanging fire with her brother—if he had been the man brought down by his own bullet? Suppose the horsemen who had killed his countrymen and put these others in such agony were sitting around her table when they arrived? Why, dear God, *why* had the ambush been at that particular spot? He watched the farm building loom nearer and wished he had never been ordered to go on that train. He had promised to return to her, but not like this . . . not as the enemy.

The soldiers spread out until they surrounded the farm, closing in warily, supported by their comrades. There was no sign of life until two black servants came from a hut, laughing together. When they saw men in khaki with rifles the laughter froze on their faces. At a jerk from a rifle they obeyed and turned back into the hut. Three soldiers ran and stood guard outside. More searched the barns and sheds, finding nothing and taking up positions facing the house itself, rifles at the ready.

The captain painfully drew his revolver and signaled Alex to do the same. Then, backed by half a dozen men of the Downshires, they approached the door. There was no sound of voices from inside, but the senior officer took no chances. Reaching out he lifted the latch as gently as he could, then nodded to his companions, raised his booted foot, and kicked the door hard. It opened with a crash and all the weapons came up in readiness to point at a young girl with a kettle in her hands, and an old man sitting at the table with a Bible. There was no one else in the room.

The captain stepped inside leaving Alex clearly framed in the doorway with a revolver in his hand. The old man stared at the captain as if he saw a manifestation of the devil. But as Alex stood helplessly with his gaze locked to hers, he knew the war had come at last to Hetta Myburgh.

## CHAPTER EIGHTEEN

It was as if her world had suddenly come to an end. Shock held her and Hetta forgot the kettle in her hand, the bubbling pots swinging above the flames, the bread rising in the oven. She forgot Oupa sitting at the table, the laundry airing on the rack. She did not see the men crowding into her kitchen. All her life, her senses were caught by that one man at the door. He was tall and strong, dressed in khaki with black leather straps and boots, and a helmet with a green, yellow and black patch on the side of it. He held a gun that was pointing straight at her. He was the enemy.

Everything that had once been sweet and wonderful now lay crushed beneath his feet. The dew that trembled in diamond drops on a summer morning would be forever dulled, the *madeliefies* dotting the veld with instant rainbow color after spring rains would be lifeless. The steenbok, exquisite, dainty, miniature, would move with ugly clumsiness. The ripe maize, the pelts of young lions, the plaintive moo of a newborn calf, the clean joyous spread of the veld were nothing now—would never be again. Her spirit died slowly and agonizingly, along with trust, hope, and the surrender of her soul.

His eyes were large and dark with pain, but it could not be as acute as hers. The face that had always been so naked before her held secrets of experience and suffering she had never seen before, but what was the full extent of suffering any person could bear? He gazed as if blinded to all the world except her, as if all life had stopped since he had left this place five months ago. Yet his arm was raised and the gun he held remained pointing at her.

"Are you alone?"

Some words pounded the silence, and a man came to stand in front of her—a man with blood on his sleeve and lines of weariness across a youthful face. She stared at him uncomprehending, not knowing or caring who he was, registering only that he had broken the contact between herself and Alex.

"Are there any men from a commando here?"

She continued to stare at him until movements beside her caught her attention, and she saw Oupa get up and seize his chair to make a swing at a soldier. She gave a cry, but the Englishman ducked and caught the chair.

"Watch it, Grandad, this rifle's loaded, you know."

All in a flash Johannes Myburgh made a lunge at the next soldier, who brought his gun up in defense.

"Hold your fire," the captain shouted, "We do not shoot civilians. Pin him against that wall, for God's sake, before he gets hurt."

Two of them grabbed the old man's arms and forced him against the wall where he stood heaving with effort, dark eyes brilliant with venom. The captain, moving with considerable pain, went across and tapped the broad chest with the barrel of his pistol.

"We have no intention of hurting anyone, but you are obviously as dull and stubborn as the rest of your people." He turned to a corporal. "Find somewhere out of harm's way, then lock him in."

"Yes, sir. Come on, Grandad. Time to cool off."

They seized him and began hustling away toward the door, but he angled his head to the captain and spat full in his face. The young English officer stiffened but said nothing as he slowly took out his handkerchief to wipe his cheek. But the soldiers were livid and prodded their prisoner with the butts of their rifles as they took him outside.

Hetta watched it all with the numbness that followed shock, feeling none of it was true. That her grandfather, so proud and wise, should be dragged from his own house, that the British had taken his farm from him was beyond bearing.

The officer came back to her, but his jaw was working with emotion and there was a sharp edge to his voice when he said, "Unless there are armed men here we shall not be aggressive, so it's useless to behave badly. It only makes an unpleasant job more difficult."

She could only stare at the cheek where Oupa had spat at him, and he gave a deep sigh before passing a hand over his face in weariness.

"Oh God, does anyone of you speak their confounded language?"

Suddenly, Alex was there beside him, the gun put away, looking at her with that same darkness in his eyes. He spoke to her in Dutch that was hard to follow because his voice was unsteady and his concentration poor.

"There was a battle down by the railway. We have men who are badly hurt. Some may be dying. We want only water, perhaps some soup, and bandages. Will you help us?"

She was a woman. Compassion was part of her. With complete lack of emotion she nodded faintly.

"First, I must ask if you expect . . . anybody . . . to come here tonight."

And if they did? She shook her head.

Alex turned to the other officer and told him in English, "It's all right. If we put the wounded in the barn, Miss Myburgh will give what assistance she can."

The captain gave a ghost of a smile. "Oh yes, I'd forgotten you had . . . er . . . connections with the family. The old boy doesn't appear to appreciate your charm half as much as his granddaughter." He began turning away and said over his shoulder, "Oh, tell her we're taking a couple of horses. The usual speech about military authorities paying for what they commandeer. I'll leave you as officer in charge of Miss Myburgh. No doubt you'll enjoy that."

For the next two hours Hetta did everything with automatic hands and movements, still feeling part of a nightmare. With complete lack of emotion she boiled kettles of water, bathed gaping wounds, tore up calico for bandages, even straightened two broken legs and bound them to boards. She poured water or soup down throats, placed ice cold clothes on feverish brows, and removed two bullets that were still lodged in limbs. She had been taught to cope with shooting accidents and wounds inflicted by wild beasts, besides all manner of sickness.

It was not until the men were all settled and the captain

was sitting in her kitchen, his jacket discarded while she dressed his arm, that feeling returned. She wished it had been possible to remain numb forever. Through all she had answered Alex in nods or a few short words when it was necessary. He had spoken in hesitant Dutch and she had answered in the same language. Not once had she looked at him.

Now he sat on the edge of her table and held the bowl of water. It was not necessary. She could have managed without his help, and the gesture made her angry. It was then she realized emotion was riding her once more: anguish and despair rushed in.

"You have to give these people credit for their country knowledge," the captain commented wearily. "Healing potions and mystic cures! There used to be an old woman in our village who could heal almost anything. Filthy stuff she used, but it worked. A witch, some called her."

"I should keep quiet," Alex said sharply. "You look done in."

"Not that this one could be called a witch. She has a certain earthy charm, for those who like womanhood in the raw."

"Keep your remarks to yourself. They are in very bad taste."

Fair eyebrows went up. "Well, well! I hadn't realized you were given more than shelter and sustenance when you spent the night here."

Alex was on his feet, slopping the water all over the table as he set the bowl down. "That's enough, damn you! Miss Myburgh understands English very well."

The captain looked at her with a glint of anger in his light eyes. "I see. Why didn't you answer me when I spoke to you?"

She was beginning to shake. He reminded her of the dark man who had come with Alex that night. There was that same arrogance, that mocking smile, that smooth voice. Lifting her head high she said in English, "If I came to your house with guns and shouted at you in Dutch, I should not expect *you* to answer."

The man held her eyes for a long moment, then gave the faintest nod.

"Yes, I'm sorry. You have been very kind, and I am a guest in your house—an unwelcome one, to be sure, but a guest just the same." He stood up, slipping his jacket carefully over his shoulders. "Is there a room where Lieutenant Russell and I can get some sleep?"

She was so full of anger, so incensed at the things he had said, so shaken at the way Alex had defended her, it was impossible to speak. Snatching up the bowl of water and bloody bandages she flung a hand to point at Franz's room and walked to the door leading to the yard. The minute she stepped outside two men appeared out of the darkness with lowered rifles. They smiled when they saw who it was and rested their weapons again.

"Sorry, Miss, can't be too careful."

The few steps to the corner of the house where she threw the water away and tossed the soiled cloth onto a pile of rubbish showed her more soldiers leaning against the corner of her barn, highlighted in the wedge of yellow light spilling from the door. They were everywhere. Thank God, Franz and Piet had ridden off only yesterday. They would not return yet.

For a while she stood there filled with anger against the dark night. It resembled her own blindness to all she had been told, and it resembled the void into which she had fallen since that door had crashed open. Out there lay the maize field where she had been ravished by her own thoughts of the man who had stood on the threshold with a gun.

It was sometime before she returned to the house, for her prayers had been long. It would have been impossible to say them in her room knowing there were those under the same roof who had marched in by force and locked her grandfather—an old man—in an outhouse.

When she reached the kitchen it was empty. With her teeth chattering she straightened the room, threw more logs on the fire, and went to her rocking chair. It was out of the question to go to her bed, so she loosened her hair until it fell long and free, took a heavy shawl to cover her shoulders, then turned the lamp low and began to rock slowly back and forth in the chair Oupa had made for her grandmother. Her thoughts were wild and sad, breaking her apart . . . but they would not go.

She sat for a very long time, until there was a vague movement behind her. She stiffened, knowing he had come from Franz's room and was standing by the table. Her hands tightened in her lap until the fingers all but snapped.

The squeaking of her chair grew slower until it stopped altogether. But she would not look away from the fire.

"I have been waiting for him to fall asleep." There was a pause. "Now I'm here the right words won't come."

Her pulse thudded in her throat. The flames threw out sparkling lights that trembled on her lashes. The room became as still as twilight on the *kopjes*. But a great storm was gathering not far off, and the thunder of it was in her heartbeat.

There was a rustle and a squeak of leather, and he was there beside her. She could see the shining boots, the khaki breeches, the brass buttons on his jacket . . . but she would not look up. The thunder grew nearer and dark clouds raced across her vision.

"Since the day I left here, I have thought of nothing else but returning. How . . . how could I guess it would be like this?"

She looked up then and saw him only through her eyes and not her heart. He stood in her kitchen with the firelight flickering over the clean lines of a jaw that betrayed the pride of heritage. He stood straight, wearing the uniform of a great empire. He was one of the hated British . . . the enemy. The chair was set violently rocking as she flung herself from it and faced him.

"I am a Boer," she cried. "Speak in Dutch!"

He drew in his breath sharply. "If that is what you want."

"What I want is for you to go . . . *go!*" She backed across the room as he moved toward her.

"Hetta . . . please . . . we had no choice. Men were dying. You saw them—you know it's the truth."

"No. I do not know the truth from you. You have told me all lies."

He took a quick step and caught her arm, but she pulled away, leaving just the shawl in his hands. Throwing it down with a quick movement he followed her until she put the table between them.

"I have never lied to you."

She saw the rapid rise and fall of his chest and knew there was anger in him. It increased her own. "Yes . . . *lies.* You said the British would not take our farm, yet they have come. Today they have come."

"We have not taken your farm."

"They are standing outside with guns—they are everywhere," she flung at him. "They have taken horses, they have broken open the apple barrels. They watch wherever I go."

He broke into English. "We were attacked near here this afternoon. We have to be on guard."

"Speak in Dutch!" she commanded, fighting back the tears. "When you are in my house you will speak Dutch."

"I will speak in any language you wish if you will only listen!" He tried again to reach her but she moved to the rocking chair once more and held it between them as her storm raged.

"I listen to nothing more you say."

He took the chair and wrenched it from her so that it fell sideways. "You *will* listen."

Defenseless she backed until the cupboard stopped her retreat, and he was standing before her. His very nearness set thunder and lightning battling within her.

"Do you think it was easy for me to come here like this, knowing what it would do to you?" he demanded thickly. "I would have done anything . . . *anything* . . . but I had no choice."

Hitting out against her own helplessness she attacked him. "Oupa is the head of my family, yet you lock him in a shed like an animal. He is an old man and his pride is great. You are the same as the others."

Her arms were suddenly seized in hands that were shaking. "You saw that we had to do it. For his own sake, we had to do it." He was in the grip of a storm as great as hers, and shook her hard. "What is it that you want? I was shut away like an animal once. Do you think *I* have no pride? When I hid in the barn, do you think I did not feel like an animal trapped by the hunters beneath? All my life I have been dealt the lash of guilt. Do you want to punish me more . . . is that it?"

Yes, she did. Her hopes and future had been woven around him, and he had crushed them today. He had drawn out of her very soul, very fibers of her body a love she had thought eternal, yet he had smashed it apart in an instant. He and his soldiers and his empire. She needed to punish him for the rest of mankind. Struggling hard in his fierce grip she lashed out in every way she could, fighting for control of the sobs that threatened to master her.

"You lied . . . all the time you lied. There would not be war . . . *you said that.* They would not take our farm,

and they are here." His grip was tightening and it made her
struggle more. "And her—your Englishwoman who looks
at you and you follow—you told me she had gone back to
England. Is that another lie?" She put back her head in
anguish and saw his face through a shimmer. "You told me
you would come back, but you return with a gun. *You are
the enemy!*"

"No–o," he groaned, snatching her against him and
bending her back in an aching curve as he covered her
mouth with his to stop the words she was saying. "Does an
enemy do this . . . and this . . . and this?"

In a flash her passion changed direction beneath the onslaught of his. He held her immobile and broke her aggression with kisses more savage than her words. Still she felt
the need to punish him and beat against his shoulders with
her fists, turning her head away, but could not help reveling in his unyielding strength and the way his mouth pursued and captured hers time and again.

"By God, if you knew how you ruled my life you would
not call me that," he said, breathing hard and shaking her
in his fervor. "You are in my mind night and day. Everything I do is for your sake. There is not a moment when I
do not want you. I have built my future and my lost pride
on your love."

In that moment she saw again only the man he was and
loved him . . . *loved him*. Her hopes and dreams began
an agonizing recovery. It was more than she could bear.

"No . . . no!" Tearing herself free, she bolted for the
door, but he caught her as she reached it and swung her
round to face him, misunderstanding the reason for her denial.

"You are saying I was wrong to do so?" he asked
harshly. "Then you are the one who has lied. Can you say
you have never loved me—that nothing else mattered but
that love? Can you say that?"

She saw the gathering of old ghosts in the tightness of his
mouth, the echo of struggling pride around his smooth jaw,
and in his eyes the hovering pain of rejection.

"No," she whispered, then more anguished, "*No*. Please,
do not look at me that way, Alex. It hurts me."

The changing lights in his eyes and the way he let out
his breath in a long sigh told her something she had known
from the time he approached her rocking chair. He reached
out and touched her hair with an unsteady hand.

"It's beautiful like this—soft and flowing." His fingers stroked the dark fall several times, then drifted across to the smoothness of her throat. "This is the first time I have seen you with your hair down. It's very exciting."

His touch on her skin sent tingles of exquisite warning through her. Only half aware of her own actions, she put up a hand to stop his caress and found it caught and put gently behind her. "Alex . . ." His lips put an end to her protest, then traveled over her cheekbone, past her ear and down her throat to rest in the hollow of her shoulder.

Memories of the maize field flooded her limbs with weakness. This was what she had wanted, had craved for, yet there was still some indefinable stirring of resistance that made her pull away.

"No, Alex."

He was close behind her, pulling her back against him while he spoke into the curve of her neck with fierce words. "Do you know what it was like to see you with him in the barn—what it did to me?"

"It meant nothing," she said desperately.

"And if it had been *you* watching *me*?"

She grew still, the sharpness of his thrust making her gasp. Whirling around to face him, she felt the desire well up to engulf her. In the dim light his hair shone with living fire. His eyes were lit by golden sparks of desire. He was vital, exciting, and alive. Her eyes closed against a picture of a pale, pale creature beneath his searching hands, and silver blonde hair spread across his body.

She was against him, locking her fingers in his thick hair and pulling his head down until his mouth was against the rise of her breast. It was the end of resistance. Sweeping her up, he carried her into her room, while she sought to drive out thoughts of a beautiful remote Englishwoman by pulling open the buttons of his jacket one by one, until her dark hair stranded across a chest that was pale against the brown of his throat.

From her pillow she demanded fiercely, "You have not been so with her?"

"No." Her bodice opened beneath his fingers.

"Swear it," she cried, half in anguish, half in ecstasy.

His head came up and she read in his eyes the denial of the whole world in defense of that moment. "I swear it. *I swear it!*"

Words were suspended as he introduced her to a throb-

bing joy she had only imagined. She moaned his name over
and over, and bit into his shoulders in rapture while tears
of a different kind welled up beneath her lashes. The fire
raged in them both, and when the leaping flames dwindled
she lay against him with wet cheeks against his chest while
he told her of the precious gift she had given.

When he took her again he was gentle and full of tenderness. Then, they slept.

It was that time just before dawn when the dying close
their eyes, infants fight their way into the world, and those
who are awake are in a limbo somewhere between the two.
The soldiers guarding the Myburgh farm saw nothing of old
Johnnie as he slipped from the native quarters and went to
the shed where his master was being kept. The men in
khaki held the key, but it was easy enough to lift the bar
from the window and open the shutter.

The prisoner was awake and, despite his years, scrambled up and over the windowsill to freedom with the help
of his servant, who thought only to return the *baas* to his
proper place in the household.

The old man had sat in the straw all night full of the
hatred of years. It was not only his hatred, but that of his
forbears, his contemporaries, and descendants. It was a
wrath he felt he shared with God. A hunting accident
had prevented his going with his son to Majuba: age had
stopped him going with his grandson. But the Lord had
sent the British to him. He had shown the way Johannes
Myburgh could avenge the many wrongs against his race.

In the forge there was an old rifle—not as good as the
one he used now, but it had a sweet and true aim. He
walked slowly, stiff with the discomfort of the night, and
thought of the many signs from God that had been given
him—the old wounded lion he had seen. Piet Steenkamp
had spoken of the lion and the springbok, and now he
knew what he must do to these men who no longer wore
red coats. He had not seen an Englishman for years, but
they had not changed—arrogant, with the faces of boys—
and they always came in force.

Through the faint lightening of dawn he made his way
along the side of the barn and crossed to the far corner of
the house where no guards had been posted. Halfway along
the wall was the window of Franz's room. The lantern
burned low showing the fair-haired officer sprawled across

his grandson's bed. The man was asleep, and there was a white cloth bound around his arm. Johannes Myburgh spat upon the ground in disgust, then moved on, muttering to himself.

He reached the next window. The lamp burned brightly in Hetta's room, and showed a scene that broke his pride, his faith, and his heart. The man with chestnut hair was pulling on his boots as he sat on Hetta's bed. He was a big man, his bare torso looked broad and muscular, and Johannes Myburgh raged inside to think of his granddaughter being forced to submit to the brute. But his rage turned to anguish when the girl rose naked from beneath her blanket and went to her seducer with smiles and teasing hands.

For a while the old man leaned back against the wall feeling acutely ill, then he stumbled to the forge where he sat weeping for a long time, calling upon the Lord to strike the girl down for her sins against her people. In the midst of his suffering the voice of the Almighty reached him, as it had always done in the past, and he went down on his knees in prayer.

Like all lovers they found it difficult to break apart, but dawn was on the threshold and both knew their first union must be put aside for a while. Hetta dressed quickly, then insisted on buttoning Alex's jacket for him. It took a long time for he kept kissing her fingers. When she braided her hair he took one swathe and awkwardly tried to copy what she accomplished with deft speed. They laughed over his efforts, and kissed with lingering joy. At last, he put her away from him very firmly and told her he must see that all was well outside.

After he had gone she remained a little longer in her room knowing no other moment would be as poignant, then went out to draw water from the pump. A soldier saw her and walked over to take the bucket inside for her. He expressed his gratitude for all she had done for his comrades the night before. She nodded and thanked him for carrying the bucket before he returned to lounge against the wall of the barn once more.

No other morning had been like this one. She was aware of herself as never before, and the tears of joy she had shed were not far away again. Every word he had said was ringing in her mind; every touch, every sensation tingled as if it were happening all over again. Sighing, half-smiling she put

kettles to boil and took bread from the cloth to slice. A
shadow darkened the doorway and she looked up joyously.
The radiance died from her face to be replaced by concern.

"Oupa! No, you must not," she cried when she saw the
old rifle in his hand. She started forward to take it from
him.

"Keep back, harlot," he cried in a voice of wrath. "You
have sinned against God, against your people, against your
brother, and against Johannes Myburgh, the head of your
house. You have eaten of the fruits of the flesh. You have
dishonored your name. The wrath of your dead father falls
upon your head. You have shamed she who bore you. You
have betrayed your kin."

Hetta felt the room spinning as the blood rushed from
her veins leaving her body icy cold. The old man seemed to
fill the doorway with his impressive size and dignity. His
voice resounded throughout the room as he denounced her,
shouted her sins aloud like the Almighty Himself. It was
terrible. She put her hands up to cover her ears, but nothing would keep out his words.

"You have taken an Englishman into your bed. He
comes, and like a harlot you give your body in lust to the
enemy of your people. You are a traitor. You have earned
the wrath of the Lord, and He has spoken to me. Vengeance is His, and I am His instrument."

There was a crash, and one of her best plates fell from
the dresser, shattered. It was then she realized the rifle had
been fired at her.

Stunned she felt her lips moving. *"Oupa!"*

There was a sharp crack, and the old man lurched forward before crashing to the ground, his rifle sliding across
the floor to within a few feet of where she stood. There was
a red stain spreading across his back.

Outside in the yard, the soldier who had helped her
carry the bucket was just lowering his rifle. "Christ, miss!
He was going to kill you. His own flesh and blood!"

Hetta stared at the man. He was big, with a ruddy face,
and dressed in khaki. There were hundreds like him—
thousands. *They will never go . . . they will take our
farms . . . if we kill half a million there will be another
half a million to take their place . . . they killed your
father . . . they are the enemy.* The voices of Franz and
Piet swam in her head as Oupa lay at her feet. He had been

with her throughout her life, and now he was gone. In an instant he was gone.

The soldier was walking toward her with his gun lowered, and she could see blood spreading over an old man's coat. The rifle was at her feet. She picked it up and put it to her shoulder. The soldier had a surprised look on his face as he fell, and it was that that stayed with her—that and the spreading stain on a beloved old man's back.

Hands seized her from behind and wrenched the weapon from her. A fair-haired man shouted words at her that did not mean anything. In the yard, two men were bending over the dead soldier. One of them was shouting.

"Did you see what happened?"

"She shot him—in cold blood."

"There were three shots."

"I saw her shoot Clarke. He was just walking toward her."

"Who fired the other shots?"

"I don't know, sir. She's a bloody murderess."

"One of the shots killed the old man. Did you see that?"

"No, but she killed Clarke. I saw her do it . . . and Mr. Russell did."

"Bloody Boer!"

They took her into the yard where the body lay. One of the two beside the dead soldier had chestnut hair. His cheeks were wet.


The polo match was exciting, according to the shouts and applause. But Judith's mind was elsewhere. She had gone to please Neil who was playing; nevertheless, it reminded her of watching Alex in England when she had been engaged to him. For the past few months she had had such determination, such high hopes of being given a second chance to win his love, but he had destroyed them four days ago during a short walk through Ladysmith. How could she possibly win a man who was so completely captivated by another woman?

Soon, she must decide—to stay or return to England. She could marry Neil Forrester, she knew, but she liked him far too much to condemn him to a wife who could not love him. He would find happiness with someone else. In time—someone who had never met an aggressive, resentful, but utterly enslaving fellow officer. She could marry a charming, unfaithful man-about-town who would leave her free to live her own life—alone.

At the conclusion of the polo match she had not solved her problem, but had practically resigned herself to the inevitable. It was only increasing her pain and inviting his further derision to remain near Alex. Neil escorted her home and regretfully had to decline an invitation to dinner due to the celebration of a past victory for the regiment. For the same reason, Mrs. Davenport was destined to spend an evening without her Colonel.

Judith went in and kissed her aunt, trying to appear in gay spirits. She gave a lively and amusing account of the match she had not watched, chatted lightly about the Midsummer Ball planned for the following month, gave her opinion of the young Lancer lieutenant who had been cashiered for helping himself from the mess funds, and declared her intention of ordering a rose-colored muslin afternoon dress.

Mrs. Davenport listened attentively and said all the right things, but when her niece began a nonstop narrative on the dog the Downshires had adopted as a mascot, she lifted a graceful hand and said, "Enough! My dear girl, you have hardly drawn breath since you came in."

Judith stopped. "I'm sorry. Are you feeling tired?"

"Not at all, but I know you very well. What is on your mind that you have to cover with such trivial chatter?"

She took a long breath, then smiled with resignation. "It's time I went back to England."

The older woman did not hurry with her answer, but nodded slowly. "Yes, perhaps it is, dear. South Africa has not been a particularly happy place for you, has it?"

"Certainly not happy . . . but I shall never forget it. I have learned things about life and human nature that would have remained a mystery to me at Richmond. I hope it has taught me the wisdom that was lacking two years ago when I thought it was possible for a man to be given away by his father, neatly parceled and fashioned to suit the receiver." She rose and went to the window to hide the silly moistness that filled her vision. "No wonder Alex hated me."

A significant silence hung in the room after that, until Judith felt there was something wrong and turned to look at her aunt.

"My dear, you will only hear this from some uncaring

person if I do not pass on what Reginald told me this afternoon. I should not like that to happen."

She grew very still. "It's Alex, isn't it?"

"Yes. I'm afraid he has become involved in a quite scandalous affair that is sure to have repercussions all the way back to London. That little Dutch girl from Landerdorp has shot one of our soldiers. Alexander saw her do it and has been forced to bring her back to Ladysmith to stand trial for murder."

## CHAPTER NINETEEN

She sat perfectly still, staring at something only her eyes could see. A shaft of sunlight struck through the barred window making a pattern on the planks of the floor, and turning her brown boots to tan in the yellow light. The shawl she wore was the same Alex had snatched from her shoulders three nights before in the kitchen of the farm; the dress the one she had slipped on so joyfully after their night of union.

The room contained no more than a trestle bed, a washstand, a chair, and a rug, but if it was not a prison cell it was the next thing to it. And yet, he realized, it was not so very different from the room in which she had slept all her life—plain, containing all that was necessary and nothing more. The one difference was that a locked door kept her within its walls now.

Alex had been with Hetta for ten minutes and it was breaking him. Nothing he had ever known had been as terrible as this—even the night on Spion Kop. His own pain he could bear—hers tore him apart. He sat on the bed talking steadily, but the girl on the chair before him had not moved once. He pleaded, demanded, threatened. He spoke in English and Dutch and left her in no doubt of her future, but his voice echoed in the stillness, heard only by himself.

She did not know he was there; had been like that from

the moment he had heard shots and run from the barn. She
was cold, almost lifeless. She had died sometime between
his leaving her melting with kisses and the moment he had
turned the corner to find her with a gun. In those few minutes she had gone from him, and he could not call her
back.

He looked at the face that had given him a wealth of
expressions and saw only a mask; the eyes so luminous in
passion stared like two brown stones; and the vibrant supple body he had known with joy now seemed no more than
a shell. The weight of what she had become bowed his
head. "Why, Hetta . . . why?" he asked yet again, knowing he would never know the answer.

When he dragged himself to his feet and called to the
guard to unlock the door, Hetta was still sitting as she had
been when he entered and gave no sign that she was in the
living world. He went back to his quarters only to continue
the self-torture there. Three people had known what happened on that morning, and two were now dead. Hetta
could reveal the truth, yet nothing he said or did brought
any response. It was as if she had locked the secret away,
and herself with it.

Two hours later he received a summons from Colonel
Rawlings–Turner. The adjutant sent him in to find the
colonel standing by his window, apparently deep in
thought.

"You wanted to see me, sir?"

The older man turned away from his reverie and walked
slowly forward. "Yes. No doubt you can guess why."

Alex could, but said nothing.

"No one is allowed to visit Miss Myburgh except the
native woman servant and the officer selected to conduct
her defense. You used your rank to gain admittance from
the guard. I trust you will not make it necessary for me to
take the embarrassing step of issuing orders to keep you
out."

Alex stiffened. "No, sir."

"This disastrous affair could not have come at a worse
time. The raising of the siege has left the gentlemen of the
press with a thin time of it newswise. They will seize on
this and wring every ounce of drama from it. Our national
popularity has rarely been as low in the eyes of the world,
and the fact that we are trying a Boer woman for murder

will bring about the use of words such as *barbarous* and *inhumane* from some quarters."

He stopped two feet away and fixed Alex with a glare. "Your name is certain to be linked with hers—a British officer and an enemy woman! Unless this affair is handled with discretion and good sense there could be a scandal of gigantic proportions that will reflect on your father as a member of the government that instigated this war. You are in a hell of a situation. I shall try my level best to get you out of it, principally because you are an officer of the regiment, but also because I hate to see a worthwhile man make a mess of his life."

There was a short moment of silence before the colonel said in an altered tone, "Alexander, you are not the first man to become hopelessly entangled with a woman against his better judgment, and you will most certainly not be the last. You must forget it and start salvaging what is left—for her sake as well as your own. This war has intensified the strength of the Boer hatred against us, and if her relationship with you is made public her people will regard her as a traitor. You must break off the association completely, and refrain from any mention of it in your evidence."

Alex felt colder by the minute. "You are asking me to play Judas. I am the only person in Ladysmith she can trust . . . the only one who could persuade her to tell the truth of that morning. If she doesn't, how can any tribunal conduct the case?"

"By using the best judicial system in the world. Personal emotion will not enter into it."

"They'll condemn her because she is a Boer."

"They'll condemn her because she is guilty. Three people saw her do it—including you. She shot a British soldier . . . one of your own men who had a wife and children in England. There is no doubt what happened."

"I know what happened. I think I shall never forget it," Alex said thickly. "Whatever they do to her now won't bring back Clarke, or old Myburgh. I desperately want to know *why* it happened. As one of the two officers present the responsibility was partially mine. The situation was completely controlled one minute then, in a flash, two people were inexplicably dead. Miss Myburgh is the only person left alive who could reveal what sparked off the slaughter." Suddenly he had to say what was inside him. "It should never have happened, but how could I guess she would ever . . . she was full of gentleness and compassion. What happened to her so suddenly?"

The colonel pursed his lips. "However one might try to cheat the inevitable, it has a habit of winning. Her roots were stronger than you thought." Surprisingly he put his hand on Alex's shoulder. "Any man who can escape across hostile veld and survive the horror of Spion Kop has the strength to pick up the pieces after something like this."

"And what about her?" he managed to get out.

The face of his commanding officer hardened. "She took her future entirely into her own hands when she pulled that trigger. You must accept that."

Back in his quarters Alex stood looking from the window at the hills that had sheltered the Boers who had held the town in siege. Trying to analyze his feelings was pointless. Everything that had made him hope and strive to keep going had been built on Hetta, and now it had all come crashing down. Her need of him had been his strength and freedom; her faith had bolstered his own. If she were lost, then so was his future!

It was sometime later when he became aware of a faint tapping on his door. His abstracted invitation to enter changed to surprise when he saw his visitor.

*"Judith!"*

She came in quickly and shut the door behind her, leaning back against it. Her hands betrayed her nervousness as she plucked at the navy blue of her skirt.

"I know I should not visit you in your quarters—that ladies are forbidden here—but there seemed no other way of seeing you alone."

"I see." It was not a brilliant comment, but the best he could manage. Her presence in his quarters—strictly compromising for any female—and his state of mind, slowed down his powers of concentration.

"Alex, I . . . I know how you must be feeling. I wanted to tell you how sorry I am and offer any help I can."

"Help," he echoed, "why?"

Faint color stole into her unusually pale cheeks. "We have known each other a long time. Surely this is one of those times when old friends can be a comfort." Her hand pushed up her shining hair with unnecessary fussiness. "No . . . I am saying this all wrong. I am offering to help because I want to very much."

He was supremely bewildered. The same outwardly, this

girl had become a stranger in manner. Hesitating and uncertain, almost embarrassed, she had taken him unawares.

"I don't quite understand."

She came into the center of his room, taking hold of the back of a chair as if for support. "We . . . we have had our differences in the past, some of which concerned . . . Miss Myburgh. I have learned how deep is your . . . regard . . . for her and can imagine how dreadfully anxious you must be." Her blush deepened. "It seemed to me you might need a friend—someone who could sympathize and who was not connected with the military."

He passed a weary hand over his hair, wishing he could go to sleep and wake up in another place, another time. "It's very kind of you, but . . ."

"Alex, it took a great deal of courage to come here. Please don't treat me like an unwelcome guest and show me the door with polite regrets." Her knuckles whitened as she gripped the chair. "Ladysmith is notorious for gossip. Even the most closely guarded secrets are common knowledge within ten minutes. I have heard what is being said and . . . and none of it is very pleasant."

"No . . . I suppose not."

She approached and touched his arms. "Please, let me help."

He looked down into the pale blue eyes and saw depths that had not been there before. Her face still bore the imprint of what she had suffered during the siege, giving her beauty a life it had previously lacked. In that moment she seemed sincere—warm, even—and his battered spirits surrendered before he knew it.

"Yes . . . thank you . . . except that I can't think of anything you can do."

"Is there any message I could take for . . . her? I know visitors are not allowed, but perhaps another woman . . ."

He took the first step into the void. "It's over. There is nothing I could say to her now." She made no comment, just stood waiting for him to continue. "In any case, she would neither see nor hear you. She has been like that since it happened."

"Would you like to tell me about it?"

He shook his head. "No."

"It's time you told somebody. You look ill."

He waved an arm wearily. "You'll hear it all from the gossips before long."

"I'd rather hear the truth from you."

"What is the truth? She is the only one who knows." He turned away to stare from the window again. Vividly the picture leaped up in his memory once more, breaking him each time it appeared. He saw Hetta standing just inside the door, a small figure in a brown dress, rifle to her shoulder. At her feet was a huddled shape. He remembered Clarke walking toward the house, the jerk of her slender body as the rifle kicked back, then the soldier folding at the knees and pitching forward. The sound of the shot seemed to have been lost somewhere in the depths of his shock. Not lost, however, was the vision of that controlled deliberate aim. She had meant to kill.

He became aware that Judith had moved up beside him. "You shouldn't be here. If someone should see you there'd be even more gossip."

Her look was steady and held a quality he was too exhausted to identify. "During the siege we had to do many unconventional things. It taught me a lot. I have shed the coat of cool morality you accused me of wearing and realize life is not a gift but a challenge. I *do* know what you are going through, Alex, believe me."

He wished she would go. His head was beginning to spin, and her face kept fading into a vision of Hetta's—not as it had been but the mask it now was. Forcing himself to focus on her he murmured, "Yes . . . thank you."

"Are you all right?"

He nodded, but she said, "I think you should lie down for a while and try to sleep." Her hand touched his sleeve again. "There is worse to come, and you are going to need someone who . . . understands. Anytime you find it too much, promise you will come or send for me."

"Of course." It was said automatically in the hope she would leave, and she did.

As Colonel Rawlings–Turner predicted, the trial of Hetta Myburgh had the pressmen buzzing like wasps. The military tribunal, well aware that the case could quickly become notorious, were determined to deal with it scrupulously but speedily. Everyone in Ladysmith knew that Lieutenant Russell of the Downshires had been conducting some kind of affair with the girl—Guy Cuthbertson had told a colorful tale of his escape from Landerdorp at many a dinner table since—but the members of the tribunal felt it was better ignored for the sake of the officer and the girl, especially since Alexander Russell was one of the witnesses for the prosecution.

The proceedings were conducted in English and Dutch, an interpreter translating everything so that the Boer girl would be perfectly clear on what was said, but she sat throughout the trial completely impassive and silent.

The defending officer, unable to get a spark of attention from the accused, based his case on temporary insanity, and produced evidence to show that the Boer girl had never previously shown militance toward the British. This involved bringing Guy Cuthbertson to tell how she had given him and Alex food and shelter knowing they were escaped prisoners.

It was during this exchange that the newsmen got their first taste of scandal. Guy said quite bluntly that the girl was hostile to him, and it was only through her friendship with his companion that he was allowed to stay. He went on to give it as his opinion that she would have handed him over to the Boer commando that used the farm that night if it had not meant betraying Lieutenant Russell also.

Taken aback, the defending officer stopped his questioning, but the prosecution was obliged to elaborate on the suggestion of her hostility, and Guy readily obliged. A Boer was a Boer as far as he was concerned, and he hated them all. This one had shot one of his countrymen and deserved all she got.

Alex heard it all with deep disillusionment. Guy had slept safely in Hetta's barn and eaten her food the next day, when a word from her could have had him shot. Had he no idea of the risk she had taken to hide them from her own people? He was arrogant in his survival, contemptuous of her simplicity, and blind to compassion.

His own evidence of that occasion was stilted. It was difficult to be objective and banish the memory of a girl struggling in the hay beneath the hands of a seducer. He told of her agreement that they could stay until dawn, because there was a storm raging and her natural humanity would not allow her to turn men out onto the veld under such conditions. He stated his conviction that she would have done the same for any human being because she had a woman's natural compassion. Asked about his friendship with her, he merely agreed he had become acquainted with

her before the start of the war, when he had been stationed
at Landerdorp.

"Lieutenant Cuthbertson states that she was hostile to
him—ordered him to leave."

"If two ragged Boer prisoners appeared out of the darkness at an isolated farm, any Englishwoman would have
had the same instinctive reaction. When she recognized a
face she knew, her fears would subside somewhat. That is
what happened in this case."

"So you admit it was only your acquaintance with Miss
Myburgh that led her to offer you shelter?"

"No. I think it was the natural instinct of a woman
brought up in a harsh land to provide hospitality to those
in need."

That neatly disposed of his relationship with Hetta as far
as the tribunal was concerned, but the newsmen were not
satisfied. At the end of the day's proceedings they swarmed
around Alex as he left and dug their probes into his inner
wounds. He fought desperately to control his temper as one
man suggested he had gone to her farm deliberately, knowing she would gladly shelter him—had gone there on previous occasions. Other, foreign, reporters tried to insinuate
that he was a Boer sympathizer who had deliberately been
allowed to escape in order to carry on working for them.
To be able to introduce a British officer who was a traitor
into the trial of a young Boer girl accused of killing the
soldier who had murdered her grandfather would be sensa-
tional propaganda for French and German readers.

The British newsmen whose employers were against the
present government saw endless possibilities for antiwar
backing. Defenseless farming folk being bullied by the military—empire-builders trampling all beneath their feet—
British officers seducing simple girls and forcing them to
betray their loyalties. They drew the line at suggesting Alex
might be a traitor—they were British enough to baulk at
such a thought—but they always enjoyed a tilt at military
aristocracy and the landed gentry had wronged too many
peasant girls and got away with it. More, this man was the
son of one of the very politicians they opposed!

Alex stood at the gates of the courthouse, surrounded by
shiny-suited men waving notebooks and pencils at him. It
was hot, he had been through some kind of hell that day
watching Hetta as she sat so still and silent while the interpreter spoke into deaf ears, and it seemed the nightmare

was not even half over. He had yet to give the evidence that would convict her.

The things they shouted at him, the suggestions they made, the insults veiled by questions, all spun around him. He could not forget her sitting across the room, so near yet a lifetime away from him now—the same girl who had looked up at him from the seat of an ox wagon with entrancing awe and trust.

"Please, gentlemen, I have nothing to say," he insisted desperately. "Kindly let me pass."

Pushing forward he found them all moving with him, a buzzing shifting mass who stung him with their words. His control began to break, but they suddenly fell back, their attention taken by a smiling girl, making her graceful way toward him.

The gleaming ash-blonde hair was piled in soft curls, her beauty enhanced by a pink parasol. In an exquisite frill-necked blouse of white organdie and a tailored skirt of blush pink that emphasized her tiny waist with a high band, she commanded every eye. Those newsmen who had been through the siege greeted her warmly and with respect; those who were new to Ladysmith goggled at this vision of a true English lady.

She reached him and tucked her hand through his arm. "My dear Alex, you will be late. Aunt Pan always takes tea at four, and she will be so disappointed if you are not there. You know how she dotes on you." A gracious smile swept the pressmen. "You must excuse Lieutenant Russell, gentlemen. He cannot break his promise to an elderly invalid who suffered so much during the siege."

In a daze Alex walked beside her through the gap made by her arrival, and down the road that led to her bungalow.

"Three months, and the town looks as it did this time last year, when we first arrived," Judith said lightly. "It's amazing how quick recovery can be."

He was collecting his wits slowly. All he could say was, "You should stay clear of this. I am not the best person with whom to be seen these days. Those men will read anything they wish into what they see."

"Nonsense! What can they read into an invitation to tea with a respectable invalid relative who happens to be engaged to your colonel? Nothing could be more proper."

He stopped and turned to her. "You know that is not what I meant."

"Alex, they are probably still watching us."

"Don't you see, by walking up to me in such a manner . . ."

She put her arm through his once more and coaxed him forward. "You were being hounded by those men. It was the easiest way of silencing them. Several are friends of mine from the siege, you know."

"You put your reputation in danger."

"That no longer worries me."

"It will worry Neil Forrester."

She looked away from him. "Neil is a very understanding person."

"All the same . . ."

"Alex, you made me a promise last week . . . and Aunt Pan *is* expecting you to tea."

To argue further was too much effort. Contrary to his expectations it was peaceful and relaxing in the company of the two women. It was as if nothing had changed. Mrs. Davenport chatted about Hallworth, Richmond Park, and the home she would have in the Cotswolds when the war ended. Judith sat with cool composure dispensing the tea, then played light pieces on the piano in a highly accomplished style. It was all very English and civilized. When he left, the swirl in his brain had stopped.

During the following days Judith sought him out frequently, and he grew accustomed to her company at a time when he felt most alone. Walking by the river, riding through the town, or sitting on the *stoep* of her bungalow, her understanding presence stopped for short periods the serpent of despair that undulated through his nightmare days and tortured nights. When they talked it was always she who led the conversation along lines of safety; when there was silence between them her calm, sweet-perfumed nearness held the darkness at bay.

The trial continued. The defense brought witnesses to show how Hetta Myburgh had cared for the wounded, supplied food and water for the ambushed troops, and even removed two bullets from the limbs of the British soldiers. The prosecution produced others who said she had been sullen and hostile, doing what she had only because there was no alternative. They told of how Johannes Myburgh had attacked them with a chair and spat in the face of their officer.

The fair-haired captain agreed that Miss Myburgh had

spared no effort to help the injured men, that she need not have applied ointments nor taken out bullets that would normally be dealt with by a surgeon. But he had to say that her manner was resentful, plainly unfriendly, and she had pretended not to understand English when he spoke to her.

The fact that Alex had spoken to her all the time in Dutch had to come out, but the captain pronounced his opinion that Miss Myburgh had been no friendlier toward Lieutenant Russell than to any of them. The old man had been actively hostile and had to be put under lock and key for his own safety, but she had been controlled in her anger. He ended by stating that Lieutenant Russell had tried to avoid going to the farm, had warned him that Boer commandoes used it as a base, but men were dying and he had had no choice.

Finally, the proceedings reached their climax—the actual killing of Johannes Myburgh and Rifleman Clarke. The captain said he had been sleeping in the house when the sound of a shot woke him, followed almost immediately by another. He ran into the main room—a kitchen—just in time to see Miss Myburgh fire a rifle at Clarke who was walking toward her in the yard outside. The soldier was trailing his gun and in no way threatening her. From what he could remember, the man looked pale and was holding out his hand in an almost protective manner. The captain wrested the rifle from the girl's hand, but she appeared to be in much the same state as she had since it happened. She had put up no resistance, nor shown any further aggression to any of them.

Corporal Marchant stated that he had been talking to Lieutenant Russell when they heard a shot. They had hardly moved before there was another. Together they ran to the corner of the barn and rounded it just in time to see the accused fire a rifle at Rifleman Clarke. No, he was not threatening her; his gun was dragging along the ground. They could not see his expression because they were behind him, but he was walking in a way that suggested he was not expecting hostility from her. They ran to Clarke and found he was dead—shot through the heart. The accused had "gone all queer" and was like that all the way to Ladysmith.

When Alex stood to give his evidence he was afraid his jaw was not going to move. Gripping the table to steady himself he was able to answer the questions put to him only

with great physical effort. He substantiated what Corporal
Marchant had said and agreed that Miss Myburgh had
been in no danger from Rifleman Clarke.

Sweat began to break on his forehead. The courthouse
was stifling that afternoon, and he could not drag his eyes
from the girl sitting alone and silent in the straight-backed
chair. He looked at the braids around her head and remembered the feel of her hair in his hands that clumsily
tried to plait the thick swathes. Her throat above the brown
dress was smooth and tormented him with recollections of
its softness beneath his lips. Her vulnerability layered him
with guilt, and her withdrawal broke him.

"So, in your opinion, this was not an act of self-defense?"

The question hung in the air too long. "I think it was in
defense of her grandfather who had been shot."

"That was not what I asked."

The room rocked. "No . . . not self-defense."

"Would you say it was a deliberate act of hostility—that
her intention was to shoot Rifleman Clarke dead?"

The answer was there, but would not come. Her face
swam before him. He felt ill.

"Answer the question, please."

"Yes."

"Thank you, Mr. Russell. I think that is conclusive
enough."

The accused was called and remained where she sat. A
civilian doctor who spoke Dutch gave his opinion that Miss
Myburgh was no longer suffering from a suspension of normality, but repeated invitations to answer the charge
against her met with no response.

At last, the summaries were presented and provided the
bizarre conclusion to a notorious case. Since two of the
witnesses to the series of events were dead, and the other
refused to reveal what happened, a hypothetical outline of
that morning had to be drawn. It was as follows.

Johannes Myburgh had been freed by his granddaughter
while one officer slept and the other had gone to check on
the wounded men. The old man had taken a rifle from a
hiding place and gone toward the house with the intention
of shooting the captain as he slept. He had already shown
his hatred by spitting in his face and attacking the soldiers.
As he crossed the yard, Rifleman Clarke had spotted him,
guessed his intent, and shot at him. As he was going forward to examine the old man, the girl had taken up the

rifle and killed him. It was impossible to determine who fired the third shot, or why.

However, all the tribunal had to decide was whether Hetta Myburgh was guilty ot the murder of Rifleman Clarke and, in the absence of any testimony from the girl herself, had to bring in their verdict on the evidence they had heard.

She was found guilty and sentenced to death.

Alex did not hear the knock on his door. The first he knew of another presence was a hand on his shoulder. The visitor's identity did not register. He was hardly conscious of his own whereabouts. Someone took the chair facing the bed where he sat with his head in his hands. Two blue shoes beneath a fall of dark satin were all he saw through his daze. He continued to stare at them for a long time, trying to understand their significance. The power of thought had deserted him. He wanted to sleep, but could not.

The evening ticked away. The glow of the setting sun had long since ceased to redden the room, and only the light from the corridor outside shining through the fanlight made it possible to see the furniture. It had grown cold, as June evenings often did, and Alex shivered. The next minute, a match flared, and the log fire began to dance with flames. The brightness made him look up. The long velvet cloak she wore was amber rich in the firelight; her face shadowy and indistinct. He thought of the farmhouse kitchen, the brown dress in the lantern glow, the enveloping dark shawl.

"I destroyed her . . . destroyed us both," he said in a voice that had a faraway sound.

"No, Alex, you could never have done that."

"All my life I have been accused of it, but this time I really am guilty." He looked into the flames and had a lightning memory of lying in a punt staring at the sun. It highlighted how he had felt that first day, riding out beneath Devil's Leap. "She held out a loving hand to me when I most needed it. For the first time I was Alex—a person in my own right. I took her hand without hesitation, without thought of what I was demanding from her. Meeting Hetta gave me my freedom, but took away hers."

It was all spilling out, the blame and the guilt. The words were for Hetta who would never hear them now. "I thought our love would prove stronger than anything in life. I thought it above the prejudice and hatred all around us. I thought nothing else could touch us. My God, how blind I was . . . how selfish!"

There was a rustle and the velvet cloak fell partially across his knees as she knelt before him, taking his hands in hers. He stared into a face that had silver shimmering streaks upon it.

"In return for my love I demanded everything, and it was too much . . . more than she could possibly give. She was right. I was the enemy."

## CHAPTER TWENTY

The proceedings of the military tribunal in the case of Hetta Myburgh were sent to the commander of Ladysmith garrison, who upheld the verdict but remitted the sentence. A strong plea for mercy had accompanied the verdict, in view of the death of Johannes Myburgh at the hands of the murdered soldier, and the girl's subsequent abnormality. But also to be considered were the political implications if the death penalty were carried out. Notoriety was to be avoided, at all costs, and the newspaper references to the relationship between a Boer girl and a Rifles officer—the son of a member of the British government—wavered dangerously on the brink of scandal. In consequence, the wheels of officialdom turned at twice their normal speed, and the prisoner was freed by the end of June. She was escorted to Landerdorp by train, given back the two horses borrowed by the military, and left to return to her farm.

It was a bitterly cold rainy day that put a cloak of menace over Devil's Leap as Hetta rode beneath it. She shivered and felt the ghosts of those who had died there touching her with bony fingers. After the confines of a room for so long, the veld seemed to have lost its natural free wildness. The ride seemed endless, the two horses the only other living creatures in her world.

Johnnie came out to the yard on her arrival; he cried unashamedly, to see her, but she slid from the saddle and walked into the house as if they were not there.

A chill hung everywhere. The small windows allowed little of the gray afternoon light into the room, but she did not fetch a lantern. Frugal ways had been part of her upbringing. Keeping the shawl around her shoulders for warmth she lost no time in clearing the range and lighting a fire. Bread must be baked—that on the table had turned green—and the small corpse of a buck hanging stiffly by the door should be cooked before it putrified further. The porridge in the pot hanging from the hook above the fire had congealed and had to be chipped from the sides. It all took time.

Only when the fire was going well, dough was rising in the hearth, and the buck had been skinned did she light the lamp and move to draw the curtains. Her foot kicked against something and she looked down. It was the broken plate from the cupboard.

The curtains remained as they were. The rocking chair creaked as she rolled slowly back and forth. The fire crackled and spread orange light over the mound of dough, but otherwise the house was silent. The flames began to die. The bread should be baking now. On the table the skinned buck lay stiff and shiny—dead far too long. Through the open doors it was possible to see Franz's bed, blankets thrown back in haste. And her own, rumpled, and with a few scattered pins upon it where she had put up her hair that morning.

On the mantle lay a pipe and a skinning knife. Beside the door hung an old coat, the smell of tobacco strong upon it. Beneath stood a pair of boots, newly finished, shaped by stiff fingers. They would never be worn. The fire went out soon after midnight; the dough turned sticky. The lantern flickered for a while, then gutted, but the rocking chair creaked on and on. The Bible, cherished book so lovingly handled, remained on the table untouched, its comforting words locked between the covers.

It was a week later, when she was hoeing vegetables in an icy morning wind, that a horseman appeared on the horizon and drew near very quickly. She let the hoe drop and walked to the house, knowing why he had come. It would be better inside.

When the door crashed open she was standing by the table, and he strode to within two feet of her.

"I have heard. Our people in Ladysmith report regularly." He put down his rifle on the table. "Did you think to hide your sins forever?"

The whip in his right hand sang through the air and sliced into her cheek, leaving a runnel of blood. "I once told you I thought God foolish to put such features on any woman with a body such as yours. Now I know it was the work of the devil. Traitress . . . Jezebel!" The whip sang again and lashed her neck where it curved into her shoulder.

She welcomed it and cried out inwardly for further punishment. There would never be enough.

"You sold your soul to an Englishman. Beneath the eyes of the head of your family, of your brother and your promised man, you consorted with the enemy of your people. Yet you denied it—here in this very room before the Bible you denied it. You are false before the Lord—an outcast."

His pale green eyes were brilliant with emotion, and she could even smell the fury emanating from his body. "You hid your weak lover from my eyes knowing he had been my prisoner. You hid him here, in the house of your murdered father, even as I sought what was mine by right." He seized her arm and pushed his face close so that the moist red lips were moving only a few inches from hers. "You were ripe, true enough, but for some English *gentleman* who thought to amuse himself. When he had done that he betrayed you. Have the British not committed enough sins against our people that you must satisfy their lust and bring your name down in the eyes of your people?"

He threw her aside so that she fell across the table. "He came here with men and murdered the father of your father, yet a Myburgh woman gave her body to that same man. I shall take my revenge of him, but first it is my right to punish you for wantonness and betrayal. I would not have a woman used by an Englishman as my wife."

The table was hard against her cheek and there was nothing to grip with her hands as he beat her. Yet, when he stopped, she lay there for a long time wishing she had not to get up.

"I should kill you, but I am not the Almighty. Vengeance is His."

He went to Franz's room to sleep, then left with his saddlebag full of bread, *biltong*, cheese, and apples from the barrels. Hetta went back to her hoeing, neither watching his retreating figure, nor heeding the agony of each movement. Her face was impassive as the rich soil parted beneath the blade she wielded.

The decision to return to England remained in the uncertain future, for Judith could not bring herself to leave Ladysmith just yet. In her saner moments she told herself ruefully no other girl would be so willing to prolong a relationship bringing sweet anguish that increased with each passing day, yet the resolution required to cut from her life a man who wanted no place in it was always just beyond her reach.

In her wild moments it was possible to feel some kind of hope that Alex would allow a bond on which she could build. For the two months since Hetta Myburgh had been brought in for trial she had been in the company of a vulnerable man. She was not foolish enough to imagine his present dependence on her meant it would be permanent, but it was heady while it lasted.

He was lost in a world that had turned upside down, and she provided the only stable thing in it. It was nowhere near what she yearned for, but enough—more than enough—to prevent her booking that ocean passage.

Since the Boer girl had been freed Alex had been subdued. That one evening when he had bared his soul in almost unconscious confession had never been repeated and, once the sentence had been remitted, Judith had sensed in him a resignation that locked away all but that part of him that he was prepared to show to the world.

He had survived the hovering scandal and the veiled hostility of those who conveniently forgot his escape from Landerdorp and subsequent action at Spion Kop and felt his loyalty was not all it should be. Anyone meeting him for the first time would see a reserved and serious young man with quiet charm, but Judith had seen him magnificently aggressive or stunningly happy. The change in him made her long to bring about a return of one or the other—anything that would light a spark within him once more.

As she dressed to go riding one afternoon, it was of Alex she thought, although her escort was to be Neil Forrester.

Buttoning the jacket of her dark green habit, she wondered yet again whether it would make any difference if she told him the truth about Neil. That old taunt about making her a good husband seemed to have turned to fact as far as Alex was concerned, but their relationship was so delicate and precious that to introduce such a topic might injure it. Besides, she had seen the far-off pain in his eyes too often to believe the Boer girl was not still firmly in his heart.

Picking up her gloves she turned for the door. She told herself constantly she must tread warily if she did not wish to lose him again, but deeply in love as she was, it was no easy thing to do. A sigh broke through as she made for the parlor, and she tried to concentrate on the man waiting there for her. Poor Neil . . . did he suffer as she did? Love was a cruel taskmaster!

They mounted and rode easily down the main street, heading for the hills. It was a silver blue day—the first after a week of low driving clouds and rain that turned the streets into a quagmire. July in Natal produced extremes of weather, but the best were days like this one. The sky went on forever, high and brilliant, above a town washed in clarity within a horseshoe of hills that threw back an unbelievable medley of colors. The air was crisp and exhilarating, pure veld air that filled a person with health and life.

The pair rode in pleasant companionship. It was a day for young people—the kind of day that set hearts leaping and the vigor of life and love surging through limbs. Judith wished it were Alex beside her. Surely such food for all the senses would kindle something inside his bruised heart!

"This is too beautiful," Neil said bringing Judith back to awareness. "I should have chosen a time when rain fell and put one in the right mood for melancholy."

"Melancholy . . . why?"

He smiled briefly. "I asked you to come today in order to say good-bye. I hoped you might feel just a little sad."

She held her breath. "The regiment is going away?"

"No," he said gently, "not the regiment. Just me. I have been seconded to headquarters to replace a fellow who has contracted typhoid. Although it does not bring promotion it is a career advantage, so I should be glad."

Judith reined-in. "Neil . . . I shall be sad. And I shall miss you."

"Truly?"

"You know me well enough not to doubt it."

He dismounted and came round to her, holding up his arms to help her to the ground. They began walking over the springy turf, and Neil continued his too eager attempt to express enthusiasm over his appointment.

"It's frightfully helpful for a fellow to be selected by those in high places, you know. Of course, it's probably because of my father, but if I do well it will persuade them I'm not too bad on my own merit. There were some green faces around the mess table, I can tell you. It's all spit-and-polish and protocol at headquarters—no bivouacs and bully beef for staff officers." His laugh was forced. "A life of luxury from now on, eh?"

"I don't think it was because of your father, Neil. The Colonel thinks very highly of you—he has said so on many occasions. I am certain it was his personal recommendation that had you appointed."

"Thanks, I hope you're right." He stopped on a jutting ledge from which there was a magnificent view over Ladysmith. Judith stood beside him feeling he had brought a mood of melancholy to the day after all.

He waved a hand at the spread of white buildings below. "One gets a Boer's-eye view, so to speak. It's easy to see how they managed to siege the place for so long. They had the perfect position here. And to the rear is the tortuous country Buller had to try and cross—again under their eye the whole time."

She looked at the tiny figures moving about the streets—miniature horses and toy carts—and felt herself grow cold. They must have sat here and watched as the moving things vanished in a cloud of dust when their shells exploded. Looking at it from this vantage point made the war seem even more terrible, more cold-blooded than it had been down there in the town.

"It seems so long ago now," she said softly, lost in recollection.

They stood for a while, watching. Then Neil said, with his eyes still on the town, "Perhaps it is just as well I am leaving."

Judith knew to what he referred and thought carefully before answering. "I have valued your friendship, Neil. Without you I am certain I should have gone to pieces many a time during those terrible months. You are a fine person. Alex once said men like you are the backbone of England. How right he was."

Brown eyes swung round to study her. "Whatever happens, it always comes back to Alex, doesn't it?"

She nodded slowly. "I'm sorry."

"No, I'm the one to be sorry. It was all too obvious that you still cared for him after giving back his ring, and I thought that natural enough. During the siege I began to hope it was not just the time and place that drew us together, but when he rode into Ladysmith with Buller that day I knew my case was hopeless. He is a damned fool," he finished bitterly.

"No, Neil, the fault has been mine from the start."

"I find that hard to believe—knowing you both."

She shook her head very faintly. "I think no one really knows Alex. Only when he is willing to share himself will there be any chance of doing so."

Neil tilted up her chin with a gentle hand and kissed her mouth softly. "That is my unofficial good-bye. Contrary to all Alex says, I am villain enough to wish him to the devil. I think he would find congenial company there."

"I think he has already been," she murmured, "and thankfully returned."

They began the descent in silence, full of their separate sadnesses. Judith was turning away from him to negotiate an outcrop when a slight movement in the trees caught her attention. Thinking it to be an animal, she was about to tell Neil he should have brought his service revolver when the branches rustled and parted to reveal a figure who stood in their path in mouse-colored jacket and breeches. She drew in her breath sharply. The man had a dark beard and wore the slouch hat adopted by Boers.

"Halt!" he said in a thick accent.

There was no time for sane thought. Everything happened so quickly her mind reeled with the horror of it all. The rifle in the man's hand went off without any apparent movement from him. Like something in a grisly mime the front of Neil's tweed jacket burst into a flower of spreading scarlet petals, and he doubled up without even a cry before rolling slowly from the back of the tall black horse. Judith watched him hit the ground and lie still, hearing a high screaming sound that was in her mind alone. Nothing came from a throat that had grown rigid and dumb.

The man moved forward and jerked his head to indicate that she should dismount. Stunned she could only stare at him. Neil was dead! He could not be; he had been given a staff appointment. A hand fastened around her leg, pulled sharply, and she pitched forward to land with a thud on the ground. A foot jabbed her in the ribs, and the man indicated the copse with a jerk of his rifle, but the grass was soft and comfortingly familiar beneath her body. She did not want to leave it for the dread unknown in the trees, and clung to it with her hands until he seized her arm and hauled her to her feet, pushing her forward.

The trees now appeared much, much taller and so thickly placed it was like night within their confines. Suddenly, it had grown bitterly cold, and the most tragic thing in her life seemed to be the fact that she had said good-bye to Neil, but not to Alex. He was lost to her forever and would never know she loved him as much as Hetta Myburgh had.

The trees began to close around her, and her legs grew so weak it was almost impossible to go on. Was there a life after death? she wondered. Would everything just turn black and remain that way forever? Terror deeper than comprehension possessed her at the thought. She did not want to die here in the dark copse. In a frenzy of struggling she tried to free herself so that she could run back beneath the open blue sky. It was imperative to reach Neil before being gunned down. To die alone would be to remain alone throughout eternity.

Her struggles halted the man, but did not free her. His grip was intense. Light green eyes held a wildness bordering on hatred, as if there were some personal element in what he was about to do. Throwing down the rifle he gripped her other arm so that she could not move. Then, and only then, did Judith realize it was not her death he desired.

*"No!"* she cried in an anguished plea. To leave Alex without a farewell was nothing now. This way, she could never return to face him.

She fought. All her strength and hopelessness went into the effort. Biting, clawing, and kicking she struggled against his overpowering strength, but slowly the battle was lost. Sobbing with the wildness of grief she felt the darkness of the copse merge with that in her mind until black was the only color in the world.

The sun was sitting on the top of the hill when Judith stumbled from the trees, shaking uncontrollably. Her wild glance fell on the horses grazing peacefully nearby, and she went to the mare, clinging to the warm hide with hands that moved convulsively. Her body felt broken. It shook with icy tremors and sagged against the beast. Her mind had gone on a flight of dementia in a bid to dismiss the horror of a short while ago, and strange words and moans came from a mouth that would not move. She had been branded forever: The finality of death would have been a mercy.

The crispness in the air turned to prefrost chill, and the sun sank lower leaving only a blush of rose-colored cirrus flaying across the sky for as far as the eye could see. It would be dark in an hour. The girl who lay white-faced and shocked across the mare longed for it. Night would hide her—as she must always hide from now on.

Suddenly, a faint sound sent her spinning around in terror, believing the bearded man had returned. It was a moment or two before cohesive thought told her the sounds were coming from the body huddled on the ground. It added a new dimension to her nightmare, and for some minutes she clung to the grazing animal, staring at the man as if he were a ghoul.

Another low moan, and his hand moved on the grass. Shaking from head to foot she moved with slow fearful steps, hardly believing what she saw. Neil's face was agonized, pale and beaded with sweat but, incredibly, his eyes opened as she knelt beside him and pushed her tangled hair from where it clung to the wet streaks on her face.

"Dear God, you are alive!" she breathed.

His mouth moved in labored manner until she could make out the words he formed with such effort. "Forgive . . . me . . . forgive . . ." Blood frothed from his mouth to end all speech. It ran in crimson bubbles down his face.

Judith's stomach heaved and she retched. Rising to her feet she ran back to the mare where she held the saddle as if it were a lifeline. God help me, she prayed, for He had given her a burden too great to bear. Minutes passed. Thoughts flew back and forth in her brain. There is nothing I can do for him. *You can take him back to Ladysmith.* He is dying: there is no hope. *There is always hope.* The journey would probably kill him. *A night on the kopje will definitely kill him.* I do not have the courage. *Find it!*

It grew even colder and the isolation, the looming nightmare of the copse, the moans of pain all pressed their overwhelming weight against the frailty of her defense. Once she had told Neil what a poor creature she was—that she shied from facing another's pain, blood, and sickness, the responsibility of lives in danger—but how could she fail him when there was no one else?

Taking a deep breath she turned until her back was against the mare and faced what she must. For several seconds she stood immobile until it was apparent that Neil was fighting to raise himself on his hands. It was enough to send her forward with a protesting cry, to sink to her knees beside him. He fell back to reveal a dark stain spreading across his clothes, and his eyes fastened on hers with desperate need. She turned back the tweed of his riding jacket with the tip of a finger and thumb. Blood lay like a thick crimson slime over torn flesh in which pieces of silk shirt and tweed were compounded. Bile rose in her throat, but she pressed her fist against her lips with a quick movement and fought the faintness the sight urged on her.

With pounding heart she got up carefully, then lifted her skirt to unfasten the ripped petticoat. When it slipped to the ground she trembled with the memory of hands tearing it from her body so short a time ago, but forced her mind back to what she must now do. Feverish hands tore long strips from the petticoat before folding the remainder into a pad to put across the sickening wound. It was all done more with the object of hiding from her eyes something she could not face than with any medical design, but once she had bound the pad in place and fastened the binding strips with the watch pinned to her jacket, the pounding of her heart was easing.

Neil had drifted off into a limbo of his own once more by the time she decided his horse was too tall for her purpose and brought the mare to stand beside where he lay. However great her determination, however urgent the need to get him to a doctor, Judith knew it could only be accomplished with the wounded man's help, and began the long task of willing him to summon his strength.

Coaxing, lifting, fighting down her own despair, she brought him from his semiconscious state and helped him to his feet beside the mare. For a long time he hung onto the pommel, racked with the agony of the slightest movement and hardly aware of her presence. Knowing he needed to marshal his courage and strength, yet watching the sun

sinking lower, Judith tried to fight her rising panic. Once
darkness fell they would be lost!

It was something of a miracle that he ever reached the
saddle but, during that time, watching him strive beyond
the bounds of endurance, a new strength came to her. Broken and without a future herself, there suddenly seemed to
be *something* that could be saved from the horror of the
afternoon. By saving him, keeping him alive, it was possible to defy the man who had destroyed her. It became a
fever burning within, a desperate urgency, a reason for existence. She must get him to Ladysmith alive or there
would be no further life for herself.

Once in the saddle, Neil succumbed to weakness, falling
comatose across the animal's neck, and all Judith's efforts
failed to rouse any spark of response in him. Filled with
determination she tore the hem from her skirt and slipped
the band through the belt he wore, fastening the other end
to the pommel as tightly as she was able. Then she bound
his wrists around the mare's neck so that he was reasonably
secure. It was not enough, for Neil was a heavy man, and
one glance told her she would have to walk beside him all
the way to ensure that he did not slip.

With the other horse tied to the mare Judith set out on
the long journey to the town below. She and Neil had
looked at it but a few hours ago when the extent of sadness
had merely been the need to say farewell: from this moment on neither would be the same person.

It was not long before the departing sun left a faint silver
light in the west that stood out against the gathering purple. There was only one path, stony and tortuous. Judith
walked blindly. With the coming of night, reminiscent of
the dark copse, she felt the scream rising within her throat
once more. Her back crawled with the sensation of moving
bracken beneath it scratching at her skin as he forced her
down. The hair hanging limply across her cheeks smelled
of the dank earth and her nostrils were full of the sourness
he had emanated. Deep in the pit of her stomach was a
pain that throbbed with every step. It was a pain she felt
would never go—a pain that degraded her in the eyes of
the world.

Yet, every step she took toward Ladysmith struck a blow
on her behalf. Battening down her silent screams, forcing
her mind to divorce itself from her body, she put one foot
before the other in a rhythmic pattern of hatred against the

bearded Boer. He would not take the life of a man who had stood no chance against his gun, a man who had been shot for no other purpose than that he had been there.

Moving now through a dense blackness that hid all save the denser shadows looming each side of the path, Judith could only trust the instinct of the horse's sure hooves on the sloping ground. Stumbling, kicking her toes on roots and stones, and clutching the edge of Neil's jacket with a hand that ached from the effort of holding him steady, she tried not to heed the wild night sounds. When darkness fell in Africa the other half of the animal kingdom stalked the veld and *kopjes*. Creatures of daylight trod warily then and headed for cover.

Time passed in leaden seconds, and Judith became like one of the country's night roamers—eyes wide and suspicious, body tense, senses stretched to the limit. When the ground leveled, and a cold wind rushed at her from the void, she bared her teeth against it and her hair whipped back into pale streaming tusks against her ears.

Soon after, the lights of Ladysmith lay ahead. They danced unsteadily before her eyes. The more she pressed forward, the further distant they appeared to float. Her legs no longer obeyed her wishes. She grew wilder and stumbled desperately forward, half-hanging to the mare. She would not be defeated.

With her breath coming now in sobs of anguish she dragged herself toward the lights of humanity, the clasp of her hand on the tweed coat tightening with every step. "Live!" she implored the man slumped across the mare. "Please, God, *live!*"

Suddenly, a man's voice from the darkness shouted, "Halt!" In her mind it was the one with the beard challenging her again, and when a shadowy figure materialized from the night and began walking toward her, she gave a cry and backed away.

"It's a woman," said a voice.

"A woman . . . what woman?"

A blinding light was full in her face as the lantern was raised. "It looks like . . . good God, it *is* Miss Burley. She's in a terrible state. Come and give me a hand."

Boots thudded on the dust road, and she stared wild-eyed at the light. The voices were English, but the tall masculine shapes frightened her. They held rifles.

"George, take a look over there. She's got a man tied to that horse."

"It's Mr. Forrester. He's dead. Christ, what's happened? Wait a minute . . . I can feel his heart beating. Get a stretcher up here quick—no, get two. Miss Burley looks just about done for."

The voices grew fainter. Neil was alive and in Lady-smith. Now she could walk away into the darkness where she must hide from now on.

The story of the dramatic arrival was circulating Lady-smith by morning, and everyone was speculating on the facts behind it. Lieutenant Forrester was in a coma, his life hanging in the balance, and Judith Burley was incommuni-cado by her own choice. Alex had been out with another armored train and did not hear of the affair until the fol-lowing afternoon when he bumped into a fellow officer as he returned to his quarters. Full of immediate concern he lost no time in riding up to the bungalow on the outskirts of Ladysmith.

Mrs. Davenport received him in the parlor, rising and going to him as he entered. "Alexander, how thankful I am that you are back!" she said with enough emotion to sur-prise him.

"I have only just heard . . . but the barest details."

"That is all anyone knows. That poor boy is dying, and Judith has locked herself in her room. I have tried to speak to her . . . Reginald has appealed to her for the facts. I do not know what to do for the best. She says she wishes to be left alone, but she looked so ill when . . . oh, Alexander, what a terrible thing to have happened. I have never seen her like this, even during those terrible days at the end of the siege."

He was shaken. Judith, cool, unemotional, assured, lock-ing herself in her room like an overwrought domestic after a servants' quarrel? It did not make sense, even allowing for a depth of feeling for Neil that he had not imagined. "How much do you know of what happened?" he asked. "She must have said something to you."

"That's just it . . . she appeared on the *stoep* when I was growing seriously worried, and burst into tears when she saw me. I could get no sense from her at all." Mrs. Davenport walked back and forth, her silk dress rustling as the skirt swung around. "If you had seen her! Hair pulled from its pins, clothes torn and muddy, blood all over her skirt! I was shocked and full of the most terrible apprehension. I put her to bed and sent for the doctor immediately, but she refused to see him."

"Refused?" Alex could hardly believe it of the girl he knew.

"Refused," Mrs. Davenport affirmed. "She seemed terrified of the man." She put her hands to cheeks that were dangerously over-bright. "He was very understanding and withdrew right away, leaving a sleeping draught for her. Before I could prepare it, Reginald arrived hoping she could shed some light on the shooting of poor Mr. Forrester." She looked at him in desperation. "That was the first I knew of what had happened."

Alex was growing more uneasy by the minute, and Mrs. Davenport's overwrought state added to his concern. That she needed reassurance was plain, but he could not give it unless he knew the true situation. Taking her arm he led her to the sofa and sat her down with firm hands.

"What did the Colonel tell you, Aunt Pan?" he asked gently. "Just tell me and I'll see if I can sort it out."

Slightly calmer Judith's aunt related how the girl had arrived on the outskirts of the town last night, leading her mare to which was tied the wounded man. Around his wound were strips of a woman's petticoat and he was secured to the animal by a strip torn from the hem of a riding skirt. Judith had been exhausted and filthy, appearing frightened when the guards challenged her. While they raised the alarm and sent for stretchers, she had left the horses and walked away into the darkness before they knew she had gone. Neil Forrester was found to have a serious wound in his stomach and was unconscious. He had been that way ever since.

"Naturally, Reginald is most anxious to know how one of his officers was shot, but all she would tell me was that a Boer did it and she brought him back to a doctor."

"When did she tell you that?" he asked.

"Last night when I took in the sleeping draught." She bit her lip. "I found her door locked this morning. She has not opened it all day. The doctor called soon after breakfast . . . but he could hardly break into her bedroom." There was a moment before she rose again and put her hand on his sleeve. "Speak to her. Persuade her to come out."

He looked at the distress on her face and frowned. "I'll

try, but I can't see that I shall succeed where you have failed."

"But yes," Mrs. Davenport assured him. "If there is one person she would want right now, it is you."

He was startled. "Well, I can't give her good news of him, you know."

She gave him a strange look. "Alexander, I don't believe you understand Judith any better than she used to understand you. Go and talk to her . . . please."

He did his best, but there was no answer to his knock—no sound to suggest the room was even occupied. Starting with gentle persuasion, his voice grew sharper as the silence continued.

"You are helping no one, Judith, least of all yourself," he said. "You have had a shock and we are all concerned for your welfare." Still silence. "Neil is still very ill, but you could help him far more at his bedside than worrying in there alone."

He stared at the door that remained shut and tried a last tactic. "Think of Aunt Pan. She has only recently recovered from a serious illness. Any kind of worry could set her back, and she is extremely anxious over you."

Baffled and angry he went back to the parlor to report failure. His anger increased at the sight of the elderly lady's distress, and it remained until he left fifteen minutes later.

It was not until he returned to his quarters and stood at the window with a drink in his hand that he admitted his anger was due to a strange sense of responsibility for the girl who had become a close companion over the past two months. He thought about the facts he had been told and grew more and more pensive. It appeared Neil had been shot by Boers before her eyes, although he had not been in uniform. It was hardly typical behavior of the enemy to gun down an apparent civilian, unarmed and escorting a woman.

But the most amazing thing about the incident was that one must assume Judith had witnessed such a tragedy, then bound the man's dreadful wound, lifted him onto a horse, and led him back to the town single-handed. There was no other explanation.

Judith had always puzzled him, but never more so than now. From the time she had agreed to their marriage he had thought her inexplicably avaricious, prim, and cold. When she suddenly released him from an engagement she had fought so desperately to retain he had wondered at her motives—and thought her sights set on a higher goal.

She was gone from his mind completely for a long time, and it was a shock to find she had been in Ladysmith all through the siege. He remembered the sense of something bordering on anger he had felt at the sight of her the day he had ridden in. The other women had looked as she had, but it had seemed particularly brutal in her case and an uneasy feeling of responsibility had pierced him.

Since then he had learned of her courage and patience while nursing her aunt. He had been told by many of the concerts she had given, and her successful teaching of children at a time when such things were inclined to be neglected. All that had suggested a personality vastly different from any she had ever displayed to him.

Taking him by surprise yet again, she had offered friendship at a time when such an association would do her reputation little good. For a girl once so sensitive to convention she had appeared remarkably unconcerned about the world. In the last few weeks he had felt close enough to her to find an easy companionship. Her cool, level-headed approach had been a peaceful island in his sea of emotion. Her undemanding presence was a welcome relief from the war that had raged in him since that terrible morning at the farm.

Now, at a time when he would have sworn he was beginning to know her, she had done another chameleon change. Neil had been shot down before her eyes, admittedly, but there had been enough horrors in Ladysmith to daunt any woman. Why had she given under the strain now? If she loved him so much, the way to help him was to be at his bedside, not grieving on her own.

She remained there the following day. Late in the afternoon, Alex, out on the firing range, received the message that Lieutenant Forrester had broken from his coma and was asking to see him urgently. Alex rode at a sharp trot to the hospital, arriving to find Colonel Rawlings–Turner outside the room in which Neil was lying. He pulled up short.

"Good afternoon, sir. I . . . I was told Neil wished to see me."

"That's right," was the gruff reply. "Won't see anyone until he has talked to you. The doctor assures me there is a chance of his survival if he is kept quiet, but you must find out what happened, my boy. If there is a Boer commando on the outskirts of this town we must search it out. Can't have anyone else picked off."

"No," Alex agreed. "I'll do my best, sir."

As he went in the nurse looked up and smiled. "I will give you five minutes," she said, and went out.

Putting his helmet carefully on the table at the end of the bed, Alex moved around to take a look at Neil. He appeared to be sleeping. Suddenly, he was angry that a man who had army tradition so strong in his veins should be shot while riding with his sweetheart, unarmed and out of uniform. If he died as a result of it, it would be a cruel twist of fate.

"Neil . . . it's Alex," he said in a low voice. "You wanted to see me, I understand."

The brown eyes opened slowly, but took a long time to register recognition. Alex smiled and perched on the side of the bed.

"We're counting on you to recover, old chap. Can't have too many rotters like me getting into the regiment, can we?"

Neil gripped his sleeve in great agitation. "Judith . . . it's Judith."

"She's all right," Alex soothed, "but awfully cut up about you."

The dark head moved from side to side on the pillow, as if tormented.

"Oh God, you've got to help her."

Alex furrowed his brow. "In what way?"

The man in the bed was breathing with difficulty, and Alex leaned nearer so that he could hear his words. The beginnings of concern were stirring inside him.

"No one else can help her now," came the rattling whisper.

"I . . . don't understand," he said slowly. "What are you trying to say?"

"It has always been you. If you let her down now . . ." He tightened his grip on Alex's sleeve. "He . . . fired before I had a chance to protect her. I tried—before God, I tried to get up—but I couldn't move. He took her at gun point . . . into . . . into the trees. *The brute took her at gun point.* Oh God, I'll never forget the way she looked . . . the way she . . ." He broke down and turned his face to the wall, but Alex no longer saw him. Hardly aware of the colonel rising to his feet in expectation, or the nurse smiling a good-bye, he strode along the corridor and out into the dying day.

The sunset's red glow reflected the throbbing behind his eyes during that gallop between the military huts toward Ladysmith. He thought of her on that first night in the rose garden at Hallworth, pure and supremely beautiful in white frosted with silver, and again of the New Year's Eve ball when he had told her the regiment was leaving. The delicate apricot of her dress had also been in her cheeks, but she had swept past him in superb style, holding her head high. More recently she had walked among a group of pressmen and silenced them with one gracious smile. She was cultured, virtuous, and courageous. She was a lady in every sense of the word.

The thought of some bestial creature violating her in some foreign woods sent the blood pounding through him in an outcry of rage. To think of her pale shimmering hair matted with earth and moss, rough dirt-engrained hands on that smooth skin; her pride falling beneath an onslaught of animal lust, set a fire of revenge rioting in his breast. He imagined her struggles, her cries, her wild prayers, and lashed his horse with the whip to make it go even faster. If only he had known sooner!

He arrived at the bungalow and jumped the low fence that marked off the garden. Throwing himself from the saddle he took the steps in one stride to burst into the parlor.

Mrs. Davenport started at his sudden violent arrival in her room and had done no more than open her mouth when he demanded to know if Judith were still in her room.

"Yes . . . but, Alexander what do you mean by this . . . this . . . ?"

He was across the room and opening the door into the far corridor. "Stay where you are, Aunt Pan, for your own safety."

Once outside Judith's room he paused to control his breathing, then said, "Judith this is Alex. Open this door at once!"

Leaving a long enough pause for her to do so, he repeated the demand in a tone loud enough to raise the roof, and added, "If you don't I shall shoot off the lock. That's no idle threat, I swear. I mean to come in."

Drawing his revolver with a hand that was unsteady he cocked it and pointed it at the lock. As he was on the point of firing it, he heard a soft click of a key turning. Slowly he replaced the gun and reached for the handle.

She was against the far wall, looking at him with eyes that were sunken and red-rimmed. Her face and throat were purple with bruises. The slender body usually carried with such grace sagged against the wall in a loose silk wrapper carelessly tied. Her pale hair hung as straight as a nun's veil.

*Dear God in heaven!* His lips moved slightly, but the words were mere thoughts as he found his throat thick with emotion. Her eyes revealed all too plainly the degradation and despair she felt beneath his gaze, and he knew her future depended on what he did during the next moments.

Moving toward her with great care he said softly, "Did you think I would not understand? Oh, my dear, if there is one person in the world who knows what it is like to fight back, it's I. We'll do it together."

For a long, long time she stared at him. Then, silently but with complete abandon, she went into his arms, and he held her until she lived again.

## CHAPTER TWENTY-ONE

October 1900. Another spring was carpeting the veld with flowers, pushing the maize shoots through the rich soil, and putting the battle cry back into the throats of the militant Boers. New leaders had arisen to replace the original ones, to rally the defeated and scattered burghers.

Joubert, who had invested Ladysmith for too long and with too much dependence on the Almighty, had died. Two other generals had been captured, and Paul Kruger, heartbroken and discredited, had fled to Holland. The British had Johannesburg and Pretoria, with full command of the railway system, and outnumbered the Boers nearly ten to one.

World opinion was still in favor of the Boers, but all appeals for armed assistance were met with embarrassed excuses. The power of Britain's navy was too well-known, and investments in South African gold made a postponement of peace a financial risk. The war in South Africa had become something everyone except the Boers wanted swept under the carpet.

With unconditional surrender hovering, the new leaders set out to inspire their people to take up an apparently hopeless crusade. Even when their hopes that public opinion in England would put in an antiwar government in the general election failed, their fire would not be quenched.

So, when the British—and the world—believed the war virtually over, a new phase of guerrilla fighting began. Small groups of Boers roamed the country in no particular pattern, blowing up bridges and sections of railway track, attacking supply columns and small outposts. They used fast horses, hid in isolated farms, struck where they were least expected—and vanished again into the veld.

There was no attempt to gain territory—the burghers knew they could never hold it—but they successfully harassed their adversaries at every opportunity and prevented peace negotiations from being approached. The great British Empire was still at war with a small nation of farmers. Sheltered and fed by their womenfolk in farms dotted all over the veld, they had a great advantage. As they kept cutting off the British supply lines, so it was decided the same must be done to them.

Orders were issued to the British soldiers to burn down any farm whose owner was known to shelter members of a commando. The livestock was to be slaughtered or commandeered; the women and children to be put into special camps for safety and protection. It was an order that met with no enthusiasm. The British had always been surprisingly controlled where other armies rushed in to rape and plunder, and putting a torch to simple farms built by the hands of the owners was not to their liking. When women and children began dying in the camps through disease and lack of supplies—most of which had been blown up by the Boers en route—they relished the task even less.

Their opinions altered when they learned that the Boers had begun a practice contrary to all rules of warfare—that of dressing in the uniforms of their enemy. Prisoners were no use to them—they had no food nor anywhere to house them—so they were stripped and turned off to return to their lines the best way they could. Then the Boers, in British khaki, rode right into camps and shot soldiers who mistook them for comrades until it was too late. After that, burning the farms seemed fair reprisal. The gentlemanly war had turned dirty.

The maize shoots on the Myburgh farm were struggling to push through despite the neglect of the fields: The cattle were thin and bow-headed. Hetta saw it all and did nothing. The crops would soon be trampled beneath cavalry hooves: The cattle would be slaughtered. She had heard how the English soldiers made bonfires of farmhouses, gleefully piling treasured pictures and hand-woven cloths onto the flames before running with burning sticks to the buildings. They stoned the poultry and galloped their thoroughbred horses among the livestock with lances. "Pig-sticking" they called it, and all the while they yelled like uncontrollable children with the excitement of destruction. Piet had said so, so it must be true.

Soon they would come up the track from Landerdorp to burn down her house. Piet had been right from the beginning—the British were taking their farms and imprisoned those upon them. They were all he had said they were. They tramped across Africa with their arrogant feet and took away freedom. They had killed her father, her grandfather, and her brother. Although Franz had not been shot, his death from fever on the bitter winter veld had been caused by his need to fight the enemy. Here, on the farm, she could have tended him, but out there where cold and exhaustion laid a man low he had had no chance. She did not grieve for him; just regarded his loss as God's retribution.

Most of the time she sat in the rocking chair looking out at the hills through her open door. The poultry would soon be finished and there would be no eggs. The storekeepers in Landerdorp would sell her nothing, neither would they buy. The remaining cattle would give poor meat, and what vegetables she had were choked with weeds. Most of the black people had drifted away: there was just Johnnie.

Day after day Hetta sat in the farmhouse just staring at the hills, never knowing when the Landerdorp commando would return for food and shelter. Piet always led them in. They took what they wanted, went where they wished, and left when they were ready. They all ignored her: she expected them to. Piet was their leader and they did what he did. Hetta Myburgh was an outcast.

The commando rode in one noon toward the end of October when the heat had been intense. The men made straight for the pump where they drank thirstily, then washed the dust from their bodies. They wrung the necks of several chickens and brought them into the kitchen, throwing them on the table for her to prepare and stew.

She began plucking, sitting on a stool by the doorway with a bowl between her feet for the feathers. Her fingers worked expertly while the men went back and forth carrying from their saddlebags piles of clothes—khaki uniforms. They would boldly wear them into the British camps. The enemy would not know they were not comrades-in-arms, until it was too late. They all seemed excited, and their voices carried to her as she worked.

"This is good warm stuff. No wonder the *rooineks* drop from the heat."

"*Ja*, we should have had these during the winter."

"*Magtig*, this is so big!"

"It is to go over their bloated bellies. Even with all their marching they stay fat."

Suddenly, there was laughter as Jan Kronje strutted the kitchen in breeches and tunic three sizes too big, saying, "Yes, *sir!*" He was only fifteen and had not filled out. He looked such a child with the big pith helmet practically resting on his shoulders on each side of his head.

"The good Lord smiled on us last night, eh?" demanded Piet joyfully as he watched the lad. "They walked right into our hands."

The laughter slowly died into an uneasy silence, until big Kobie van Heerden said, "It was not right to kill them, Piet. You should not have done that. They had surrendered; we had their rifles."

"*Ja*," several agreed in a murmur.

In an instant Piet was thumping the table and shouting in a voice vibrant with hatred, "Are you all women?"

"We are men," said Kobie quietly, "but we are not animals. Shooting helpless prisoners is not human, it is not necessary."

The gentle defiance sparked off a stream of unrestrained speech that echoed beneath the rafters. Although Hetta could not see him, she knew well enough how he looked— eyes ablaze, mouth wet with fervor, and arms waving wildly. His words went right through to her bones.

"Is it *necessary* to raze farmsteads built by honest toil in the sight of God? Is it *necessary* to cut the throats of sheep, or trample the crops, or slaughter calves with lances? Is it *human* to take women and children into captivity to die from pestilence and hunger? Is it *human* to oppress a whole nation for the sake of supremacy?"

After the roar of the lion, the gentle *klipspringer*. A slightly built man in his thirties spoke for the first time. He had a British uniform in his hands that he had not put on.

"We could have our farms, our women, and children. We could have peace." He held out the khaki clothes. "This is destroying us. We can never win; they dare not lose. To continue is against the will of the Almighty. He has shown us that we must wait. The time is not right for us to rule this land—He has made that plain. The truth and honesty of our cause is gone. We are doing things that ought not to be done. How can we condemn the godless English when we sin against humanity ourselves? We should be on our knees to the Lord, not defiling His name with our deeds."

Piet walked over and stood before the speaker. "You should not be on your knees, Koos, but on your stomach. You are like the snake that twists around the sturdy tree for support."

Dark eyes looked back unflinchingly. "No, Piet, I have fought as well as any man in this commando. I love my country, my farm, and my family, but the longer we go on defying the British the more farms they will burn, and the more innocent people will die. The hatred will go beyond appeasement. If our land is scorched, our women and children imprisoned, the burden is ours. What started as a crusade has turned into madness. After what I saw last night, I want no place in this commando." He held out the uniform. "Give this to a disciple of the devil. I will have none of it."

Piet struck the man across the face with the back of his hand. "So we have another traitor—a man who will bow to the British. This place breeds them." He moved back twisting his hands together in frenzy. "Get back to your land, if it is still there; and your woman, if she is not in bed with an Englishman."

The man remained quiet, saddened rather than angry. "See, you are already proving my words right, Piet Steenkamp. Six months ago you would not have said such a thing to your neighbor. You are no patriot, you are a madman. Who else would strip men naked, then shoot them as they stood?" He dropped the uniform on the floor and walked past Hetta, whose hands had become stilled in the midst of plucking the chickens.

Piet swung around and crashed his fist on the table. "Now is the time for all traitors to come forward. Who else will go with him? I want no one with a weak belly."

The boy Jan Kronje struck a pose in his outsize uniform and mimicked in perfect English, "I say, has any of you chaps a weak belly?"

Piet threw out his arm and knocked the boy off-balance with a blow to the head. "Silence, *Boetie*. You know nothing, yet."

The others looked at him uneasily while the boy got to his feet, greatly shaken. No one said anything until Piet began to laugh.

"I shot them naked so that the uniforms would not be full of bullet holes. It takes a clever man to do that, eh?"

Hetta heard his laughter and recognized the strange note that frightened her more every time she heard it. She believed it also frightened the men for they began to join in, their laughter as forced and desperate as his.

They went to various parts of the farm to sleep while Hetta cooked the hens, then sat around the wooden table to eat. She put plates before them, but they neither thanked her nor acknowledged her presence. They talked freely of their plans to raid Landerdorp that night to destroy a supply train that was on a siding. In British uniforms it would be easy to approach the tiny depot and enter the rail yard. They knew the layout well enough, and with young Jan Kronje to answer in Oxford English any challenge from guards, they could plant explosives with ease.

When Piet went to check on the horses, and Hetta cleared away the plates, the men spoke among themselves of the coming action. It was the first time they had posed as British soldiers and were not certain they liked the idea. They had heard that Lord Kitchener had ordered the troops to shoot any Boer prisoners caught wearing khaki uniforms.

"They would not kill prisoners," said one.

"It is what we have just done."

"No, it was Piet. We did not do it. It was wrong."

"I sometimes think he is too wild."

"Then why do you follow him?" cried the hero-worshiping Jan. They ignored him.

"It is because of the English officer. He has wanted this since he saw him in Landerdorp last week. He has taken the woman. Now he wants to kill him."

"It is his right."

"*Ja*, it is his right."

"When he has avenged Johannes Myburgh, the wildness will go from him."

"Perhaps. I think it is more than that."

"He cannot kill every Englishman."

"He will try."

They laughed to relieve their tension, and it brought a return of bravado that set them on their feet to don khaki. Piet came in to approve their appearance and tell them it was time to set out. They were to ride to the hills then lie low until the guard changed at two A.M. Full of bluster they gathered up their saddlebags filled with explosives and left without a glance at the girl standing so still in the corner.

Hetta hardly noticed their departure. After five months of blessed emptiness, a pain was stirring deep within her. *The English officer*. Alex was back in Landerdorp! When the men were out of sight she moved to the door and stood for a long time looking at the stable where her horse was hanging his head over the door. At last, she turned away and went to sit in the rocking chair, setting it in motion with leaden feet.

The night stretch of guard duty was always painful. A man was at his lowest ebb just when he should be most vigilant. An attack in the early hours of the morning brought out sharp reflexes from the men taking part, but for those patrolling, staring out into darkness for long hours on end, the fight against sleep was hard.

For Alex the duty also meant too much time for thought. Landerdorp evoked painful memories. Colonel Rawlings–Turner had sent him back for a twofold reason, he knew. To show his confidence in a subaltern whom gossip had said was the lover of a Boer girl from the district. To force Alex to banish his ghosts by facing them.

For the first few days he had been haunted by the need to look constantly toward Devil's Leap, and every woman walking in the street or driving an ox wagon quickened his pulse. He would do nothing if she should appear, yet he hoped for just a sight of her, hoped she would look as she had done before the tragedy. He knew it was over, that there was nothing they could say to each other now. In that respect, he had banished her ghost.

But the colonel had not taken into account the depth of the love that had been between Hetta and himself. Because of it he would never forget her. Because of it he could not understand why she had freed her grandfather. She must have known what the old man was likely to try. Because of it he could not believe she had meant the sleeping captain to be shot as he lay on a bed in her house. The desire to know the truth of what happened that morning after she had left his arms would never be banished. Here in Landerdorp he asked himself why more often, knowing the answer lay out on the veld beyond Devil's Leap, a four-hour ride away, and knowing he could never go there.

Restless, he got up and walked to the window of the first-floor room above the station office. From there he had a good view across the yard and sidings lit by lamps at the corners of the sheds. He set his thoughts onto more practical matters.

After a while, movement to his right caught his eye. Half a dozen soldiers appeared from the shadows near the yard gates. He frowned trying to think who they could be, then called through the open window, "What are you men doing?"

A high light voice answered, "Guard returning from duty, sir."

Alex took out his watch. He was surprised to find it was only two-thirty. The night seemed long. He watched the soldiers as they crossed the yard and went behind the engine shed. They looked very slovenly—uniforms creased and baggy—and they marched like new recruits. He moved across to check the duty roster, then looked up at the wall with another frown. They were all old soldiers who would know better than to turn out looking as if they had slept in their uniforms . . . and which of them spoke like a youth with a polished Oxford accent?

Feeling distinctly uneasy, he clattered down the stairs to where a corporal and three riflemen were on duty. They had only just taken over and had not yet begun patrolling the yard. Something bothered him about the men he had seen crossing below, but could not think what it was until half way through his questions to the corporal.

"Has there been a change of duty roster which has not been reported to me? Did you pass the outlying guards as you . . . Got it!" he exclaimed. "The flashes on their helmets were not Downshires. By God, where have they gone?"

In three strides he was at the door, and there his fear became a reality. It was only a brief glimpse he had of a man sliding from the shadows to cross an exposed area, but he had no doubts. The "British soldier" had a thick black beard and a face he had seen before through the bars of the nearby bull cage and from the hay loft of Hetta's barn.

Turning back into the room he shouted, "Corporal, sound the alarm! There are Boers in British uniforms all over the yard. Fix bayonets and use those if you can. For God's sake don't shoot unless you are certain he is not one of our own men." He nodded at two of the guard. "You come with me. Some were heading toward the siding. Corporal, send up reinforcements when they arrive."

With that he began to run, drawing his revolver as he went. The minute the alarm was sounded shots were fired. In a flash, all the lamps were shattered by Boer bullets, and the yard became as black as night. Alex ran on, his thoughts flying.

Seeing that face again, remembering a vivid and primitive scene in the haystack below, he suddenly knew who had taken Judith at gunpoint into the woods . . . and he knew why. But even as the rage roared up into his brain a voice told him personal vengeance must be put aside in this moment.

On a siding stood the supply train bound for Northern Transvaal, delayed because a section of track had been destroyed farther up the line. It provided the perfect prize for a roving Boer commando, and the guard such a tiny garrison could provide was nowhere near adequate. With the attackers in khaki uniforms those guards would be overcome easily.

His eyes were growing used to the darkness, now. He signaled the two riflemen to slow down and approach with more caution. To the rear and left came the roar of explosions and rattling rifle fire. Alex guessed Boers were creating skirmishes all over Landerdorp to prevent the garrison from concentrating on the rail yard. The leaping yellow light from a burning store shed threw up the outline of the supply train backed by a steep grassy embankment just ahead of them.

There were eighteen cars, all told, carrying sacks of letters and parcels; huge consignments of boots, blankets, and medical supplies as well as tents, fodder, light field guns, and all kinds of ammunition. The cavalry remounts were all in the stock yards waiting for the track to be repaired. To lose the train would be costly.

They had slowed to a walk, and Alex halted the two men beside some trees while he sized up the situation. As he had suspected, those guarding the train had been overcome and killed—fooled by the khaki uniforms. Their bodies lay along the side of the track. In the faint intermittent light from the burning building figures could be seen moving among the cars, planting sticks of dynamite in each. There must have been ten against their three, but the fuses were being lit and any number of reinforcements would be useless unless they arrived immediately . . . and Alex knew they were engaged in fighting elsewhere.

Thinking quickly he sent one man up a tree beside them. He was an excellent marksman and should be able to pick off anyone who came within range. Telling the other to take the left end of the train, he turned to the right and worked his way toward the last car.

He could see the bright moving lights as the flames traveled along the fuses and knew time was of the essence. They had been set off one after the other, and the dynamite would go up in sequence all along the row of cars, starting from each end.

Knowing it was just as essential to stop them from lighting more fuses as to put out those already alight, he fired as he ran. He hit a man in the act of planting explosives in the truck and saw him fall. Another he wounded in the leg, and sent him scrambling away up the embankment.

A dash across an open stretch that invited bullets to bite into the ground around him, then he had reached the first fuse, already half burned through. Stamping out the flame was easy enough once the sticks of dynamite had been removed from their wedged position beneath the sliding door, and he moved from one truck to the other conscious of time and increased rifle fire.

The Boers were not fools and soon realized what was happening. Halting in their tasks they turned their guns on those at each end of the train. The rifleman was killed immediately, bullets from four different guns finding their mark, and Alex felt one skim his helmet before another burned against his neck sending blood trickling down inside his collar. A Boer was brought down by the man in the tree. Alex was alone. With the need to hug cover he could no longer move quickly, and the fuses were burning with deadly speed.

At that moment he spotted his personal quarry twenty yards ahead of him, placing explosive sticks in a crack of the car that Alex knew contained shells for long-range guns. If that went up the whole rail yard would go with it. He thought rapidly. To move into the open brought the danger of being killed, so he played them at their own game.

Speaking in Dutch he called in a low voice, "Piet, I'm trapped. Help me!"

The man had lit the fuse and halted his forward progress to look back along the train in Alex's direction. Staying half-hidden so that all that was visible was a khaki uniform he said, "Over here. Help me!"

It worked. Piet Steenkamp sidled and dodged back toward the sound of the voice. Alex cocked his revolver. There was a long moment during which they faced each other as men as well as enemies. Alex saw it all in his face—the determination, the endeavor, the endurance. But he also saw implacable hatred, fanaticism, and contempt. Then the pale eyes registered shock, the mouth started to curl, the finger began to squeeze the trigger. But he had met another as expert with a gun as himself. He slipped to the ground, dead before the bullet left his own gun.

Alex stared down at him, a crumpled form in the hell glow of the fires springing up all around them. He had not done it for Judith, he realized, nor for Hetta—nor even for Spion Kop. It was because of the British uniform he wore.

There was no time for the luxury of reflection. One glance told him the fuse on the ammunition car had advanced very fast. The little dancing flame was moving inexorably toward the neat cylindrical sticks. Abandoning his cover Alex made a dash for it, but it ended ten yards too short when shots hit him in the back, punching him onto the ground in an agony beyond anything he had endured at Spion Kop. Unable to stop himself, he rolled back and forth hoping to relieve the stinging pain that was eating right into his chest.

Movement made the anguish worse. He lay on his side, gasping in air to offset the need to cry out. The redness of the sky reminded him of that merciless sun that had burned into him as he lay on a plateau eight months ago. It all came back like a nightmare he could feel.

It almost seemed he was back there in reality, for he heard moans nearby as he had done then. Twisting his head slightly, he saw a soldier face downward beside the train—one of the guards who had been taken unawares and shot. He was not dead, as Alex had supposed, although there was a pool of blood beside him. He was not dead—a hand was moving convulsively on the ground. Suppose the others were still alive!

In desperation he raised his head to look at the ammunition car. The fuse had a matter of inches left, that was all. Slowly, with a strength of will he did not know he had, Alex dragged himself to his knees, then into a crouching, pain-racked stance.

Swaying on his feet he peered through the sweat drenching his eyes. There were only two inches left on the fuse. Staggering and lurching toward it, he knew only that he must not fail. It danced before his eyes, and he frowned to aid his focus on the small traveling light. Twice he fell, but the agony in his body concentrated into agony of mind as he thought of the consequences if he did not put out that light in time. It was such a small flame; he could not let it roar into an eternal holocaust.

It was a mere inch away from the bound sticks of dynamite and there was no time to unwedge them. Falling against the side of the car with a sobbing breath he closed both hands around the flame and pressed them tightly together. His palms sent shooting raw agony up his arms, but he gritted his teeth and maintained the pressure until he was certain the flame had gone out.

He had no sensation of gladness or relief, just utter weariness that threatened to drive him back to the ground. To counteract it he reached out a reddened palm for the long handle on the sliding door. At that moment, there was a roar and a sheet of blinding light from the next truck that sent a wall of resistance thumping against him, throwing him backward. Blackness, total and lasting, overtook him.

The sun had gone down long ago; the fire in the kitchen had burned low. It was a bare hour before midnight. The girl in her rocking chair was there in body only, for her spirit had returned to a summer day when she had heard an amused voice and looked up at a man who at once fascinated, overawed, and called to her. It had been that sense of appeal, that reaching out that had captured her from the beginning.

As she stared into the embers she remembered the sun catching his hair as he rode to meet her from where he had always waited below Devil's Leap. She saw again the joy on his face that came alive with expression more and more as the weeks passed. He had respected the boundaries she had put upon their meetings and on their relationship—until she had ridden to him one morning knowing it was not enough.

She saw him again walking with a woman who had only the claim of a diamond to take him away, and knew his pain as he went . . . and her own as she had watched him go.

Then, the memories rioted through her one after the other—wild anguished memories that covered every shade of passion and fear. She heard his voice stumbling over Dutch words, remembered his eyes bruised with shock. Once more she could see the bull cage and his hands gripping the bars; then a figure coming from the darkness of her barn into the light shed by the lantern she held. He had been wet and exhausted—a man from the veld—and she had known him to be *her* man forever.

The returning life within her reached every part of her body to pound it with the echoes of her love for him. In memory she saw Alex standing in the light of her own kitchen.

"*I have been waiting for him to fall asleep. Now I am here the right words won't come.*"

"*You are the enemy!*"

"*Does the enemy do this . . . and this . . . and this?*"

"Alex!" With a long anguished cry she left the rocking chair, rushed from the house leaving the door wide open, and released her horse from the stable. There was no time for a saddle—no time for anything. It was a long, long ride to Landerdorp, and the attack would begin at two A.M.

The horse thundered across the open veld but did not move fast enough for the girl upon its back, nor for the man in Landerdorp who had asked himself *why* so many times.

She had known she was too late when she left the farm, but the red glow in the sky ahead did not turn her back. With the horse lathered and winded, she rode on, her body throbbing with more words . . . her words. *"Swear you have not been so with her"* and his husky reply, *"I swear it . . . I swear it!"*

The chill of the night pushed through her dress, but she was not conscious of it. She rode as if driven by an impulse beyond her control. The veld sounds were all about her, but her ears were deaf to them. She burned with all that had ever been between them; she heard only the words he had spoken from their first meeting. Alex, oh Alex!

At the entrance to the *nek* Hetta slid from the horse's back and began scrambling up the rocky sides leading to Devil's Leap, holding her skirt bunched in one hand. In her wildness she set stones slithering down to crash below, and her hands grew raw from the sharp flint edges she grasped during the climb. Breath was rasping in her throat like sobs, but her eyes were dry.

Up and up she went, heedless of effort or danger until she reached the point above Devil's Leap. There, her grasping hands dropped to her sides, the skirt of her dress ballooned around her as she straightened for a view across to Landerdorp, so short a distance away. Her stillness became almost death; her breathing almost nonexistent.

The little rail depot was a cluster of vague shapes that were thrown up intermittently by the glow of fires when the smoke thinned. She recognized the crack of rifle fire. Then, as she watched, a deep thud was immediately followed by a flash of extra vividness that lit up the far-distant railway cars that stood upon the lines within the yard. Her hand moved to catch at her throat, and she closed her eyes against the sight below.

"Forgive me," she whispered, not certain to whom she spoke.

She turned, knowing what she must do. The veld wind blew more sharply across the ledge that jutted out over the *nek*. It gave an atmosphere of isolation, almost of limbo, yet she forced herself to climb down onto it. In the darkness of night there was no sign of the edge, nothing to show when one would take a step into space. All around was blackness and the whispers of those who had stood there before her. Shrinking back against the rock, she stood listening to them, feeling an affinity with the damned.

Into her mind came the words she had spoken. *The black people believed it was a magic place. If the man was possessed by devils, those devils would persuade him to climb back up and continue his wickedness. Those lying in wait killed him with their spears. If he was blameless, the gods would bear him safely down when he leaped into the* nek *and send him happily on his way.*

She was possessed by devils, there was no doubt. Her own people turned their backs upon her, the souls of Oupa and Franz denounced her. Piet had called her wanton, a traitress. There was no alternative but to climb back up and face the spears that awaited her.

Still she stood there, hearing an echo of his voice from that day so long ago. *"There is no choice but disaster. Once a man set foot on Devil's Leap he was lost, whatever happened."*

*"You make it sound very sad."*

*"It is."*

She turned and began climbing.

# *EPILOGUE*

The young lieutenant who took out a party of men to the Myburgh farm had recently arrived from England, but he had read of the events that had taken place there earlier in the year. Naturally, he did not condone the shooting of a soldier, but burning peoples' homes was a little too barbaric for his taste. The senior officer who had sent him did so to introduce an untried boy to the realities of a particularly poignant war.

The soldiers forming the burning party were all old campaigners. Battle-hardened they felt that the Boer girl who owned this farm would get her just desert when left in a camp at the mercy of the other Boer women. Female tongues could inflict worse wounds than many a lash.

It was a day at the start of December when the heat was intense. The men rode drowsily, cursing the sun that had been their enemy on so many occasions. They wanted to go home to a pleasant island where buxom women and rosy-cheeked children awaited them. They had begun by feeling their traditional tolerance for the enemy, but now the Boers were dead and would not lie down.

Six months ago, if the Boers had acknowledged defeat each of these men would have been happy to shake their hands. Now, although they did not approve, they would play the same dirty game in this stupid war. That was what the Bible-thumping bastards believed in—an eye for an eye—so that was what they would get.

It was a long ride to the farm, and when they drew near the lieutenant ordered them to approach with caution. It appeared quiet, but they could easily be ambushed by the commando known to use it. They saw a sturdy house, built in Dutch style, with particular care and attention to detail. The outbuildings were also of stone, standing alongside the house itself to form a pleasing picture—unlike some ramshackle places they had seen on the veld.

There was little movement apart from the ripple over the maize fields, and a few grazing beasts. Reluctantly the men had to admit there was a vivid savage beauty about this country they cursed so often, and a farm like this one might be a heaven on earth if it were not so far from civilization.

Their caution was not needed. They rode into the yard to find the place deserted except for an old native who was hoeing a vegetable patch. He had to stay beside his master, he told them, and indicated a grave beneath the shade of some trees. The others had gone.

They chaffed him, as they did anyone they could not quite understand, but he continued with his hoeing and took no notice when they kicked open the door of the house.

Now that they had arrived the actual business of striking a match was difficult. The whole place was neat and polished; the trundle beds made up ready for occupation. The curtains looked freshly washed; firewood was stacked beside the range. There was a pair of new leather boots standing beneath a coat that hung on a peg. A pipe stuck from the pocket.

Hetta Myburgh had gone, according to the old native. They did not understand it. What reason could a woman have for cleaning from floor to ceiling a house she was about to abandon before it was burned to the ground? It made them uneasy, made what they were about to do seem worse than before.

Suddenly, the corporal of the party had had enough. He turned to his officer and asked permission to begin. The boy looked pale and uncomfortable, but reluctantly nodded his head.

The furniture caught quickly, and the blaze brought out something in the men that needed little encouragement. The feeling that the missing girl was somehow striking a last blow by polishing her house ready for the burning was pushed down by retaliation. Soon they were ripping down curtains, smashing the windows with their rifles, and pulling shelves from the walls. Several tried in vain to break up a rocking chair, but it was too solidly built, and they threw it onto the fire in one piece, giving a shout as the flames began to lick round it. Everything they could lay their hands on went onto the crackling pile: Hetta Myburgh appeared to have taken nothing with her.

It was not long before the soldiers were forced to leave the house, and they stood for a moment outside watching the stone walls blackening with smoke. Then, someone ran with a blazing piece of wood to the barn and touched the end to the low-piled hay. The flames ran through it with a loud crackling noise, leaping up to lick around the loft above before running on to surround a row of barrels containing apples. The roof crashed down sending a shower of sparks flying out. They settled on the roofs of the native huts, which were soon burning fiercely.

The madness really took hold then. A few men mounted their horses and began chasing the cattle, whooping and poking the poor beasts with their bayonets. The lieutenant called them back, but they were past hearing. The maize was flattened by pounding hooves. Flames failed to travel through the green stalks and turned into thick foul-smelling smoke that hung over the fields. What fowls there were met with a quick death and were slung from saddles ready for the return.

Before long, the wide incredible sky was blurred by smoke, the home built with such hardship and endeavor stood blackened and in ruins, surrounded by piles of dark ashes. The scene that had struck the men as one of fascinating wild beauty was now stark, desolate, and accusing.

They sobered quickly, the orgy of destruction lying like a leaden weight on their breasts. The boy officer felt sick and told himself it was the accursed sun. With unspoken accord the men mounted and prepared to leave, telling themselves it was the heat and a country that got under a man's skin that made them feel the way they did. They rode off, passing the old native who was still hoeing vegetables near the grave of Johannes Myburgh.


It was a very different December that year from the last. The heat, the rain, the flies, and the dust were still there in Ladysmith, but one could walk in the streets without fear of falling shells, there was enough to eat and drink. No one strained his eyes to catch the flash of the heliograph, or listened constantly for a relief column that could not break through.

The hospital was full of sick and wounded, but no longer overcrowded and lacking supplies. There was a neat, orderly atmosphere, an antiseptic hush along the corridors that made Judith want to tiptoe.

The nurse smiled at her as she reached Alex's door. "Now the patient will be happy. He has been asking after you for the past hour."

Judith smiled back. "He knows I always come at the same time each day."

"To an impatient man two o'clock never seems to come. You'll find Lieutenant Russell waiting on the *stoep* for you."

"How is he?" Judith asked quickly.

The nurse spread her hands. "He is a strong man. The wounds are healing well, under the circumstances. As for the rest, who can tell? They all take it in different ways. It depends on a man's strength of character . . . and those who are closest to him."

"Yes, I see," said Judith quietly.

She went into the hospital room closing the door silently behind her. His chair was out on the *stoep* where he could feel the benefit of any slight breeze, but she did not go out for a while. She just stood watching him for a few moments, as she always did, trying to marshal her courage. When she was ready her feet made a determined sound on the floor, and he turned quickly.

"Hello, Alex. I'm glad you're out here. It's terribly hot indoors today," she began.

His face had lit up. "Judith! Thank you for coming."

"Not at all," she said with a little laugh. "I might tell you I am glad to get away at times. Since Aunt Pan became Mrs. Rawlings–Turner she talks of nothing but 'Reginald's Regiment.' They argue most dreadfully, you know."

He smiled faintly. "An ideal pair."

"I suppose so. They look very happy."

"I'm glad. She was a widow far too long."

Judith took a deep breath before saying, "Life is funny, isn't it? She came out to South Africa determined to get *me* married."

"And was hoist with her own petard," he finished for her. "She always meddled too much in your life. It won't work with the Colonel." He moved restlessly in the chair. "What's the latest gossip?"

Disappointed with his answer she said sharply, "I don't listen to gossip." Then she relented. "I'll tell you three things that will interest you, however. Neil went down to Durban this morning. He sails in the hospital ship on Friday. There is a message for you. He said . . ." she faltered slightly, then continued with determination, ". . . he said the regiment did not appear to have suffered from accepting rotters, after all."

A broad smile crossed Alex's face. "He'll go far, that boy. What's the next thing?"

Uncertain of his reaction she approached the topic with care. "We are very distantly related, aren't we, Alex . . . *family*, I mean?"

"I suppose so," he murmured. "Why?"

"I . . . I thought Sir Chatsworth ought to hear the news from someone other than the mere official notice, so I wrote to him. He appears to have been very grateful for my thoughtfulness, judging by his reply. There is a letter addressed to you, also."

She watched him as a series of expressions crossed his face, loving him, longing to turn the key that locked him away inside himself.

"Do you want to know what he writes?"

"Not really," was the firm reply. "It's far too late now. The only bond that held me to him was one of guilt and I'm free of it at last. He had his reasons for doing what he did, but I can never forgive him for making me so desperately unhappy. Leave him with his dreams of Miles."

Judith was shaken. He had never spoken so frankly about his father before, and she sensed that he meant what he said. She put back into her bag the unopened letter, feeling that she would someday hear the full story and understand.

"And the third?" he asked, breaking into her thoughts. "You said you had three things to tell me."

"Yes." Now that the moment had come she lost her courage. Until today Alex had been quietly subdued, but there was an aggression in him now that reminded her of their engagement days.

"Well?"

"They went out to the Myburgh farm and burned it down—destroyed everything."

He was upset, it was obvious from the clenched hands on the chair and the way his jaw worked just above the bullet scar on his neck.

"When they arrived the place had been abandoned. She . . . she must have guessed we would have to do it. I thought you would like to know." He nodded but said nothing, and she went on, "It was better than being put in a camp, Alex."

"Yes," he said slowly. "I think that would have killed her." Then, after a long pause. "Thank you, Judith. You are a very good friend."

It was her perfect cue, yet it took all her will to lead in from it. "I want to be more than your friend, Alex. We . . . we have grown to understand each other, to depend on the other's company. Over the past weeks we have spoken of things no other person could hear. Now, more than ever we need our combined strength." She swallowed nervously. "I still have the engagement ring."

"I told you before to return it to my father," he said stiffly.

"I . . . I'd rather put it back on my finger."

Suddenly, he was blazingly angry. "Oh no, Judith, I want no noble self-sacrifices from you."

"It wouldn't be that, Alex."

"Of course it would," he snapped. "You would be tying yourself to a man who is blind. There is no reason for such a course, I assure you. I am learning Braille very quickly, and when they allow me out of this damned chair I'll walk very well. Hallworth has wide doorways and broad shallow stairs, thank God, and I shall hire a man as my personal servant—probably a soldier who has been invalided out of the regiment. I have been making decisions only this morning and have it all planned. I shall invest in the railways—join the board of directors of one of the companies. I have always wanted to do that. It's a pity I have to leave the regiment . . . but I was never much of a soldier."

She closed her eyes in acute sadness as she thought of the Victoria Cross he was to receive for his action at Landerdorp that had saved men's lives and cost him his sight. When she opened them he was still talking about his plans for the future, flinging the words at her in angry defiance.

Cutting across them she cried, "If we are considering self-sacrifice, it would cut both ways, Alex. My chances of marriage are somewhat slender. What man would want a woman who . . . ?"

"That's enough," he broke in harshly. "I thought I had made it clear to you that the past is best forgotten. Surely you don't imagine that I intend to go back on my word, that my plans for the future leave no place for you for as long as you need me. In time, you'll feel secure again, forget all that has happened to you here. In England you will make new friends, build a life that is free from horrors, find happiness with someone who cares no more than I do for what has gone before. In England . . ."

Sitting there with the sun burnishing his hair as it lay in small tongues against the back of his neck, the thick lashes half-closed, the sturdy shoulders squared aggressively, he was again the man in the rose garden on a beautiful English June evening so long ago. *A resentful and unwilling bridegroom!* She had taken refuge then in her pride. For both their sakes she must not make the same mistake again.

Kneeling beside his chair she touched his arm, and he stopped in midsentence, surprised at her nearness. "Don't fight me, Alex. You have been doing that far too long."

He grew still and wary, as if sensing the determination that had overtaken her. "Sometimes, that is the only way to survive."

"No, there is another way," she told him softly. "From that moment we met again at Hallworth I have wanted to be your wife. I still wanted it when you sailed away so gladly for two years, and I followed you for that reason. When I gave back the ring it was like surrendering the dearest thing in the world. All these months I have told myself if you survived I would say the words my pride and your anger would not let me say. I love you, my dearest. I always have . . . so much that if I lose you this time, I know I couldn't go on."

He sat perfectly still, looking at her with eyes that could only hold a memory. Then his hand reached out and found her face, brown fingers touching her lashes gently.

"Don't," he murmured. "There was a girl long ago who cried over love for me . . . and so did Hetta. This time there must be no tears."

"This time?" she whispered.

His voice grew faraway. "All my life I seem to have been heading in wrong directions. Twice I thought love could overcome all obstacles in its path. Now I believe life and I have come to terms, but I have been trying to plan a future without you in vain. We have surely overcome all the obstacles . . . but is your love strong enough to wait for me to catch up?"

She put her hand over his as it rested against her cheek.
"It has not faltered yet: I am certain it never will."

His kiss was sweet and full of promises she knew he
wanted to keep. They had both lost something in this wild
country, but they would turn their backs on it and rebuild
their lives, together, until their love was as strong and free
and eternal as the veld.

Far out on the veld a small dark-haired girl driving an
ox wagon had joined several more of her kind. They were
trekking north away from the British, as their ancestors
had done.